The Fiery Angel

CLASSICS OF RUSSIAN LITERATURE

The Fiery Angel

A Sixteenth Century Romance

BY
VALERI BRIUSSOV

TRANSLATED BY
IVOR MONTAGU
AND
SERGEI NALBANDOV

HYPERION PRESS, INC.
Westport, Connecticut

Published in 1930 by Humphrey Toulmin, London
Hyperion reprint edition 1977
Library of Congress Catalog Number 7623872
ISBN 0-88355-475-5 (cloth ed.)
ISBN 0-88355-476-3 (paper ed.)
Manufactured in the United States of America

Library of Congress Cataloging in Publication Data

Briussov, Valerii IAkovlevich, 1873-1924.
    The fiery angel.

    (Classics of Russian literature) (The Hyperion
library of world literature)
    Translation of Ognennyi angel.
    Reprint of the 1930 ed. published by H. Toulmin,
London.
    I. Title.
PZ3.B7812Fi   1977   [PG3453.B7]   891'.7'3'42
ISBN 0-88355-475-5   76-23872
ISBN 0-88355-476-3 pbk.

5

I. Foreword by the Russian Editor

THIS XVIth Century narrative here presented to the reader has reached us in but one extant manuscript, now in private hands. The owner, by whose courtesy we are enabled to publish the Russian translation before the appearance in print of the original, intends to provide the German edition with a detailed critical introduction. Those interested are referred to his essay, which will provide an exhaustive description of the manuscript, and an examination in detail of the question of its authenticity, the time of its writing, its historical importance and so forth—here we shall confine ourselves to a few words only upon these points.

The manuscript has the form of a ledger in quarto of two hundred and eight pages of bluish paper, the four last being blank, and the whole bound in parchment, with clasps. It is written in Gothic script, and though not entirely devoid of dialect peculiarities, is in that "middle-Germanic" language in which books were being published in Germany at the very end of the XVth and the beginning of the XVIth Centuries; only the dedication is composed in Latin. The manuscript is nowhere in the handwriting of its author, who says himself that the confession was written towards the end of 1535 A.D., but is a transcription made considerably later, probably as late as the very end of the XVIth Century, by someone unknown to us and, we may surmise, a Catholic. The state of preservation of the manuscript leaves little to be desired, for every line is legible and the few imperfect passages can easily be reconstructed from the context.

The scrupulous care of the author, his strict desire to describe impartially and correctly everything that he lived through, can be placed beyond any doubt. In the XVIth and XVIIth Centuries sorcery and magic were not so much popular superstitions as definite sciences, expounded in books by the most eminent naturalists and jurists. The vague witchcraft and fortune-telling of the Middle Ages grew in the epoch of the Renaissance and the Reformation into a beautifully developed discipline of sciences, of which the scientists numbered more than twenty (see for example the work of Agrippa, " *De Speciebus Magiae* "). The best intellects of those centuries not only believed in the possibility of commerce with the devil, they even consecrated special treatises to the subject. Thus Jean Bodin, for example, the famous author of " *De Republica*," acknowledged by Buckle as one of the most remarkable of historians, wrote an immense compilation proving the existence of witches ; Ambroise Paret, the reformer of surgery, described the nature of demons and the forms of possession; Kepler defended his mother from an accusation of witchcraft without impugning its rationality ; and so forth. Popes issued special bulls against witches, and at the head of the well-known " *Malleus maleficarum* " is placed the text : " *Haeresis est maxima opera maleficarum non credere*," i.e., " Not to believe in the doings of witches is the highest heresy." The number of sceptics was very small, and among them an important place should be assigned to the Iohann Weier mentioned in this account (or, in another transcription of his name, Jean Wier), who was the first to recognise in witchcraft a special form of disease.

In rendering the manuscript into Russian, we have taken into consideration the fact that its author paid considerable attention to the literary aspect of his narrative. Accordingly, we have not thought it necessary to reproduce the minor stylistic peculiarities of the original, and our translation must be regarded as a free translation. At the end of the narrative will be found the most essential translator's notes.[1]

V. B.

[1] Mr. Briussov was apparently prevented from fulfilling his intention, for no notes are found in the Russian edition. This edition, from which the present version has been made, was published in 1908 and 1909 in two volumes—the hiatus occurring after the tenth chapter of the manuscript. It is now out of print. Its *soi-disant* "editor," Mr. Valeri (Yakovlevitch) Briussov (*b.* 1873, *d.* 1924) was a distinguished poet—the accepted head of the Symbolist school of Russian poetry, a critic, translator and playwright, and an exceptionally erudite man. A selection of his short stories (*The Republic of the Southern Cross*, Constable) has been published in English, and the reader desiring further particulars regarding him is recommended to D. S. Mirsky's excellent *Contemporary Russian Literature*, 1881-1925, Routledge.

I. M. and S. S. N.

II. The Manuscript

Non Illustrium Quiquam Virorum
Artium Laude Doctrinaeque Fama
Clarorum
At Tibi
Domina Lucida Demens Infelix
Quae Multum Amaveris
Amandoque Perieras
Narrationem Haud Mendacem
Servus Devotus
Amator Fidelis
Sempiternae Memoriae Causa
Dedicavi
Scriptor

The Fiery Angel

or a True Story in which is related of the Devil, not once but often appearing in the Image of a Spirit of Light to a Maiden and seducing her to Various and Many Sinful Deeds, of Ungodly Practices of Magic, Alchymy, Astrology, the Cabalistical Sciences and Necromancy, of the Trial of the Said Maiden under the Presidency of His Eminence the Archbishop of Trier, as well as of Encounters and Discourses with the Knight and thrice Doctor Agrippa of Nettesheim, and with Doctor Faustus, composed by an Eyewitness.

14

Contents

Contents

Amico Lectori

*The Author's Foreword in which is related his Life
prior to his Return to German Lands*

IT is my view that everyone who has happened to
be witness of events out of the ordinary and not
easily comprehensible should leave behind a
record of them, made sincerely and without bias.
But it is not only the desire to advance so intricate a
matter as the study of the mysterious powers of the Devil,
and of the spheres permitted to him that induces me
to embark upon this unadorned narrative of all the
marvellous events I have lived through during the last
twelve months. I am attracted also by the possibility
of opening my heart in these pages, as if in dumb
confession before an ear unknown to me, for I have no
one to whom my tragic story may be uttered, and,
moreover, silence is difficult to one who has suffered
much. In order, therefore, that you, gentle reader,
may see how far you may have confidence in my guile-
less story, and to what degree I was able rationally to
appreciate all that I witnessed, I desire, in short, to set
out my tale.

First I shall explain that I was no youth, inexperienced and prone to exaggeration, when I encountered
that which is dark and mysterious in nature, for I
had already crossed the line that divides our lives
into two parts. I was born in the Kurfürstendom of
Trier at the beginning of the fifteen hundred and fourth
year after the Materialisation of the Word, February the
fifth, St. Agatha's day, which happened on a Wednesday,

17

in a small village in the valley of Hochwald in Losheim. My grandfather was barber and surgeon in the district, and my father, having obtained for the purpose the privilege of our Kurfürst, practised as a physician. The local inhabitants always highly esteemed his art, and probably to this day, when ill, they have recourse to his attentive care. There were four children in our family : two sons, including myself, and two daughters. The eldest of us, brother Arnim, having studied with success his father's craft, both at home and in the schools, was received into their corporation by the Physicians of Trier, and both my sisters married well and settled down : Maria at Merzig and Louisa at Basel. I, who had received at Holy Baptism the name of Rupprecht, was the youngest of the family, and still remained a child when my brother and sisters had already become independent.

Of my education I must speak in some detail, for, though I forfeited school tutelage, yet I do not consider myself any lower than some of those who pride themselves on a double or a treble doctorate. My father dreamed that I should be his successor, and that he would hand down to me, like a rich heritage, both his practice and the respect in which he was held. Almost before he had taught me to read and write, to count upon the abacus, and the rudiments of Latin, he began to introduce me to the mysteries of the preparation of drugs, to the aphorisms of Hippocrates and the book of Iohannitius the Syrian. But from childhood, all sedentary occupations requiring no more than attention and patience have been hateful to me. Only the insistence of my father, who held to his purpose with senile stubbornness, and the pleas of my mother, a woman of kindness and timidity, forced me to achieve a measure of success in the matters studied.

For the continuance of my education, father, when I had reached fourteen years of age, sent me to the City of Köln on the Rhine, to his old friend Ottfried

The fiery Angel

Gerard, thinking that my application would increase by competition with my school-fellows. However, the University of that city, from which the Dominicans were just then conducting their shameful dispute with Iohann Reuchlin, was ineffective in stimulating in me a special zeal for learning. In those days, though some reforms had been begun, there were among the docenti practically no followers of the new ideas of our time, and the Faculty of Theology still arose amongst the others like a tower over roofs. I was made to learn by heart hexameters from the " *Doctrinale* " of Alexander and to penetrate into the dead " *Ars Dictandi* " of Boethius. And if I learned something during the years of my stay at the University, it was certainly not from the lectures of the schools, but only from the lessons of the ragged, wandering tutors who appeared from time to time in the streets of Köln itself.

I must not (for that would be unfair) describe myself as devoid of abilities. True, often was I tempted from the working desk and the binding of asses' skin—away into the mountains and forests, to the rustle of verdure and the wide and distant spaces, yet, endowed with a good memory and quick understanding, I have later been able to gather together a sufficient stock of information and enlighten my intellect by the rays of philosophy. What I have since chanced to learn of the works of the Nürembergian mathematician Bernhard Walther, of the discoveries and reflections of the doctor Theophrastus Paracelsus, and still more of the entrancing views of the astronomer Nicolaus Koppernigk living in Frauenburg, enables me to think that the beneficent revival that in our happy age has regenerated both philosophy and the free arts may one day move to the sciences. (But these must be familiar to everyone who confesses himself, in spirit at least, a contemporary of the great Erasmus, wanderer in the valley of the humanities, *vallii humanitatis*.) In any case, both in the years of my youth—unconsciously, and as adult—

19

after reflection, I never set high store by learning gathered by new generations from old books and not verified by the investigations of experience. And, together with the fiery Giovanni Pico di Mirandola, author of the divine " Discourse on the Honour of Man," I am ready to pour out my curses upon the " schools where men busy themselves in seeking new words."

Avoiding the University lectures at Köln, I threw myself, however, with the more passion into the free life of the students. After the strictness of my paternal home, I found to my taste the gay drinking, the hours with frail companions, and the card games that take one's breath away by their sudden turns of fortune. I quickly familiarised myself with these riotous pastimes, and with the general noisy bustle of the city, filled with eternal fuss and hurry, that are the characteristic peculiarities of our days, and on which our elders look, puzzled and incensed, remembering the quiet times of the good Emperor Friedrich. Whole days did I spend in pranks with my bosom friends, days not always innocent, migrating from drinking house to bawdy house, singing students' songs and challenging the artisans to fight, and not averse from drinking neat brantwein, a practice that fifteen years ago was far less widespread than now. Even the moist darkness of the night, and the tinkle of the street chains being fastened, did not always send us to our rest.

Into such a life was I plunged for nearly three winters, until all these diversions came near to ending unhappily for me. My untried heart flared up with passion for our neighbour, the baker's wife, sprightly and pretty—with cheeks like snow strewn with the petals of roses, lips like corals from Sicily and teeth like pearls from Ceylon, if one may use the language of the poets. She was not disinclined to favour the youth, upright and sharp of repartee, but she desired from me those small presents, of which, as remarked Ovidius Naso of old, women are ever greedy. The money sent me by my father was insufficient to satisfy her capricious tastes, and so, with one of my wildest school-fellows, I became involved in a very nasty business, that did not remain undiscovered, so that I was threatened with imprisonment in the city gaol. Only owing to the strenuous intercessions of Ottfried Gerard, who enjoyed the goodwill of that influential Canon of distinguished intellect Count Hermann von Neuenar, was I freed from the trial and sent home to my parents for domestic punishment.

It was then that there began for me that unscholastic schooling to which I am indebted for the right to call myself an enlightened man. I was seventeen. Not having received at the University even a bachelor's degree, I settled down at home in the miserable state of a parasite and a disgrace, shunned by all. But I found in our secluded Losheim one true friend, who loved me humbly, who soothed my embittered soul and led me on new paths. He was the son of our apothecary, Friedrich, a youth, slightly older than I, ailing and strange. His father loved collecting and binding books, especially new ones, printed ones, and he spent on these all the surplus of his income, though he read but seldom. But Friedrich gave himself up to reading as to some maddening passion, he knew no greater ecstasy than to repeat aloud his beloved pages. And when I was not wandering with an arbalist over the crests and slopes of the neighbouring mountains, I used to visit the tiny garret of my friend, at the very top of the house, under the tiles, and there we would spend hour after hour surrounded by the thick tomes of antiquity and the slender volumes of our contemporaries.

Thus, helping each other, now stubbornly arguing, now uniting to admire, in the cool days of winter and the starry nights of summer, we read all that we could obtain in our secluded backwater, transforming the

garret of the apothecary into a veritable academy.
In those ancients of whom I had heard no mention at
the University, either at the *ordinarii* or the disputes—
in Catullus, Martialis, Calpurnius, we found passages
of beauty and taste for ever unexcelled, and in the
creations of the divine Plato we looked into the remotest
depths of human wisdom, not comprehending all, but
moved by all. In the compositions of our own age,
less perfect but nearer to us, we learnt to be conscious
of that which, heretofore, had lived and swarmed
within our souls, but had no words. We recognised
our own, yet heretofore nebulous, views in the inex-
haustibly amusing " Praise of Folly," in the witty and
noble—whatever one says—" Sponge," in the mighty
and merciless " Triumph of Venus," and in the
" Letters of Obscure Men " which we read six times
from beginning to end, and to which antiquity itself
can oppose perhaps Lucian alone.

Around us, meanwhile, great events were thundering,
still fresh in the memory of all. It was a time of which
the saying goes to-day : he who did not succumb in the
year '23, did not drown in '24, and was not killed in '25—
must give thanks unto the Lord for a miracle. However, occupied by discourses with the noblest intellects,
we were scarce disturbed by the black storms of current
life. We could find no sympathy for the attack on
Trier by the Knight Franz von Sickingen, whom some
glorified as a friend of the righteous, but who in fact
was a man of olden temper, sprung from the ranks of
robbers, who hazard their heads to despoil a passing
traveller. Our Archbishop repulsed the invader, thus
showing that the times of Florisel of Nicea have
become mere grandfather's tales. For the two following
years popular riots and revolts swept through the
German lands like a Satanic roundelay—serfs broke
into the villages and castles, burned, slaughtered and
tormented. The dreamer Friedrich thought at first
that this hurricane of blood and fire would help to

establish better order and justice in the land, but I never expected anything of German peasants, still too wild and ignorant. All that resulted justified me and the bitter words of the writer : *rustica gens optima flens pessima gaudens.*

Great dissension was caused between us by the first rumours about Martin Luther, that " invincible heretic," who then, already, had not a few followers among the ruling princes. People nowadays assure us that in those days it was as if nine-tenths of Germany cried " Long live Luther," and in Spain they afterwards declared that with us religion changes like the weather, and that may-beetles fly between the three churches. But the dispute about Transubstantiation and Sanctifying Grace interested me personally not at all, and I have never been able to understand how Desiderius Erasmus, that unique genius, could interest himself in monastic preachings. Conscious with the best men of my time that faith consists in depth of heart and not in outward show, I felt for that reason no constraint either in the company of good Catholics or in the midst of fanatical Lutherans. Friedrich, on the contrary, who found in religion gloomy precipices to terrify him at every step, regarded the books of Luther as a shining revelation, though me they pleased only by a degree of strength and floridness in the style, none the less rather unpolished—and our discussions at times slipped gradually into insulting quarrels.

At the beginning of the year '26, immediately after Holy Easter, sister Louisa came to our house with her husband. Life with them in the house became quite unbearable for me, because they, untiringly, rained reproaches on me that I, in my twenties, still remained a yoke on the shoulders of my father and a millstone in the eyes of my mother. About that time Knight Georg von Frundsberg, the glorious vanquisher of the French, was commissioned by the Emperor to visit our lands for the purpose of enlisting recruits. Then

it came into my mind to become a free landsknecht,
for I saw no other means of changing my way of
living, that was ready to go stagnant, like the water
in a pond.   Friedrich, who had dreamt that I should
earn fame as a writer, was very sad, but found no
reasons to dissuade me.   And I declared to my father,
definitely and determinedly, that I had chosen the
military craft, since the sword became me more than
the lancet.   Father, as I had expected, flew into a rage and
forbade me even to think of a military career, saying,
" All my life I have repaired human bodies, I do not
desire that my son should mutilate them."   Neither I
nor my friend had money for me to buy arms and
clothing, so I decided to leave the parental roof sur-
reptitiously.   At night, I remember it was, on the 5th of
June, unnoticed I made my way out of the house,
taking with me twenty-five Rhine guldens.   I remember
well how Friedrich, accompanying me till I reached
the entrance to the field, embraced me—perhaps for
the last time, weeping by the grey willow standing pale
as a corpse in the moonlight.

I, on the other hand, felt in my heart that day no
heaviness of parting, for a new life shone before me,
like the depth of a May morning.   I was young and
strong, the enlisting officers accepted me without
question, and I was allotted to Frundsberg's army of
Italy.   It will be readily understood by everyone that
the days that followed were not easy for me, one has
only to remember the nature of our landsknechts—
men riotous, coarse, untutored, ostentatious in the
gaudiness of their dress and the floridness of their
speech, seeking only where they might drink deeper or
seize richer booty.   It was almost frightening to me,
after the witticisms, tempered as a needle, of Martial,
and the arguments of Marsilio Ficcino, soaring as the
flight of a hawk, to share in the unrestrained jests of
my new comrades, and sometimes the whole life
appeared but an oppressive nightmare.   My officers,

24

however, could not fail to notice that I was different from my comrades both in learning and behaviour, and as, moreover, I could manage the arquebus well and was ready and willing for any task—I was constantly singled out and given occupations more suited to me.

As a landsknecht I made all that strenuous march into Italy, when we had to cross the snow-clad mountains in the cold of winter, ford rivers up to our throats in water, camp for whole weeks in the engulfing mud. It was then that I took part in the capture by assault of the Eternal City, on the 6th May of the year '27, by the united Spanish and German troops. With my own eyes I saw the infuriated soldiers loot the churches of Rome, commit violations in nunneries, ride wearing mitres through the streets on Papal mules, throw the Holy Sacrament and the Relics of the Saints into the Tiber, set up a conclave and declare Martin Luther pope. After that I spent about a year in the various cities of Italy, acquainting myself more closely with the life of the country, a land truly enlightened and still remaining a shining example to the other nations of the world. This enabled me to become familiar with the entrancing creations of the Italian painters, whose works are so superior to those of ours, except of course to those of the inimitable Albrecht Dürer— amongst them, moreover, the creations of most recent times, those of the ever lamented Raphael d'Urbino, his worthy competitor Sebastiano del Piombo, the young but all-embracing genius Benvenuto Cellini, whom we also encountered as an enemy in the field, and Michael-Angelo Buonarotti, who despises somewhat the beauty of form, but is yet powerful and original.

In the spring of the following year, the lieutenant of the Spanish detachment, Don Miguel de Gamez, approached me to his person as physician, because I had gained a certain familiarity with the Spanish language. Together with Don Miguel I had to travel to

Spain, whither he was despatched with secret letters to our Emperor, and this journey resolved my fate. Having found the court at the City of Toledo, we found there also the greatest of our contemporaries, a hero equal to the Hannibals, Scipios and other great men of antiquity—Hernando Cortes, the Marquis del Valje-Oaxaca. The reception arranged for that proud conqueror of Empires, as well as the narratives of those who had returned from the country so entrancingly described by Amerigo Vespucci, persuaded me to seek my fortune in that blessed haven for all the failures of this earth. I joined a friendly expedition, organised by German settlers in Seville, and set sail with light heart across the Ocean.

In the West Indies I entered at first the service of the Royal Audiencia ; but soon, having seen proof of how unfaithfully and unskilfully it conducts its affairs, and of how unjustly it rewards abilities and services, I chose rather to execute commissions for those German houses that have factories in the New World, for preference for the Welzers who own copper mines in San Domingo, but also for the Fuggers, the Ellingers, the Krombergs and the Tetzels. Four times I made forays to the West, to the South and to the North, searching for new veins of ore, for fields of gems— amethysts and emeralds, and for a forest of precious timbers : twice under the command of others, and twice personally commanding the expeditions. In this way I marched through all the lands from Chicora to the port of Tumbes, spending long months among the dark-skinned heathen, beholding in the log-palaces of the natives riches so vast that before them the treasures of our Europe are as nothing, and several times escaping the destruction that hung over me as if almost by a miracle. In my love for an Indian woman, who concealed beneath her dark skin a heart that could feel both attachment and passion, it was my lot to experience powerful agonies of soul, but it would be out of place

26

to relate of them here at greater length. I may say in short—that, just as those soft twilight days spent at the books with dear Friedrich educated my thoughts, so these terrible years of wandering tempered my will in the flame of trial, and endowed me with that most priceless attribute of man—faith in myself.

It is certainly quite erroneous for people in our country to imagine that across the Ocean gold is to be gathered from the earth merely by stooping down, but, none the less, after spending five years in America and the West Indies, I contrived, by unremitting industry and toil and not without the help of luck, to put by an adequate sum in savings. And it was then that the thought came to me to travel back to German lands, not with the object of settling peacefully in our almost sleepy township, but with the worldly desire to parade my successes in front of father, who could not but think of me as the ne'er-do-weel who robbed him. I shall not conceal, however, the fact that I was also filled with a burning longing and weariness for home, that I had never thought to feel for my native mountains, on whose slopes, embittered, I used to wander with my arbalist, and that I passionately wanted to see my dear mother, as well as the friend whom I had left behind, and whom I hoped to find still alive. Even then, however, I was firmly decided that, after having visited the home village and re-established connection with the family, I should return to New Spain, which I regarded as my second fatherland.

In the early spring of the year '34, I sailed away in a ship of the Welzers from the port Villa Rica de la Vera Cruz, and after a stormy and difficult journey we arrived in the wealthy city of Antwerpen. Several weeks of my time were spent in accomplishing the various commissions I had undertaken to fulfil, and it was only in the month of August that, at last, I could set out upon the journey to the Rhine lands. From that moment, properly, begins my narrative.

Chapter the First

How I first met Renata and how she related to me her Whole Life

FROM the Netherlands I decided to go overland, and I chose the route through Köln, for I wanted to see once more that city in which I had known so many pleasant hours. For thirty Spanish escudos I bought an excellent horse, capable without strain of carrying both me and my baggage, but, fearing robbers, I tried to assume the appearance of a simple sailor. I exchanged the gay and relatively sumptuous dress in which I had strutted about in luxurious Brabant for the outfit of an ordinary seaman, dark brown in colour and with breeches tied below the knee. But I retained my reliable long sword; for I placed no less faith in it than in Saint Gertruda, patroness of all land travellers. I set aside a small sum in silver joachimsthalers for my expenses on the journey, and my savings I sewed in the lining of a broad belt in golden pistoles.

After a pleasant five days' journeying in the company of casual strangers, for I travelled without undue haste, I crossed the Maas at Venloo. I will not conceal the fact that when I reached the regions where German dresses began to flicker past me, and my hearing was assailed by the glib—oh, so familiar—speech of home, I was seized by emotions perhaps unworthy of a full-grown man! Leaving Venloo early, I reckoned to reach Neuss by the evening, and accordingly I took leave of my road companions at Viersen, for they purposed visiting Gladbach on the way, and turned, already alone, on to the Düsseldorf highway. As there was need to hasten I began to urge on my horse, but stumbling, it injured its ankle against a stone—and this insignificant occurrence gave rise, as direct cause, to the long series of remarkable happenings that it became my fate to live through after that day. But I had long observed that it is only insignificant happenings that prove the first links of those chains of heavy trial which, unseen and unheard, life sometimes forges for us.

On a lame horse I could advance but slowly, and I was still far outside the town when it became difficult to see in the grey twilight, and from the grass there rose a pungent mist. I was riding at that time through a thick beech forest, and was foreseeing not without misgivings a night spent in a place totally unknown to me, when suddenly, rounding a bend, I espied, in a small clearing at the very edge of the road, a little wooden house, all asquint, lonely, and as if it had lost its way. The gate was closely shut and locked, the lower windows more like large arrow-slits, but under the roof there dangled on a rope a half-broken bottle, indicating that here was a hostelry, and, riding up, I began to hammer on the shutters with the hilt of my sword. At my firm knocking, and at the furious barking of the dog, the hostess peered out, but for a long time she refused to let me in, questioning me as to who I was, and why I rode that way. All unsuspecting what future I was demanding for myself, I insisted with threats and with curses, so that at last a door was unlocked to me and my horse led away to its stall.

Up a rickety staircase, in darkness, I was conducted to a tiny room on the second floor, narrow and uneven in width, like the case of a viola. Whilst in Italy a softly laid bed, and an appetising supper with a bottle of wine, can always be found even in the cheapest hotels, travellers in our country—except the rich, who carry dozens of stuffed bales with them on mules—still have to be content with black bread, inferior beer and a night on old straw. Stuffy and narrow seemed my first shelter in my native land to me, especially after the clean, almost polished bedrooms in the houses of the Netherland merchants whose doors had been opened to me by my letters of recommendation. But I had experienced worse nights indeed during my arduous travels across Anahuac, so, drawing my leather cape about me, I tried as soon as possible to nod my head off into sleep, not heeding a drunken voice that sang in the lower hall a song new to me, the words of which, however, became fixed in my mind:

> *Ob dir ein Dirn gefelt*
> *So schweig, hastu kein Gelt.*

How surprised should I have been, if, as I fell asleep, some prophetic voice had told me that this was to be for me the last evening of one life, after which another was to begin! My fate, having transported me across the Ocean, had held me on my journey exactly the right number of days, and then brought me, as if to a destined march-stone, to this house so distant from town and village, where the fatal meeting awaited me. A learned Dominican monk would have seen in it the obvious expression of the will of God; an enthusiastic Realist would have found in it reason to deplore the complicated linkage of causes and effects, that do not fit into the revolving circles of Raymundus Lullius; while I, when I think of the thousands and thousands of chances that were necessary for me to chance that very evening on my way to Neuss into that small wayside inn—I lose all sense of differentiation between the ordinary and the supernatural, between *miracula* and *natura*. I can only suppose that my first meeting with Renata was, in a smaller way, just as miraculous as all the marvels and buffetings that later we lived through together.

31

Midnight, probably, had long passed, when I suddenly awoke, roused all at once by something unexpected. My room was bright with the silver-blue light of the moon, and the stillness around was as if all earth, and heaven itself, had died. But then, in this stillness, I distinctly heard in the next room, behind a partition of planks, a woman whisper and cry out feebly. Though wise is the proverb that says the traveller bears enough to worry about on his own back and should not pity the shoulders of others, and though I have never been distinguished by exaggerated sentimentality, yet the love of adventure, to which I have been inclined since childhood, could not fail to rouse me to the defence of a lady in distress, to protect whom, indeed, as a man who had spent whole years in battle, I had a knightly claim. Rising from bed and unsheathing my sword half way, I left my room and, even in the dark passage in which I found myself, easily distinguished the door to the room from which the voice had come. I asked loudly whether anyone required protection, and, when I had repeated these words a second time and no one had replied, I thrust at the door, breaking a small bolt, and entered.

It was then that I beheld Renata for the first time.

In a room as cheerless as my own and also lit brightly by the moonlight, there stood, in shaking terror, a woman stretched against the wall, her hair loose and flowing. No other human being was there, for all the corners of the room were clearly lit and the shadows lying on the floor were clear-cut and distinct; and yet, shielding herself, she thrust out her arms in front of her as if someone were advancing towards her. In this movement there was something terrifying in the extreme, for one could not fail to understand that she was threatened by some invisible apparition. Seeing me, the woman, uttering a fresh cry, rushed to meet me, fell on her knees before me as if I were a messenger

from Heaven, seized me convulsively and said, panting :
" At last it is you, Rupprecht ! I have no more
strength ! "

Never, before that day, had Renata and I met, and
she saw me as much for the first time as I saw her, and
yet she called me by my name as simply as if we had
been friends from childhood. I tried not to show my
surprise and, laying my hand lightly on her shoulder,
asked whether it were true that she was being pursued
by an apparition. But the woman had no power to
answer me and, weeping and laughing by turns, she
pointed with her trembling hand where, to my eyes,
there was nothing but a ray of moonshine. I must not
here deny that the unusual nature of all the surrounding
circumstances, together with the consciousness of the
presence of inhuman powers, had seized my whole
being with a dull terror that I had not experienced
since early youth. More to soothe the frantic lady than
because I myself believed in the efficacy of the act, I
unsheathed my sword completely, and, grasping it by
the blade, I pointed the cross-like hilt before me,
repeating some mystic words taught me by an Indian
who invoked the demon Anjan. But the woman,
beginning to tremble, fell on her face as if in a convulsion of imminent death.

I did not think it proper to my honour to flee from
thence, though I realised immediately that an evil
demon had now taken possession of the unfortunate
creature and was fearfully tormenting her from within.
I swear by the pure blood of Christ—never till that day
had I witnessed such convulsions nor suspected that a
human body could be so incredibly distorted ! The
woman stretched out painfully and in defiance of all
natural usage, so that her neck and breast became as
firm as wood and as straight as a cane, then she suddenly
bent forward so that her head and chin approached her
toes and the veins in her neck became monstrously
taut, then, by reversal, she miraculously thrust herself

33

backwards, and the nape of her neck became twisted
inside her shoulder, towards the small of her back and her
thigh high raised. I watched these ecstasies of torment
as if made of stone, practically without horror and without curiosity, as I would watch a representation of the
torments that await us in hell.

Then the woman ceased to knock herself against
the hard planks of the floor, and the distorted features
of her face little by little became more endowed with
reason, but she still bended and unbent convulsively,
again protecting herself with her hands, as if from an
enemy. I guessed then that the Devil had come out of
her and was outside her body and, drawing the woman
to me, I began to repeat the words of the holy prayer
that, I have heard, is always employed at exorcisms:
Libera me, Domine, de morte aeterna. In the meantime the moon was already setting beyond the tops of
the forest, and, in measure that the morning twilight
took possession of the room, shifting the shadow from
the wall to the window, the woman who lay in my arms
came gradually to. But the darkness still breathed on
her, like the cold tramontana of the Pyrenean Mountains, and she trembled all over as if from the frost of
winter.

I asked: had the spirit departed.

Opening her eyes and glancing round the room, as if
recovered from a swoon, she answered me:

" Yes, he dissolved, for he saw that we were well
armed against him. He can attempt nothing against a
strong will."

These were the second words that I had heard from
Renata. Having uttered them, she began to weep,
shivering in a fever, and she wept so that the tears
rolled down her cheeks without restraint and moistened
my fingers. Reflecting that the lady would not recover
warmth on the floor, and in a measure reassured, I
raised her without effort, for she was of small stature
and slight, and carried her to the bed that stood near by.

34

There I covered her with a coverlet that I found in the room and tried to soothe her with quiet words.

But the woman, still weeping, became seized by yet another access of excitement, and, catching my hand, said :

" Now, Rupprecht, I must relate to you the whole story of my life, for you have saved me and it is your right to know everything of me."

In vain I persuaded the lady to rest and sleep—she, it seemed to me, did not even hear my words, but, firmly clasping my fingers and looking away from me, began to talk quickly—quickly. At first I did not understand her speech, with such impetuosity did she pour out her thoughts and so unexpectedly did she turn from one subject to another. But gradually I learned to distinguish the main flow in the unrestrained torrent of her words and I realised that she was, actually, telling me of herself.

Never afterwards, even in the days of our most trusted intimacy, did Renata relate to me so consecutively the story of her life. True, even that night, not only did she keep silence about her parents and the place where she spent her childhood, but even, as I later had the opportunity of convincing myself without doubt, she in part concealed many later events, and in part related them falsely—whether intentionally or owing to her weakness I do not know. None the less, for a long time I knew only of Renata that little she related to me in this feverish story, therefore I must give it here in detail. Only, I cannot manage to reproduce exactly her disordered speech, hurried and disconnected, I shall have to replace it by a colder narrative.

Naming herself by that single name which alone I know, even to this day, and mentioning her first years so perfunctorily and obscurely that her words were not retained by my memory, Renata at once came to the event that she herself considered fatal to her lot.

The Fiery Angel

Renata was eight years old when for the first time there came into her room, in a ray of sunshine, an angel, as if all flaming, and clad in snow-white robes. His face shone, his eyes were blue as the skies, and his hair as of fine gold thread. The angel named himself—Madiël. Renata was not frightened in the least, and they played, she and the angel, all that day with dolls. After that the angel came often to her, nearly every day, and he was always gay and kind, so that the girl came to like him better than her relatives and playmates. With inexhaustible inventiveness did Madiël amuse Renata with jokes or stories, and, when she was upset, he comforted her tenderly. Sometimes with Madiël came his comrades, also angels but not flaming ones, clothed in capes of scarlet and of purple; but they were less kind. Strictly Madiël forbade Renata to tell anyone of his secret visitations, and even had Renata disobeyed his request, no one would have believed her, for they would have thought her lying or pretending.

Not always did Madiël appear in the image of an angel, but often in other guises, especially if Renata had little time to be alone. Thus in summer Madiël would often fly to her as a huge flaming butterfly with white wings and golden antennæ, and Renata would conceal him in her long tresses. In winter he sometimes took the shape of a distaff, so that the girl could carry him with her everywhere without parting from him. Sometimes, also, Renata would recognise her heavenly friend in a plucked flower, or in a tiny coal that fell out upon the hearth, or in a nut that she broke with her teeth. At times Madiël would come into Renata's bed and, snuggling to her like a cat, pass with her the time till morn. During such nights the angel would carry Renata away on his wings, far from her home, and show her strange cities, famous cathedrals and even the shining abodes that are not of this earth— and at daybreak, without knowing how, she would always find herself again in her bed.

36

The Fiery Angel

When Renata had grown up somewhat, Madiël declared to her that she should be a saint, like Amalia of Löthringen, and that that was the reason and purpose for which he had been sent. He spoke to her a great deal of the sacrifice of Jesus Christ, of the blissful submission of the Virgin Mary, of the mystic paths to the sealed gates of the earthly paradise, of Saint Agnes, inseparable from her meek lamb, of Saint Veronica, eternally standing before the image of her Saviour, and of many other things and persons that could not but guide her thoughts into pious channels. According to Renata's words, even if she had previously had doubts whether it were true that her mysterious visitor was a messenger from Heaven, they could not but dissolve like smoke after these conversations, for a servant of Satan could certainly not have pronounced such a quantity of saintly names without experiencing extreme pains. Further, Madiël even appeared once to Renata in the image of Christ Crucified, when from his pierced and fiery hands streamed a flame-crimson blood.

The angel insistently exhorted Renata to lead the strict life of a saint, to seek purity of heart and clarity of mind, and she began to keep all the fast days established by Holy Church, to visit Mass every day and to pray a great deal in the solitude of her room before the image of the crucifix. Often did Madiël force Renata to submit herself to cruel trials : to go out into the frost naked, to hunger and abstain from drink for many days and nights on end, to flagellate her thighs with knotted ropes or torture her breasts with sharp points. Renata spent whole nights on her knees, and Madiël, remaining with her, would strengthen her in her exhaustion, as the angel strengthened the Saviour in the Garden of Gethsemane. At Renata's urgent request Madiël touched her hands, and on the palms showed sores, like the stigmata of Christ's wounds upon the cross, but she concealed these wounds

37

carefully from everyone. In those days, because of her divine aid, there appeared in Renata the gift of working miracles and, like the most devout King of France, she healed many by a single touch of her hand, so that in the whole district she was famed as holy.

Having attained development, and remarking that maidens of her age had sweethearts or betrothed, Renata approached her angel with an insistent demand that she too should be bodily joined, and to him, for according to his own words love was higher than all else, and what could be sinful in the closest possible union of those who love ? Madiël was much saddened when Renata thus made known to him her passionate desires ; at these words—thus she related—his face became all ashy-flaming, like the sun looked at through smoked mica. He firmly forbade Renata even to think of matters of the flesh, reminding her of the bliss unbounded of the righteous souls in Heaven, where enter none who yield themselves up to carnal temptations. But Renata, not daring to insist openly, decided to attain her aim by cunning. As in the days of childhood, she prayed Madiël to pass the night with her in her bed—and there, embracing him and not releasing him from her arms, she urged him by all means to unite with her. But the angel, inflamed with vast anger, dissolved himself into a column of fire and vanished, scorching Renata's hair and shoulders.

After that the angel did not appear at all for many a day, and Renata fell into an extreme state of gloom, for she loved Madiël more than all the children of men, more than all the fleshless creatures and the Lord God Himself. Days and nights did she spend in tears, astonishing all those around her by her unconsolable despair ; she lay for long hours like one dead, beat her head against the walls, and even sought voluntary death, thinking, if only for a single moment in the next life, thus to see her beloved. Unceasingly she addressed prayers to Madiël, beseeching him to return

38

to her, promising with due solemnity to submit in all
matters to his righteous choice if only she might feel
once again the nearness of his presence. At last, when
strength was already leaving Renata, Madiël appeared
to her in a dream, saying : " As you desire to join me
in bodily union, so will I appear to you in the image of
a man ; wait for me seven weeks and seven days."

Roughly two months after this vision, Renata made
the acquaintance of a young Count who came to their
lands from Austria. He was clad in white garments ;
his eyes were blue and his hair as if of fine gold thread,
so Renata at once recognised him as—Madiël. But
the visitor did not want to show that they knew one
another, and he styled himself Count Heinrich von
Otterheim. Renata tried by all means to attract his
attention, not even disdaining the help of a sorceress
and the use of love philtres. Whether these unworthy
means were effective, or whether the Count sought
Renata of his own accord is not known; in any case he
disclosed to her his heartfelt love and requested that
she secretly leave the parental roof with him. Renata
did not hesitate a moment, and the Count, at night,
drove away with her and lived with her in his family
castle on the River Danube.

Renata spent two years at the castle of the Count
and according to her words they were as happy as no
one else in the world has been since the fall of our fore-
father in Paradise. They lived constantly close to the
world of angels and demons, and they engaged in a
great scheme that was to bring happiness to all the
peoples of the earth. One thing alone grieved Renata
—nothing would persuade Heinrich to confess that he
was Madiël and an angel, and he stubbornly persisted
that he was a loyal subject of Duke Ferdinand. However, towards the end of the second year of their life
together, the soul of Heinrich suddenly became possessed by dark thoughts ; he became gloomy, sad and
sorrowful and all at once, in the night, without giving

anyone warning, he left his castle, riding off no one knew whither. Renata waited for him several weeks, but without her protector she knew not how to defend herself from the attacks of evil spirits, and they began to torment her without mercy. Not desiring to stay longer in the castle, where she was no more mistress, she decided to leave and to return to her parents. The fiendish powers left her no peace, even on her journey, and perhaps to-night, had I not hastened to her assistance, they would have destroyed her for ever.

Thus related Renata, and I think her narrative occupied .more than an hour, though here I have rendered it much more shortly. Renata spoke without looking at me, expecting from me neither contradiction nor agreement, as if not even addressing herself to me, but as if confessing to some invisible confessor. Neither in relating of incidents that had undoubtedly shaken her cruelly, nor in speaking of matters that to most would seem shameful and that the majority of women would prefer to conceal, did she betray either emotion or shame. I must note that the earlier part of Renata's story, though she then spoke much more incoherently and disconnectedly, I retained clearly. All that happened to her after her flight from the parental home, on the other hand, remained very confused to me. I learned later that it was in that latter part of her narrative that she had concealed a great deal and, more particularly, related much not in accordance with reality.

Scarcely had she uttered the last words, than Renata suddenly weakened entirely, as if her strength had just been enough to tell the story to its end. She glanced in my direction as if with surprise, then sighed deeply, fell with her face into the pillow and closed her eyes. I wanted to get up from her couch, but, softly embracing me with her arms, with tender compulsion she made me lie next to her. Not surprised by anything that might happen in that unusual night, and

The Fiery Angel

obedient, I lay down on the bed next to this woman, then still a complete stranger to me, not quite knowing how to behave towards her. Affectionately she encircled my neck and, pressing against me with almost naked body, she immediately fell asleep, soundly and undisturbed. It was already light with the blue light of dawn, and after what we had experienced I almost laughed to see how we both lay, strangers in a strange hostelry in a forest wilderness, yet embraced in one bed like brother and sister beneath a parental roof.

When I had convinced myself that Renata was sleeping quietly, I carefully freed myself from her embrace, for I felt the need of fresh wind on my face and to be alone. Attentively I gazed at the face of the sleeping woman, and it appeared soft and innocent, like the images of children in the pictures of Fra Beata Angelico at Fiesole; almost incredible did it seem to me that, so short a while ago, the Devil had possessed this woman. Softly I left the room, donned my tall hat and made my way down, and, as everybody in the house was still asleep, I drew back the bolts of the door myself, and straightway found myself in the wood. There I walked along a solitary path amidst the heavy trunks of beeches, dearer to me than the slim palms and guaiacums of America, and listened to the early chirruping of the birds, that greeted me as a familiar language.

I have never belonged to the number of those persons who, following the philosophers of the peripatetic school, maintain that in nature there are no disembodied spirits, denying the existence of demons and even that of holy angels. I have always held, though before meeting with Renata I had never actually been a witness of anything miraculous, that both observation and experiment, the two primary foundations of knowledge, prove undeniably the presence in our world, side by side with mankind, of other spirit forces, who are considered by Christians to compose the spiritual armies

41

of Christ and the hordes of Satan. And I remembered
also the words of Lactantius Firmianus, who maintains
that at times guardian angels are tempted by the charms
of young maidens, the souls of whom it is their duty
to protect from sin. None the less, many details in
the strange narrative of Renata seemed to me hardly
credible and indeed inadmissible. Admitting that this
woman I had encountered actually was in the power of
the Devil, I was unable to distinguish where the deceits
of the Spirit of Evil ended and where her own lies began.

Thus tormenting myself with guesses and misunderstandings, I wandered at length along the paths of the
unknown forest, and the sun was already risen high
when I returned to the roadside hostelry in which I had
spent the night. At the gate stood the hostess, a
corpulent woman, red-faced and of stern appearance,
more like the leader of a band of robbers, who, however, recognising me, greeted me with all courtesy,
calling me lord knight. I decided to use this convenient opportunity to find out about the mysterious
lady, and, approaching, I enquired with a voice of
indifference, as if I only desired to gossip for want of
something better to do—who was the woman whose
room was next to mine.

And this, roughly word for word, was the unexpected
answer that the hostess gave to me:

"Ah, Lord Knight, it were better you did not ask
me about her, for my kind heart led me, maybe, to
commit a mortal sin when I gave asylum to a heretic
and one who has signed a pact with the Devil. Though
she is not from our parts I know her history, for I was
told it by a good friend of mine, an itinerant merchant
from her part of the country. This woman who pretends to be so modest is in truth nothing but a whore,
and by various machinations she penetrated into the
confidence of Count Otterheim, a man of most noble
family, whose castle is a little below Speier, on the
Rhine. She so ensorcelled the young count, who, already

in his early childhood, had lost his parents, persons
worthy and respected, that instead of taking unto
himself a fair wife and serving his master, the Kurfürst
of Pfalz, he occupied himself with alchymy, magic and
other deeds of blackness. Would you believe it, from
the day this besom took up habitation in his castle,
each night they altered their shape—he into a were-
wolf, she into a were-wolf bitch—and scoured the
neighbourhood ; how many they slew during that time
—children, foals, sheep, it is hard to say. Then they
brought evil and blight upon the people, caused the
milk of cows to run dry, called up thunder, ruined the
crops of their enemies, and committed hundreds of
other crimes by means of their magic powers. But
suddenly the Saint Crescentia of Dietrich appeared in
a vision to the Count and denounced his sinful conduct.
The Count then became penitent, accepted his cross,
and set off barefoot to the holy grave of God,
ordering his servants to drive his concubine from
the castle, whence she went, wandering from village to
village. If I gave her shelter, Lord Knight, it was only
because I then knew nothing of her history, but, seeing
how, by day and by night, she now pines and moans
for her sinful soul cannot rest, I shall not endure her
to stay another four-and-twenty hours, for I do not
wish to abet the Enemy of Mankind."

This speech of the hostess, who related a great deal
more that I do not remember, filled my soul with shame
and remorse. I was not of course distressed at the fact
that I had spent a few hours in bed with a woman who
might really have been guilty of repulsive crimes, for I
do not admit the possibility of transmittance of spiritual
infection by mere contact and, moreover, I had no
reason to believe all that the hostess had told me. But
from her words I could at least see without question in
how many particulars this lady had deceived me in her
nocturnal relation of her life, if only in that she had
persuaded me that the castle of her paramour stood in

an Austrian archdukedom, when in reality it was here,
in the neighbourhood, on our native Rhine. It appeared to me as though my companion of the night,
seeing in me a newly arrived and simple sailor, had
wanted to befool me, and this thought so fogged my
mind with indignation, that I forgot even the obvious
signs of possession of the unfortunate creature by the
Devil, of which I had myself been recent witness.

But even while I stood before the hostess as she
continued her plaints, not knowing what to do, the
door opened and upon the threshold appeared Renata
herself. She was attired in a long cape of silk, blue in
colour and with a hood that covered her face, and in a
pink bodice with white and blue trimmings—as are
dressed the noble ladies of Köln. She held herself
proud and free as a Duchess, so that I scarcely recognised in her the devil-distracted creature of my night's
vigil. Probably, in the modest attire of a Spanish
mariner, I looked to her a pauper and a simpleton.
However, finding me with her eyes, Renata walked
straight towards me with her light step, that always
suggested the flight of a bird.

I took my hat off before the lady, and she said
hurriedly but commandingly:

" Rupprecht, we must ride away from here at once,
immediately. I cannot stay here, not an hour more."

It must be thought that the voice of Renata contained
some especial charm for me, or that at our very first
meeting she had taken the opportunity to attract me
by some secret means of witchcraft known to her, for
despite that which I had been thinking of her only a few
moments ago, I found nothing to say in contradiction
of her words, indeed accepted them as an order dis-
obedience of which was impossible. And when the
hostess of the hostelry, suddenly changing her polite
tone to one extremely rude,' began to demand from
Renata the money she owed her for her room, I
hastened to say that everything would be paid her

44

fairly. Then I asked Renata whether she had a horse
to continue the road, for in such remote districts it is
not easy to find a good one.

" I have no horse," said Renata to me. " But from
here it is not far to the town. You can lift me into your
saddle and lead the horse by the rein. And in the town
it will not be difficult to buy another mount."

She ordered me and all my goods about as if I were
her servant or a bought slave.

And, to justify myself in my own eyes in a measure,
I thus addressed myself:

" What matter even though I spend some coins and
some days extra in travel. The girl is attractive and
worth such a sacrifice; and, after the labours of my
journey, I am entitled to the usual diversion. And,
moreover, she laughed at me yesterday and I must
show her that I am not so simple and uncouth as she
supposes. Now, I shall amuse myself with her during
the journey, until she bores me, and then I shall leave
her. And as far as the fact that the Devil is after her is
concerned, that is hardly my business, and I am not
likely to be frightened of any devil in my relations with
a pretty woman, I, who never feared the redskins with
their poisoned arrows."

Thus I reasoned with myself, trying to convince
myself that my meeting with Renata was merely a
droll incident, one of those that men, smiling, relate to
their fellows in alehouses, and, deliberately, with self-
importance, I felt my taut and heavy belt, reminding
myself of the song I had heard the evening before:

Ob dir ein Dirn gefelt,
So schweig, hastu kein Gelt.

Fortifying our strength in the inn with milk and
bread, we made ready to depart. I helped Renata to
mount my horse, which had quite recovered overnight.
To the bundle with my goods was added another
package, though not a heavy one. Renata was as

merry as a turtle-dove, laughed a great deal, joked and parted on friendly terms with the hostess. At last we struck the road, Renata on horseback, I walking by her side, holding the horse by the rein or leaning on the pommel. All the inhabitants of the inn crowded at the gate to see us off and take leave of us, not without mockery. And I was ashamed to turn my head and look at them.

Chapter the Second

That which was foretold us by the Village Witch and how we spent the Night at Düsseldorf

FROM the hostelry, for a time the road still led through the woods. It was cool and shady, and Renata and I talked without tiring, the while we slowly made our way onward. I was not a stranger to society, despite my soldier's life, for in Italian cities I had often had occasion to visit both carnival masques and theatrical performances, and later, in New Spain, I used to attend the evening gatherings in local wealthy houses, where reigns by no means the barbarism of a wilderness, as many think, but where, on the contrary, elegant ladies play the lute, the zither and the flute, and dance the algada, the passionesa, the mauresque and the other latest dances with their cavaliers. Trying to show Renata that under my rough sailor's jacket hid one who was no stranger to education, I was happily surprised to find in my partner's conversation a sharpness of wit and a breadth of knowledge unusual in a woman, so that involuntarily all my mental faculties took guard, like an experienced fencer meeting unexpectedly a skilful blade in his opponent. Of the manifestations of the night we said not a word, and one might have imagined, to see how gaily we were talking, that I was peacefully escorting a lady away from some sumptuous tournament.

To my question whither we should turn our way, Renata replied without hesitation—to Köln, for there she had relatives with whom she would like to stay a

while ; and I was glad that I had not to alter the route
I had chosen. The thought that our strange acquaintanceship was not long to last caused me deep pain,
and yet at the same time was not altogether displeasing
to me ; only, I thought secretly to myself that I must
not waste time, if I wished to recompense myself for
what I had missed on the previous evening. Accordingly, I sought to give the conversation a free and easy
turn, like that of a dialogue in Italian commedia dell'
arte, and, encouraged by the cordial smiles of my
companion, who maintained, none the less, a degree
of the aloofness of one higher in rank, I dared at times
to kiss her fingers and make subtle hints. And I do
not know whither we should have sailed on the dangerous waves of these frivolous jests if a new and unexpected incident had not chanced suddenly to overturn
all calculations, as a storm overturns a caravel keel
upwards.

The matter was so—I suggested to her that, passing
the tiny Neuss, we should go on to spend the night at
Düsseldorf where we should find hostels of the finest
class, and thence to Köln—by the convenient route
along the Rhine. Renata agreed with the easy condescension of a princess, and we turned out of the wood
on to the big main road, where we soon fell in with both
single travellers and parties escorted by a guard. But
passing through the open fields under the direct rays
of the sun was quite tiring, both for Renata who was
riding in a saddle not adapted to a lady's seat, and
for me who had to hurry to keep pace with the steady
progress of the horse. To while away the torrid hours
we sought shelter in the well-peopled village of Geerdt,
which lay in our way. And here Fate, already scheming
the horror of the days to come, laid a second ambush
for us.

It surprised us at once as unusual that everything
in the village was arranged for the repose of travellers,
and that many of those who had been journeying on

the same direction as ourselves also made a halt at Geerdt. I enquired the reason of this from a peasant woman, in whose house we rested and ate our midday meal, and with pride and vainglory she informed us that the village was famed far and wide in the district for its witch, who could foretell the future with surprising skill. Not only from places in the neighbourhood, according to the words of our informant, did dozens come daily, but many came from far distant villages and cities, even from Paderborn and Westfalen, to learn their fate, for the fame of the witch of Geerdt had spread throughout all the German lands.

These words were to Renata as the whistle of a snake-charmer, it was as if she immediately forgot all else and desired to go straightway to the witch. In vain did I persuade Renata to rest awhile, she did not even desire to finish her midday *merenda*, and, hurrying me, she kept on repeating:

"Let us be going, Rupprecht, let us be going at once, otherwise she will be tired and will not see so clearly into the future."

We were conducted to a small house on the outskirts of the village. At the entrance, standing or reclining on logs strewn about it, there waited a whole crowd of people, as at a church porch on Christmas Eve. These people were of most varied type, such as rarely happen to foregather together, noble ladies clad in silks and velvets and travelling in closed carriages, burghers in dark broadcloth, huntsmen in green jerkins, peasants in upturned caps, even beggars, thieves and all manner of scoundrels. Talk in all the Rhine dialects was to be heard, even in Dutch and Rotwelsch. It was as if some ruling prince had halted in a small township, and suitors and suite were crowded before his resting-place.

One had to wait one's turn, and listen perforce to the conversations which were going on all around, and which entertained Renata a great deal, though to me they seemed boring. However, here for the first time did I learn how infinite is the sea of superstition, and how much the justifiable fear of the power of sorcerers and the tricks of witches is augmented by childish and unreasoning prejudice. As was fitting in such circumstances, the talk was of various signs and fortune-tellings, of amulets and talismans, of secret spells and incantations, and I was surprised no less by the knowledge in these matters shown by the richly-clad ladies, than by that of the beggars without coats to their backs. I, like anyone else, had as a child chanced to see old women passing a hen around the pot to prevent the bird running from home, or, in the morning when they combed their tresses, spitting on the hairs left on the comb to escape the evil eye, or had heard them trying to cure themselves of back-ache with the words *sista, pista, rista, xista*, repeated ten times, or of flea-bite by exclaiming *och, och*—but here a dam burst before me and a whole stream of superstitions poured forth upon me like a flood. Interrupting one another, they spoke of how to protect oneself from witchcraft with sulphur, how to enchant a girl by throwing her a toad, how to divert the eye of a jealous husband by means of knotted cords, how to cast spells to increase the yield of vines, what stockings best aid a woman in the pains of child-birth and of what material a bullet must be cast that it may never miss its aim—to listen to them one would have thought that signs attended every step in life.

I remember that there was a beardless, doddering old man, dressed like a medicus, all in black; he praised the witch without ceasing, speaking thus:

" You'll do well to believe me! As if I didn't know fortune-tellers and witches! For more than fifty years have I followed them; ever seeking those I might believe. I have been in Dalmatia, and further than that, sailed across the sea to Fez, to the muchazzimins. I have tried fortune-telling with bones and with wax, with cards and with beans; chiromancy, crystallomancy, catoptromancy and geomancy; even had recourse to goety and necromancy; and the horoscopes that have been prepared for me—even I cannot remember! Only every one lied to me, and the tenth of the prophecies did not come true. But here the old beldam reads in the past as in a printed book, and speaks of the future as if she sat in council with the Lord God daily. Of my past life she has told me what I had forgotten myself, and what lies in wait for me she just reckons on her fingers!"

Listening to this senile chatterer, I thought that I too might have lost faith in fortune-telling had I been deceived for a good half-century, and also I wondered whether it were worth while to peer into the future when one was already waist-deep in the grave. But I had no desire to argue with anybody, and while Renata, still not having abated her proud manner, asked questions about amulets and love potions, I patiently awaited our turn to enter the house.

At last a red-haired lad who was addressed as the son of the witch beckoned to us with his hand, and having taken from us the fixed price, eighteen kreuzers each, let us through the door.

Inside the house was twilight, for the windows were hung with deep-red cloths, and it smelt stuffily of dried herbs. Though it was very hot outside a fire burned in the stove. In the light of this twilight, I discerned on the floor a tom-cat—an animal beloved of all magic; beneath the ceiling hung a cage, and in it what appeared to be a white blackbird. The witch herself, an old woman with a wrinkled face, sat at a table against the back wall. She was clothed in a special kind of gown, such as witches always wear, adorned with the images of crosses and horns, and her head was swathed in a red kerchief ornamented with sequins. Before the witch stood jars of water, packets containing roots, and various other odds and ends—and all the while, muttering something, she kept threading through these with her fingers.

Raising towards us her eyes, her sunken and piercing eyes, the old creature mumbled amiably :

" Well, you pretty ones, what come you here to seek from grandmother ? There's no warm bed here, only bare planks. But that's nothing, that's nothing, be patient, all will have its turn. Time was for strawberries, time will be for apples. So you want me to tell you your fortune, little poppets ? "

Not without disappointment did I hear all this coarse patter, and even the remnants of curiosity left me. But the beldam, still muttering like one drunk, shuffled about with her hands, found an egg and broke the white into the water, which clouded. Peering into the cloudy shapes that wound and unwound in the water, the witch began to foretell us our future, and her words seemed to me but a feeble deception :

" I see a journey here for you, sweet children, but not a far one. Whither you are bound, go thither ; there awaits for you the fulfilment of your desires. A stern man threatens to part you, but you are bound one with a leather strap. A warm little bed, a warm little bed awaits you, my pretty ones ! "

The old creature went on mumbling for a little and then beckoned us towards her, saying :

" Come nearer, baby fledglings, and I shall give you a little herb, a good herb : only once a year it blooms, just once only, in the night of the eve of the day of St. John."

Expecting no harm, we approached the witch. But suddenly her mouth twisted in her wrinkled face, her eyes became round like the eyes of a pike and black as two coals. She quickly stretched forward and, clutching at my coat with fingers crooked like an iron hook, no longer muttering, she hissed snake-like :

" My boy, what is this, this that you have upon you ? On the coat, you, and you too, my beauty, on the bodice ? Blood—where is it from ? Such a lot of blood—where does it come from ? The whole coat is blood and the

whole bodice is blood. And it streams, the blood, oozes
and smells."

And she snuffled with the nostrils of her hooked nose,
inhaling the scent, and her whole body trembled either
with joy or terror. But I felt uneasy at this hissing and
these words, and Renata near me tottered so that she
might straightway have fallen. So I tore myself free
from the clutches of the ape, overturned the table so
that the glasses broke and the water ran, and, catching
Renata in one arm, I laid the other hand on the hilt
of my sword, shouting :

" Away, witch ! Else I pierce your damned body
like a fish ! "

But the beldam in fury still clutched at us, howling,
" Blood ! Blood ! "

At the noise, the son of the witch ran in and felled
his mother from her feet with a blow of his fist, then began to rain on us obscene curses. It appeared as though
such happenings were no novelty to him, and as though
he knew how to behave when they arose. As for me,
I hastily bore Renata out into the fresh air, and, not
listening to the questions of those who were waiting
their turn, I hurried to the home where we had left
our baggage and our horse.

But after this occurrence all the gaiety and talkative-
ness of Renata was as if mown down by a scythe, and
she uttered no word nor did she lift her eyes. When
our horse had been girthed and I had helped Renata
into the saddle, she drooped like a broken reed and the
reins fell from her hands. In her movements and
actions she probably resembled exactly the remarkable
automaton of Albertus Magnus.

Thus, sadly, we departed from Geerdt and made our
way along the road towards the Rhine. To discourage
Renata from believing in the prophecies of the witch,
I tried to picture to her all that had happened reflected
in a comic mirror, relating to her all those cases, even
those of which I had only heard, in which predictions

53

had not come true or had been turned to ridicule. I told her how a prophet foretold a near death to the Duke of Milan, Gian Galeazzo Visconti, and a long life for himself, and was immediately slain by the Duke. Further, I related how Henry the VIIth, father of the present English King, asked an astrologer much given to prediction : was it known to him where he would pass the night ? And, when the astrologer replied Nay, said " I can see into the future better than you : you will spend it in the Tower of London "— whither the unhappy astrologer was at once taken. I also told her of a certain youth, to whom a gypsy exactly appointed the day and hour of his death, and who by design therefore ran through all his ample fortune by about that very time, and then, seeing that he was ruined and death yet tarried, ended his life by a thrust of his sword. And I related too of one to whom a seer explained that he would die of a white horse, and who thenceforward began to avoid all horses, even chestnut, pied and black, but perished by an inn sign with the picture of a white horse falling upon him in the street.

By these and similar stories I sought to enliven the spirits of Renata, though the wild prophecy of the witch pressed upon my soul too like a fallen rock. But as Renata did not show in any way that she was listening to, or even noticing my words, I gradually became silent also. We rode in silence, straight towards the blue of the eastern edge of the sky. The horse, tired by its load, stepped wearily, and I, tired too from the miles I had walked, studied carefully the image of Renata, dissecting it, like a connoisseur studying the heads of marble figures.

It was then for the first time that I saw plainly the features of Renata's face, with which later my glances became so familiar, and I realised that she was in no way beautiful. Her nostrils were too thin, and the line of her chin to her ears swept almost slant, while her ears themselves, in which glittered golden earrings, were placed unevenly and too high; the eyes were cut not quite straight and the eyelashes too long. Everything in her face was irregular, but there was in it a charm, distilled, perhaps, by some magic means, or with the aid of some Cleopatrian mystery. Judging from the face, I would almost have thought Renata Italian, but she spoke our language like a mother-tongue, and with all the peculiarities of the Meissen dialect.

After an arduous ride, and after crossing the Rhine, we reached Düsseldorf, the capital of Berg, a city that has grown rapidly in the last few years owing to the enterprise of its Duke, and that even now can rank with the most handsome towns of Germany. In the city I found a good hostelry under the sign "*Im Lewen*," and for a fair price obtained two of the best rooms, for I wanted Renata to receive both that luxury of surrounding that was her due and all the possible comforts of a journey. But Renata seemed to me not to notice my efforts, and one might well have thought that, amidst the polished furniture, the tiled fireplaces and the mirrors, she perceived no difference from the bare, uneven benches of the country inn.

The host, taking us for rich people, invited us to dine at his table, or, as the French say, at the *table d'hôte*, and he served us very diligently, especially praising some chicken fried in almond milk; and the good Rhinewine from Bacharach. But Renata, though present in body at our table, was far away in thought, and she hardly touched the dishes and took no part in conversation, though I made various efforts to blow the breath of life into her. I related of those wonders of the New World that I happened to have witnessed, of the steps in the temples of the Maya flanked by giant, hewn masks, of immeasurable cacti, in the trunks of which can stand a horse and rider, of the perilous hunt of the grey bear and the spotted ounce, and of my

lone adventures, not forgetting to embellish my tales
with quotations now from the opinions of a contemporary writer, now from the verses of a poet of antiquity.
The host and his wife listened mouths agape, but
Renata, suddenly, breaking into the middle of my
speech, rose from the table and said :

" Are you not weary yourself, Rupprecht, of chattering of such trifles ! Farewell."

And without adding another word she turned and
left, though this was rather impolite, as I think now.
But at the time I only felt confusion, and fear lest she
might be angry with me and, jumping up, I hurried
after her.

In her room Renata silently seated herself in the
corner on a chair, and there she remained, motionless
and speechless. I, not daring now to open a conversation, timidly lowered myself on to the floor next to her.
Thus we stayed in the solitary room, holding no speech,
and from a distance we might have seemed some lifeless creation, carved by a skilled hand and made of
painted wood. All the gayness, all the lack of ceremony
with which we had conversed in the beech forest, had
now evaporated, leaving the bottoms of our souls dry.
I felt myself gradually lapsing into a condition of dumb
helplessness, and it seemed to me as if I could now
neither utter a word nor attempt a movement. Thus,
probably, feel animals when they grow paralysed
beneath the staring eye of the rattlesnake.

On my left through two large open windows could
be seen the tiled roofs of the twisting streets of Düsseldorf, and the belfry of the church of Saint Lambert,
triumphant above the house-tops. The bluish eve
spread softly across these triangles and rectangles,
breaking up the clearness of their lines and merging
them into shapeless masses. And that same bluish
evening flowed into the room and swathed us with
the white sheets of a shroud. I watched, in the darkness, as brighter and brighter glittered the semi-

circular earrings of Renata, and more and more distinct grew the outlines of her thin white hands, and now I could no longer turn away my glance. As all around had become enveloped in the silence of the night, it must be assumed that much time had elapsed, but we did not note its passage, nor hear its steps, nor know of it.

And now at last, with an effort of will as though I were taking a decision of greatest importance, committing some perilous deed, I tore my eyes away from Renata, tore my soul away from the silence, and spoke :

" Perhaps you are tired, noble lady, and wish to rest. I shall leave. . . . "

My voice seemed to me very unnatural, but the sounds broke that magic circle into which we had been bound. Renata lifted her immobile face ; her lips parted, and when she uttered the words it was as if a dead woman spoke, by a miracle :

" No, Rupprecht, you must not go away. I cannot remain alone ; I am in fear."

Then, after a few moments of silence, as her thoughts slowly unrolled, she spoke again :

" But she said that we should ride on whither we were bound, for there awaits us the fulfilment of our desires. So, in Köln we shall meet Heinrich. That I knew even before she spoke, and the hag only read it in my thoughts."

Daring sparkled up in me like a tiny flame from under the ashes, and I answered :

" Why should your Count Heinrich be in Köln if his lands are on the Danube ? "

But Renata did not notice the barb concealed in my retort, and, catching only one expression she clutched at it feverishly.

In her turn she demanded :

" *My* Count Heinrich ? How *mine* ? Is not all that is mine at the same time also yours, Rupprecht ? Is there between us a line, a boundary that divides your being from mine ? Are we not one, and the ache of my heart does it not pierce your heart ? "

I was struck by this speech as by a club, for though I was by then already completely subject to Renata's charms, yet I had not imagined any relation such as her words assumed. I did not even find anything to reply, while she, leaning her pale face towards me and placing her soft hands on my shoulders, asked gently :

" Do you not love *him*, Rupprecht ? Can one not love *him* ? But he is of the Heavens above, he is but one."

Once more I could not find an answer, and Renata quickly fell to her knees and drew me to stand close to her. Then, turning to the open window, to the brilliant, moonless stars, she began to speak in a voice meek, low, but clear, a sort of litany, to each prayer of which I had to intone a response, like a church choir.

Renata spoke :

" Give me to see once more his eyes, blue as the skies themselves, and his eyelashes sharp as needles ! "

I had to intone :

" Give me to see ! "

Renata spoke :

" Give me to hear his voice, sweet, like the bells of a tiny temple submerged beneath the waters ! "

I had to intone :

" Give me to hear ! "

Renata spoke :

" Give me to kiss his white hands, hands of mountain snow, and his lips, not vivid, but like rubies beneath a transparent bridal veil ! "

I had to intone :

" Give me to kiss ! "

Renata spoke :

" Give me to press my bared breasts to his breast, to feel how his heart slows, and then beats quickly, quickly, quickly ! "

And I had to intone :

The Fiery Angel

" Give me to press ! "

Renata was tireless in the invention of more and more new praises for her litany, composing them like a monk his prayers, and surprising me with the elaborateness of her comparisons, like those of a meister in a contest of meistersingers. I had no power to resist the witchery of her appeals, and, deprived of will, I muttered the responses, that pierced my pride like thorns.

And then Renata, pressing herself against me, looking into my very eyes, asked me, seeking to torture herself with her questions :

" And tell me now, Rupprecht, is he not handsomer than all else ? Is he not an angel ? But I shall see him again ? I shall caress him ? And he me ? If only once ? Only once ! "

And I answered in my despair :

" He is an angel. You will see him. You will caress him."

The moon of yesterday rose into the skies and pointed the column of its light at Renata, and under the moonbeam the darkness of our room moved. The bluish light at once revived the previous night in my memory, and all that I had learned about Renata, and the resolves to which I had later pledged myself. With even measured tread like the march of well-drilled troops, there passed through my head such thoughts as these :

' And what if this woman is once more mocking you ? Yesterday she mocked, pretending the evil-doing of the Devil, and to-day she mocks, pretending the madness of sorrow. And in a few days, when you have been dropped like a fool, she will be making jest of you with another, and letting him make free with her, in the spirit of this morning.'

With these thoughts I became like a drunken man and, suddenly seizing Renata by the shoulders, I said to her, smiling :

" It is not fitting to give yourself to sorrow, pretty lady, shall we not turn now to a pastime gay and pleasant ? "

Renata shrank back from me in fear, but I, bracing myself up with the thought that otherwise I might become ridiculous, drew her to me and bent over her, intending to kiss her.

Renata freed herself from my hands with the strength and agility of a forest cat and cried out to me :

" Rupprecht, the Devil inhabits you ! "

But I replied to her :

" No devil is in me, but you think to play with me in vain, for I am not such a simpleton as you suppose ! "

Again I seized her, and. we began to wrestle, very hideously, and I gripped her fingers so strongly that they creaked, and she beat and scratched me furiously. At one time I had already felled her to the floor, feeling for her at that moment nothing but hatred, but she suddenly plunged her teeth into my hand and slipped out with a lizard-like twist. Then, sensing that I was the stronger, she bent all double, her head fell on her knees, and there happened to her that same fit of tears as yesterday. Seated thus on the floor—for I in confusion had let her drop—Renata wept in despair. Her hair fell around her face and her shoulders trembled pitifully.

At that moment an image rose in my imagination : a picture by the Florentine painter Sandro Filippepi, which I saw by chance at the house of some grandee in Rome. On the canvas was depicted a stone wall of crude blocks tightly wedged into one another ; an arched entrance set in it was firmly barred by iron gates ; and near it, on a ledge projecting forward, was seated an abandoned woman, dropping her head on her hands in the inconsolability of her sorrow. Her face was not visible—only her dark hair. Garments were strewn around. And nowhere was there anyone else.

The Fiery Angel

This picture had made the strongest impression on me, I know not whether because the painter knew how to render in it emotion with an especial vividness, or because I saw it on a day when I myself had experienced a great sorrow—but never was I able to recall this work without my heart contracting painfully, and bitter grief rising in my throat. And when I saw Renata, seated in the same pose, dropping her head and weeping with the selfsame inconsolability—the two images, the one revealed to me in life and the other created by the painter, rose one upon the other before me, merged, and live till this day inseparable in my soul. Even then, the moment I pictured to myself Renata, once more lonely, abandoned, before the gates thus mercilessly closed upon her—inexhaustible sorrow flooded into my heart and, kneeling again, I tenderly moved Renata's hands from her face and said to her, with a catch in my voice, but solemnly :

" Forgive me, noble lady. In truth the Demon possessed me and blinded my feelings. I swear to you by the salvation of my soul that nothing like this will ever happen again ! Accept me once more as your true and humble servant, or as your elder and willing brother."

Renata lifted her head and looked at me, at first like some small hunted beast when the hunter gives it its freedom, then trustingly and childlike, and she took my face affectionately between the palms of her hands and replied :

" Rupprecht, dearest Rupprecht ! You must not be angry with me and ask of me what I cannot give. I gave all to my friend from Heaven, and for men I have left neither kisses nor words of passion. I am an emptied basket from which another has taken all the flowers and the fruit, but even empty you must carry it, for fate has bound us together and our fellowship was long ago inscribed in the Book of the All-knowing."

Again I swore never to leave her, as one swears before an altar in the hour of betrothal, and my oath was honest, though later it once seemed to me as though I should break it.

Rising then from my knees, I said that I would take my leave, and would go into the other room we had engaged, so that Renata might rest alone freely. But she stopped me, saying :

" Rupprecht, without you I should be in fear ; *they* would fall upon me again and torment me the whole night through. You must remain with me."

Not ashamed, as children are not ashamed, Renata quickly took off her dress, then her footwear, and, nearly naked, she laid herself into bed, under the blue canopy, calling me to her, and I did not know how to refuse her. So, this second night of our acquaintance we passed under one coverlet, but remaining as strange to each other as though separated by iron bars. And when it happened that an understandable excitement again overcame my will, and, forgetting my oaths, I strove again for tenderness, Renata quietened me with sad and cold words, so passionless and thereby so cruel, that all the blood became numbed in me, and I fell on my face impotent, like a corpse.

Chapter the Third

*How we came to live in the City of Köln and how
we were deceived by Mysterious Knockings*

LWAYS whenever possible I kept to the wise
saying of the French:

> *Lever a six, diner a dix,*
> *Souper a six, coucher a dix,*
> *Fait vivre l'homme dix fois dix.*

So the next day I woke much earlier than Renata
and, again slipping carefully from her sleeping embrace,
I went into the adjoining room. There by the window,
through which young and handsome Düsseldorf
sparkled in the morning sun, I considered my position.
I felt already that I lacked the strength to leave Renata,
that I either had been charmed to her by some magic
power, or borne naturally into gentle bondage by the
Mother of Love—the Cyprian.

Boldly reviewing my position, like a warrior who
finds himself fallen into danger, I now addressed myself
thus: "Very well, abandon yourself to this madness
if already you cannot overpower it, but be circumspect
lest you lose in this abyss your whole life, and perhaps
your honour. Mark to yourself beforehand terms and
limits, and beware overstepping them when your soul
is aflame and your mind powerless to give counsel."

I took out of the belt the coins sewn within it, and
divided my savings into three equal shares: one share
I decided to spend with Renata, another I desired to

63

give to my father, and the third I kept for myself, so that, returning to New Spain, I should be able to live there an independent life. At the same time, I resolved that I should not stay with Renata for more than three months, whatever wind might blow upon our life together, for after the happenings of the night I did not trust completely her words about the relatives who were supposed to be waiting for her in Köln : and the immediate future soon showed me how correct I was in that surmise.

Having thus thought out everything reasonably and soberly, I went to the host of the inn and for a fair price sold him my horse. Next I went to the river quay and bargained with one of the barges that were descending the Rhine with Netherland goods, for her to take us as far as Köln. Then I acquired various necessaries proper to a journey with a lady, such as— a pair of cushions, soft coverlets, victuals and wines ; and at last I returned to the hostelry.

Renata displayed real joy at seeing me, and it seemed to me that perhaps she had imagined I had flown secretly and left her. We breakfasted together in care-free spirit, once more without recalling the torments of the night, as if in daylight we were quite different beings. Immediately after the meal we walked over to the barge, for she was quite ready to set sail. The barge was of goodly bulk, with steep sides, and two-masted, and we were given on board a large cabin situated in the bow part of the vessel, which was raised high and terminated in a peaked roof. I spread blankets on the floor, and, in such accommodation, an envoy of the Great Mogul himself might have travelled without fatigue.

We cast off from the docks of Düsseldorf soon after noon, and travelled without much adventure until Köln itself, two days and nights, spending the hours of darkness riding at anchor. During all this journey, both by day and by night, Renata remained very calm and reasonable, and she showed no signs either of deceitful gaiety, as on the day when we were riding to Geerdt, or of dark despair, as during the night spent under the sign "*Im Lewen.*" Very often she joined with me in being enchanted by the beauty of the places past which we travelled, and engaged with me in conversation upon various matters of common life or art.

Certain words said to me by Renata at this time I think it necessary to enter here, as far as I remember them, for later I found in them the key to the riddle of certain of her actions.

They were uttered when the owner of the barge, a stern mariner named Moritz Krock, broke into our conversation and it happened to turn to events that had taken place just about that time at Münster. At first glance Moritz had not the appearance of a fanatical reformer, he was attired in ordinary sailor's clothes, like myself, and carried on the duties of his profession, but he spoke with such fervour of the new prophet from Leyden, whom he called "Iohann the Righteous, mounted upon the Throne of David," that I began to doubt whether he were not himself one of the re-baptised. Having related to us how the citizens of Münster had destroyed images, organs and all church properties, and lumped together all their goods to have and use in common, how they had established twelve elders, according to the number of the twelve tribes of Israel, and placed Iohann Bockelszoon at their head, and how the Münsterners, fortified by the armies of Heaven had successfully repulsed the episcopalian landsknechts, Moritz continued, as if delivering a sermon :

"For a long time we men hungered and thirsted, and there came to pass the prophecy of Jeremiah : 'The children shall cry out for bread and there shall be none shall give unto them.' The darkness of Egypt enveloped the vaults of the temple, but now they

resound with hymns of triumph. The new Gideon
has been hired by the Lord as day-labourer at a
groschen a day, and he has sharpened his scythe to
mow the yellowed fields. Forged are the lances on the
anvil of Nimrod and his tower is ripe to fall. Elijah
is risen in the New Jerusalem and the true prophets
of the true Apostolic Church fare out unto all lands—
to preach a God who is not dumb, but liveth and
speaketh ! "

To this arrogant speech I replied, with circumspection, that it was as dangerous for new thoughts discovered by learned men to become the property of the
people, as for daggers to be distributed to children as
toys. That the pomp of the church, as well as of many
church institutions, perhaps even the monastic, so often
plunged deep in riches, did in truth not correspond to
the spirit of the teaching of Jesus Christ, but that it
was impossible to better the matter by riot and force.
That, lastly, life must be rejuvenated not by abolishing
dogmas and robbing princes, but by educating minds.

It was here that Renata joined unexpectedly into
the conversation, though I had thought that she had
not been listening at all to Moritz' words and had been
busy studying the currents of the river, and she said :

" Only those who have never known what faith
means can speak of such things. Who has but once
experienced with what bliss the soul is received into
God—will never even think of a necessity to forge
lances or sharpen scythes. All these Davids marching
against Belials—these Luthers, these Zwinglis and these
Iohanns—are the servants of the Devil and his henchmen. What a deal we talk of the crimes of others, but
what if we were to turn our glance upon ourselves, and
look as if into a mirror—were to see our sins and our
shame ? Ah, then would we be horrified, and flee into
the cell of a monastery as the stag flies from the huntsman. It is not the church we must reform, but our
own souls, that are no more able to pray to the Almighty

and have faith in His word but must ever be desiring
to reason and prove. And if you, Rupprecht, thought
as this man here, I would not stay with you a moment
longer, but would rather throw myself head foremost
into this river by our side than share a cabin with a
heretic."

These words, that seemed to me very unexpected at
the time, Renata uttered with passion, and, quickly
getting up, she walked away briskly. And Moritz
also, having looked at me not without suspicion, walked
away and began to abuse his mates.

We never returned to the subject, but Moritz shunned
us, and we were left on the barge in complete solitude,
which I preferred. After the angry words of Renata,
I endeavoured to conciliate her and pay her more
attention, to show her more openly how much store I
set upon her affection; for example, the whole night
until daybreak, which Renata spent sleepless in the
cabin, I remained with her and at her request softly
stroked her hair, until my hand grew almost numb.
Renata, apparently, was grateful to me and treated me,
during these hours and next morning as well, with a
kindness quite exceptional. Thus our friendly calm
lasted until our very arrival at Köln, where it suddenly
snapped like a rigging rope at the onset of a tempest.

In the decline of the second day of our journey, there
appeared far off the tops of the churches of Köln, and
it was with a heartfelt emotion that I pointed out to
Renata the spire of Saint Martin, the squat roof of
Saint Gereon, the narrow tower of the Brothers
Minorite, the enormous massive of the Senate House,
and at last the giant torn in two, the unfulfilled grandeur
of the Cathedral of the Three Kings. When we approached more nearly and I could distinguish the
streets, the houses, and the old trees still standing, my
emotion was roused to its highest pitch, and I was ready
to weep with ecstasy, for a moment forgetting Renata.
This circumstance, judging by everything, did not

escape her cat-like observation, and she at once amended her amiable attitude towards me, becoming stern and unbending, like a reed that stiffens in the frost.

Our barge docked at the Netherlands quay in the midst of other vessels, both sailing and rowing, at the time when the confusion on the quays was at its height. Having taken leave of Moritz and clambered ashore, we plunged from our solitude on board ship as if into the first circle of the Inferno of Alighieri, where are heard :

Diverse lingue, orribilie fevelle,
Parole di dolore, accenti d'ira,
Voci alte e fiochi. . . .

Everywhere lay unladed goods, barrels and cases, everywhere crowded men, sailors, mariners, dock-hands, clerks of the merchant houses, carriers and simple idlers ; here too drove up carts for the carriage of heavy merchandise ; wheels squeaked, horses whinnied, dogs barked, men bustled and swore, and we became surrounded by traders, and Jews and carriers, all offering their services. But as soon as I had picked a lad out of the crowd, and bidden him carry our baggage, Renata, without any warning, turned to me and, in a voice quite changed, spoke thus :

" Now, Master Knight, I would thank you. You have rendered me great service by escorting me hither. Go now your ways, and I will find me shelter in this town. Farewell, and may God protect you."

I thought that Renata was saying this out of exaggerated courtesy, and began to remonstrate politely, but she replied to me, now quite firmly :

" Why seek you to intrude into my life ? I thank you for your pains and your assistance, but now I require them no longer."

Taken aback, for then I as yet knew little the soul of Renata, all woven of contradictions and surprises like a cloth of many-hued yarn, I reminded her of the

68

oaths we had exchanged, but Renata turned to me for
a third time, with indignation and not without rudeness :
- " You are not my father, nor my brother, nor my
husband ; you have no right to detain me by your side.
If you think that by spending a few guldens you have
bought my body, you are mistaken, for I am not a
woman from a house of pleasure. I go where I list, and
you cannot force me to stay with you by threats if
your companionship be distasteful to me."

In despair, I began to speak volubly, much of what I
said I cannot now recall, at first reproaching Renata,
then humbly beseeching her and clasping her hands
to retain her, but she shrank away from me with
contempt, and perhaps even with disgust, and replied
shortly but stubbornly that she wished to be alone.
Strangers began to take note of our dispute, and when
with especial insistence, I urged Renata to follow me
she threatened to seek protection from my assaults with
the city reiters, or simply with any good people.

Then, deciding on hypocrisy, I spoke as follows :
" Noble lady, my knightly duty does not permit me
to leave a lady alone, in the evening, amidst a crowd
of strangers. The streets are not safe by twilight, for
robbers and misbehaving revellers are abroad. I do
not fear to face the guard, for my conscience is guiltless
of any crime, but to part with you now I will not agree,
for anything in the world. Lastly, by all that is holy, I
swear to you that to-morrow morning, if you still desire
it, I shall give you final and complete freedom, shall
not burden you with my presence, and shall not dream
of attempting to trace where you have gone."

Probably realising that I would not relent, Renata
submitted with that indifference with which submit
those sorely ill, to whom all is one, and, closing her cape
to conceal her face, she followed me through the city
gate. I ordered the baggage to be carried to a widow
of my acquaintance, one Martha Ruttmann, who since
the death of her husband had lived by letting out rooms

to travellers. She dwelt not far from the church of
Saint Cecilia, in an old, low, two-storied house,
herself living below, and letting out the upper floor for
money. To reach her we had to traverse the whole
town, and Renata did not let slip a word the whole way,
nor did she bend back the edge of her hood.

To my surprise, Martha at once recognised in the
sunburnt mariner the beardless scholar who had
caroused at her board in the years gone by, and was
as glad to see me as if I had been a relative; she
began to spoil me, prattling:

"Ah, Master Rupprecht! Did I ever hope to see
you again? Look, all these ten years I've not forgotten
you! Master Gerard did say that you ran off with the
landsknechts, and I thought that only your bones were
left, whitening somewhere in the fields of Italy. And
look, what a strapping and stern and handsome man
you have become—the spit and image of St. George
on the holy painting! Step upstairs; there I have rooms
disengaged and ready: there's not much business now
—everyone tries to get into the hostelries, so that affairs
are slack, trade goes down, it's not as in bygone days."

In a quiet voice I ordered her to prepare all the
upstairs rooms for myself and my wife, saying that I
should pay in good Rhine gold, and Martha, sensing
money in my purse as a hunting dog senses game,
became even twice as polite and admiring. Walking
backwards before us, she led the way to the upper floor,
but, while Martha fussed, getting everything ready
for the night and questioning me with many gossiping
asides, Renata played throughout the dumb part in a
comœdia, not even unveiling her face, as if in fear that
she might be recognised. But as soon as we were left
alone, she at once said to me commandingly:

"You will sleep, Rupprecht, in that room there, and
do not dare to come to me unless I call."

I looked Renata in the face and made no sound in
reply, but I walked out with such a weight upon my

soul as if I had been condemned to be branded with a
hot iron. I wanted either to weep, or to thrash this
woman who had so strange a power over me. I gritted
my teeth and said to myself: " All right, all right then ;
if only you give me the chance, I shall repay you alb
for alb "—and at the same time it seemed to me as
though it would be heavenly bliss only to sit once more
at Renata's bedside and stroke her hair until my hand
was exhausted. Not daring to disobey her injunction,
I agonised in bed, like one drunk, to whom the world
sways like the deck of a caravel, until weariness over-
mastered my bitter-angry thoughts. Till the morning,
however, nightmares suffocated me and I seemed to
see the beldam of Geerdt, astride on my bosom, roaring
and drinking blood as it spouted from my breast, while
Renata with a youth in flaming robes floated past
through a blue garden amid gigantic lilies, and I
crawled after them like a toad, my heavy limbs powerless to part from the earth.

None the less, the habit of the camp woke me with
its drum at the customary hour, and I had time to put
myself in order and freshen my head before Renata
summoned me. But she called in a voice stern and
callous, and when I heard the comfortless words that
she addressed to me I felt as though I were swallowing
all the green waters of the ocean waves with not one
tiny sail on the whole horizon.

This is what Renata said to me, not mentioning anything of her yesterday's intention of leaving me :

" Listen, Rupprecht ! We must find Heinrich this
very day, I do not wish to wait one day longer. We
must find him, though we have to tramp through the
whole town. Let us go then ! "

I would have replied to this commanding speech that
I could be of but little help in the search for Count
Heinrich, never having seen him face to face, but so
imperative was Renata's gaze that I found neither
words nor voice, and when, lowering her hood, quickly

and determinedly, she rushed out into the street, I moved after her like a shadow tied to her. And never will I forget those frantic rushings from church to church, through every street, that we carried out that day! Not once, but many times, did we comb the whole of Köln from Saint Cunibert to Saint Severin and from the Holy Apostles to the shore of the Rhine, and it became clear that Renata was not for the first time in this city. First of all she dragged me to the Cathedral, but, tarrying there but little, she rushed to the Town Hall, circled round it, scanning the Market and the Square, and past Hürzenich she nearly ran to the ancient Mary of the Capitol. At the leaf of this sumptuous trefoil we wearied silently for some time, Renata with greedy eyes studying every figure as it appeared far away upon the street, and I, at her side, making a supreme effort of will to appear unconcerned and care-free. Then Renata seized me by the hand and dragged me quickly, quickly, either pursuing or fleeing from pursuit, first towards Saint George, where the masons, who were building a new and luxurious porch, gazed at us in astonishment, then to Saint Panteleon. And later still we encountered Saint Gereon with his holy hosts, were sighed after by the eleven thousand immaculate virgins who rest with Saint Ursula, glared at by the huge eye of the Minorites, and at last we came back to the quay side of the Rhine, beneath the shadow of the imposing tower of Saint Martin, where Renata waited with such certainty and confidence as though it were here that she had been foretold a meeting by a voice from Sinai, while I dully watched and studied the bustling life of the docks, saw how the vessels sailed up and away, and the lading and unlading of many-hued barges, marked how men fuss and fret, always busying themselves over something and always hurrying somewhere, and all the time I reflected that they had no concern with two strangers, hiding near a church wall.

Ϯbe ϯierⅉ Hngel

It was, judging by the sun, long past noon, when I
at last dared to address a summons to Renata :
  " Should we not return home ? You are tired ;
dinner is prepared for us."

But Renata looked at me with contempt and replied :
" If you are hungry, Rupprecht, go and dine ; I feel
no need."

Soon again we resumed our disorderly running
from street to street, but with each hour it became more
disorderly, for Renata herself was losing faith, though
with stubbornness and obstinacy she still carried out
her purpose : inspecting the passers-by, tarrying at the
cross-roads, peering into the windows of houses. Before
me flitted familiar buildings—our University, and the
Bursaries, where my schoolfellows used to live, Kneck
College, Laurence's, the XVIth. Houses, and other
churches again—Saint Clare, Saint Andrew, Saint
Peter—and though I knew Köln well before, from this
day I know it as though I had both been born in it
and spent my whole life only within its walls. I must
say that I, a man accustomed to difficult marches
across the savannah, and to whom it has happened for
whole days on end to pursue a fleeing enemy, or on the
contrary myself to retreat from pursuit—I felt myself
overcome and nearly falling from tiredness, though
Renata seemed tireless and unchanged : she was
possessed by some frenzy of seeking, and there was no
power to stop her and no means to bring her to reason.
I do not recollect after what journeyings and twistings
we found ourselves in the evening once more in the
neighbourhood of the Cathedral, and there, vanquished
at last, Renata sank down upon a stone, leant against
the wall and remained motionless.

I seated myself near by, not daring to speak, and
prey to a dull, numb weariness that filled all my limbs
like thick lead. Above my eyes towered the grey bulk
of the forepart of the Cathedral, with its temporary
roof, with towers as yet unbegun, but none the less

73

imposing in the boldness of its design. And strangely
enough, at this moment, forgetting my condition and
Renata, forgetting weariness and hunger, I began, as
I now remember well, to reflect upon the details of the
Cathedral and its building. I recalled the plans of the
Cathedral, that I happened to have seen, and the stories
of its construction, the names of the good craftsman
Gerhard and of His Eminence the Archbishop Heinrich
von Virneburg, and I decided for myself that, like its
brothers the Cathedral of Saint Peter in Rome and the
Cathedral of the Birth of the Holy Mother of God in
Milan, never would it be fated to rise in its proper
grandeur ; to raise to its heights the heavy materials
required for its completion, and to erect perfectly the
arrows of its spires according to their plan—are tasks
far surpassing our means and forces. While, if ever
human science and the art of building attain such a
measure of perfection as to render these tasks possible
and easy, men will of course have lost so much of their
primitive faith that they will no longer wish to labour
to enrich the House of God.

My meditation was interrupted by Renata herself,
who said to me shortly and simply :

" Rupprecht, let us go home."

I rose with difficulty and followed Renata like one
in irons ; but, in thinking then, not without relief, that
all the events of the day were done I was mistaken :
the most startling lay yet in wait for us.

When we reached our home I bade Martha prepare
food for us, but Renata did not want even to touch
anything and, as if with great difficulty, she swallowed
a few baked beans and would not drink more than two
mouthfuls of wine. Then she went to her bed and
stretched herself on it in complete prostration, like
one paralysed, weakly warding off my touches and, to
all my words, only shaking her head negatively.
Approaching, I lowered myself to my knees near the
bed and looked silently into her eyes, which suddenly

74

became staring and devoid of meaning or expression—and thus I remained for a long time, in this posture, which thenceforward and for many weeks became habitual to me.

This was the very hour that fate chose to add yet another link to the chain dragging me to my perdition, and to transform me, for the first time, from a spectator and observer of devilish schemes to their accomplice and abettor. With that same frankness with which I relate of myself in this book both the good and the bad, I want to relate this event also, that I may show how the Devil knows means by which, hardly perceptibly, he may lead a man astray, to his own ways.

While we were thus plunged into darkness and silence, as into some black depth—there suddenly sounded above us a strange and quite exceptional cracking knock upon the wall. I looked round surprised for, apart from us two, there was nobody in the room, and at first I did not say anything. But after some interval, when the selfsame knock occurred a second time, I softly asked Renata:

" Did you hear that knock ? What can it be ? "

Renata answered me in an indifferent voice :

" It is nothing. That happens often. It is the tiny ones."

I asked her again :

" What tiny ones ? "

She answered me quietly :

" The tiny demons."

This reply so interested me that, though I was reluctant to worry Renata in her weakened state, nevertheless I dared to question her, seeing that she understood something of which I had only a nebulous conception. With great reluctance, and pronouncing the words with difficulty, Renata informed me that the lower demons, who are always present in human circles, occasionally manifest their presence to those who are not protected from them by knocking on the walls and different

objects, or by moving various things. To this Renata
added that when, by her acquaintance with Madiël, her
eyes were opened to the secret world, she even saw these
very demons, who are always of human appearance and
clothed, unlike angels, in capes, not light or brilliant,
but dark, grey or smoke-black in colour, but that they
are however, enveloped in a kind of glow, and in
moving they float noiselessly rather than walk, and to
disappear they dissolve like clouds.

I must not conceal the fact, and I will say here and
now, that Renata later gave another explanation of the
knockings that to many will perhaps appear more
simple and natural, but, from everything, I gather
that it was this first one that was true, and even if she
were mistaken about them, it was only in that she did
not recognise in them the usual devices of the Devil,
who seeks ever to enmesh the soul in his dubious webs.
But at that time I had no occasion even to reflect upon
what she said, for I gave myself up wholly to a feeling
of astonishment at the nearness to us of the world of
demons, that, for the most of human beings, is as if
situated on the further side of some inaccessible ocean
that can be traversed only in the galleys of magic and
sorcery. And, moreover, while Renata spoke, the
knockings sounded gay upon the wall above her bed,
as if confirming her words. But as never, and in no
circumstances of my life, did the torch of free experi-
mentation, lit in my soul by the books of the great
humanists, flicker out in me, addressing myself to the
knocking being I asked with extreme daring :

" If you who make these knockings are truly a demon,
and if you hear my words, knock thrice."

At once, clearly, there resounded three knocks, and
at the moment they were as terrifying as if an invisible
hammer were knocking through my skull at my brain.
But quickly, overpowering this weakness, with renewed
daring and not comprehending the dark abyss towards
which I was thrusting myself, I asked again :

"Are you a friend to us or an enemy? If a friend—knock thrice."

Immediately sounded three knockings. After these Renata, too, rose in her bed, and her eyes became alive again as she asked:

"In the name of God I conjure you, Knocker, speak! Do you know anything of my master, Count Heinrich? If you know, knock thrice."

Three knocks sounded.

Then an uncontrollable trembling seized Renata and, sitting up, she seized my hand and, pressing it with her thin fingers, she quickly began to put questions to our conversationist, one after another; where is Count Heinrich? how soon will he return? when will she see him? how angry is he with her?—questions to it would be very difficult to reply with knockings. But, intervening, I tried to bring some system into the conversation and established that three knocks would always mean an affirmation, two a negation, after which we only had to put our questions in such a way that they could be answered by a single "yes" or "no." It did not then occur to me that commerce with infernal powers might be sinful, or even dangerous, indeed I was even ready to pride myself on the new method of demonomancy I had invented, and a long conversation ensued between us and our guest.

We asked him: who is he, whether he be a demon? And that he answered us, yes. Then we asked him, what is he called? And by going through a number of names and all the sounds of the alphabet, we learned that his name was Elimer. Then we asked him whether he knew Count Heinrich, and that he answered us, yes. We asked whether Count Heinrich were in Köln, and to that he replied, no. We asked, would Count Heinrich arrive in Köln, and to that he replied, yes. We asked: when? soon? not to-day? perhaps to-morrow? and learned that it would be to-morrow. Then, continuing our questioning, we learned that we must await Count Heinrich the next evening, not going out anywhere, in this very room, that he will find his own way to Renata, that he has not forgotten her, that he is not angry with her, that he has forgiven all, loves her as before, and wishes to be with her.

All these answers were to Renata as the words of the Saviour ' *talipha, kumi* ' to the dead virgin. She too revived, and, forgetting her weariness, she tirelessly put one question after another, nearly always about the selfsame thing with the words but slightly altered, only to hear once more this ' yes ' so sweet to her. And when in the affirmative knocking there was some especial hope for her, she fell back into the pillow with a light sigh as if in ecstasy, swooning for a moment as if after some rapturous exaltation, and softly spoke to me : " You heard, Rupprecht, you heard ? "

Thus it continued for more than an hour, until the knockings, at first growing weaker as if he who knocked was tiring, finally ceased altogether. But even after their cessation Renata for a long time could not quieten down, and, happy, she repeated to herself and me her questions and the answers of the demon, or made me repeat them, assuring me and herself " But I knew that I should see Heinrich here ! But I felt so and I said so ! For I had reached the limit of agony, and more weariness my heart could not have borne ! " And Renata condescendingly stroked my hair and my face, gave me her hand to kiss, and pressed herself against me as if accustoming herself to the future caresses of her lover, and I found no release for my despair, but had to listen to her voice and touch her fingers with my lips. And the torment of her raptures lasted until long after midnight, despite our weariness, and I listened to Renata rejoicing like a child, still kneeling by her bed, so that at last, when she bade me go to my bed and sleep, I could scarcely stand upon my numb legs.

It may easily be understood that my second night

in my lonely room was no better than my first, and once more, and with good reason, my soul had occasion to withstand the assaults of the dark thoughts that marched against it, buckled in steel and with lances tilted. To my heart's content I gave myself up to thinking of the terrible connection that exists between the life of men and the life of demons, and of the new road on to which had swerved suddenly all the events of the past few days.

And this was the attempt I made the next morning, saying to myself that in a defeat the vanquished can only place hope and reliance upon his own extreme meekness and the mercy of his conqueror. When Renata called me to her, I delivered the following speech, carefully thought out and fully prepared:

"Noble lady! I desire to express openly that which you have probably guessed from my silence. Not simple courtesy, not knightly duty, keep me longer at your side, but something much greater, a feeling of which neither man nor woman should be ashamed. I gave you my oath to be your true servant and your faithful brother, but I shall remain for you also a worshipping adorer. Having known you, I fully realise that I shall never desire to be near another woman, and that which you have disclosed to me of the bestowal of your love does not in any way deter me. I do not hope for any liberty, but nevermore can I endure to be without you, or the wish to kiss your sleeve sometimes and watch your gliding step. Whatever may betide, even if fate has decreed the fulfilment of your happiness, take me into your service, allow me to be your body-guard and with this right arm defend from danger you and him whom you have chosen."

I will not say that everything in this, rather exaggerated, speech was sincere to the end, and that I should truly have liked to do all I said, but none the less it was along this slope that my thoughts slid, even if they did not reach the bottom—and if Renata had demanded

79

the fulfilment of my promises, perhaps I would have performed all that I had offered, as if upon the boards. But Renata, having heard me through, said, her brows puckered :

" Do not dare even to think of anything of the kind, Rupprecht. You are the last shadow of this epoch of my life too full of shadow. I return into the world, and you must disappear as the darkness of the night at the rising of the sun. How can you think that when Heinrich is with me I could endure to look at you and know you kissed my hands and lay in one bed with me ? No, as soon as Heinrich crosses the threshold, you must leave by another door, leave this city, slip back into your unknown, that I may never hear of you any more ! This you must swear to me by the Passion of our Saviour on the Cross, and if you be untrue to your oath, then may your judgment be harder than that of Judas ! "

Then I asked Renata :

" And what if in the morning, on leaving the house, you behold upon the threshold my corpse with my own dagger in my breast ? What will you say then to your Heinrich ? "

Renata answered :

" I shall say that it is probably some drunken passer-by, and that I shall be glad when the corpse is removed by the reiters."

After that I gave the oath exactly as she asked, and obeyed Renata in everything without argument, or demur, though I knew not, and did not desire to think, how I should behave in the evening. Renata, on the contrary, was rational and meticulous, which I had not expected her to be. She sent me to buy her a dress, for apart from the sumptuous one she always wore and her blue travelling cape she had no other attire, and also to obtain her many trinkets, both those suited to a journey and for the beauty of her face, apparently desiring to use all means to be especially

attractive to Count Heinrich and also not to be a
burden to him. She displayed the greatest heed and
forethought about all kinds of trifles, and despite the
rain, which did not cease all day, she made me many
times return to market and wander from one merchant
to another.

In such cares the time passed till evening, and nothing
had been omitted or forgotten by the hour when the
twilight, fallen early owing to the clouds, began to fill
the room with heavy darkness. I know not whether
my emotions were those of a man, who, having suffered
torture in prison, now awaits the appointed hour at
which he is to be led forth to execution, but there was
in me a dull weakness and a stubborn stupidity. I
drifted down each minute, as a boat with no helmsman
drifts down a rapid stream.

Scarcely had the darkness thickened perceptibly when
the knockings on the wall sounded again, and Renata
asked hastily whether it were our acquaintance of
yesterday—Elimer. The answer was given that in truth
it was he. Then began a repetition of the previous
evening, with this distinction, that the first knocking
demon was soon joined by other demons, who also
gave us their names: Rizzius, Ulrich, and others that
I cannot remember. Each had his own peculiar
knockings—thus, Elimer knocked clearly and definitely, Rizzius so that he was hardly heard, Ulrich
with such blows that one might fear the wall would
break. The demons willingly answered all our questions, as far as was possible, by knockings, and they
were not at all abashed by the names of the saints,
or of the Lord God Himself, uttered by Renata. At
the same time there flared up in various parts of the
room, near the floor, flames like those on a marsh, and,
rising to the height of two elbows, they went out,
diffusing. But by this time even my very soul was
carried away towards all that is implied by the expression of Horace, *scire nefas*, and even the obvious

stigmata of Hell no longer weakened me nor dismayed my will.

I now regret that, having dared to embark upon such a doubtful undertaking as commerce with knocking demons, I did not profit by the conversation to find out more concerning their nature and power. But that evening both Renata and I were so engrossed by the expected coming of Heinrich, that I had not in me enough curiosity to conduct a long inquisition. I had time to find out only that in their world there are rivers and lakes and trees and fields, and that it is inhabited partly by devils previously created by God as good beings, but who rebelled with Lucifer, and in part by the souls of people who have died and who, though they are unworthy of Hell, have not obtained the hope of Purgatory and are condemned to weary on earth until the Second Advent, that they are glad to converse with human beings, who appear to them as tiny flames in darkness, but that they cannot approach all of them, only those who have special faculties.

This was the little that I thought of asking. But Renata put an interminable number of questions to each who spoke, leading indeed all to one end : whether it be true that Heinrich will come to her to-day ? And all those that gave answers replied to her only ' yes.' Then Elimer told us that we must wait for Heinrich in the darkness that surrounded us : that he will enter on the stroke of midnight : that he is already in the town and changing his attire. At this last answer Renata desired by all means to know every detail of his new costume, and she tirelessly mentioned all the garments that her Heinrich had worn, and also named all the items and accessories of manly attire, and all the colours of cloth, so that Elimer might be able with a simple ' yes ' to depict all the image of Heinrich. We learned that he wore the green costume of a huntsman, such as is worn in Bavaria, with brown frogs, a green hood, a light belt studded with gems, and blue boots.

Then Elimer said that Heinrich had already left his dwelling and was coming to us, that he was passing now along one street, now along another, that now he was approaching the doors of our house. My heart beat so fiercely that I heard its dull beats, and for the last time I questioned the demon:

"If the Count is entering the outer door, knock thrice."

Came three knocks. I repeated:

"If the Count is mounting the staircase, knock thrice."

Came three knocks. In a hoarse voice Renata said to me:

"Rupprecht, begone and do not return."

Her face looked terrifying to me and, swaying like one wounded, I walked towards an exit into a gallery, whence it was possible to descend into the courtyard of our house, but, noticing that Renata, drunk with expectation, was not looking at me, I tarried by the door, for an invincible curiosity urged me to look, if only once, upon the face of this Count, then still mysterious to me. But minutes went by and the Count did not appear, and no steps were heard behind the door, and all around was quiet and unchanged. Many minutes passed, and carefully I approached Renata who stood at the table.

Gasping, Renata asked:

"Elimer! If Heinrich is near knock thrice!"

There was no answer and she asked again:

"Elimer! If you are here knock thrice!"

There was no answer, and in extreme despair Renata exclaimed for the third time:

"Rizzius! Ulrich! Answer—will my Heinrich come?"

There was no answer.

Suddenly the whole of her strength left Renata and she would have fallen as if struck by a bullet, had I not caught her. I do not know whether the demon with

83

whom we had just conversed so friendlily, or her former
enemy, entered into her, but once more I was witness of
a terrible torment like that of the country inn. Only it
seemed to me as though this time the spirit did not
enter the whole body of Renata, but possessed only a
part of it, for she was able to defend herself in some
degree, though all her body writhed and turned horribly,
twisting out the limbs as though the bones would break
through muscle and skin. Again I had no means to
help the racked creature, and could only look into
Renata's face, completely distorted as if someone else
looked out from her eyes, and watch all the monstrous
twists of her body, until at last the demon released her
of his own will, and she rested in my arms, feeble, like
a tender bough draggled in a whirlpool. I carried
Renata to her room, into her bed, where she wept long
and helplessly, now altogether speechless, unable to
utter a word.

Thus ended the second day of our stay in Köln and
the fifth day of my acquaintance with Renata. Those
five days, despite the multitude of the various incidents
compressed within them, have remained chiselled in my
soul with such vividness that I can recall the minutest
events, nearly every word spoken by Renata, or by
me in reply to hers, and all my thoughts, as though they
had taken place but yesterday. And if I had not thought
it necessary to be short, for the description of yet more
remarkable happenings is still before me, I might have
related that which I experienced in this short time with
many further details than I have set down here.

Chapter the Fourth

*How we lived in the City of Köln and that which I
saw at the Sabbath*

NOT only, no doubt, the sufferings to which the
demon who tortured her had subjected Renata,
but also the despair that had replaced her
tantalising hopes—made her as weak as if she
had been through a long and complicated illness. The
morning after that night in which we had in vain waited
for Count Heinrich, Renata was quite definitely not
strong enough to rise from her bed, could not move her
left hand, and complained that she felt as though a
sharp nail were being hammered into her head—so
she had to spend several days in bed. It was my great
happiness to care for her like a nurse, to feed her and
give her to drink as one would a small, helpless child,
to watch over her tired sleep and search amongst my
poor store of medical learning for means to alleviate
her condition. Though Renata accepted my ministra-
tions with the queenly condescension usual to her, I
could justly conclude, both from the expression of her
eyes and from isolated sentences, that she valued my
faithfulness and my care, and this rewarded me to
overflowing for all my recent sufferings. And after the
first five days with Renata, which had been like an
incessant whirlpool amongst rocks, there now came for
me days soft and sad, but sweet, each so like the last,
that one might have taken them for but one day, only
reflected in many mirrors.

Returning now in thought to that time, I feel the

talons of sorrow clutching at my heart, and I am
inclined, with murmur against the Creator, to regard
this memory as the most cruel of His gifts. And yet I
cannot restrain myself from describing, though shortly,
the apartments in which our tragic fate was accomplished, and the even daily tenor of our life that, in
spite of all changes, remained constant until the fatal
hour of our first parting.

As Renata spoke to me neither of the relatives that
she had made believe to possess in Köln, nor of her
desire to leave me, I took care to prepare for her more
comfortable quarters. I chose for her that room, out
of the three on the upper floor, which was destined by
Martha for the most exalted of her lodgers, and which
accordingly was furnished with a certain luxury. At
the wall to the right of the entrance, on a small podium
mounted by three steps, stood a handsome wooden bed,
with a half-canopy also of wood, and decorated with
cloth, pillows edged with lace and a satin coverlet.
Another considerable feature was the fireplace of
coloured tiles of rare workmanship, such as often one
does not find even in Milan, and against the outer
wall was stood a large wardrobe, carved and with inlaid
decorations. Between the windows was placed a handsome table with curved legs, in the corner behind the
bed a folding prie-dieu, and the furniture of the room
was completed by chairs, a lectern for reading, and a
large Italian mirror hung on the left of the entrance.
I remember the interior with the utmost vividness and
now, as I write these words, it seems to me as if I have
only to rise at any time and open the door—and once
more I shall walk into the room of Renata and see
her with her head drooping on the carved desk of the
lectern or pressing her cheek against the cold glass
circles of the window.

The room of Renata was separated from mine by a
narrow corridor that gave on to a covered gallery, which
half encircled the house and from which one could

descend straight down by a staircase, without passing
through the lower floor. My room, which was destined
by Martha for less wealthy lodgers, was furnished
plainly, but none the less better and more pleasantly
than the rooms in regular hostelries. And there was
at our disposal another, yet a third room, much smaller
and quite separate, the entrance into it being straight
from the landing of the inner staircase; at first we
had not thought of using this little closet and I paid
for its rent only to escape neighbours. In fact, apart
from us, there lived in the small solitary house only
Martha, a woman who, though it is true she loved to
gossip, did not willingly entertain guests, and so even
in gay and noisy Köln we were as much cut off from
people as Merlin in the charmed wood of Viviane.

Old Martha was convinced that my young wife and
I were enjoying ourselves, and of course she in no wise
suspected how strangely we passed our days. Receiving from me a good allowance, she served us
willingly and with care, effecting all my commissions
and watching well over our table: in the morning for
breakfast we usually received fried eggs, sausage,
cheese, eggs in shell, baked chestnuts and fresh rolls;
and in the evening at supper—mutton, sucking-pigs,
geese, carp, pike, and I usually had at the same time
a bottle of Rhinewine or Malvasia. Martha was
surprised that I did not wish to renew any of my
former friendships with anyone, and many times she
tried to persuade me to visit the aged Ottfried Gerard,
my former teacher, but I, on the contrary, strictly
forbade her even to mention my arrival in Köln.
However, Martha did not obey my order very faithfully,
for at times attempts were made to greet me in the street
by persons among whom I recognised not only my
former drinking companions, but even magisters or
the University—however, I made them understand
that they were mistaken in their greetings and took
me for another.

87

The Fiery Angel

During the illness of Renata and the first days of
her convalescence we spent whole hours in conversation,
and now she listened with great eagerness to my stories
of New Spain, wondering at the great deal I had seen
during my life. Sometimes she caressingly stroked my
face with her fingers, saying, as if to a small child:
" What a clever learned Rupprecht I have ! " But
for a long time we spoke not a single word hinting
either of Count Heinrich or of the power of the hostile
demons who threatened Renata, and when—as happened several times—we heard in the evening darkness
again the familiar knockings, we hastened to blow up
the fire and talk of other things, and the knockings
ceased of themselves. At such times, however, the
obvious nearness of unseen foes confused not only me
but Renata with cruel fear, and then she did not send
me away to my room, but allowed me to spend the
night with her—sometimes at the foot of her bed,
sometimes again under one coverlet, though as man
and woman we remained strangers to each other. And
I even found in this torturing nearness a special charm
and sweetness, as if one were to enjoy the deep cuts of a
sharp blade insensibly dividing the flesh.

Towards the very end of August, Renata was so far
recovered that we began to take long walks in the town,
for the most part wandering to the shore of the Rhine,
somewhere up its stream, beyond the Hanseatic quay,
and there sitting on the ground we watched the dark
and mighty waters of the great river, unchanged since
the day of great Cæsar who forded them, yet changing
every minute. This uniform view, day after day,
brought ever new thoughts to our minds and new
words to our lips, and our conversations seemed as
inexhaustible as the Rhine itself, though it is quite
possible it only appeared to us that we were conversing
continuously. In any case I felt vividly as though all
the chaos of knowledge and information that I had read
in various books and gathered during the changing

fortunes of my life—now passing under the clear scrutiny of Renata, by agency either of her severe condemnations, or of her penetrating corrections—was gradually being welded to one enormous and unified mass, as from molten pigs of iron is welded a shapely bell, that can sound far and high.

However, with all the meekness and submissiveness of Renata, there yet lived in her an unsatisfied weariness that would not release her heart from its poisonous fangs, so that as the strength of Renata grew, there revived in her all the stubbornness of her desire, flung like the hand of a compass always toward one point. I had no other occupation than to watch over the transparency and cloudlessness of the horizon of Renata's soul, and soon I noticed that nefarious signs were foretelling another storm, for no more was I a novice in the navigation of those latitudes. But, though I was warned, the storm blew so impetuously that I had no time to reef in my sails, and the galleas of my life was once more whirled round like a child's top.

As lately as that evening, going to sleep, after a long talk during which we had touched upon all matters, from the fate of our Empire to the lyric verses of the Spanish poet Garcilaso de la Vega, Renata had spoken tenderly to me : " Dearest Rupprecht, at last I am rested a little. I feel as though I had died and were now living a second life, beyond my due. There is no blood within me and there can be no human happiness in me, but there is still in this world your care and your caress." Lulled by these words, I fell asleep on the wooden planks of the podium, near Renata's bed, couched more sweetly than others on a bed of down, and, sensing through my slumber the nearness of the satin coverlet, I said to myself happily : " She is near."

But in the morning, waking suddenly as if jarred, I saw above me the eyes of Renata weary with gloom as she sat up in the bed, her mouth awry, and, somehow

realising at once the change that had occurred in her, I
exclaimed in despair :

" Renata, what is the matter with you ? "

I addressed her thus because she herself had asked
me to call her by her name and to address her familiarly,
as friends do one another, but she answered me :

" What could there be the matter with me ? Nothing
at all—I am as well as yesterday ! "

I said :

" But why is your face so sorrowful ? "

Renata spoke with that brusqueness that invariably
showed in her during her fits of moodiness :

" Do you suppose that I can laugh for ever ? I am
not one of those who are ready to dance with no reason !
And why should I rejoice ? What is there in my life that
is so gay ? "

I walked out of Renata's room and for a long time
stood near the door leading to the gallery, gazing at
the brown tiles of the neighbouring roofs, and it was
only after a considerable lapse of time that I dared to
return to Renata and see that she was sitting at the
window ledge, her face deathly and expressionless. At
first I offered her breakfast, but she shook her head
without uttering a word ; and when I called to her to
walk to the river's bank she said to me severely :

" What do you want me for ? Nobody is keeping you
—go if you think it amusing to walk through dirty
streets, amidst sweating and noisy crowds, and if you
want to convince yourself that the Rhine is still there
in the same old place ! "

From that conversation onwards Renata fell for
many days into a dark depression, from which it was
impossible to shake her by any argument or by any
effort. When I tried to persuade her that it was unreasonable and harmful thus to abandon herself to
despair, she either remained silent in reply, or bluntly
exposed to my view all the imperfection and ugliness
of the world, doomed to sin and suffering, as compared

with the divine beauty of the promised Eden, and she pointed out that a Christian has no reason to rejoice, indeed it is only proper for him to weep. She could find an inexhaustible store of arguments against the pleasures of life and no magister could have conducted a dispute with such cleverness as that with which she proved to me that there are thousands of just causes for despair—so that I, at last, could not find what to retort, what to say in answer.

The favourite pastime of Renata now became the visitation of churches, whither she went forbidding me to follow her. But I naturally disobeyed her injunction and, shielded behind pillars, watched in the Church of Saint Cecilia, or of Saint Peter, or in yet some other, while Renata stayed whole hours bent in prayer, her eyes glued to the altar, hearing through the whole Holy Mass without a single movement. Despite the fact that the Faith is in our days strongly shaken by reform and heresies, nevertheless the temples were for the most part full, both of sorrowing souls come to seek comfort of the Almighty, and of idlers come from habit, or to meet a gossip, or to wink to a pretty neighbour. We were soon picked out as a strange couple by all this varied conglomeration, and it came to me to hear, bandied about in whispers, many and various stupid rumours regarding us. But Renata of course did not notice the curiosity she excited, and I paid no attention, for it gave me an inexpressible delight just to look at Renata and imbibe her image with my eyes, as the drunkard imbibes the juice of the vine with his lips. It was there and within those walls, as I stood listening to the rhythmic harmony of the organ and imagining at times that it was the Mexican forest that rustled around me, that the thought was born in me to take Renata beyond the Ocean, and I think to this day that, had I been able to execute this purpose, I could have saved both her life and her soul.

In these evenings, which we spent together, we now

exchanged rôles, as champions fighting with rapiers exchange places, for it was I who became the listener and Renata untiringly talked to me about herself, comforting and torturing herself with reminiscences. Too well do I remember how in her rich room, by the light of two wax candles and with curtains drawn, we two would sit facing each other with glasses of Malvasia —for, though she refused food, Renata drank wine willingly—and thus spent almost whole nights through. Once more Renata made up her mind to talk to me of Count Heinrich, relating to me still further and further particulars about him, describing his eyes and his eyebrows, his hair and his body, repeating those of his words that she remembered, relating minute incidents of their lives, depicting to me their mutual caresses in such detail that my jealousy flared up like a burning flame. Renata began often to compare me with her lover, and she experienced the greatest joy in exposing to me all the baseness of my soul and all the common-ness of my face, as compared with the angelic features of Madiël and the godliness of his thoughts. Not infrequently the exaltation created in Renata by her words once more discharged itself in an uncontrollable flood of tears, and we two would drink this mixture of Malvasia and tears, until at last I would carry the helpless Renata to her bed and, also crying, kiss her feet and the hem of her dress.

This life of ours also lasted about a week, and I suppose my heart would have borne the tension of continuous pain for no longer space. But the emotional ecstasy of Renata ended as suddenly as it was born, and thereafter she spent a whole Sunday kneeling nearly all day in the Church of the Holy Apostles, raining reproaches on me with especial cruelty in the evening—and on the Monday morning she changed to a tenderness, that was yet false by all appearances, and instead of going to Mass bade me walk with her, as in those other days of ours, to the Rhine. I went uneasy in heart, for in truth these present hours were only the outer image of our former friendliness, and only a make-shift of our recent intimacy. Though—as I often afterwards became convinced—Renata would many times say that which one could not regard as true, yet she did not know how to tell a lie, having schemed a lie, and her pretending was so obvious that it roused in my soul not so much indignation as compassion. I made no sign that I saw through her play-acting, and I waited to find out whither the plot would lead me, until, at home, Renata after many insignificant words said to me:

"Answer me, Rupprecht, tell me whether you love me more than the salvation of your soul?"

I assured her of my love with an oath, being interested to see whither this question would lead. But Renata, several times requiring me to confirm my assurances, showed no desire to go into explanations, and only continued to show me an exaggerated tenderness.

In the morning of Tuesday (it will be seen in a moment why I remember exactly what day it was) Renata unexpectedly asked me to give her money, and I hastened to offer her some gold coins. But she took only a few silver joachimsthalers and went out, throwing on her cape, and with especial strictness forbidding me to follow her. Though once again I did not obey her request, she contrived this time to deceive my surveillance, as watchful as that of a spy of the Inquisition, and to lose herself somewhere amid the narrow passages near the market. I had to wait for her alone with growing uneasiness, while fearsome thoughts came into my mind, that she had left me, and only towards evening did she reappear, very tired and pale, carrying with her a small bag containing some objects. And even all that quite childish joy that possessed me on seeing the returned Renata could not dumb in my soul the sly voice of curiosity.

Contrary to her custom, Renata asked for food, then

she wanted to drink some wine, and then invented other delays, postponing the conversation she had planned, and only when the darkness began to gather, the darkness that always gives courage, did she begin to speak, not without solemnity. Roughly, what she said to me was this :

" Dearest Rupprecht! You see well that I can no longer live in this fashion. All my soul will stream out in tears : either I shall have to be put in my coffin or I shall become so ugly that even I would not desire to show myself to the eyes of him whom I love. One of two courses must be chosen : either life, and then to occupy oneself with its cares, or death—and then honestly to offer it one's hand. But you know and see and realise that I can live only if Heinrich is with me. To revive I must hear his voice ; to be happy, I have only to look into his eyes. With him I can accomplish all and Heaven itself is open to me, but without him I gasp like a fish on the shore. I must find Heinrich, and he will tell me whether I am condemned to life or to death. But where across the length and breadth of all the German lands shall we seek one man, who indeed is so powerful that if he chooses he can even cease to be among men ? To examine every town and village in our search—is it not the same as to feel throughout a haystack to find a lost thin silk thread ? Is it not clear that to make such an effort is to tempt the Lord Himself ? "

Surprised at the sobriety and consecutiveness of the speech of Renata, who at times could reason like an excellent scholastic, I replied that I considered her logic correct and waited to hear what *ergo* she would deduce from her *quia*. Then in a voice much more excited and with a face much more inspired, Renata began to speak, thus :

" You have been witness, Rupprecht, that I have prayed. I have sent to the Creator all the prayers in my power, and pledged all the vows a woman has

94

strength to fulfil, and perhaps even more! But the Lord has remained deaf to my murmuring and there is only One Power that can help me—only One to whom I can now apply. But I shall never agree to soil my soul with a deadly sin, for my soul is given to Heinrich, and he is light and he is pure, and nothing dark must come near him. Therefore you, Rupprecht, who have sworn that you love me more than the salvation of your soul, must take even this sin and this sacrifice upon yourself."

At first I failed to grasp the purport of this speech, and replied to Renata by asking her of what Power and of what Other she was thinking, but Renata looked at me mysteriously, with a face like the images of the Maya, and only approached to me her big eyes, not saying a word, until suddenly I understood and cried out:

" You speak of the Devil, Renata ! "

And Renata replied to me :

" Yes ! "

Then there ensued a discussion between us. However I may have been enmeshed by my passion for this woman, however ready I may have been to obey her least sign, to do what was pleasing to her, yet such an unheard of request stirred my whole soul to its very depths. I said first of all that it was hardly possible the Lord God would not know how to distinguish the really guilty one, and that even if I were to lose my soul by having recourse to the help of the Enemy of Man, she would no less lose hers for sending me to do this work, for the murderer is ever less guilty than he who bribes him; further—that it was doubtful whether the Ruler of Hell himself could render any assistance in such an undertaking, for he is busy catching human souls, and not in taking poll-lists of the population, where who lives, and especially was it unlikely that he would know about Count Heinrich, for he by Renata's own description, was a saint, and

95

certainly not subject to the rule of the subterranean
powers, being able to blind and divert the eyes of the
servants of Beelzebub at his will; lastly, that most
decidedly I did not know the roads leading to the
Realms of Tartary, that much of the stories of pacts
and contracts with the Devil were mere grandmother's
tales, that perhaps magic itself was but deceit and mis-
apprehension, and that in any case we should not find
it easy to hire a guide capable of directing us in good
faith straight to Satan.

Thus I spoke with irritation, at times myself not
believing my own words, and now for the first time
allowing myself to be rude and even mocking in my
treatment of Renata, but she, opposing me weakly,
invited me to watch what she was about to do. From
the small bag she had brought, she took out a few
sprigs of herb: heather, verbena, wolf's bane, orache,
and yet another herb with white flowers, the name of
which I do not know. With her left hand Renata
plucked the leaves from the herbs and threw them
over her head on to the floor, but then she gathered
them again and placed them on the table in a circle.
Next she plunged a knife into the table surface in the
middle of the circle, tied its handle round with string,
passed the end of the string to me and said, looking
at me attentively:

" Command it thrice to milk, in the name of *Him*."

Silently watching all this bedevilment, I involuntarily
pronounced thrice:

" In the name of the Devil, milk ! "

Immediately from under the knife poured a few
drops of milk, and Renata joyfully clapped her hands,
embraced my shoulders and kept on exclaiming:

" Rupprecht ! Dearest Rupprecht ! You can ! You
have the power ! "

I, quite angry by this time, demanded that she should
cease to fool me with her tricks, but Renata, changing
her joyful tone to a caressing one, began to persuade

me, pressing against me as against a lover and looking into my face:

"Rupprecht! What matters the salvation of your soul if you but love me? Must not love be above all, and must not all be sacrificed to it, even the Bliss of Paradise? Do what I desire, for my sake, and after Heinrich you shall be the first for me in the whole world. And who knows, perhaps the Righteous Judge will not condemn you for that you have loved so much, and will not sentence you to the Burning Gehenna, but only to the temporary tortures of Purgatory. And I with my Madiël—I swear to you by the Virginity of the Mother of God—we will not forget to send prayers after you even from the Gardens of Paradise!"

I might say that I yielded to the temptation of a woman, as Samson to that of Delilah, or Hercules to that of Omphala, but, not wishing to lie, I must confess that two considerations quickly flashed through my mind. The first—that truly a sin committed for another weighs only half-weight on the scales of justice, and two—that perhaps I should be guilty of no real sin in my consent, for it was scarcely possible that Renata could really find means to confront me with the Devil. Thus I was not simply yielding to her tender insistence, but, none the less, like a cool-headed gambler placing a heavy stake, at last I answered Renata that I no longer had strength to refuse her prayers, and that for her happiness I was ready to sacrifice my life, both this and the life eternal. Renata, however, when I had pronounced this solemn oath, became deeply serious, and, suddenly kneeling before me, she humbly kissed my knees, so that my soul became prey both to confusion and shame, and I knew not what to do or what to say, and in truth desired to yield up for her both my life and my soul!

I wish to describe all that followed with especial care, for I shall have to speak of controversial matters, doubted by many in these times and not entirely comprehensible to me myself. To this day, though I have travelled far from that night, I cannot say with perfect confidence whether all that I experienced was a terrible truth, or a not less horrible nightmare, the creation of imagination, and whether I sinned before Christ in actual deed and word, or in thought only. Myself, however, I incline to the second opinion, though not to such an extent as not to seek shelter with God's Mercy, which, being inexhaustible, alone can acquit me in case the horrors and blasphemies of that night prove not imaginary. So I shall refrain from attempting any decision, and will relate all that my memory preserves—exactly as if it actually occurred.

From the Wednesday morning, Renata began to prepare me for the task I had undertaken, gradually, as if by chance, mentioning one thing or another to acquaint me with the black substance of all I had to accomplish and as yet knew but vaguely. Not without trembling and revulsion did I learn that the road she had chosen for association with the Devil was a visit to the hideous dances of the Sabbath, where the Prince of Darkness appears to his faithful, and that I should have to utter words of blasphemy and perform shameful rites. But that temptation of curiosity, that Thomas Aquinas calls the fifth of the deadly sins, burned in me so furiously, ever increasing, that myself I questioned Renata about the minutest details of that which awaited me at the gathering, and my heart beat with the ecstasy of a boy who walks for the first time into the embraces of lust. I will add, moreover, that in such measure was I then blinded by my passion for Renata that, when startled by her knowledge in matters of witchcraft, I asked her suddenly whether her learning came from her own experience, and she answered me, No, but from the confession to her of an unfortunate woman, I scarcely doubted her denial and was still willing to believe in her purity.

In the evening all was ready and I even sought to

hasten the time, rather than tarry. But Renata, on the contrary, was sad as Niobe, at times her eyes filled with tears, and more often than usual she coupled with my name the word ' dearest.' And when the hour of darkness came and I could commence my forbidden traffic, Renata escorted me to the door of our third, remote room, stood for a long time on its threshold without the heart to part from me, and at last said:

" Rupprecht, if there be in you but one trace of hesitation, abandon this undertaking: I renounce all my prayers and return to you all your oaths."

But *ni Rey ni Roche*, as the Spaniards say, could stop me now, and I replied:

" I shall fulfil all that I have promised you, and I am happy that I perish for your sake. Trust me to be brave and to betray neither myself nor you. You are my love, my Renata!"

Then for the first time we approached our lips and kissed like lovers, and Renata said to me:

" Farewell, I shall go pray for you."

I expressed doubt lest a prayer might not be harmful to such an undertaking, but Renata, sadly shaking her head, said:

" Never fear, for you will be far from hence. Only, beware of pronouncing holy names yourself. . . ."

Breaking off her speech, she shrank back suddenly; as she walked away, I followed her with my glance, but, when she had disappeared behind the door, I sensed in me that clarity of mind and resolution of will that I invariably feel in the hour of danger, especially before a decisive battle. Remembering the instructions of Renata, I shut the door and shot the bolt to, locking it, and carefully covered all the chinks, while the window was already curtained with blinds. Then, in the light of a lamp filled with fat, I opened the case with the ointment that Renata had given me and tried to determine its composition, but the greenish greasy mass did not betray its secret: there came from

99

it only the pungent smell of herbs. Stripped naked, I
lowered myself to the floor, on my spread cape, and
began to rub this ointment firmly into my chest and
in my temples, under my armpits and between my
thighs, repeating several times the words: " *emen—
hetan, emen—hetan,*" which mean " here—and there."
The ointment slightly burned the flesh and my head
began to turn from its odour, so that soon I scarcely
was aware what I was doing, my arms hung limp, and
my eyelids fell over my eyes. Then my heart began to
beat with such strength it seemed as though, tied upon
a string, it leapt away from my chest a whole elbow's
length, and this caused me pain. I was conscious of
the fact that I lay upon the floor of our room, but, when
I tried to raise myself up, I was already powerless to do
so, and I thought : so all the tales of the Sabbath are
babbling nonsense, and the much talked of miraculous
ointment is only a sleeping draught—but at that very
moment all went dark before me and I suddenly saw
myself, or imagined myself, high above the earth, in
the air, quite naked, astride as on horseback a woolly
black goat.

At first my head was all fugged, but then I made an
effort and entirely mastered my consciousness, for upon
it alone could I rely as my guide and protector in the
miraculous journey I was making. Having taken stock
of the animal that bore me through the astral spheres,
I saw that it was an ordinary he-goat, obviously of
flesh and bone, with rather long and matted wool, and
only when it turned its head towards me did I notice
a devilish quality in its eyes. I did not then wonder
how I had left my room, which had a fireplace, though
of very narrow chimney, but later, however, it was
explained to me that this circumstance alone cannot
serve as proof of the imaginary nature of my journey,
for the Devil is an *artifex mirabilis* and can expand
and contract again the bricks of a stove with a speed
invisible to the human eye. Similarly I did not think,

during the flight itself, of the question what power could sustain above the earth matter so heavy as the he-goat with the weight of my body, but now I think it must have been that same infernal power that enabled Simon Magus to rise in the air, as witnesses Holy Scripture.

In any case, my hell-steed maintained itself very firmly in the streams of the atmosphere, and flew forward with such impetus that I had to cling with both hands to its thick hair to avoid falling, and the wind created by the terrific speed of its movement whistled past my ears and was painful to my eyes and chest. Having adjusted myself to the sensations of a man in flight, I began to look around me and down, and noticed that we were keeping well below the clouds, at about the height of small mountains, and I was able to make out various districts and villages as they followed one another below me like a geographical map. Of course I was quite unable to take any part in determining the choice of route, and obediently flew whither my he-goat hastened, but by the fact that we encountered no towns on our way, I concluded that we were not flying along the stream of the Rhine, but most likely towards the south-east, in the direction of Bavaria.

I suppose that the aerial journey lasted not less than half-an-hour, perhaps even longer, for I had time to get quite used to my position. At last there rose up before us out of the darkness a remote valley between two bare peaks, lit by a bluish-green light, and, as we approached it, more and more distinctly voices were heard, and the figures of various beings became visible bustling hither and thither in the valley, on the shores of a lake that shone like silver. My he-goat descended low, almost to the earth, and, riding me right up to the crowd, he suddenly tipped me off on to the ground, not from a great height, but yet so that I felt the hurt of the bump, and disappeared. Hardly had I had time to rise when I was surrounded by several frenzied women, as naked as I was myself, who lifted me up with shouts : " A new one, a Novice ! "

I was dragged across the whole assembly, my eyes, blinded by the sudden light, at first distinguishing nothing but various grimacing jowls, until I reached the side, at the entrance to a wood, where, beneath the branches of an old beech-tree, loomed dark a group of beings, whom I took to be men. There the women who led me stopped, and I saw that there was Someone seated on a high wooden throne and surrounded by his suite, but in me there was no terror, and I was able to study his appearance rapidly and clearly. The Seated One was enormous in stature and made like a human being down to the waist, like a hairy he-goat below ; his legs ended in hoofs, but his hands were like human hands, so was his face human, red-sunburnt, like an Apache, with large round eyes and a medium beard. He had the appearance of being not more than forty years old, and there was in his expression something sad and rousing compassion, but this feeling disappeared as soon as one's glance rose above his high forehead, to see, emerging distinctly from his curly black hair, three horns : the two smaller ones behind and the larger one in front, and round the horns was placed a crown, apparently of silver, that emitted a soft glow, like the light of the moon.

The naked witches placed me before the throne and exclaimed :

" Master Leonard ! He is new ! "

Then sounded a voice, hoarse and devoid of inflections as though he who spoke was not accustomed to pronouncing words, but strong and masterful, which addressed me, saying :

" Welcome, my son. But dost thou come to us of thine own free choice ? "

I replied, by my own free choice, as I had been instructed to reply.

Then the same voice began to ask me further questions, of which I had been warned, but which I do not wish to repeat here, and thus, step by step, did I perform the whole blasphemous ritual of a black novitiate. Thus, first of all I pronounced a denunciation of the Lord God, of His Holy Mother the Virgin Mary, of all the Saints in Paradise, and of my faith in Christ, the Saviour of the World, and after that I gave Master Leonard the two convened kisses. For the first he benevolently gave me his hand, and as I touched it with my lips, I noticed one peculiarity: its digits, not excepting the thumb, were of equal length, crooked and clawed like those of a kite. For the second, rising, he turned his back upon me, so that above me rose his tail, long like that of an ass, and I, playing my rôle to the end, bent down and kissed his he-goat's rump, black and emitting a nauseating odour, but yet strangely reminiscent of a human face.

And when I had performed this ritual, Master Leonard, still in the same unchanging voice, exclaimed:

" Rejoice, oh my beloved son, and accept my sign on thy body and bear it throughout the ages of ages to come, Amen ! "

And, bending his head towards me, he touched my breast with the point of his larger horn, above the left nipple, so that I felt the pain of the prick and from under my skin oozed a drop of blood.

At once the witches who had brought me clapped their hands and shouted for joy, and Master Leonard, seating himself on the throne, pronounced at last those fatal words for the sake of which I stood before him.

" Now ask of me what thou wilt, and thy first desire will be fulfilled by us."

With perfect self-control I replied:

" I desire to know, and I beg of you to inform me, where is now the Count Heinrich von Otterheim, known unto you, and how am I to find him."

As I said this I gazed into the face of the Seated One and saw how it hardened and became overcast and terrible, and it was not he, but someone else standing near the throne, small of stature and hideous, who answered me:

"Thinkest thou that we do not know thy double-dealing. Beware playing with matters that are stronger than thou. And now begone, and perhaps later wilt thou receive an answer to thy insolent question."

In no wise frightened by the threatening tone, for the naturalness and humanity of everything that was happening instilled no terror into me, I was about to reply, but my guides whispered into my ear: "No more! Later! Later!" and dragged me away from the throne almost by force.

Soon I found myself amidst a variegated crowd, which was making merry as at the Feast on Saint John's day, or at the Carnival festivities at Venice. The field on which the Sabbath was being held was rather large, and probably used often for that purpose, for it was so trampled that no grass grew upon it. In places, here and there, fires that burned without fuel rose from within the earth, and they lit all the district by a greenish light like the light of fizgigs. Amidst these flames there bustled, jumped and grimaced three or four hundreds of beings, men and women, either quite naked or barely covered with shirts, some with wax candles in their hands, and also hideous animals of human appearance, enormous toads in green caftans, wolves and wolf hounds upright on their hind legs, apes and long-legged birds; here and there beneath their feet crawled and twisted repulsive serpents, lizards, salamanders, and tritons. In the distance on the very shore of the lake, I could make out some small children with long white staffs, who, not taking part in the merry-making, were grazing a herd of toads of a lesser size.

One of the naked witches who were leading me took an especial interest in me, and showed no sign of leaving me when the others, dragging me into the

crowd, dispersed in various directions. Her face
attracted me by its gaiety and pertness and the young
body, though with breasts drooping, seemed yet fresh
and responsive. She held my hand firmly and,
snuggling against me, told me that she was known at
the night feasts as Sarraska, and was persuading me:
" Come and dance." I saw no reason to refuse her.

By this time shouts were heard in the crowd: " A
roundelay ! A roundelay ! " and everyone, as if performing a well-known rite, began to gather into three
large circles, locked one within the other. Those in the
medium one stood as is usual in village roundels, but
those in the least and the largest stood reversed, with
their faces turned outwards and their backs turned
inwards. Now were heard the sounds of music: flute,
violin and drum—and then began the devilish dance,
that started to grow more rapid with every movement,
at first reminding me of one of the Spanish *danses de
espadas* or of the *sarabande*, and then like nothing
upon earth. As I and my companion had got into
the very outer circle of the roundelay, I could only
barely see what was taking place in the other circles:
it seemed as if the least was furiously wheeling from
left to right, and those in the second furiously jumping
up and down, while in ours the main figure of the dance
appeared to consist in us, turning half-way and not
unlocking our hands, knocking our buttocks against
each other.

I was quite out of breath when at last the music
stopped and the dance ended, but hardly had the
dancers broken the circles than the sound of singing
was heard, coming from the direction of the throne.
The Seated One, accompanying his singing with the
sound of a harp, sang in a hoarse and heavy voice a
psalm, to which we all listened in respectful silence.
And, when he ceased, we all began to sing in chorus
the black litany, in form like a church litany, while to
its prayers, all the words of which I could not quite

understand, the usual responses were heard : " Miserere
nobis ! " and " Ora pro nobis ! "

Meantime came bustling among us some small but
active creatures in red velvet tunics sewn with small
bells, and they laid tables very smartly, covering them
with white cloths, though, as one could see, these
attendants performed their duties without the help of
hands.

Sarraska, who had recovered her breath during the
singing, again began to urge and hurry me :

" Behan, Behan, come quicker, let us take our seats
or none will be left, and I am terribly hungry."

Having decided to conform to the customs of the
place, as I have done always and everywhither fate
has carried me, I followed the young witch, and we were
among the first to seat ourselves at the table, around
which were placed wooden benches of the commonest
kind. Very soon the litany was over, and with the
greatest noise and yelling the whole concourse followed
our example, filling the benches, pushing and quarrel-
ling for seats. The attendants in velvet tunics began
to place various dishes on the table, all simple in the
extreme : cups with cabbage soup or oatmeal, butter,
cheese, plates with bread made of black millet, bottles
of milk, and quarts of wine, which, when I tried it, proved
sour and of low quality.

Above all sounded the buzz of unceasing talk, roars
of laughter, whistling and giggling, but I made use of
the fact that our seats were at the side to endeavour to
question Sarraska about various details of the festival
I did not properly understand; and she, greedily
stuffing her stomach with the proffered dishes, very
willingly satisfied my curiosity.

I asked her who were these attendants who served
the dishes, and she said that they were demons, and
armless, who performed their work with the aid of
their teeth, and wings that they concealed beneath
their capes. And then and there she called one of

these attendants to her, to show him to me closer, and it was strange to me to see how the naked woman turned here and there in front of us the smallish mannikin with an idiot face, and wings like those of a bat in place of hands.

I asked next how it was that they were none of them afraid to dance amid the columns of fire. But Sarraska laughed out loud and told me that the fire does not burn, that it is only the priests who try to instil fear by pretending that the fires of Hell cause suffering, but that in reality they are like soapy froth, and she wanted to drag me forward to convince me of the fact, but I was careful to do nothing to attract the attention of the whole company to myself.

Again I asked, whether the serpents and tritons that crawled about our feet might not harm us, but Sarraska, laughing again, assured me that these creatures were pets and harmless, and at once she dragged a snake from under the table and wound it round her breasts, and the snake tenderly licked her neck with its forked tongue and playfully nibbled at her scarlet nipple.

At last I asked whether there were Sabbaths more lively than to-day's, and at this question Sarraska's eyes sparkled and she said to me:

" Of course ! To-day is the most ordinary of gatherings, such as is held every Wednesday and Friday, but what took place here on the Feast of the Assumption, or, wait, what will there not be on the Holiday of All Saints ! At such times more than a thousand people are gathered together, stolen babies are baptised, weddings celebrated, obits held in memory of the dead ! Then there is rejoicing, oh what a joy it is to dance, to sing, and to caress ! Sometimes there are wolves that give pleasure with which no man can compare ! And, for a treat, sometimes, we cook ourselves children's meat in milk ! "

And with these words Sarraska's teeth somehow

The Fiery Angel

glittered peculiarly in her mouth—white and sharp
teeth; and when I asked again, not without revulsion:
whether it were really true that human flesh was so
tasty and wolves' caresses so agreeable, she only
laughed slyly in reply. Then I asked her whether it
had occurred to her to experience the caresses of demons
and whether they gave joy. She, not ashamed, declared
to me that they do, and a great joy, only their seed is
as cold as ice. But then she drew quite close to me and,
shamelessly touching parts of my body, she began to
speak to me thus:

" What is the use of recollecting the past, my precious
Behan ? To-day I love you, and you are more desirable
to me than any incubus. Look, already they are putting
out the fires and soon the cock will crow—come with
me, then."

When, however, I shook my head in negation and
tried to free myself from her embrace, Sarraska asked
me why I was so sad. I told her that Master Leonard
had promised to give me an answer to a question of
great importance to me, but till now he had made no
reply.

Sarraska then told me:

" Don't you be sad, precious Behan! I was his
betrothed last Friday and he is very kindly-disposed
towards me. I will go and ask him; he will not
deny me.

Having said this Sarraska slipped from the bench
and ran off, and, left by myself, I began to take a look
round. In truth the fires were already going out and
only a few of them still weakly smouldered near the
ground, and before my eyes the benches began to
empty quickly, for the moment had come for the
participants in the Sabbath to give themselves to the
last and most ignoble stage of the feast. The tender music
of flutes rose above the lawn, through the thickening
darkness hands reached out for hands, and the mingled
bodies began to sink to the earth with soft sighs, here

108

and yonder, between the tables, and on the shores of the lake, and far away under the trees. Here I saw the ugly coupling of a youth with an old woman, there the hideous toying of an old man with a child, here the shamelessness of a maid giving herself to a wolf, or the fury of a man caressing a wolf-bitch, or a monstrous bundle of many bodies plaited in one caress—wild outcries and gasping breath sounded upon all sides, increasing and drowning the sound of the instruments. Soon the whole lawn was become one Sodom come to life, a new feast of Codrus, a horrid madhouse in which all were seized with the fury of heat and threw themselves upon one another, hardly seeing who was before them : man, woman, child or demon—and the invincible odour of lust rose from these dark, heaving masses, drugging me also, so that I felt rise in me that same fury of the male, that same insatiable thirst for embraces.

And, at this very moment, Sarraska appeared in front of me rejoicing, and said :

" It is accomplished, accomplished ! He said to me : Has not my true servant already given him the answer : whither you are riding, ride thither ! ' If he confirms it—it must be true ! "

After these words, assuming that my sadness must have been blown away, the witch silently embraced me with her arms and drew me after her towards the beginnings of the wood, close to me like a lizard, and whispering to me disconnected words of caress. The temptation of lust penetrated into me, through the nostrils, and through the ears, and through the eyes. And Sarraska with her warm body as it were scorched all my body, so that I allowed myself to be led without hindrance. Beneath the thick branches of a walnut tree we fell to the ground, on a little island of moss, and in that moment I remembered neither my oaths nor my love, but only gave myself up to joy, that darkened my reason and deprived me of will. But suddenly, while I was still weak after these transports, right in front of me I saw the face of Renata amidst the green leaves, and awareness flared up in me like lightning, and remorse and jealousy seared me painfully. Renata was quite naked, like most of those participating in the Sabbath, and on her face was the same expression of sensual heat as on those of the others—and, apparently not seeing me, she made her way as though seeking some-one, through the beginnings of the wood. I leaped up like a wild boar breaking from a trap, thrust away Sarraska who sought to hold me back, and, as she passed, flew after her with the sad and angry cry:

" Renata ! Why are you here ? "

Renata, as if recognising me, flung herself away in fright, disappearing in the darkness, but I flew after her amidst the black bushes, stretching out my hands, furious and ripe to kill if I caught her. But she, appear-ing only for moments, disappeared again, the trunks of trees barred my way, branches whipped my face, while behind me sounded screams, whistlings and cries of the chase as though I were being pursued, and everything whirled in my head, and at last I could see nothing around me and fell to the ground, as if into a deep well, head foremost.

Later, when I came to, and, with a great effort, opened my eyes and looked around, I saw that I was lying alone on the floor of that small room in which I had smeared myself with the magic composition. In the air still hovered the strangling odour of the oint-ment, all my body ached as though I had been jarred by falling from a height, and the pain in my head was such that I could scarcely think. However, summoning all my strength, I managed to sit up, and at once tried to take stock of the meaning of all that which filled my memory. And for quite a long time I sat motionless, thinking and drawing conclusions.

Cbapter the Fifth

How we studied Magic

MY conclusions assailed me from two sides, like the warriors of two enemy hosts, and it was not easy for me to weight the scales of my understanding on to one side, for in both cups could I place new and ever new considerations.

On the one hand there was much to sustain the view that my dread aerial journey to the Sabbath had been merely an apparition of sleep, called forth by the poisonous vapours of the ointment I had rubbed into my body. The cape on which I had recovered my senses was crumpled and rucked into folds exactly as it would have been after a human body had lain on it for a prolonged period. Nowhere on my body were there any signs of my journey of the night, particularly, I noted, there were no scratches or sores on my legs from the barefoot dance upon the meadow or the hunt through the woods. And lastly—and this was the most important— on my breast could be perceived no trace of the prick of his horn, with which Master Leonard had seemed to brand upon me the eternal mark of the Devil, *sigillam diabolicum.*

On the other hand the connectedness and consequence of my memories far exceeded that usually associated with dreams. My memory informed me of details of the devilish games heretofore entirely unknown to me, and which I had not the slightest cause to invent. Moreover, I had quite clearly been conscious of taking part in the witches' roundelay in body and not in spirit, if

one admit, that is to say, the possibility of the separation
of spirit from body during life, which the divine Plato
is ready to recognise but which is much doubted by
the majority of philosophers.

Finally it occurred to me that there was to hand a
trusty method of resolving my doubts. If all that I
had seen had been real, then Renata, giving me the
slip, must have followed me in my flight through the
air, and now must either yet tarry away from home or
else lie in her bed as tired as I. With a new access of
rage and jealousy, I hastily began to dress and put
myself in order, which was not easy for me to accomplish
for my hands yet shook and darkness kept coming into
my eyes. In a few minutes I was already in the corridor,
where the fresh morning air pouring into my chest
somewhat reinvigorated me, and, with heart beating, I
opened the door of Renata's room. Renata was sleeping
quietly in her high bed, and there were no signs of her
having spent the night as I had spent it, for there was
no trace of the smell of the ointment, which would
have shown that she had resorted to the magic rubbing.

At that time, this seemed to me an invincible argument in favour of my not having quitted the realm
of dreams, and yet I was seized not by a feeling of
joy, in that the deeds and words of the night, by which
I had destroyed the eternal salvation of my soul, were
but dreams—but by a staggering sense of shame. It
appeared to me extremely ignoble that I had been
unable to perform that which I had promised Renata,
or to penetrate to the throne of the Devil, though this
is easily achieved, it seems, even by quite insignificant
persons. I fancied at the same time, that my dream
had maybe been sent by the Devil himself, desiring
once more to laugh and mock at my helplessness, and
the thought struck me like a humiliating slap in the
face. And in this moment, while I gazed on the sleeping
Renata, there was born in me, and immediately hardened, that resolve that governed my subsequent actions

during the many weeks that followed: the resolve to
try my strength in open contest with the spirits of
darkness whom I had encountered in my path through
life, and who so far had tossed me about like a ball.

Meanwhile, Renata, roused by the creaking of the
door, slightly opened her eyes. Another feeling—
remorse that I could have suspected Renata of deceit—
forced me to rush impetuously towards her, to sink
to my knees with a kiss upon her hand, and to utter
words she could not have understood.

" Renata! Beloved! I thank thee! And thou wilt
forgive me! "

Renata, still sleeping, was at first unable to understand what it was all about, but then she remembered
everything and asked quickly:

" Rupprecht, have you been there? Did you see
Him? Did you ask Him? What did He answer? "

These cruel questions, which showed me that Renata
quite overlooked the fact that I was exhausted to the
point of fainting and thought only of her Heinrich,
somewhat sobered me. I replied to her that the ointment had proved ineffective, and that, instead of carrying me to the place where the witches hold their revels,
it had only sent me to sleep and given me visions of the
Sabbath. But at the same time, as if in delirium, I
began to declare that I now took it upon myself to
accomplish her purpose for her, that not much was to
be obtained by approaching the Devil as a pauper
a moneylender, for he hearkens only to those who
command him as a master a servant, and that, in fine,
one must penetrate into the world of demons by means
of the power of knowledge, not by the doubtful spells
of sorcery.

In the excited state in which I then was, I wanted at
once to lay before Renata my whole plan of studying
secret sciences, and it was only at her oft-repeated
request, almost against my will, that I consented to
relate to her all that which seemed to me only an evil

dream. However, in this narration I concealed two circumstances from her : one, that I had not withstood the temptation of Sarraska, and two, that the image of Renata herself had appeared to me amidst the other apparitions of the night. Renata treated my recollections as entire reality, by no means agreeing with me that they were only an hallucination, and she considered the words of Him who presided over the feast of the night a confirmation of the prophecy of the witch of Geerdt. But I laughed without restraint at myself, at Renata and at my aerial journey, saying that if it were a reality, it was an absurd one; if a dream, then a lying one ; if a prophecy, an inconclusive one.

I was eager at once to take up without delay the new task that confronted me, but my incontrollable weariness and the recent exhaustion prevented me. And soon the ache in all my limbs, and a cruel headache, even forced me to take to my bed, and the remainder of that day I spent in a state of semi-coma, through which the images of the Sabbath whirled before me like an incessant wheel: naked witches, handless demons, round dances, the feast, the caresses, Master Leonard. I remember as if in a dream that Renata came from time to time to my bed and laid her cool hands on my burning forehead, and it seemed to me then as though the involuntary tenderness of those fingers immediately cured all my pain.

On the morning of the following day, I woke as usual once more brisk and strong, but finding, still, that my decision of the previous day had taken root in my soul and spread wide its branches, like the tree that was grown in a few hours by the Hindu gymnosophist. I soon confirmed to Renata, quite coolly and quite definitely, that I intended to undertake the study of magic, since I saw no other means of rendering her the service she expected of me. Renata listened to me with close attention and, however unexpected it may have been on the part of her who was the first to attract

me to demonomancy, then declared to me that she
definitely opposed my scheme, and she did not tarry
to put before me, with no little effect, all the difficulty,
the danger, perhaps even the hopelessness of the task
that I had planned.

Thus Renata told me that the study of magic requires
many long years and much preparatory labour, that
the most profound secrets are never entrusted to books
but only passed from lip to lip, from master to pupil
among the initiated, and that, lastly, she would not
accept such a sacrifice from me and absolved me from
my oaths.. But I had replies to all these arguments:
I said that as a knight I could not abandon a lady without first attempting every imaginable means to her
salvation, that for the attentive eye and mind the hints
preserved in books on magic are in themselves sufficient;
that I wanted not to penetrate into all the *arcana* of
the forbidden sciences, but only to obtain a sufficiency
of information for certain purely practical purposes—
and so forth.

But when it became thus apparent from the conversation that I did not wish to yield my purpose, Renata
sought to frighten me, and, betraying her close acquaintance with magic commerce, she spoke to me,
broadly as follows:

" You do not know, Rupprecht, the sphere into which
you desire to enter. There is in it nothing but horror,
and the magi—they are the most unhappy of men.
The magician lives under the continual threat of painful
death, only by unsleeping activity and extreme concentration of the will can he restrain the furious spirits that
are ready every moment to tear him in pieces with their
ravening fangs. A whole host of inimical monsters
attends every step of the magician, watching only lest
he may forget, or omit, some tiny safeguard so that they
may hurl themselves ferociously upon him. Imagine to
yourself a beast-tamer spending his days and nights in
a cage of mad dogs or poisonous snakes, the fury of

which he can barely harness with whip and hot iron, that is the life of a magician. And in recompense for this unceasing torment, he obtains only the forced service of lesser demons, ignorant and far from all-powerful, always treacherous, always ready for betrayal and every baseness."

These remarks of Renata were sweet to me, like the light of the sun through rain, for here, for the first time, did I see in her concern for my fate, but, notwithstanding, I replied without hesitation :

" I am prepared to agree that all may be as you say, but fear has never yet had power to restrain me. Evil spirits are a creation of the Lord, though deprived of His grace, and, like everything in nature, except the Personal and Almighty Will of the Creator, cannot but be subject to natural laws. It thus remains only to learn these laws, and we shall have power to govern the demons, as now one uses the powers of the wind for the progression of ships. No doubt the wind is immeasurably more powerful than man, and at times storms shatter shipping to splinters, but usually the captain contrives to bring his cargo to the quay. I know that I expose our ship, and you upon it, to great danger, increasing sail under storm, but we have no other course."

After these words of mine our discussion came to an end.

Later, events occurred to convince me that Renata, in opposing me, spoke much against her own conviction, and that magic and secret sciences had for her a yet greater force of attraction than for me. However, playing her part, for quite a long time she made belief to despise my occupations, and showed no desire to render me the slightest help in my work, and I had to surmount the first, and as always the most difficult, bends of the new road quite alone and without counsel.

In the years of my scholastic life I had known a book dealer who lived on the Red Mountain, an old eccentric by the name of Jacob Glock, with whom, when penniless, I had used to pawn or to whom I had used to sell my textbooks. Into his shop, then, did I plan to cast my fisherman's line, for I remembered that he had been interested in books on astrology, on alchymy and magic, and perhaps himself had been immersed in the search for the philosopher's stone.

The shop of Glock had not altered at all in the ten years that had passed, and I felt myself a student again when, crossing the threshold, I found myself in a darkish, cramped room, with only one door leading to the street and no windows, choked full with bundles of various books, old and in manuscript, new and printed, second-hand or fresh from the press, in gay covers or in leather bindings with clasps. In the midst of many-storied shelves, tidy columns of quartos and unruly heaps of polemical pamphlets, sat Jacob Glock himself on a broken bench, as if monarch of all these manuscripts, opusculi and folios, locked up in his shop like the winds in the cave of Aeolus. Seeing me, Glock lowered his glasses to his nose, replaced upon his lap the etching he had been studying, turned towards me his unshaven chin, and sat waiting to hear what I had to say, without recognising me as an old acquaintance.

Remembering the character of Glock, I began by roundabout, introducing myself as a travelling scholar and saying that, having heard much of his rich collection and having in view the composition of an opus on certain questions of theology, connected with magic, I had come especially to the City of Köln to acquire the necessary books. After listening to my oration, Glock looked at me for a long while, shuffling his lips as old men do, then lifted his glasses back to his eyes, took up the etching and said:

" I trade only in books approved by the Church. Go to the fair at Frankfurt; there you will obtain all that you need."

I understood that the old man was afraid lest I

might be a spy of the Inquisition, and I tried to assure
him to the contrary by all means, adding, moreover,
that in bygone years his business had been famed all
over Germany for containing, like the treasury of
Crœsus the Lydian, matter to satisfy all tastes.

Yielding to flattery, Glock grumbled in reply:

" Bygone days ! A great deal was true in bygone
days ! Is our Köln what it was in bygone days ? Then
we reckoned the number of students here as equal to
the number in all the other German Universities
combined, and now there are fewer here than in any
other. For what purpose should the Kölnians now
need books, when our rectors are like the drunkard
Bommelchen or when priests like Reiss, who does not
even know his Latin letters, are appointed to the
Church of the Holy Apostles !

Thus our conversation was engaged ; I agreed with
the old man, recalling to him the happy days of Köln,
brought the conversation round to books and printing
presses, and humbly, for a whole hour, listened to him
singing the praises of the good printers from Ulrich
Zell to Iohann Soter, hymns to the incomparable
editions of Aldo Manutius and Henri Estienne, and em-
barking on discussions respecting the advantages of the
various scripts and various types, such as Gothic, Roman,
Antiqua, Bastard, Cursive. In recompense, the old
man, in taking leave of me, said more good-naturedly :

" And, dear sir, call again ; we shall rummage
through these piles together—perhaps we may find
something suitable for you : there's quite a lot that
gets blown into this shop of mine by the strong wind—
te-he-he ! "

Of course I did not fail to call on Glock again on the
following day, and he greeted me like an old friend.
After once more torturing me with his discourses for
no little time, he then handed me a tiny opusculum,
printed in Köln : " *Das Geheimniss der heiligen
Gertrudis zur Erlangung zeitlicher Schätze u. Güter,*"

one of the most incomprehensible compositions that I have ever read, and quite useless to me, and for which, moreover, he charged me the incongruous price of five guldens. But, in return for that, Glock allowed me one day later to rummage in his treasures, and I picked out several manuscripts filled with incantations and magic drawings, and with the tempting titles: "*Buch Mosis und dreifacher Hollenzwang*," "*Mächtige Beschwörungen der hollischen Geister*," "*Hauptzwang der Geister zu Menschlichen Dienster*" and so forth, for which I had again to pay lavishly. Then, continuing to dive like a pearl diver day after day into these waves of books, I extracted with Glock's benevolent help almost a whole library, and he also persuaded me not to despise even books directed against magic, such as, for example, the absurd old book with bad drawings of Ulrich Molitor "*De laniis et phitonicis mulieribus*," the empty opusculum of Martin Plantsch "*De sagis maleficiis*," the famous compilation of Institor and Jakob Sprenger "*Malleus maleficarum*," which has the direct purpose of rendering easier for judges the recognition, denunciation and punishment of witches, and even the treatise of the ill-famed Dominican, enemy of the humanists, Jakob Hochstraten: "*Quam graviter peccant quaerentes auxilium a maleficis*."

And when Glock found that he had palmed off upon me all his stale goods, rotting in his shop, he opened me a book-case in which he kept the strictly scientific dissertations on the subject, and there opened up for me as it were a New World, yet more remarkable than the fields and valleys of New Spain. Here at last reached my hands the works of Albertus Magnus, Arnald de Villanova, Rogerius Bacon, Robert of England, Anselm of Parma, Picatrix of Spain, the compositions of Abbot Trithemius, and amongst them his striking "*Philosophia naturalis*" and "*Antipalus maleficorum*," the opus of Peter of Apponia "*Elementa*

magica," in which fullness of breadth is joined to
clarity of expression, and, after all these, the book that
brought into system all the knowledge thus accumulated
and illumined it by the light of a truly philosophic
attitude to phenomena : " *Henrici Cornelii Agrippae
ab Nettesheym, de Occulta Philosophia libri tres,*"
with the fourth part in manuscript. This last work
Glock also sold me dearly, saying that the edition was
a secret one, and pointing in confirmation to the fact
that neither the place of printing nor the year was
indicated on the title-page ; but later I found that it
had been printed at Köln only a few months before,
and under privilege of His Majesty the Emperor at
that—and only the supplementary fourth part was, in
a degree, a rarity, since the author, fearing persecution,
had not given it to the printing press.

None the less, I harboured no ill-feelings towards
Glock, though he did manage to drag a great deal of
money out of me and to bore me not a little with his
discourses. But he at least provided me with all the
books I needed, and in his senile prattle occurred not
a few observations not only useful to me, but actually
indispensable. I let such expressions in his speech as
" wizard's vinegar," " the raven's head," " the green
lion " and " the red lion," " the sails of Theseus " and
other kindred matters quite useless to me slip past my
ears, as well as all his stories of the famous alchymists
and their fabulous enrichments, but I seized on each of
his priceless hints regarding questions of operative magic,
carefully remembered all his explanations of magic
terminology, and learnt how to extract use from his
anecdotes about famous magi, necromancers and
theurgists. If I achieved some success in the discipline
I was studying, for that I am indebted not a little to
this good old man, who, though dreaming of the
transmutation of lead into gold, did not forget, however, to mine silver out of the pockets of others by more
conventional methods.

The Fiery Angel

These visits of mine to the shop of Glock, which here
I have described only shortly, lasted several weeks, but
of course I did not waste all that time, but returned
home immediately, seating myself at the desk and poring
my eyes over the pages of the folios. My zeal for this
work was so strong that, no doubt, had I in my time
studied the " *Sententiae*," " *Processus*," " *Copulata*,"
" *Reparationes* " and all the other text-books with the
same diligence, it would not have been my fate to sack
the town of the Holy Father with the riotous Lutherans,
nor would I have visited the prairies of Anahuac, but
passed my life in peacefully reading lectures, as
magister, from a pulpit in one of the Universities.
Devouring volume after volume, passing from treatise
to treatise, learning new mysteries after new mysteries, I yet ever felt myself not fed to the full, like
the Scylla of Virgil, and my mind in those days became a sort of swallower of inscribed and printed
papers.

In such measure was I carried away by my work,
that, for the time being, even the voice of passion died
down in me : I looked on Renata with eyes that were
somehow more blind, and her words made a lesser
impression on me.   More—I was in no way prey to
worry when, on several occasions, having spent the
whole day in meditation and moodiness, she suddenly,
without uttering a word, put on her cape and departed
for long hours, unknown to me, returning only late
at night.   I was not disturbed in any way when she
began wilfully to mock my work, and wilfully addressed
me with insulting words, calling me hard-working
but devoid of gifts. Completely given up to research,
reasonings, deductions, I felt my soul as if encased
alive in a block of ice, I knew that the heart of my
love still beat, and that it did not suffer from the fact
that its wings were motionless.

One morning, however, after one of her disappear-
ances of this kind, Renata, quite suddenly and as

simply as if it were her custom, pushed *two* chairs to the desk and said to me:

"Well, Rupprecht, it is time to begin work!"

I looked at Renata with surprise and gratitude, kissed her hand and we sat down side by side. From that day—it was at the end of the month of September—we continued the study of secret philosophy and operative magic together.

As I hope that my narrative will not only serve as matter entertaining to the reader, but perhaps be of use and aid to anyone caught in that same snare that entrapped me, so I wish here, in a few short words, to relate what Renata and I learned from the books we read, though, of course, I have no hope of exhausting that immeasurable ocean called the sphere of secret or forbidden sciences.

I presume that it will be permitted to me to set aside the futile tales of theologues and scholists, who think that any given science can be founded on quotations from the Holy Scriptures alone. The writers of that worthless pack express pretensions to know every smallest detail of the demons, their exact number, as well as all their names. Some of these know-alls, for example, affirm that demons are divided into nine categories: the first, where are gathered the false gods, is ruled over by Beelzebub, the second, where are the false prophets, by Python, the third, with the inventors of all evil, by Belial, the fourth, where are the avengers of crimes, by Asmodeus, and so forth. Others communicate the exact hierarchy of the demons, among whom there is, it appears one emperor—Beelzebub, seven kings: Bel, Pursan, Bilet, Paimon, Belial, Asmodeus, Zapan, twenty-three dukes, thirteen margraves, ten counts, eleven praesusi, and a multitude of knights, and all of these are mentioned by their names. A third group pictures the court of the Master of Hell, relating exactly that at the court of Beelzebub the Grand Chancellorship is held by Adramelek, the

Treasurer is Astaroth, the Great Chamberlain—Verdelet, the Chaplain-in-Chief—Kamoos, and naming with no less exactitude not only all the ministers of Hell and their lords of battle, but also the envoys of Hell at the various European courts. It is but too obvious that all these constructions are based on general ideas and are a mere imitation of the contemporary construction of a state upon earth, while true science can only be based on experiment, on observation and on the trustworthy evidence of eye-witnesses.

On the other hand, in books really worthy of attention, very often we could find no answers to questions that we might rightfully have proposed, for serious investigators conform not with the curiosity of their readers, but with the limits of their knowledge. For the nature and life of demons is in such measure difficult of study that, to this day, despite the noble and disinterested efforts of scientists old and new, and, moreover, of such colossi of science as Albertus Magnus, the Abbot Trittenheim and Agrippa of Nettesheim—there yet remains in that sphere a great deal uncertain or entirely unknown. Indeed it would be useful to inscribe, at the head of every discussion upon demons, the just words of one of the manuscripts that we read : " To comprehend the nature of demons and their power is as difficult for a human as for an ant to comprehend the philosophy of the universal doctor Thomas Aquinas."

However, this is the general conception of these matters to which we attained after a diligent and honest study of the library I had collected :

Demons belong to the number of reasoning beings created by God and are divided into three species. The first are named " of heaven " (*coelestes*), they inhabit the upper spheres and accomplish exclusively the will of God, round whom they revolve, as round a definite centre. The second are named " of the worlds " (*mundani*), for to them is entrusted the inspection and

care of the worlds, and to be distinguished among
their number are the demons of Saturn, Jupiter, Mars,
the Sun, Venus, Mercury, the Moon, also of the twelve
signs of the Zodiac, the thirty-six celestial decuriae,
seventy-two celestial quinariae, and so forth. The
third are named " of the earth " (*terrestres*), and are
divided into four orders—fire, water, air and earth—
and live permanently amidst human beings, interfering
invisibly with our affairs, and, as should of course be
expected of them, the demons of fire react for preference
upon our mind, those of the air—upon our senses, of
the water—upon our imagination, of the earth—upon
our body and its lusts. Although not one particle of
the earth is free from these demons, yet some of them
manifest themselves more in one place, others in another,
so that there are yet separately classified the demons of
the night and of the day, of the North and of the South,
of the East and of the West, sylvan demons, demons of
the fields, of the mountains, house demons or familiars.
And as regards the total number of demons, the
investigators do not agree among themselves upon that
question and it can only be said that their number
must be very great, surpassing hundreds of millions.

As regards the bodies of demons, there exists wide
dissension among the investigators, but one is forced
to the conclusion that demons have bodies that are
fluid, of thin composition, but immortal, not subject to
decay, not in ordinary cases perceptible to our senses—
sight and touch—and able to penetrate through all
kinds of matter. The bodies of the higher demons,
however, composed of the finest ether, are finer than
those of the lower demons, into the composition of
which enter fire and air, and still finer than those of
the lowest, which consist of elements of water and earth.
To render themselves visible, demons have to form for
themselves bodies of firmer substance, adopting the
appearance sometimes of a nebulous figure, or of a
spirit of fire, or of a bloodless, corpse-like, human

being. The body proper of a demon does not require food and therefore has no natural functions, likewise a demon has no sex and does not feel lust, and thus cannot multiply in a natural way. However, for purposes of evil, demons are often enabled to unite bodily with men and women as *succubi* and *incubi*, and a demon that appears in one instance as a *succubus* preserves the seed thus admitted to use in another instance when required to play the part of an *incubus*.

All demons can enter into commerce with humans, but the *celestial* demons do so only when they so will or at the Lord's command, while the *earthly* demons are too weak and insignificant for their help to be of service to humans, so that magi are accustomed to invoke the *worldly* demons. To invoke a worldly demon one must know his name, his character and his appropriate incantation. Many demons in conversing with humans have communicated their names, that is how we know of them, for example, the twelve demons of the Zodiac: Malchidaël, Asmodel, Ambriël, Muriël, Verchiël, Gamaliël, Zuriël, Barchiël, Aduachiël, Ganaël, Gambiël, Barchiël. But, in the opinion of investigators, their names can also be calculated artificially: from the Hebrew letters corresponding to the ciphers of the celestial signs, by going through the whole celestial circle by degrees, beginning at the sign of the given demon, when we go upwards we obtain the names of the good demons, when downwards those of the evil ones. The character or seal of a demon consists of his sign joined to the monogram of his name. The sign is formed of six roots, corresponding to the six star longitudes, to which are also adduced the planetary longitudes and the lines connecting them, and the monogram is written out in one of the antique alphabets admitted by the magi—Egyptian hierogly- phics, Old-Hebrew letters, specially altered Latin letters or, finally, in cipher letters. The incantation, which is the chief element of the invocation, is com-

posed by the magus by agreement with the demon, and
in the incantation is indicated all the characteristics of
the demon as well as a persuasive appeal to appear
and perform the request, and the whole is strengthened by
the power of the secret names of God.

The force of the incantation resides in the magic
significance of figures, which Pythagoras himself has
demonstrated and no serious investigator can deny,
and in case the whole ritual of the invocation is performed exactly, the name of the demon written out
correctly and the incantation pronounced without errors,
the demon cannot fail to appear before the magus
and cannot fail to obey his command, as a steel needle
properly magnetised cannot fail to turn North. It is
worthy of present note that various demons have shapes
beloved of themselves and in which they usually appear
before the invocator. Thus the demons of Saturn
appear slim and elegant, with an angry countenance,
their complexion is dark, their movements like gusts
of wind ; before their apparition is seen a surface white
as if covered with snow, often they take the shape of a
bearded king riding on a dragon, or an old woman
leaning on a staff, or a four-faced creature, or an owl,
or a scythe, or a juniper tree. The demons of Jupiter
appear of middle stature, the body rather sanguine,
their complexion is rufous, the movement impetuous,
the countenance meek, the speech cringing ; before
their apparition human beings devoured by lions are
often seen ; often they take the shape of a being with
naked sword riding on a stag, or a man wearing a
mitre and in long robes, or a maiden decorated with
flowers, or a bull, or a peacock, or a sky-blue robe.
The demons of the Moon appear enormous, fat and
phlegmatic ; their complexion is like a dark cloud,
the expression is troubled, the eyes like rubies and full
of moisture ; they have teeth like boars, are bald and
their movements are like the rocking waves of the sea ;
before their apparition it rains ; often they take the

shape of a king riding on a hind with a bow in his
hands, or a small boy, or an arrow, or a roe-deer, or a
huge centipede, and so forth.

Concealed in all these various shapes, the demons
enter into conversation with the invocator, speaking
his tongue, at first they try to cheat him, but then, if
he does not yield to them, they submit to his desires
and execute obediently everything possible to their, it
must be said, rather limited power.

Such are, on very general lines, the characteristics
of demons and the ritual of their invocation.

These data, that I have narrated here on four smallish
pages, Renata and I gathered during nearly two months,
studying diligently, like the most studious of scholars,
to the very end of October. Renata did not know Latin,
and consequently the books that were written in that
language—and these were a majority—I had to translate to her word for word, but in no wise was her
collaboration a burden to me. On the contrary,
Renata in many ways facilitated my study, for, with
incredible ease, she knew how to explain the concealed
meaning of certain statements or to supplement that
which was only hinted at in the printed page—this,
at the time, I regarded as her serpentine penetration,
but I am now prepared to explain it by the fact that this
occasion was not the first on which she had approached
the sphere of the secret sciences, she knew and had
heard of magic operations a great deal that remains
unknown to the majority. And I am convinced that
it was only these recollections of Renata, together with
the chance remarks of Glock, that made it possible for
me to master so complicated a science as magic in so
short a time as ten weeks.

It is noteworthy that, after joining me in my work,
Renata suddenly as it were changed completely, and
during the four or five weeks that we laboured together
she remained constantly in a pleasant mood and there
was none of the usual strangeness in her behaviour.

Her zeal and diligence soon exceeded mine, and she spent whole days without tiring, at her book studies from grey morning to black night, forgetting both church services and town festivals. Not seldom did it happen that when I was already dropping with fatigue and my brain refused to take in more, Renata still had no wish to leave the lectern and, reproaching me, opened another tome. She was ready without respite to delve with the spade of reason into the dark mines of the printed pages, night as well as day, and never did her arm weaken in the work, and never was her joy blunted when we brought to light from these depths a new nugget of gold.

However, there was an explanation for this indefatigableness of Renata, for, when she had approached nearer to the secrets of magic, she soon came to believe, blindly and stubbornly as always, that with their help she really would be able to regain the love of her Count Heinrich. But for my part, on the other hand, plunging into the study of the secret sciences, I gradually lost sight of my primary purpose, and was soon quite disinterestedly carried away by my work like a true adept. Overcome by the majesty of those vistas that opened before me—the vistas of the world of demons into which our world of humans is thrust like an islet into the ocean—for a time I forgot about Count Heinrich and about the oath I had given to Renata. I was so happy in sailing, she at my side, upon the seas of books, manuscripts, designs and calculations that, though at last I saw beyond the breakers the shore to which I myself steered the ship, somehow I could not feel rejoicing and I did not hasten to make port. And when, after we had mastered the essentials of ceremonial magic, Renata began to hurry me to apply our knowledge to the matter in hand, for a long time I still found pretext to postpone the decisive day, pleading the insufficiency of that knowledge.

At last, in the first days of the month of November

that had crept on us unheeded with its cold winds and long twilights, no objections remained to me and I saw the necessity of yielding to Renata's insistence. From book and theoretical studies we turned to practice, and undertook the final preparations for the precarious experiment, which were as yet by no means easy, for we had carefully to acquire the rare objects needed, and to make ready, with every precaution, the necessary instruments. In this too, Renata helped me as patiently and as cheerfully, day by day more convinced that the hour of her reunion with Count Heinrich was at hand, and telling me so with extreme heartlessness as if not noticing the torment it caused me. While, in me, the closer approached the appointed day, the more there rose in me ill-forebodings like ghosts, and, standing in the corners of my soul, they gloomily nodded their heads both at the words of Renata and at my replies.

It was first suggested that I should act alone as invocator, for Renata believed that participation in the matter would tarnish her soul, which she wanted to keep pure for her Heinrich. I tried to overcome this consideration, pointing out that we were seeking power over the demons not for base gains, but for a good purpose; and that to force the evil spirits to tremble and obey is a worthy deed, not disdained by many of the Holy, as, for example, Saint Cyprian and Saint Anastasius. After some hesitation, Renata agreed with me, but rather, it seemed to me, because she did not entirely trust my abilities as a magus and was afraid that I should either forget, or be unable to perform, something vital. Thus we approached the decisive experiment together, *magister cum socio*.

I want to describe in all its details the invocation that we performed, so that an experienced and learned man, if this Narrative should fall into his hands, shall be able to determine what we omitted and what, therefore, accounted for the pitiful and miserable failure of our undertaking.

129

The day we selected, after many discussions, was a Friday, the 13th day of November, because the demons of Friday, which is consecrated to Venus, are especially apt to return women the affections of their lovers; the field of operations was that selfsame closet from which I had attempted my unsuccessful aerial journey to the Sabbath. On this date, we assembled there all we might require for the invocation, and we also took steps to ensure that there should be none other in the whole house that evening except ourselves, for the loud noises might have evoked the suspicions of our Martha. We prepared ourselves for the experiment by forbearance from all food, complete abstinence from wine and the concentration of our thoughts upon our single purpose.

The first care of the invocator is always the magic circle, for it serves as defence against the attack of inimical demons from without, and that is why on the execution of this circle, according to the name of the invoked demon, the distribution of the constellations, the place of the experiment, the time of year and the hour—a great deal of attention is always lavished. We first drew the magic circle on paper, and transferred it in charcoal on to the floor of the closet only on the day of the experiment. It consisted of four concentric circles, the largest of a diameter of nine elbows and enclosing three perfect circles set one within the other, the outer, middle and inner of these three being set each a palm from the other. The middle ring thus formed was divided into nine equal parts, and in these houses was inscribed: in the first, turned straight towards the West, the secret name of the hour we had selected for the invocation, that is, the midnight of Friday, *Nethos ;* in the second the name of the demon of that hour, *Sachiël ;* in the third—the character of that demon ; in the fourth—the names of the demon of that day, *Anaïl,* and of his servants *Rachiël* and *Sachiël ;* in the fifth—the secret name of the time of year, that is, autumn, *Ardaraël;* in the sixth—the names of the demons of that time of year, *Tarquam* and *Guadbarel;* in the seventh—the name of the root of that time of year, *Torquaret;* in the eighth—the name of the earth at that time of year, *Rabianara;* in the ninth—the names of the sun and the moon by which they are known at that time of year, *Abragini* and *Matasignais.* The outer ring was divided into four equal parts and in these houses, turned due West, North, East and South, were inscribed the names of the demon of the air who was in command that day, *Sarabotes rex,* and his four servants: *Amabiel, Aba, Abalidoth, Flaef.* The inner ring was also divided into four parts, and in these houses were inscribed the eternal divine names: *Adonay, Eloy, Agla, Tetragrammaton.* And, lastly, the space within the inmost circle, where the invocators were to stand, was divided into four sectors by a cross, and without the circles, at the four corners of the world, were drawn five-pointed stars.

When the time of midnight approached, carefully locking all the entrances of our dwelling, and having once more ascertained that there was no one within it but ourselves, we entered the experimental closet. Here Renata and I robed ourselves in new dresses of pure white linen, specially prepared, long and concealing our feet, and held at the waist by belts made of the same material. On our heads also we placed linen headwear, resembling mitres, on the front part of which was written the Divine Name, our feet we left bare. While robing, we recited the established prayer: *Anco, Amacor, Amides, Theodonias, Anitor, per merita angelorum tuorum sanctorum, Domine, induam vestimenta salutis, ut hoc, quod desidero, possim perducere ad effectum.* In our hands we took each a magic wand, made of wood, unbranching, and with a metallic point like a tiny sword. Then, not yet entering the circle, we laid on a table, placed to one side and covered with a white linen cloth, a parchment with the sign of the pentagram and the name and character of the demon *Aduachiël*, for the sun was then at the sign of the bowman, and on a wooden tripod, placed at the very edge of the circle itself on its western side, we laid the *librum consecratum*, that is, the book in which were faithfully transcribed all the incantations we intended to pronounce that day. Near the tripod we lit two candles of pure wax, and, on the four five-pointed stars—four earthen lamps, filled with pure vegetable oil and with a burner made of vegetable fibre.

When all had been thus prepared, I looked at Renata and saw that her excitement had reached its utmost limits—her hands shook, her face was pale and she could hardly stand. Then I turned to her like a *magister* to his *socio:* "Friend, remember the importance of this hour," and hastened to begin the experiment. Having sprinkled all around with holy water, pronouncing the established words : *Asperges me Domine*, I firmly entered the magic circle from its western side through a door left by us there in drawing it, and, when I saw that Renata had followed me, I locked the door with the sign of the pentagram. In my soul at that moment there was coldness and sorrow, but I remembered clearly all I had to do.

Turning to the four corners of the world, I called the twenty-four names of the demons on guard that day, six to each corner, then the names of the seven demons who govern the seven planets, then those of another seven to whom are entrusted the days of the week, the seven colours of the rainbow and the seven metals. In the meantime, Renata, having become accustomed to the duties of a disciple, sprinkled the lamps with the fumigators prepared by us, into the composition of which entered : lavender, the powder of bracken and verbena, the oriental resin of styrax, and, particularly, the ointment of the plant nard, dedicated to the day of Venus, and from the lamps there rose streams of aromatic smoke, which, gradually spreading, began to cloud the room with an indefinite bluish mist.

Then I commenced the invocation proper, trying to speak in a tone of voice that should be welcoming, but yet commanding. First I read some church prayers that protect the invocator, and then I pronounced the summons to the demons of the air, which begins with the words : *Nos facti ad imaginem Dei, dotati potentia Dei et ejus facti voluntate per potentissimum et corroboratum nomen Dei, El, forte admirabile, vos exorcisamus.* I could hear the voice of Renata giving me the responses to my prayers. Soon I noticed, or it appeared to me, that in the swaying smoke of the incense there formed and flickered various shapes, probably lower spirits, attracted by the odour of the nard, and I directed at them the point of my wand, forbidding them to touch us. Believing then that the time for the extreme invocation had come, I pronounced the last of the preparatory words : *Ecce Pentaculum Solomonis quod ante vestram adduxi praesentiam,* and so forth.

There blew into my face a cold wind, which lifted my hair, and at that moment I was convinced no less than Renata, of the success of the experiment. Glancing at her I saw that her trembling had not calmed and that she was nearly dropping with exhaustion. So, hastening, I began to walk round the circle from west to east, pronouncing the main invocation addressed to the demon Anaël.

Audi, Anaël ! ego indignus minister Dei, conjuro, posco, urgeo et voco te non mea potestate sed per vim, virtutem et potentiam Dei Patris, per totam redemptionem et salvificationem Dei Filii et per vim devictionem Dei Sancti Spiritus. Per hoc devinco te, sis ubi velis, in alto vel abysso, in aqua vel in igne, in aere vel in terra, ut tu, dæmon Anaël, in momento coram me appareas in decore forma humana. Veni ergo cum festinatione in virtute nominum istorum Aye Saraye,

*Aye Saraye, Aye Saraye, ne differas venire per nomine
æterna Eloy, Archima, Rabur, festina venire per
personam exorcitatoris conjurati, in omni tranquillitate
et patientia, sine ullo tumulto, mei et omnium hominum
corporis sine detrimento, sine falsitate, fallacia, dolo.
Conjuro et confirmo super te, dæmon fortis, in nomine
On, Hey, Heya, Ia, Ie, Adonay, et in nomine Saday,
qui creavit quadrupedia et animalia reptilia et homines
in sexto die, et per nomina angelorum servientium in
tertio exercitu coram Dagiël angelo magno, et per nomen
stellæ quæ est Venus et per sigillum ejus quod quidem
est sanctum—super te, Anaël, qui est præpositus diei
sextæ, ut pro me labores. El, Aty, Titeip, Azia, Hyn,
Ien, Minosel, Achadan! Va! Va! Va!*

I had time to make three rounds of the circle while
pronouncing this invocation. In the bluish smoke
around swayed devilish faces, and everywhere from the
floor of the room rose streams of mist, in miniature
resembling those I had seen at the Sabbath. But in
vain did I wait to see appear before me in vision the
image of little girls at play, that would serve as indication of the apparition of the demon of Venus. Passing
Renata thrice I saw that she was in a state of extremest
tension, with eyes opened as if in ecstasy and supporting
herself with an effort by means of the wand, which she
used as a staff. Knowing, however, that to attract the
demon into one's sphere whole hours of labour are
often required, as yet I did not lose hope and I began
to pronounce the more forcible invocations:

" *Quid tardas? ne morare! obedito præceptori tuo
in nomine Domini Bathat, super Abrac ruens, super-
veniens. Cito, cito, cito! Veni, veni, veni!* "

A confused rumble was now filling the room, as
though wind or rain were coming towards us along the
foliage of tall trees. The expectation of something as
yet unseen and striking seized me with all its power;
my flesh and my reason were taut and ready, either for
defence or attack. But at this moment, while I was

facing the tripod and staring into the swaying mist, there sounded behind me, where Renata was, a knock, as deafening and as sudden as if our house would split. With an involuntary cry, I turned round and saw that one of the lamps, the one near which Renata stood, had gone out. I flew there with the magic wand, pointed forward, for I knew that access within our circle to evil spirits had thus been opened, but it was probably already too late. Encountering Renata's face, I hardly recognised it, for it was distorted and twisted, and it must be supposed that one or several demons, making use of the breach in the circle, had seized and possessed her. Renata, who a moment ago had hardly had the strength to stand up, suddenly pushing me aside with extraordinary force, rushed with her wand uplifted towards the other lamps. I had neither the strength of will nor means to stop her, and she, though of course her hand was guided by him who concealed himself within her, destroyed not only the other three lamps, but also the two wax candles with a few blows of the wand. We were plunged into complete and utter darkness and around us rose, if it were not a deceit of our senses, a wild howling, a roaring of laughter and whistling.

In this moment of danger, I realised that the magic circle could no longer protect us, for in any case it was broken, and therefore, loudly repeating the words of release : *Abi festinanter, apage te, recede statim in continenti !*—I dragged Renata with all my strength away from the room. On the threshold, hurriedly unlocking the door, I pronounced the final exorcism, considered especially powerful : *Per ipsum et cum ipso et in ipso.* I think that never, not in the most ferocious battle with the redskins, did I stand in such danger as in that room, filled with inimical demons and like that cage of mad dogs and poisonous snakes of which Renata warned me. Probably only my extreme presence of mind saved us from death, for I just managed to open the door and lead Renata first into the fresh air of the corridor, and then into the moonlight that streamed into her room.

But Renata's face remained terrifying and quite unlike her, for it even seemed to me as if her eyes had become larger, her chin more pointed, her temples more prominent than normally. Renata threw herself furiously about in my arms, tore off both the mitre and the linen robe, and incessantly shouted words in a hoarse, almost masculine voice, not her own. Listening, I realised that she spoke in Latin, though, as I have already mentioned, she knew nothing of that language. The import of her words was terrible, for Renata heaped curses on me, on herself, on Count Heinrich, uttered furious blasphemies, and threatened me and the whole world with the most fearful calamities.

Though I have never had much confidence in the protection of holy objects, yet, in this my horrible position, expecting at every moment that all the un-shackled demons would hurl themselves at us out of the room of invocation, there was nothing better left for me than to drag Renata to the small altar in her room and there hope for God's help. But Renata in her frenzy refused to approach the holy crucifix, shouting that she hated and despised it, and raising her clenched fists at the image of Christ, and at last she fell to the floor in that same fit of convulsion of which I had already twice been a witness. But never yet had I spent such hopeless hours bending over the tormented creature, and watching the rending of her body by the demons that had seized her, perhaps even by my fault.

Little by little, my fears calmed down and I began to feel that we were already out of danger; in the same gradual, natural way, passed the torment of Renata, and the demon that was in her, shouting at me for the last time that we would yet meet, left her. And we two, prostrate on the floor near the crucifix, were like shipwrecked mariners, who have attained to some small

rock, but have lost all and are certain that the next
wave will wash them down and swallow them for
ever. Renata could not speak, and silent tears rolled
down her face, and I had no words to comfort or to
cheer her. Thus we stayed, silent, on the floor, till
dawn came and we had to take care to remove all
traces of our nocturnal experiment. I carried Renata
in my arms to her bed, for she could neither walk nor
stand, and myself, not without some trepidation, entered
the room of invocation.

The smoke of the incense filled it, and the broken
fragments of the lamps lay on the floor, but no other
damage had been done and no agency hindered me in
tidying the room and effacing from the floor the traces
of the magic circles I had drawn with such care.

Thus ended our experiment in operative magic, for
which we had prepared for the length of more than
two months, and on which first I, and then Renata,
had set such rich hopes.

After that day, Renata relapsed again into that black
despair from which she had been raised awhile by her
studies and her faith in their success; and this new
fit of depression by far surpassed all the earlier ones
in its strength. Previously she had found in herself
the will and desire to argue and to prove to me that
she had many reasons for sadness, but now she did not
want to speak, nor to listen nor to answer. During the
first few days, ailing, she lay in bed motionless, turning
her face to the pillow, not moving a muscle, not opening
her eyes. Later, still in the same state of indifference,
she would spend hours sitting on a bench, her eyes
fixed on a corner of the room, busy with her thoughts
or altogether idle, not hearing when her name was
spoken, like a wood-carving by some Donatello, at
times, however, feebly sighing and only thus showing
signs of life. Renata would have sat the nights through,
also, in this posture, had I not persuaded her to lay
herself down in her bed with the fall of darkness, but

several times I had proof that, none the less, she spent the greater part of the time till morn sleepless, with eyes wide open.

All my efforts to arouse in Renata any interest in existence remained fruitless. She could not glance at the magic books without a shudder; and when I broached to her a repetition of our experiment, she shook her head in refusal and contempt. At my invitation to come out into the town, into the streets, she only shrugged her shoulders silently. I also tried, not without ulterior motive, to speak to her even of Count Heinrich, of the angel Madiël, of all that was most sacred to her, but most often Renata did not even hear my words, or at last made painfully always one and the same reply: " Leave me alone ! " Only once, when I had attacked her especially insistently with my prayers, Renata said to me : " Do you not understand that I *want* to torture myself to death ? Of what service is life to me, when I have not, and never can have, its chiefest joy ? It is good for me to sit here and remember —then why do you urge me to go somewhere where each new impression will be painful to me ? " And after this long speech she fell once more into her state of lethargy.

This recluse, immobile life of Renata, and the fact, moreover, that she almost completely abstained from taking food, soon affected her so that her eyes sank like the eyes of one dead and became woven round with a blackish wreath, her face became greyish, her fingers transparent like dull mica, so that I, trembling, felt that her last hour was definitely approaching. Sorrow tirelessly graved in the soul of Renata a black pit, deeper and deeper plunging its shovels, and lower and lower sinking its bucket in the shaft, and it was not difficult to foresee the day when a blow of its spade would hack through the thread of life itself.

138

Chapter the Sixth

Of my Journey to Bonn, to Agrippa of Nettesheim

IT is no easy matter to stop a cart that has settled down to run along one road, and so I too could not immediately turn off that road along which, during the last months, I had been rushing full tilt. Even after the failure of this first experiment, I was still unable to force myself to think of anything but incantations, magic circles, pentagrams, pentacles, the names and characters of demons. . . . Once more, I carefully went through the pages of the books we had so often studied, trying to find out the cause of our failure, only to convince myself that we had performed everything correctly and according to the advice of science. I should certainly not have failed to repeat the experiment, even without the help of Renata, had it not been that I was deterred by the thought that, as I could import no new element into my methods, I had no right to expect any new result.

In this my uncertainty there began to flicker, like the light of a beacon in a white shore mist, one scheme, which at first I dismissed as inaccomplishable and hopeless, but which later, when the idea became familiar, seemed perhaps accessible. I had learned from Jacob Glock that the writer whose work on magic was my most valuable find amongst all the treasure of books I had gathered, and who at last had presented me with that thread of Ariadne that led me out of the labyrinth of formulæ, names and incomprehensible aphorisms— Doctor Agrippa of Nettesheim, resided a bare few hours' ride distant from my place of habitation : in the City of Bonn, on the Rhine itself. And so, more and more, I began to ponder over the idea that I might turn, for the solution of my doubts, to this man, initiated into all the mysteries of the hermetic sciences, and knowing, no doubt, from experiment and from relations with other scientists, a great deal that it would not be proper to communicate in print *profano vulgo*. It seemed to me an impertinence to disturb the labours or repose of a sage with my private affairs, but, in my heart of hearts, I did not think myself unworthy of a meeting with him, and I did not think that he would find my conversation either ridiculous or dull.

For advice, as yet undecided on my course, I visited Glock's shop ; it was already a long time since I had been there and he was very glad to see me, for he was pleased to have in me a humble listener. This time I had to endure a voluble panegyric to Bernard of Treves, one of the few to discover the philosopher's stone—and only when the foundation of ecstatic words dried up, or perhaps Glock's throat became parched, did I attack the exposition of my case. With circumspection, I explained that my studies of magic were now nearing their end, that, none the less, the conclusions I had reached differed widely from those generally held, and that, accordingly, before expressing my views in a composition, I should like to subject them for consideration to a true authority in such matters ; here I mentioned the name of Agrippa and expressed the supposition that Glock, whose beneficial labours were renowned all over Germany, might be able to give me aid in such a matter.

To my great surprise, Glock not only received my proposal with no little attention, but expressed readiness to help it, and there and then he promised to secure me an introductory letter to Agrippa from his printer, with whom he, Glock, was on terms of friendship. This promise I accepted as an *omen bonum*, and I wondered whether it were not the goddess Fortuna herself who had assumed for that day the doddering shape of the old bookseller to help me on my way, as, in the songs of the divine blind poet, the goddess Minerva assumes the shape of the aged Mentor.

Two days later, Glock kept his promise, and did indeed send me a letter, of which the inscription stood as follows: *Doctissimo ac ornatissimo viro, Henrico Cornelio Agrippæ, comprimis amico Godefridus Hetorpius*—and then it seemed to me that it would have been even unworthy to withdraw from my enterprise. Of course I was disturbed at having to leave Renata, but by staying at her side I could in no way alleviate the heavy malady that cut her life at its root. I tried to talk over my plan with Renata, but she showed no wish to penetrate the meaning of my words, and begged me with a pitiful sign of the hand not to torment her with explanations, so, shutting my lips tightly, I decided to act at my own risk, went to buy myself a horse and got out from the corner my travelling bag, which had grown all over dust.

And when, on the very day of my departure, in the early morning, I went into Renata's room to take my leave, and told her that, though I left, I rode on our joint business, she thus replied to me:

" We—you and I, can have no joint business together: you are alive, I—dead. Farewell."

I kissed Renata's hand and walked out, as if in truth from a room where stood a coffin and funeral candles smoked.

Between the towns of Köln and Bonn lay only a few good hours riding along the Emperor's highway, but as winter weather had set in already, and snow might be expected at any moment, the road was in bad condition, and I had to journey the whole day long, from morning dawn till darkness, not once resting in the village inns, at Godorf, Wesseling, Widdig, Gerzel, and even having almost to spend the night not far away from the town. I should also mention that my new clothes, of dark brown woollen cloth, that I had had made for me in Köln and was wearing for the first time on this visit to Agrippa, reached a very sad state, and even my trusty comrade—the sea-cape that had seen the tempests of the Atlantic, failed to protect them in any way. However, throughout the whole duration of the journey, I was in so brisk a mood as I had not known for a long time, for, having left Renata on the first occasion after several months, it was as though I had recovered my lost self. I experienced the sensation of walking from a dark cellar suddenly into clear light, and my solitary journey along the Rhine to Bonn seemed to me the immediate continuation of my solitary road from Brabant, while the recent days with Renata—seemed like a painful nightmare at one of the wayside halts.

However, I never forgot the purpose of my journey, and I was pleased with the thought that I was to see Agrippa of Nettesheim, one of the greatest scientists and most remarkable writers of our time. Yielding to the play of imagination, of which everyone is probably aware, I visualised to myself in every detail my visit to Agrippa, and word after word did I repeat mentally the speeches that I intended to address to him, and that I expected to hear in reply, and some of these, not without difficulty, I even composed in Latin. I wanted to believe that I should appear before Agrippa not as an inexperienced disciple, but as a modest young scientist, not devoid of knowledge and experience, but seeking instruction and advice in those highest spheres of science that are as yet not sufficiently elaborated, and among which it is not derogatory to enquire one's way. I imagined to myself how Agrippa would at first listen to my discourses not without misgiving, then with joyful attention, and how, at last, astonished by my intellect and the rich store of my information, he would ask me with surprise how,

at my years, I had yet succeeded in achieving a so rare
and many-sided learning, and how I would reply to
him that my best guide had been his works. . . . Not
a few other, no less foolish, unbelievable, and simply
unthinkable conversations did my childish vanity
prompt in me, as it dived suddenly out of the bottom
of my soul during the hours of my difficult road along
the cold and deserted fields of the Archbishopric.

Cold and tired, but still in possession of my spirits, I
reached the gates of Bonn after the third bell had
already sounded from the tower, in complete darkness,
and obtained a *laisser-passer* from the night watch not
without difficulty, so I was unable to be very particular
about the choice of my night shelter and eagerly
accepted a room in the first hostelry that came handy,
I seem to remember, under the sign of " The Golden
Vine."

On the morning of the following day, the host came
to me, as is the custom in small hostelries, ostensibly
to enquire whether I were in need of anything, but
rather for curiosity, to worm out of the new guest who
he be. I greeted him not without gladness, for I had
to make enquiries about where Agrippa lived, and,
apart from that, I was pleased to show that I came to
visit so important a man. And as the host proved a
native of long standing, I heard from him, apart from
the intelligence about the street where the house of
Agrippa stood, also the town gossip concerning the
latter :

" How should we not know Agrippa ? " said the
host. " Every one of our urchins knows him from
long since and, to tell the truth, shuns him ! Little
good is spoken of him, and very much that is evil.
They say that he practises Black Arts and consorts
with the Devil. . . . In any case he sits like a barn-
owl in his nest, and sometimes does not show himself
on the streets for weeks on end. That he cannot be
so very good a man may be judged from the fact that

he has brought two of his wives to the grave and that
the third, a bare month gone by, has just divorced him.
However, I trust your kindness may excuse me if he
be your good acquaintance, for I speak only from hearsay, and what will not folk say in their chatter! One
cannot hear the half of it!"

I hastened to assure him that I had no friendship
with Agrippa, but only monetary transactions, and the
host, reassured, but lowering his voice, began to relate
to me all manner of fables concerning the illustrious
guest of his town. Thus he related that Agrippa always
kept several familiar demons who lived with him in
the guise of dogs; that Agrippa read of all that
happened at the various ends of the earth upon the
disc of the moon, and thus knew all the news without
messengers; that, possessing the secret of the trans-
formation of metals, he often settled his accounts with
coins that had all the appearance of fair ones, but later
reverted to pieces of horn or dung; that he would show
to noblemen all their future in a magic mirror; that
in his young days, when attached to the person of the
Spanish general Antonio de Leyva in Italy, he secured
by magic means success to his chief in all undertakings;
that once Agrippa was seen finishing a public discourse
in the town of Freiburg at ten o'clock in the morning
exactly, at the same moment as, already, he was beginning another public discourse many miles away, in the
town of Pontimussae—and a great many other equally
doubtful stories.

I listened to these foolish tales with pleasure, not
because I believed them, but because I thought it
flattering to be going to the house of so remarkable
a man. And when, by my calculations, the hour
propitious for the visit had arrived, once more arranging
my clothes, I left the hostelry with a proud air, and as
I walked along the street, I wished secretly that the
passers-by might notice whither I was bound. Remembering now these vain dreams of mine, I cannot but

smile, bitterly and sadly, for Fate, that toys with a man as a cat with a mouse, contrived to laugh at me with fine cruelty. Instead of the rôle of *triumphator*, assigned to me by my amour-propre, it condemned me to play rôles far less honourable: those of a street brawler, a senseless wine-bibber, and a schoolboy whom his teacher reprimands.

By the indications given me, I quite easily found the house of Agrippa—at the edge of the town, near the wall itself, rather large, though only three-storied, with many outbuildings, ancient, forbidding, and entirely detached from any other houses. I knocked at the door, then, not obtaining an answer, repeated my knocking, and at last, pushing open the door, which proved to be unlocked, I entered a vast and empty hall and, guided by the sound of voices, penetrated further, into a second room. There, by a broad table, round a tureen containing some steaming viand, sat chattering and laughing gaily four young men, whom I took for house servants. Hearing the squeak of the opening door, they stopped talking and turned to me, and from under the table there rose and came forth, growling and baring their teeth, two or three thorough-bred dogs.

I asked politely:

" May I see Doctor Agrippa of Nettesheim, who, I am informed, resides in this house ? "

One of those at his midday meal, a tall, strapping lad with the features and accent of an Italian, rudely shouted at me in reply:

" How dare you enter a strange house without knock-ing ? This is neither a beer shop nor the Town Hall ! Begone, before we show you the way to the door ! "

This shout was so much contrary to my expectations that it acted upon me like a slap on the face—at once I lost control over myself and, in an outburst of irres-ponsible anger, shouted in reply words equally sharp and unwise, which ran something as follows:

"You are mistaken, friend, in saying that I entered without knocking! But in this house, it seems, the lackeys tipple instead of attending to their duties! Go, enquire of your master how you should receive his guests, for here is an introductory letter to him from one of his friends."

My words had a most violent effect. One of those sitting jumped up with furious curses and flew at me with clenched fists, overturning the bench, another rushed to his support, a third on the other hand tried to restrain his comrades, while the dogs began to attack me with barking and growling. I, seeing myself unexpectedly involved in an inglorious brawl, drew my tried sword from its sheath, and retreated towards the wall, brandishing it and declaring that I should spit through anyone who approached to within the nearness of a thrust. For a few minutes it all reminded me of the halls of King Ulysses before the beginning of the slaughter of the suitors, and it might easily have happened that, owing to the inequality of forces, I might have paid with my life for my arrogance, and no one, of course, would have paid any concern to the murder of an unknown passer-by.

Fortunately, however, the quarrel had a more peaceful issue, for the voices of the more reasonable prevailed, convincing us that we had no cause for a bloody encounter. One of the young men, called, as I soon learned, Aurelius, caused us to separate, by delivering to us the following speech:

"Master traveller and my comrades! Do not permit the god of strife—Mars—to triumph in this house, dedicated to the goddess of wisdom—Minerva! Master traveller is at fault for treating us like servant-folk, but we too are guilty, in that we greeted a noble gentleman thus contemptuously and impolitely—let us therefore offer each other mutual apologies, and discover what be the reason for the misunderstanding, soberly, as befits thinking people."

146

To tell the truth I was glad of this turn to the affair, which saved me from a purposeless, yet dangerous fight, and, having grasped that I saw before me not the servants of Agrippa, but his pupils, I politely explained to them once more the object of my visit, named myself, showed the introductory letter, and explained that I had come from another town especially to hold converse with Agrippa.

Aurelius answered me:

" I do not know whether you will succeed in seeing the teacher. He has a custom of working in his study without leaving it for several days and nights on end, and no one in the house dares to worry him during that time, so that even his meals and drink are left for him in an adjoining room. There are put for him also all the letters that are sent to him, so, if you will hand us yours, we shall include it in that number."

After a declaration in such terms, there was nothing better left for me to do than to hand over to Aurelius the letter from Hetorpius and make my bow, satisfied that thus happily had solved itself my first adventure in the house of Agrippa, an adventure in which I had not played an entirely dignified part. It must be, however, that that day belonged to the number of unlucky days, *dies nefasti*, for Aurelius and I both took it into our heads to smooth over the traces of the stupid quarrel, forgetting the proverb that he who tries to win back loses doubly. First Aurelius persuaded all his comrades to shake hands with me, and one by one he introduced them:

" This one," he said, pointing to the one with whom my exchange of words began, " is the eldest of us, hailing from Italy, and we call him Emmanuel; as one who was born in the South he is irascible and unrestrained; this—is little Hans, the youngest among us, and not only by name is he Iohann, but also by the love the teacher bears him; and this one is a capable fellow, a brain and a fist of which there are

few, by name Augustin ; and, lastly, you see before you
myself—Aurelius, a meek man, as you yourself have
seen, and therefore hoping to inherit the earth."

Not only did I shake hands with them all, but
offered, to our misfortune, as a sign that no misunderstanding remained between us, to drink a quart of
wine in one of the taverns. Having consulted among
themselves in low tones, the pupils agreed to my
invitation and, without delay, the five of us set forth
from the house of Agrippa to the hospitable roof of the
best hostelry in the town, under the sign of " The Fat
Cockerels."

When we had taken our seats in the large and, at
this yet early hour, quite deserted room of the hostelry,
with our glasses in which sparkled the joyful Scharlach-
berger, and with each a round of good southern cheese,
we soon forgot our recent angry looks at one another.
Wine, in the phrase of Horatius Flaccus, *explicuit
contractæ seria frontis*, smoothed the wrinkles of our
brows, and our voices grew loud, brisk and cheerful,
so that an outside observer might have taken us for
ordinary bottle companions, with no secrets dividing
us. But in vain did I try to bring the conversation
round to mysterious sciences and magic, thinking that
the pupils of the great magus would, at their glass,
boast of their frequent intercourse with demons—their
thoughts were furthest from such matters. Healthy
and jolly, they chattered of everything on earth : of
the successes of Lutheranism, of their love adventures,
of the approaching festivals of Saint Catherine and
Saint Andrew with their quaint and amusing ritual—
and I felt myself once more a student amidst my long-
vanished Kölnian bottle companions. Only young
Hans held himself aloof, drank little, and was like a
maiden who, out of prudery, says " marching companions " instead of " breeches."

When, at last, I began to ask directly of Agrippa
and his present life, there rained from all lips complaints

148

I had by no means expected. Augustin confessed that
they were now living through a very lean time, and that
the teacher was being hard pressed by his creditors,
while he had practically no other income besides that
from the sale of his works. Aurelius added that,
because of this constraint in money matters, Agrippa
had been forced to accept service with our Archbishop,
and that the latter entrusted him with such unworthy
occupations as the organisation of festivals and their
supervision. Lastly, Emmanuel with curses attacked
the third wife of Agrippa, from whom the latter had
just been divorced, saying that all these misfortunes
had been brought upon them by that woman, and by
all means praising his late wife, Jeanne-Louise, towards
whom he, Emmanuel, had seemingly been not im-
partial. Emmanuel began also to relate of the good
times they had all known in Antwerpen, where Agrippa
had flourished under the protection of the now deceased princess Margaret of Austria ; when their house
had been animated, gay, ever brimming with laughter
and jest ; when the teacher, his wife, his children and
his pupils had composed one friendly family. . . .
Unfortunately the god Bacchus was skipper of our
conversation, and the end of the story, not having made
port, sank somewhere beneath a storm of unexpected
jokes and mockeries from Augustin. One thing only
was I able to conclude with certainty : that Agrippa,
even if he knew how to make gold for others and how
to provide success for others, made no use of his crafts-
manship for himself.

A little while later, however, we headed once more
for interesting shores, for my tipsy companions began
to press me to tell them on what business I had come
to visit Agrippa. I felt unable to say a word about
Renata to these care-free fellows, and so I only mentioned
shortly that I desired to ask for some advice on questions
of operative magic. To my just surprise, this reply
was greeted with a unanimous outburst of laughter.

"Well, friend," said Aurelius, "you certainly have not hit the mark! You will have to go back laden with the same baggage as that with which you came!"

"Does, then," I asked, "Agrippa to such an extent protect his knowledge of the secret sciences and share it so unwillingly?"

Here Hans intervened in the conversation after having remained silent almost the whole time:

"How insulting it is," he exclaimed "that the teacher is always looked upon as a sorcerer! Will Agrippa of Nettesheim, one of the brightest intellects of his century, be ever paying for the infatuation of his youth, and be known only as the author of that weak and unsuccessful book 'On the Philosophy of the Occult'?"

Astonished, I pointed out that the book of Agrippa on magic could not be considered in any sense unsuccessful, and that, moreover, it had only just appeared in print, indicating, surely, that the author himself, even now, must acknowledge it as of a certain importance.

Hans replied to me indignantly:

"Have you then not read the foreword to the book, in which this is explained by the teacher? His book was spread all over Europe in incorrect transcriptions, with foolish additions, like the incongruous 'part four,' and the teacher preferred to publish his original text so that he should be responsible only for his own words. But, in the book itself, there is nothing beyond the exposition of the various theories studied by the teacher as a philosopher. He has assured us himself that never, not once in his life, has he engaged in such foolishnesses or absurdities as the invocation of demons!"

Hardly had Hans uttered these vehement words when his companions began to tease him, reminding him that not so long ago he himself had believed in invocations. Confused and blushing, almost with tears in his eyes, Hans asked them to be silent, saying that he was then but young and stupid. But, as a stranger, I asked that it be explained to me what they were talking about, and Augustin, roaring with laughter, told me that Hans, soon after he had entered the house of Agrippa, had taken secretly from the latter's study a book of invocations and grimoirs, and desired, after tracing the circle, at all costs to invoke a spirit.

"The most comical thing of all," added Hans, who had now recovered his composure, "is that the people are now telling the following story about the incident. They declare that the pupil who stole the book did really invoke a demon but did not know how to get rid of him. So the demon killed the pupil. Just at that moment, Agrippa returned home. So that he should not be regarded as having caused this death, he commanded the demon to enter the body of the pupil and betake himself to the crowded square. There, it appears, the demon left the dead body he had re-animated, so that there should be many witnesses of the pupil's sudden and natural death. And I am convinced that this preposterous fable will presently be incorporated in the teacher's biography, and given far more credit than the true stories of his works and misfortunes!"

After that, all four of them discussed demons and invocations for a few more minutes, but all the time in a tone of contemptuous jest, and they questioned me not without slyness as to where, and in what remote corner of the earth, I had picked up in the field my faith in magic, now discarded by all because of its uselessness. And I, listening to these hare-brained speeches, truly felt myself like Luther, who, arriving in Rome from his remote and tiny township and expecting to find a centre of piety, found only debauch and godlessness.

In the meantime, the host of " The Fat Cockerels " diligently replaced the emptying quarts with others filled to the brim, while my companions drank heartily

The Fiery Angel

with the insatiable thirst of youth, and I drank to stifle in me a feeling of humiliation and uneasiness—and thus our cheerful conversation gradually became a riotous gaiety. Our tongues began to pronounce words indistinctly, and in our heads spun roseate whirlwinds that made all seem pleasant, attractive and easy. Abandoning the theme of magi and invocations, we passed to subjects of conversation more suited to the state of our thinking abilities.

Thus, at first discussion arose about the relative merits of the various kinds of wine: the Italian Rheinfal and the Spanish Canary, the Speier Hensfüsser and the Würtemburg Eilfinger, and also many others, the while the pupils of Agrippa showed themselves connoisseurs no less expert than monks. The discussion threatened to develop into a fight, for Emmanuel shouted that the best was from Istria and offered to smash the skull of anyone who thought differently, but all five of us were pacified by Aurelius, who suggested a song:

> *Klingenberg am Main,*
> *Würzburg am Stein,*
> *Bacharach am Rhein,*
> *Wachsen die besten Wein!*

Poetry, probably as the voice of a Muse, quietened all, but a moment later there arose another argument about where women are best. Emmanuel again praised his Italy and especially the houses of pleasure in Venice, but Augustin maintained that there was no better place than Nürnburg, where recently a nunnery had been closed down and the nuns had all gone over to the brothels. The discussion, however, was conducted without any observation of the rules governing disputes, and as soon as I happened to mention that I had been in Rome, Emmanuel flew into a frenzy of ecstasy, clutched me in his embrace and kissed me, shouting: " He has been to Italy! You hear!—he has been to

152

Italy!" In order to allay the passions aroused also in this case, Aurelius suggested that we should agree to decide the best women were in Bonn, and that it should be proved at once. With shouts of joy the comrades agreed to the reasoning of Aurelius and declared that they had never heard a smarter *quodlibetarius*.

Striking up some jolly song, but not firmly erect upon our feet, we adjourned under the leadership of Aurelius to somewhere the other side of the town, frightening the peaceful passers-by. The freshness of the winter air, however, soon sobered me and when, at a corner, little Hans gave me a wink, I at once understood and hastened to follow the signal. The military diversion thus planned by us happily succeeded, and soon we were left alone in a deserted alley.

"It appeared to me," said Hans, "that you were not particularly anxious to continue the debauch, and I consider such pastimes both pernicious and useless. Would you, therefore, like me to see you home?"

I replied:

"You are perfectly right. I thank you and very heartily beg of you to render me this true service, for the wine in this town seems twice as strong as anywhere else in the world, and without you the only way I could find is the one leading into the nearest ditch."

Little Hans laughed good-naturedly and took the closest interest in me. Not only did he see me to my hostelry, but he put me to bed, where I was immediately engulfed in turbid sleep. And when, several hours later, I awoke, not quite refreshed, of course, and still with a strong headache, but with my consciousness aired—I saw that Hans had not abandoned me and had prepared me a potion and some supper.

"I am a medical man," Hans explained to me, "and I did not think it right to leave a patient in such a state as yours, though I remembered the saying of Hippocrates: *Si quis ebrius repente, obmutescat . . .* "

By chance this happened to be one of the aphorisms
still firmly fixed in my memory from childhood, and
consequently I was able to continue:

"... *quo tempore crapulæ solvi solent vocem edat.*"
We both laughed at so schoolboyish a truth, and this
laugh did more to bring us closer together than all our
preceding conversations.

Hans was about twenty years old, or perhaps less.
He was not tall of stature nor handsome of face, to
which latter his roundish eyes slightly protruding
under the steeply-carved brows gave an almost comic
expression, but his young features disclosed intelligence
and were agreeable. In the conversation that immediately ensued between us, this beardless youth showed
penetration, great learning in scientific matters, and
even a knowledge of the world. And so, under the
urge of a momentary impulse such as governs our
actions more often than the hand of cold reasoning,
and perhaps not altogether unaffected by the influence
of the tipsiness that had not yet entirely passed off, I
related to little Hans that which I had hidden from his
elder comrades: why I had come to Agrippa, and, in
general, what I had had to go through during the past
few months, keeping, of course, silence about the name
of Renata and the place of our residence. It is well,
however, to remember in my justification that for a
long time I had had no opportunity of speaking openly
with any human being, and that all these painful
matters I had experienced had remained in my soul
like a heavy weight, oppressing it, and for long seeking
egress.

Hans listened to my lengthy and impassioned confession with the attention with which a doctor receives
the recital of his patient's symptoms, and, after a short
meditation, he answered me thus, speaking like a tutor
to his pupil:

" I do not doubt the accuracy of any of your words.
But, apparently, you have studied medicine very little

and in any case are unaware of the new and very remarkable discoveries made in this sphere. Whereas I am lucky to have had as my guide in this science, a sage like our teacher, who, though he has ceased to practise, still remains one of the greatest physicians of his century. We know now that there exists a special disease, that cannot be termed madness, but is yet kin to it, and may be called by an old name—melancholy. This disease afflicts women more often than men, for their sex is the weaker of the two, as is denoted by the word itself, *mulier*, which is derived by Varro from *mollis*, tender. In a state of melancholy all the sensations become altered under pressure of an especial fluid that spreads over the whole body, and thus persons affected by the disease commit deeds to which it is impossible to ascribe any reasonable purpose, and are constantly subjected to inexplicable and rapid changes of mood. Now they are gay, now sad, then straightway deprived of all volition to an extreme degree—and all this without any visible cause. In the same way, they lie without any reason : pose as persons they are really not, or else accuse themselves or others of invented crimes, and especially do they like to play the part of victims and martyrs. Women of this type, sincerely believe their own stories and genuinely suffer their imaginary misfortunes; believing themselves possessed by the Devil, they do actually experience agony and throw themselves about in convulsions, in which they force their bodies to twist in such a way as is impossible for them to achieve consciously, and, generally, by means of their imagination, they can contrive to drive themselves to death. From the number of these unfortunates are filled the ranks of the so-called witches, who should be treated with soothing potions, but against whom the Popes issue bulls and the inquisitors erect bonfires. I suggest, therefore, that it is one of these women that you have met. What she related to you of her life was of course a fable, and there never was a Count Heinrich ; later she strove by all means in her power to remain in your eyes a remarkable and deeply-unhappy woman, and for this, of course, she is not to blame, for she has been compelled to it by her malady."

Having listened to this lecture, I reminded Hans of what I had told him regarding my flight to the Sabbath and our invocation of the demon Anaël, but Hans retorted to me thus :

" It is high time to cease believing in such old wives' tales as the Sabbath : a darkening of the senses, fancy—that is what Sabbaths are. You were of course in the power of. a strong sleeping drug given to you by your acquaintance, and here and now I will tell you the composition of that drug : there entered into it—oil, parsley, banewort, wolfe's bane, beccabunga, perhaps also the sap of other plants, but the chief elements were —the herb called belladonna by the Italians, henbane, and a little Theban opium. The ointment thus composed, when rubbed into the body, produces a state of profound lethargy, in which appear with great vividness the visions of such matters as were being thought of at the moment of falling asleep. Some medical men have already carried out experiments, and made women who thought themselves witches rub in the magic ointment under their supervision. And what was the result ! It was proved that these unfortunates had lain prostrate in sleep upon the selfsame spot, though they had wakened fully convinced of various incredibilities about their flights and dances. It is equally absurd to believe that various words, Chaldean or Latin, no better than our German ones, and some lines called characters, can have power over the forces of nature and over the Devil. I am satisfied that, during your experiment of invocation, what you took for the shapes of demons was naught else than the smoke of the incense, and what broke your first lamp was not one of the evil spirits, but that very assistant of yours, who, of course, was in a fit of frenzy at the time."

I could find then no replies to these reasonings, for my head was tired that day, and also because I had lost the habit of learned disputation, and so I stood before little Hans like an opponent who has dropped his sword, or like a pupil shamed, whom his tutor chastises with a ruler. This position of mine, however, did not prevent me from giving its due to the skilfulness of Hans' reasoning, and, even then, I told him that, if he could manage to find a basis for his opinions, and to support them with a sufficient number of examples, he would write an exceedingly remarkable, and perhaps useful composition. And I still firmly hope to come across such a book, that will make the name of my young friend—Iohann Weier—widely known.

Taking leave of me, Hans particularly advised me to call at their house the next day, for it was to be a Sunday, and it might be expected that Agrippa would leave his study. I agreed with him that it would not be proper if, having left the letter of introduction, I were not to appear in person at the house, but, after all I had heard from Agrippa's pupils, I did not expect of course anything of importance to me to result even from a meeting with him. This second night at Bonn I spent with none of the spring dreams of my first, and all my sterile flowers of my hopes drooped their heads to the very ground, as if in a drought.

Nevertheless, the next day, in the hour after midday mass, I again knocked at the door of Agrippa, and this time Emmanuel, Augustin and Aurelius greeted me as a good friend, only scolding me good-naturedly for having left them "in the lurch" in so unfriendly fashion the night before. Yesterday in the house of Agrippa had awaited me staves and the fangs of dogs, while to-day I was slapped on the shoulder and jestingly named *amicissime*, so that I might well convince myself that there is no better match-maker than Bacchus.

Yet more, because Aurelius and his companions really felt well disposed towards me, or because they wanted to atone for their reception of yesterday, or, lastly, because simply they were glad of a newcomer, being bored in their solitude—anyway that whole day they devoted to me, and, each vying with the other, tried to procure for me various distractions.

Aurelius undertook to show me over the whole house, and we walked through twelve or fifteen rooms, of which some were uninhabited and not fitted with any furniture at all. In the others the furnishing was of the oldest, beginning with once sumptuous, though now altogether worn-out, pieces, and ending with objects quite cheap, purchased as required, and placed helter skelter, with no elegance whatever. In the rooms recently occupied by the third wife of Agrippa, all was left in extremest disorder, as if the habitation had just been ransacked by German landsknechts; but even the tidiest of the rooms reminded one more of a carpenter's shop than of the house of a philosopher.

Aurelius acquainted me further with all the inhabitants of the house, and, first of all, with two of Agrippa's sons, Heinrich and Iohann, boys of about ten years, who did not make on me the impression of being either intelligent or educated; the other two sons of Agrippa were away at that time. With the children lived an old servant, Maria, a kind-hearted simpleton, who had not quitted Agrippa for the last fifteen years, but who appeared unable to join three words together coherently. The other maid-servant, Margarita, was only by a little younger, but also by as little brighter, and the man-servant, a tall lad, who answered to the name of Antheus, gave the impression of being a complete imbecile. Thus it was easy to guess that life in that house was not of the gayest, and I had to acknowledge that, next to the pupils, the brightest of its inhabitants were the six or seven dogs, big, well-bred, and with high-sounding names: Tara,

Zickonius, Balassa, Musa, which wandered proudly through all the rooms as if they were their hereditary possessions.

Aurelius, who never let slip a chance of assuring me that Agrippa did not practise sorcery, told me of these dogs as follows :

"The teacher so loves dogs that with some of them he never parts, even at night, and sleeps with them in one bed. On the death of one of his favourite dogs, *Filiolus*, his friends even composed several epitaphs in Latin verse. But among the populace stupid rumours are in circulation, pretending that Agrippa keeps familiars in the guise of dogs."

In the same way, when showing me the room adjoining the study of Agrippa, in which his food was placed and newly arrived letters were deposited, Aurelius said to me:

"The imperial post obtains a goodly income from the teacher, for several letters reach him daily. He is in correspondence with Erasmus, and with many crowned heads and with archbishops, and even with the Pope himself, not to mention ordinary scientists and his numberless admirers. It is from them that he learns news of all the corners of Europe, while the superstitious imagine he obtains it by magic means."

After the inspection of the house and a satisfying though very modest dinner, my new friends took me for a walk round the city, from street to street, and soon we had traversed the whole of it, for Bonn is not big, and even been beyond the gates, from whence there is a handsome view of the Siebenbergen. Also, I feasted my eyes on the churches of Bonn, especially the five-towered cathedral—indeed one of the most handsome creations of our ancient architecture. The streets that day were full of people, on holiday, and it was pleasant to wander in the midst of the crowd, dressed up in vivid, many-hued garments, to exchange winks with unknown maidens, and to study the young gallants in winter capes and feathered hats. Augustin knew the inhabitants of the whole city by name, and of nearly every passer-by, man or woman, he managed to whisper into our ears a merry anecdote in the manner of the *Facetiæ* of Poggio, which made us laugh gaily.

About five of the clock we returned home and Aurelius, having found out that Agrippa had not yet opened the doors of his study, suggested a game of chess. I left the board to Aurelius and Emmanuel, and for my own part offered to bet with Augustin on the success of either one of them, according to his choice. The boys came from their nursery to watch the game, and with them Maria, who considered herself a member of the family. We all crowded round the table at which the players sat and two of the dogs, taking place near by, watched the movings of the pawns and knights with no less attention than ourselves. And no one who had chanced to see the two chess-players, engrossed in their moves, the two stake-holders who watched them, the two boys sucking their fingers, and the good old nurse, would have thought that this idyllic family scene, worthy of the pen of Sannazzaro, was being enacted in the house of the great magus Agrippa, who, as the stories have it, drags the moon down out of the sky and raises the bodies of the dead from their graves.

I staked on Emmanuel, trusting to his inventiveness, but Aurelius proved far more cunning in the art of Damiani ; and, making his moves slowly and with more forethought, he soon definitely pressed his opponent. Playing without coolness, Emmanuel was angry and would by no means acknowledge himself beaten, but he would probably not have escaped mate, had there not rung suddenly from the room of Agrippa a summons, the sound of his bell. All that were in the room were set in motion : the boys frightenedly whisked behind the door, Maria shuffled after them, Hans rushed upstairs to obey the call, and Emmanuel,

making use of the general confusion, shuffled the pieces
on the board as if by a momentary impulse, and thus
no one could tell how the game would have ended.

A few minutes later, Hans returned from the teacher
and announced that Agrippa had read my letter and
was ready to receive me immediately, and that at the
same time he summoned to him all his pupils.

Thus was fulfilled my fondest wish, thus was realised
the aim with which I came to Bonn—but already, as I
climbed the narrow staircase to the upper storey on which
Agrippa's study was situated, I found myself no longer
possessed by the hope of obtaining the solution of those
doubts that assailed me, gnawing at me, but only by the
curiosity of a traveller inspecting the local sights. In
the meantime the pupils took a friendly interest in me
and, interrupting each other, gave me various advice
on how to conduct myself with Agrippa, reminding me
to speak louder, for the teacher was somewhat strained
of hearing, or warning me that the teacher loathed
monks, or suggesting that I should always address the
teacher as "*magister doctissime*," and the like. Before
the door of the study of Agrippa we had to halt once
more, while Hans ran on again, and only after this,
at last, the door was opened and I entered the holy of
holies.

The study of Agrippa reminded one at first glance
rather of a museum or the library of a monastery—
so cumbered over was it with cases laden with books
and folders, as well as with stuffed animals and various
instruments and appliances of physics ; even on the
benches and on the floor were strewn manuscripts,
designs, papers of all kinds. Here and there reposed
layers of dust, or rose a musty smell, but the sun,
penetrating through the narrow Gothic window, lit up
the scene almost welcomingly and vividly. At a
broad desk, also heaped with folios and ledgers, as if
himself buried in papers, there sat in a high armchair
a man of small stature, not yet aged, lean and clean

shaven, with a raspberry-coloured skull cap on his white hair and with a loose gown, edged with fur. I recognised Agrippa, for he was very like his portrait printed on the cover of the book " *De Occulta Philosophia* " ; only the expression of the face seemed to me to be somewhat different : in the portrait it is good-natured and open—but in Agrippa himself there was something contemptuous or fastidious in the features, perhaps because the lips somehow senilely drooped, and the tired lids half concealed the glance of his sharp and lively eyes. At Agrippa's feet, with its head on his knees, sat his favourite black dog, of medium size, with fuzzy hair and remarkably intelligent, as if human eyes, which, as I learned later, was called " Monseigneur."

Entering, I paused with a bow on the threshold, but Agrippa, greeting me with a nod of his head as if he were a ruling monarch accustomed to the granting of audiences, said to me :

" Welcome, Master Traveller. My friend Hetorpius writes to me of you. In my old age I have few, very few friends left to me, but that is why every word of theirs is a duty to me. Pray be seated and be welcome in this house, though you have brought me bad news."

These last words confused me a little, and, taking a place near the desk amongst his pupils, I knew not what to say, but it was Agrippa himself who resumed the conversation. Taking from the desk the introductory letter I had brought, and showing it to us, he delivered, not without rhetoric skill, a whole oration destined apparently for my benefit alone, for in it he communicated nothing new to his pupils :

" Hetorpius, in introducing you "—he said—" writes me at the same time that he dare not print my ' Apologetic Letter to the Senate of Köln," and that, in general, no printing house in Köln will accept it beneath its presses ! I recognise the usual weapons of my antagonists, for their wiles have persecuted me my whole life long! In Antwerpen the local scientists succeeded in obtaining an interdiction preventing me from practising as a medicus, though I had administered to the people in the time of the plague when all the other physicians of the town were fled in every direction! In Köln I was prohibited from delivering lectures though in Dola, Torino and Pavia, I had had more listeners than all the other magisters together. The Emperor, in whose service I was as historiographer, found it unnecessary to pay me my remuneration and at Brussels my creditors flung me into jail for my debts! Lastly, whenever I try to publish my works yet worse thunder falls upon me: in Paris one of my books was burnt at the condemnation of the Sorbonne, and in Germany its printing was opposed by the inquisitor himself, who scorned the privilege granted me. Against my writings clamour and howl doctors, licentiates, teachers, bachelors, rhetoricians of all colours, and all the uncountable crowd of idlers in cassocks, hoods and mantles, barefooted and in sandals, black, white, grey and of every coat: in one word all the makers of syllogisms and the hired sophists, whose eyes truth blinds like those of owls. But I do not fear attack, I shall know how to defend myself both from open accusations and hidden calumnies. Now they prevent me from causing to be printed a letter, restrained to a considerable degree. What of it, then? I shall write another, merciless, add to it vinegar and mustard, but reduce the oil, and shall yet publish it in another town, in London if need be, if need be, in Constantinople!"

By delivering these thundering diatribes in my presence, Agrippa, no doubt, hoped that through me they would become known to various circles of people, for he took me for a friend of Hetorpius. But I, seeing the necessity to answer, replied with circumspection, that I did not take it upon myself to be judge of the dispute between Agrippa and the clerics, nor, still less, of his dispute with His Majesty the Emperor, but that,

of course all the persecutions of which he spoke were
an honour to him, for against an insignificant person,
not the inquisition, nor the theologues, nor the scientists
would have directed their attacks.

Profiting by a moment's silence, Aurelius reminded
the teacher that I had come with a definite purpose, to
ask his advice. Agrippa, as if he only just recollected
about me, turned to me and, angrily throwing Hetorpius'
letter on the desk, asked :

" What is it then, young friend, that you desire of me ?
In what way can Agrippa, who is, as you see, hunted
like a fox by a pack of hounds, be of service to you ? "

I hastened to reply that I felt myself like Marsyas
questioned by Apollo, and that I could plead forgiveness for my audacity only in the fame of Agrippa,
spread over the whole of Europe, and in the fact that,
for the elucidation of questions not answered in books,
one could apply, in the whole of Germany, only to his
knowledge, his intellect, his experience. Further, I
related, some circumstances in my private life had led
me to engage in operative magic, that, from amongst
the books written on this subject, I could not but single
out the composition of Agrippa, and that, having studied
all that was set out in his book, I yet found a multitude
of points dark to me, and desired to enquire of each
the explanations of the author himself.

Agrippa, having heard me, frowned and said with
vexation :

" It must be that if you have read my work, you have
not done so very attentively, or have not properly
understood that which is written, otherwise you would
not turn to me with such questions ! In my foreword it
is stated, clearly and firmly, that the magus must not
be a superstitious man, nor a sorcerer, nor a demonist,
but a sage, a priest and a prophet. I regard as true
magi, the Sibyl who prophesied of Christ in the times
of paganism, and those three kings who, having learned
from the miraculous cosmic mysteries of the birth of

the Saviour of the World, hastened with gifts to the manger-cradle. Whereas you, apparently, like the majority, seek in magic not a means to the mysterious knowledge of nature, but sundry cunning means to bespoil your neighbours, to seek riches, to enquire about to-morrow's day: but for such knowledge it is necessary to go to magicians and charlatans, and not to a philosopher. My book ' On the Philosophy of the Occult ' was written by me in youth and contains many imperfections, and, what is more, it provides only a survey of all that has been said about magic, so that the searching mind may trace in it all the branches of that science, but never have I advised any-one to plunge himself into experiments in goety, dark and deserving of discouragement ! "

Seeing that Agrippa shirked a direct answer, I made up my mind, none the less, to force him to one, even if by heroic measures, and accordingly I spoke thus to him:

" Why then, teacher, having investigated carefully the spheres of magic and found there only delusions, did you not endeavour to divert others from fruitless occupation with that science, but on the contrary, hasten to publish a work that you yourself considered imperfect ? It may be, perhaps, that it was composed by you in your youth, but do not forget that you added to it two forewords written quite recently, and in which you speak of magic with great reverence, and do not in any way reveal your contemptuous attitude towards it. Do you not thereby offer a great temptation to knowledge-seeking readers, and will I not be right if I remind you of the words of the Evangel that as for him who shall lead astray but one of these little ones, it were better for him that he should have a millstone hanged about his neck and be drowned in the depth of the sea ? "

During my speech, Aurelius made sign to me with his eyes for me to desist, but I am not accustomed to remain outlaughed, and I spoke calmly to the end. Agrippa, also, was cut to the quick by my words, and his appearance underwent a sudden change, for his self-assurance and arrogance became as if extinguished, and he said to me with irritation :

" I had weighty reasons for publishing my composition, of which you, young man, have probably not the slightest inkling. To explain these to you would be quite out of place, apart from the fact that a special oath forbids me to touch upon certain questions among the uninitiated."

The sternness of the answer could only increase my insistence, and I, who had not feared to put questions to the Ruler of the Sabbath, certainly did not withdraw before the wrath of Agrippa of Nettesheim. Continuing to press him, I at once flung at him a new question, and to me it seemed as if my clear voice rattled like a pair of dice, leaping on the table for some decisive stake:

" *Magister doctissime !* But I do not claim that you disclose to me your arcane secrets ! Only, being one of those tempted by your book, I but, with all modesty, ask that you answer me, what is the nature of magic, truth or delusion, science or no ? "

Agrippa glanced up at me, but I did not lower my eyes before his, and while our two glances were harnessed together I experienced a feeling as if, hand in hand, we both stood upon the edge of an abyss. For a moment I believed that now—now, Agrippa was about to tell me something singular and inspired— but, lo, already before me again there sat in a high armchair an aged scientist, in a loose gown and framboise skull-cap, who, having mastered his indignation, replied to my impertinent questions in a voice a trifle, a shade irritated, but firm and even :

" There are two kinds of science, young man. One is that which is practised nowadays in Universities, which peers into each object separately, tearing the whole flower of the cosmos into its component parts, into root, stem, and petal, and which, instead of knowledge, provides syllogisms and commentaries. In my book 'On the Uncertainty of Knowledge,' a book that cost me many years of labour but brought me only mockery and accusations of heresy, there is explained fully what I call pseudo-science. Its adepts—the pseudo-philosophers—have fashioned out of grammatica and rhetoric instruments for their own false deductions, changed poetry into childish fabrication, based upon arithmetic, foolish divination and a music that corrupts and weakens instead of fortifying, turned politics into an art of deceits, while theology they use as an arena for logomachy, for a battle of words devoid of any meaning. It is these very pseudo-philosophers who have also distorted magic, which the ancients considered as the peak of human knowledge, to such an extent that in our days naturalistic magic is become no more than recipes for poisons, sleeping-draughts, fireworks and the like, and ceremonial magic—merely advices upon how to enter into commerce with the lower forces of the spiritual world, or how to make use of them piratically and unawares. As I will never tire of disputing and ridiculing false science, so I will always denounce false magic. And yet in a human being there is nothing more noble than his faculty of thought, and to rise by power of thought to the contemplation of substances and of God Himself—that is the perfect aim of life. It must, in fine, be remembered always that everything in this world is directed to one end, everything revolves around one point, and through this point everything is connected, one with another, everything is in determined clear connection with its fellow: stars, angels, men, animals, herbs! One soul animates the Sun in its race round the earth, the heavenly spirit submissive to the will of God, tormented Man, and the simple stone that rolls down the mountain slope —and only by a varying degree of intensity does this soul manifest its permeation of varying kinds of matter.

The science that studies and examines all these cosmic relationships, that establishes the connections between all the varying kinds of matter and the routes along which they exercise influence upon each other, this science is magic, the true magic of the ancients. It sets as its task the co-ordination of the blind life of the investigator's soul, and, as far as possible, of other souls as well, with the divine plan of the Creator of the World, and it demands for its fulfilment an exalted life, a pure faith and a mighty will, for there is no mightier force in our world than will, which is able to achieve the impossible and to perform miracles! True magic is the science of sciences, the complete incarnation of the most perfect philosophy, the solution of all mysteries, attained through the revelations of the initiated of different centuries, different countries, and different peoples. Of this magic, young friend, it seems you have learned hitherto nothing at all, and, in conclusion of our conversation, I would have you turn from divinations and sorceries to the true stream of knowledge."

After this ambiguous speech, there was nothing else for me to do but, rising, once more ask to be forgiven for the trouble I had caused and take my leave. I threw a last glance in the direction of Agrippa, and of his pupils, crowding round his chair with every demonstration of admiration—and left the room, thinking that I was taking leave of this circle for ever, and not suspecting that I was yet once again to meet the great sorcerer, nor in what strange circumstances!

On the landing of the staircase, Hans and Aurelius caught me up, desiring probably to make up for the unpleasant impression created by the audience, for they tried by all manner of means to explain away the sternness of Agrippa, saying that he had been very much upset by the letter of Hetorpius. In the short conversation that here took place between us, Aurelius said:

The Fiery Angel

" I didn't suspect, not I, that the teacher still secretly believed in magic."

And Hans, with the arrogance of youth, added :

" He is a great man and a scientist, but not of our generation."

Both Hans and Aurelius convincingly begged me to remain in Bonn for one day more, assuring me that the teacher would treat me more benevolently on the morrow, but I firmly refused to trouble Agrippa again, especially as I had lost all hope of his assistance in my undertaking. I did, however, thank the two youths for the help they had given me, and Hans amicably escorted me to the door of the house, where, in parting, we gave each other promises to exchange letters.

On the next day I rode back, heading north. Snow had fallen in the fields and it was rather cold, but the road had improved considerably and riding was far easier than it had been three days before. The horse stepped briskly out over the soft white carpet that covered the hard, frozen earth.

When, on a later occasion, I carefully thought over all my visit to Agrippa, and attentively considered all his words, I came to the conclusion that not all of them should be given credence. During those short minutes that I stood before Agrippa, an unknown traveller, he had no reasons for opening his soul, for expressing frankly his hidden thoughts on a matter so responsible as magic. It seemed as if he used not even to express them before his pupils, so that their sceptical speeches were perhaps a reflection not of the final opinion of the philosopher, but only of that solitude to which great men, forced to hide themselves even from those nearest them, are ever doomed ! And now, after my second meeting with Agrippa, I do not so much as doubt that he believed in magic far more than he ever desired to show, and that maybe it was to this very goety that the hours of his solitary studies were dedicated.

169

But all these considerations had not as yet come into my head at the time of my return journey from Bonn. On the contrary, I felt as if the stern words of Agrippa and the sober speculations of Hans had chased away like a fresh wind the fog of the mysterious and miraculous in which I had wandered during the last three months. With genuine astonishment I asked myself how it was that, for a whole quarter year, I had been unable to step out of a circle of demons and devils— I, who was accustomed to the clear and well-defined world of ship's rigging and military marches. With the same astonishment I sought an answer to the question how it happened that I, who not once heretofore had failed successfully to cure the heart wounds and scratches of the arrows of the little winged god, now found myself bound with such strong shackles to the waist of a woman who rewarded me only with contempt or condescending coldness. Reviewing, not without the colour mounting to my cheeks, my life with Renata, I now found my behaviour absurd and foolish, and was indignant with myself for so slavishly having submitted to the whims of a lady, of whom I did not even know whether she had any right to attention. To justify myself in a measure, I was ready, with considerable inconsequence, to think once more that Renata was maintaining me by her side by means of some magic philtre or spell.

At last there came into my mind the oath I had given myself at Düsseldorf, and that had not once occurred to me during the last few weeks : not to stay with Renata for longer than three months, and, in any case, not for longer than the time during which I should spend a third of the money I had saved. Three months since that morning had elapsed six days before, and the limited amount had already been almost spent. Under the influence of such meditations, the thought flickered through my mind not to return to Köln at all, but to abandon Renata to her own lonely fate and,

turning my horse, to ride south of Bonn in the direction
of my parental Losheim. However, I had not the
courage to do this, principally because I was tormented
by my longing for Renata, but also because honour
did not permit me such treachery.

Then I said to myself: when I return home, I
shall speak to Renata frankly and honestly, I shall
point out to her that her search for Count Heinrich is
sheer madness, remind her that I have come to love
her passionately and with all my heart, and offer her
to become my wife. If she can, before God and man,
give me an oath to be a faithful and a loyal wife,
we shall repair together to Losheim and, having
obtained the benediction of my parents, go to live
beyond the Ocean, to New Spain, where Renata's past
will be forgotten like a before-morning dream.

Lulled by these dreams of peaceful happiness, I
felt easy and free, and sang beneath my breath a gay
Spanish song: " *A Mingo Revulgo, Mingo*," and
unceasingly urged on my horse, so that it was while it
was yet daylight that the city walls of Kōln rose before
me, dark above the white snow.

Chapter the Seventh

How I met Count Heinrich

AVING reached our house, tired but cheerful, I knocked at the door to summon Martha, handed over to her the reins of my horse, and asked :

" Where is Mistress Renata ? "

To my surprise, Martha answered me thus :

" She appears to have got better, Master Rupprecht. When you were gone she spent whole days walking in the town, and yesterday she only returned home very late."

Of course a sharp barb lay hidden in Martha's words, for already, for some time, she had felt unfriendly towards Renata, and her thrust did not strike amiss. " How is it," I said to myself, " that Renata, who, when I am home, pretends that she is like one paralysed and cannot rise from her bed, Renata, who refuses for whole weeks to cross the threshold of her room, as if she were bound by some vow—the moment she is left alone, walks along wintry streets until the darkness of the night ! This might even enable one to credit the suggestions of Hans Weier, that all her illness is only imagination, all her sufferings—only play-acting ! "

Indignant and almost in a rage, I ran up the stair to the upper storey, where, on the landing, leaning against the balusters, Renata already awaited me ; her face was pale and betrayed extreme emotion. Seeing me, she stretched out her hands to me, took me by the shoulders and, without allowing me to say a word or herself pronouncing any greeting, said :

172

" Rupprecht, he is here."

I replied with the question:

" Who is here ? "

She explained:

" Heinrich is here ! I have seen him. I have spoken with him."

As yet not quite believing Renata's words, I began to question her:

" Could you not have been mistaken ? Perhaps it merely seemed so to you ? It may have been someone else. Did he himself admit to you that he was—Count Heinrich ? "

And Renata drew me into her room, forced me to sit down, and, nearly straining against me, bending her face close, so close, began in gasps to relate to me what had happened to her in Köln during the two days I had been absent.

According to her account, on Saturday, at the hour of the evening mass, while, as was her custom, she was wasting herself at the window in cold weariness, she suddenly heard a voice, soft but clear, as if that of an angel, which repeated thrice: " He is here, near the Cathedral. He is here, near the Cathedral. He is here, near the Cathedral." After that Renata could neither reason nor tarry, but, rising and throwing on her cape, she hastened at once to the Cathedral, on the Square, at that time crowded with people. Five minutes had not passed when she distinguished in the crowd Count Heinrich, who was walking with another young man, their arms round each other's waists. From excitement at this apparition, of which she had too long dreamed, Renata almost fell unconscious, but some force, as if from within, supported her, and she followed them, walking, across the whole town, until they entered a house belonging to Eduard Stein, the friend of the humanists.

The following day, a Sunday, Renata stood on guard near that house from early dawn, firmly resolved

to wait for the appearance of Heinrich. She had to
wait a long time, the whole day long, but she paid no
attention to the surprised glances of the passers-by or
the suspicious looks of the reiters, and only the thought
that Heinrich might have left the city during the night
made her tremble. Suddenly, when it was already
near twilight, the door opened and Heinrich appeared,
in company with the same youth as yesterday, conversing with animation. Renata walked after them, keeping
in the shelter of the walls, and she followed close upon
all their route as far as the Rhine, where the friends
took leave of each other : the stranger turned towards
the shipping, and Heinrich made as if to return. Then
Renata came out from the shadow and called him by
his name.

According to Renata's words Heinrich recognised
her at once, but she would have been happy had it
not been so, for, scarcely had he realised who was
before him, when his face became distorted with
indignation and hate. Renata caught hold of his hand,
he freed himself with a shiver of disgust and, thrusting
away the fingers that stretched towards him, tried to
walk on. Then Renata fell upon her knees before him
on the filthy quay, kissed the hem of his cape and said
to him all those words she had so often said to me ;
how she had waited for him, how she had searched
for him, how she loved him and entreated him to kill
her there and then, for of his thrust she would die bliss-
fully, like a saint. But Heinrich said that he neither
wished to speak to her, nor see her, that he even had
no right to forgive her ; at last, tearing himself free
from her hands, he disappeared, almost running, leaving
her alone in darkness and isolation.

Renata delivered the whole of this narrative at one
breath, speaking in a very firm voice, and selecting
accurate and picturesque expressions, but, on reaching
the end, she suddenly lost at one and the same time
both strength and will, and burst into tears : as though

the wind that had driven the ship of her soul had died suddenly down, and the sails begun pitifully to droop against the rigging. And at once she sank heavily to the floor, for despair always dragged her to the ground, and, drooping with face averted, she began to weep and sway herself about, repeating helplessly the selfsame words, heeding not my tender consolations, nor my searching questions.

I confess that Renata's narrative, though that day I had been, it is true, further from her in thought than ever before, made a staggering impression upon me: my heart throbbed convulsively and my soul as if filled with the black smoke of an explosion. The thought that someone had dared to treat proudly and contemptuously a woman before whom I was accustomed to kneel was unbearable to me. However, I did not allow myself to be overcome by anger and jealousy, but sought clearly to unravel that which had transpired, though it assailed me as a disorderly and impetuous hurricane. And as soon as Renata had regained at least a degree of ability to speak coherently, I demanded that she should repeat the words of Heinrich to me more exactly:

Still swallowing her tears, she exclaimed :

" How he insulted me ! How he insulted me ! He told me that I was the evil genius of his life. That I had ruined his whole fate. That I took him away from Heaven. That I—am from the Devil. He told me that he despised me. That the memory of our love was revolting to him. That our love was filth and sin into which I had enticed him by shameful deceit. That he, that he—spat upon our love ! "

Then I asked how could Heinrich have said that Renata took him away from Heaven ? Was it not he himself, of his own free will, who carried her to his castle to live with him as his wife and one nearest to him ? And since at that hour all the customary dams in Renata's soul were shattered by the impetuous flood of her sorrow, without even attempting to defend herself, she fell with her face upon my knees and exclaimed with a final sincerity so unusual to her:

" Rupprecht! Rupprecht! I hid from you the most important point of all! Heinrich never sought human love! He should never in his life have touched a woman! It was I, it was I, who forced him to betray his oath. Yes, I took him away from Heaven, I deprived him of his exalted dreams, and for that he now despises me and hates me!"

Continuing to stalk the truth carefully, as an animal stalks its prey, I discovered from Renata, question by question, all that she had concealed from me about Heinrich in her first story, and of which she had never let hint drop during the three months of our life together. I learned that Heinrich was member of a Secret society that required on entry a vow of chastity. This society was to have bound together the entire Christian universe with a hoop tighter than the Church, and to have stood at the head of the entire earth with more power than the Emperor and the Most Holy Father. Heinrich dreamed that he would be elected Grand Master of the order, and lead the vessel of humanity out of the deep abysms of evil into the roadsteads of truth and light. He had called Renata to join him only for the purpose of assisting him with his experiments in a new, godly magic, for he required that special power that is latent in some persons. But Renata, thinking Heinrich the incarnation of her Madiël, had approached him with but one aim—to possess herself of him, and, despising no means, she achieved the triumph of her purpose. Heinrich, however, after a short time during which his reason had been blinded by love, had felt horrified at what had been committed, and, in bitter remorse, fled his home castle, like a country infested with the plague.

Such an explanation of events seemed to me to have much more the appearance of truth than that which

Renata had given me before, and, at last joining into
one whole the separate threads of her story, I asked
her :

" If you yourself admit that you are guilty before
Count Heinrich, that you deprived him of his fondest
dreams and took away from him the sacred aim of his
life, how is it that you are astonished at his hating you ? "

Renata slowly rose from the floor, looked at me with
her eyes become suddenly dry, and then spoke in a
quite new voice, firm like steel :

" Perhaps I am not astonished at all. Perhaps I
am even gladdened that Heinrich hates me. I do not
bewail him, but myself. I am not sorry that he is lost
to me, but it causes me shame and bitterness to have
been able to have loved him so, to have given myself
thus to him. I, myself, hate him ! Now I know with
certainty that of which long ago I had suspicion.
Heinrich deceived me ! He is—a mere man, but an
ordinary human being, whom I could seduce and who
can be ruined, and I in my madness imagined him to
be my angel ! No, no, Heinrich is only Count Otterheim,
a failure as Grand Master of his order, while my Madiël
is in Heaven, eternally pure, eternally beautiful,
eternally unattainable ! "

Renata joined her hands as if in prayer, and I
thought the moment propitious to acquaint her with
all that of which I had dreamed and thought on my
journey back from Bonn. I said :

" Renata ! Thus you are convinced that Count
Heinrich is not your angel Madiël, but a simple mortal,
who for some time loved you and whom you loved,
perhaps even owing to your self-deception. Now this
love is dead in him, as well as in you, and your heart,
Renata, is free. Remember then that another is near
you to whom that heart is more precious than all the
gold fields of Mexico ! If, with equanimity of soul,
even though without passion, you can stretch out your
hand to me and give me a promise of faithfulness in

the future, I shall accept it as a miserable beggar a kingly alms, as a hermit accepts grace from Heaven! Here once more, Renata, I kneel before you—and in your hands alone does it lie to transform your whole horrible past into a dream fading away into forgetfulness."

Renata rose after my words, straightened herself, lowered her hands on to my shoulders and spoke thus :

" I will be your wife, but you must slay Heinrich ! "

Retreating a step, I replied asking whether I had heard aright, for once more had Renata completely upset with her words all my idea of her, as a child tips over a bag dropping to the ground all the objects it contains—and Renata repeated to me, her voice very calm, but obviously affected by extreme excitement:

" You must slay Heinrich ! He must not be suffered to live after giving himself out as another, as one immeasurably higher than he. He stole my caresses and my love from me. Slay him, slay him, Rupprecht, and I will be yours ! I shall be faithful to you, I shall love you, I shall follow you everywhere—both in this life and in the eternal fire the way to which will be opened for both of us ! "

I retorted :

" I am no hired assassin, Renata, no Neapolitan ; I cannot lay in wait for the Count round a corner and thrust a dagger into his back—my honour will not allow me to do that ! "

Renata replied :

" Can you not find reasons for challenging him to combat ? Visit him as you visited Agrippa, insult him or force him to insult you—has a man so few means of disposing of a rival ? "

That which struck me most of all in this speech was her mention of Agrippa, for until that moment I had been convinced that Renata, having been unconcerned with the things of this world, had not known the object

of my journey. As to the request itself—to slay Count
Heinrich, I should be a hypocrite if I were to pretend
that it horrified me. It was only the unexpectedness of
Renata's words that confused me, but in the depths of
my soul they found immediately a sympathetic echo,
as if someone had struck a brass shield in front of
deep grottoes and the many-voiced echo, dying out in
the distance, long repeated the sound. And when
Renata began to press me, as an opponent his enemy
chased into a crevice, to tear consent out of me, as one
panther a lump of meat from the claws of another—I
resisted without much pertinacity, just for appearance's
sake—and gave her the oath she awaited.

Hardly had I pronounced the decisive words when
Renata changed her whole attitude. Suddenly she
remarked that I was exhausted by fatigue after a rather
trying journey; and, with a care that manifested itself
in her so seldom, she hastened to take off my travelling
clothes, brought me water to wash, and found me some
supper and wine. She suddenly became to me as the
kindest, most domesticated of wives to her beloved
husband, or as an elder sister to a younger brother
fallen ill. Ceasing to speak of Count Heinrich as
though she had forgotten all about our bitter conversation and my oath, Renata began at supper to question
me about my journey, showing interest in all that had
befallen me, and discussing with me the words of Agrippa
as in the happy days of our joint studies. When, seeing
through the window a completely black sky, inwardly
conscious that we had already crossed the threshold of
midnight, I desired, having kissed Renata's hand, to
retire to my room, she said softly to me, dropping her
eyes, like a bride:

" Why do you not wish to remain with me ? "

Why did I not wish to remain ? But how dare I
dream of remaining ! It was already a very long time,
the course of many weeks, since it had last been given
to me to spend the night near Renata, and the memory

of my former intimacy with her seemed as something illusory and unattainable.

This time Renata did not desire me to stay on the wooden podium, near her bed, but called me to lie next to her again, as in the first days. This time Renata pressed herself to me with all her body, like a mistress, kissed me, sought my lips, my hands, all of me. And when, drawing back, I said to her that she must not tempt me, Renata answered me:

" I must! I must! I want to be with you! To-day I want you! "

Thus, unexpectedly, came to pass my first union with Renata as man with woman, on a day when I least of all expected it, after a conversation that least of all led to it. This night became our first bridal night, after we had spent not a few nights in one bed as brother and sister, and after we had lived for several months side by side like modest friends. But when, in the torture of this unexpected bliss, nearly drunk with the accomplishment of all that had heretofore seemed so impossible, I bent, exhausted, over the lips of Renata to thank her with a kiss for my ecstasy, I suddenly saw that her eyes were once more full of tears, that the tears were streaming down her cheeks, and that her lips were twisted in a smile of pain and despair. I exclaimed:

" Renata! Renata! Can it be that you are weeping? "

She replied in a strangled voice:

" Kiss me, Rupprecht! Caress me, Rupprecht! Have I not given myself to you! Have I not given you all my body! More! More! "

Almost in terror I fell face downwards on the pillows, ready to weep and gnash my teeth, but Renata drew me forcibly towards her, compelling me to be the live instrument of her torture, an executioner willing but trembling in horror, racking and crucifying herself with insatiable thirst on the wheel of caresses and the cross of lust. She deceived me again and again with pretended tenderness, tempted me with passion perhaps not artificial, but not destined for me, and flinging her body into fire and upon the teeth of saws, moaned with the bliss—of feeling pain, wept with the last of all joys—the despising of herself. And till the very morn lasted this monstrous playing at love and happiness, in which the kisses were sharp blades, the calls to joy—the menaces of an inquisitor, the elixir of lust—blood, and our whole bridal couch—a black torture cell.

That evening, when in the name of love murder was demanded of me, and that night, when in the name of love tortures were demanded of me, remain as the most horrible of my deliriums, and the slumber of exhaustion that freed me from these diabolical visions granted me a favour greater than in the grant of all the rulers of the world.

In the morning I awoke more exhausted than if I had been confined for half a year in a subterranean prison : my eyes could hardly look upon the light of day, and my consciousness was dull, like inferior glass. But Renata was at times as if of metal, hard and resilient, knowing no fatigue, and when I first met her glance—it was the same as it had been on the eve. Everything was still hazy to me, so that I was ready to doubt whether we two were alive, but Renata called to me already, with merciless insistence :

" Rupprecht ! It is time ! It is time ! We must go to Heinrich at once ! I desire you to slay him soon, not later than to-morrow ! "

She gave me no time to gather my thoughts, she hurried me as on a ship in the hour of shipwreck when every moment is precious, and it was now I who submitted with the meekness of the android of Albertus Magnus. Without arguing, I dressed myself as smartly as I could, buckled on my sword, and followed Renata who led me along the deserted morning street, silently, unheeding of my words, as if in obedience to someone's invincible will. At last we came to the home of Eduard Stein, large and sumptuous with cunning balconies and stucco frames round the windows, and, with the one and only word " here," Renata, pointing out to me the heavy, chiselled doors, quickly turned and walked away as if leaving me alone with my conscience. However, even without looking after Renata, I felt at once that she would not go far, but would hide behind the nearest turning and wait for my reappearance at that door, so that, rushing up, she might grasp at once from me the news of our success.

To tell the truth, I was so confused by the whirlwind of events that twirled me round that, contrary to my custom, I had no time attentively and narrowly to reflect upon my position. Only when grasping, in knocking, the door handle, of massive and refined workmanship, did I remember that I had not prepared the words of my conversation with Heinrich, and that in general I had no idea what I should do on entering this rich house. To tarry, however, there was no time, and with that courage with which a man, shutting his eyes, plunges into the deep, I knocked firmly and loudly metal against metal, and when a servant opened the door, I said that I must at all cost see Count Heinrich von Otterheim who was staying in the house, upon important business that brooked of no delay.

The servant led me through the entrance hall, filled with tall, but elegant cupboards, then along a broad staircase with handsome balustrading, then further through an antechamber hung with pictures depicting various animals, and at last, knocking, opened a small door. I saw before me a narrow room with a panelled, decorated ceiling, with carved friezes along the walls and set all with wooden lecterns for books, from behind which came forward a young man, dressed elegantly, like a knight, in silk with slashed sleeves, with a golden chain on his breast and a multitude of small golden decorations. I realised that he was Count Heinrich.

The Fiery Angel

For a few moments, before beginning to speak, I studied this man with whom, without his knowledge, my fate had so long been miraculously linked, whose image I had tried so often to imagine, whom, at times, I had thought to be either a Heavenly spirit or the creation of a diseased imagination. Heinrich, outwardly, seemed to be not more than twenty years old, and in all his being, there was such a surplus of youth and freshness as it seemed as though nothing in the world could crush, so that one was inspired with awe and reminded involuntarily of youth eternal, with which mankind is endowed by the mysterious elixir in which the philosopher's stone of the alchymists is dissolved. Heinrich's face, beardless and half-youthful, was not so handsome as it was striking: his blue eyes deeply set under his somewhat thin lashes seemed like shards of the azure sky, the lips, perhaps a trifle too full, folded themselves involuntarily into a smile like that of an angel on a holy image, and his hair, in truth like golden threads, for it was dry, sharp and thin and lay separately almost to strangeness, rose above his forehead like the nimbus of a saint. In every movement of Heinrich there was an impetuosity, not as of one running, but as of one flying, and had anyone insisted that he was a denizen of Heaven who had assumed human shape, I should perhaps have seen, sprouting behind his boyish shoulders, a pair of white swan's wings.

Count Heinrich was the first to break the silence, of course not long, but which had seemed protracted, by asking me what service he could render me, and his voice, that I heard now for the first time, seemed to me the most beautiful thing about him—singing, easily and quickly travelling through all the steps of the musical scale.

Gathering all the forces of my wit, trying to speak fluently and easily, but yet not knowing even how I intended to terminate each sentence the first words of which I had begun—I embarked on a respectful speech.

I said that I had heard a great deal about the Count, as
a remarkable scientist, who, while yet young, had
penetrated the forbidden mysteries of nature and all the
secret doctrines, from Pythagoras and Plotinus to the
teachers of our days; that from early childhood I had
been drawn by an insatiable desire to comprehend the
highest wisdom, to the search for the primary cause of
all matter; that, by diligent and unremitting study, I
had attained a certain height of understanding, but
that I had become convinced, without room for doubt,
that no man could penetrate the last mysteries by
personal efforts alone, for the initiated, even from the
days of Hiram, the builder of Solomon, had transmitted
the basic truths only verbally to their disciples: that
it was only as member of a society, in which the revelations of the peoples of remotest antiquity—the Hebrews,
Chaldeans, Egyptians and Greeks—were handed down
in succession as if from father to son, like the sacra-
mental grace of the Church, that it was possible to
achieve one's aim on the road to knowledge; that,
knowing the Count as one important and influential in
the most considerable of these societies, which are each
connected with the other by the oneness of their tasks
and the oneness of their aim, I had recourse to him with
the request—that he would help me to enter, as a
humble disciple, the ranks of one of them.

To my astonishment this half-boastful, half-hypo-
critical speech, in which I had tried to show off all my
meagre information about the mysterious orders of the
initiated—was greeted by Count Heinrich as something
worthy of attention. Taking me, probably, for an
initiate, though one standing outside the societies,
Heinrich hastily and with extreme politeness pointed
me to a bench, sat down himself and, looking into
my face with sad and candid eyes, spoke to me as he
would to a near friend:

"First answer me"—he said to me—"are you
related to us by the basic inclinations of your spirit?
184

Are you animated, as we are, by hatred of the Beasts of the East and of the West? Have you accepted, as your first and final guide, the emblem of the Son of God, lit by the light? Do you thirst to rise to the Gates of Heaven, along the seven steps of lead, tin, brass, iron, bronze, silver and gold?"

In truth, I understood little of all these strange questions, but similar expressions were no novelty for me who had just recently perused a multitude of books on magic, and, though the hour seemed to me the most important of my life, I was unable to master a sly temptation that beckoned me to discover how far the initiated understand each other. Recalling a few mysterious expressions I had encountered in the " Paemandra " and compositions of a like kind, I tried to reply to Heinrich in the language of his speech, and I took the greatest care that my words should have no relation to his, for this peculiarity I had noted in all the mysterious questions and answers. I said:

" The emerald tablet of Hermes Trismegistus announces that that which is above resembles that which is below. But the pentagram, with its head pointing up, manifests the victory of the ternion over the binary, of the spirit over the flesh; and with its head pointing down—the victory of sin over good. All numbers are mysterious, but for preference the units express the divine, the tens—the heavenly, the hundreds—the earthly, the thousands—the future. How think you then that I should have come to you if I had not known how to distinguish the upper abyss from the lower abyss?"

No sooner had I uttered these quite empty words, than I regretted my joke, for Heinrich rushed at me with the trustfulness of a child, and exclaimed in such ecstasy as if I had disclosed to him something remarkable and previously unknown:

" Ah, you are right, you are right! Of course! Of course! I understood at once that we were talking to the same purpose! And I was in no sense trying to test you! I only desired to warn you that, on the road to which you strive to attain, there are more thorns than sweet berries. The truth of truths is not opened at our secret meetings, like some little casket. The first word we address to the novice is—sacrifice. Only he who longs to sacrifice himself can become a disciple. Have you thought of the forerunners: the light Osiris slain by the dark Typhan? the god-like Orpheus torn to pieces by the Bacchantes? the divine Dionysius killed by the Titans? our Balder, the son of light, who fell by the arrow of the cunning Loki? Abel, murdered by the hand of Cain? Christ crucified? Two hundred years ago the Knights of the Temple paid with their lives for the highness of their aims and for the nobility with which they said to the rulers: ' Thou shalt be king only while thou shalt act justly.' Vergilius Maro describes the two doors from the world of shadows: the first is of ivory, but through it fly out only deceitful spirits, the second is of horn. I ask you only—do you pass through the door of lesser splendour by your own free choice? "

Heinrich spoke all this with a passionate eagerness, pronouncing each word as though it were especially precious to him, or as though it were now rising to his lips for the first time in his life. Looking at this half-youth, half-child, in whom there was so much inner fire that an infinitesimal cause, like the light-hearted questioning of a stray traveller, was sufficient to fan it into tongues of flame—I felt wilting and dying in me all my hatred of him, all my malevolence. I listened to the remarkable roulades of his voice, that seemed to open before me blue, far-off vistas, looked into his eyes, that, as it seemed to me, despite the animation of his speech, remained sad as though holding in their deeps despair that had plunged therein—and felt like a snake that crawls from under a stone to bite, but is magicked by the tune of an African charmer. There

186

was a moment when I was almost ready to exclaim:
" Forgive me, Count, I have unworthily been mocking
you!" But, checking my thought with horror on so
dangerous a path, I shouted to myself "beware!"
and hastened to take control over my soul, as a horseman
over a runaway horse. And immediately, to give
myself an opportunity of recovering my composure, I
threw out another few words to Heinrich, saying to him:

" I fear no trials, for I have long been unable to
endure the knowledge freely accessible to us, which, in
the expression of one sage, involves the assimilation of
the scientist to his science, *assimilatio scientis ad rem
scitam*. I seek that knowledge spoken of by Hermes
Trismegistus as a wise sacrifice of soul and heart. And
is it for him who seeks to fear roadside thorns?"

Heinrich seized upon these words as upon a precious
discovery and, as if able to speak endlessly on any
subject, at once poured himself out in a long and again
inspired speech. And again, without my wishing it,
the phrases of this speech, delivered with an eagerness
fit to convince and talk round his best friend, imprinted
themselves in my memory so sharply that it is not difficult for me to resurrect them, almost word for word.

" I understand you, I understand you "—he said—
" only you are still mistaken in supposing it is within
our power to hand out true knowledge, like a gift.
Mystic knowledge is called so not because it is being
wilfully concealed, but because it is of its nature hidden,
in symbols. We have no peculiar truth, but we have
emblems bequeathed to us as a heritage by antiquity,
by that first people of the earth that lived in commerce
with God and His angels. That people knew not the
shadows of matter, but matter itself, and thus the
symbols they left behind exactly express the substance
of being. Eternal Justice required that, since we had
lost this direct knowledge, we should attain bliss
through the font of blindness and ignorance. But
now we must unite all that has been gathered by our

reason to the revelations of antiquity, and only of
that union will come perfect knowledge. But believe
me, a pure soul and a pure heart will help in this
matter more than all the counsels of the wise. Virtue—
that is the true philosopher's stone."

At this point in his speech, Count Heinrich made
pause, then, with a changed face and slightly wandering
glance, he added, softly and in measure:

" You too are aware that the days and the hours are
fulfilled. You too, when silence comes, hear the sound
of the opening of the gates. Softly, softly, hark! Do
you hear—the steps are approaching! Do you hear—
the leaves are falling from the trees ? "

These last words of Heinrich he pronounced in a
voice that died away, making sign to me to keep silence,
all tense, as if he really heard the sound of steps and the
noise of falling leaves, and, bending to me, near, so near,
his eyes, large and maddened, so that I felt alarmed and
ill at ease. I tore my gaze away from Heinrich's gaze,
and, suddenly recoiling against the back of the bench,
I changed my tone and said to him firmly and harshly:

" Enough, Count, now I understand all that I wished
to know."

Heinrich looked at me uncomprehending and
enquired:

" What have you understood and what did you wish
to know ? "

I replied:

" I have finally discovered that you are a deceiver
and a charlatan, who has somewhere stolen the shreds
of mystic knowledge and makes use of these stolen
goods to pose an an initiate and a master."

At this unexpected attack, Heinrich involuntarily
rose from the bench and, continuing to stare straight
at me, made a few paces forward, as if desirous of
demanding explanation of me. I waited without
moving, not lowering my eyes, but before reaching
me, Heinrich subdued his emotion and said humbly:

"If you think thus, we have naught to talk about!
Farewell! ..."

But I, urging myself down the slope, shouted at him:
"Now it is you who are mistaken, thinking that
you will pay thus cheaply for a deceit! There are
sacred matters that may not be made a jest, and words
that may not be uttered in vain! I call you to answer,
Count Heinrich von Otterheim!"

Heinrich answered me with a face of fury:
"Who are you to come to me and suddenly address
me in that tone? I shall not listen to you!"

I replied solemnly:
"Who am I? I am—the voice of your conscience
and the voice of revenge!"

As I spoke thus, I showed myself the eyes of Heinrich
and reminded myself that Renata loved them, his
hands, and told myself that she had kissed them, all his
body, and tried to imagine how she had caressed it with
ecstasy. As if with a huge bellows I blew up in my soul
the fire of jealousy, and, like a general to his soldiers,
I gave to my words the command: "courage!"

Meanwhile Heinrich, probably thinking me a madman, said to me: "We shall speak later!"—and desired
to leave the room. But I, in fear that if I did not make
use of this meeting it might not repeat itself, barred his
way and shouted, this time in earnest passion:
"You, who speak of virtue, you I accuse of dishonour! I accuse you of having behaved towards a
lady in a manner unbefitting to a knight! You carried
away a maiden to your castle by deceit for your base,
and perhaps even criminal purposes. You then
spurned her and abandoned her. And when here, in
the street, she begged you for indulgence, you insulted
her in a way in which no man should insult a woman.
I throw you my glove, and you will take it up, if you
be a knight!"

The effect of my words, which were not thought out,
and which by all considerations I should not have said,

surpassed my expectations, for Heinrich jerked away
from me like a wounded stag, then, in extreme excitement, grasped a book from a lectern and, scarcely
aware what he was doing, began to fumble its pages
with trembling fingers, then at last turned round, and
asked me in a strangled voice:

"I do not know who you are. I can accept a
challenge only from one equal to me in station. . . ."

These words made me lose the last vestige of self-
control, for, though I have no reason whatever to be
ashamed of my descent from an honest medicus of a small
town, yet I felt in Heinrich's question an undeserved
insult, branding me, not for the first time as a matter
of fact, as a man not of knightly house. And in this
moment I could find nothing more dignified than,
drawing back my head, to say with cold pride:

"I am as much a knight as you are, and you will
take no shame by meeting me in fair combat. So send
your friends to-morrow, at noon to the Cathedral, to
make terms with mine. Else it remains for me only
to slay you as a coward and one who knows no honour."

Having uttered these words, I felt how disgraceful it
was for me to lie at such a moment, and I was seized
with shame and indignation, so that without adding
anything I almost ran out of Heinrich's room, quickly
made my way down the sumptuous staircase, and, with
an angry gesture, made the servant open the door before
me. My face was plunged in the fresh wind of the light
winter's day, and my eyes into the clear blue skies, as
into a tank of clear spring water, and I stood for a long
time uncertain whether all that had occurred was real.
Then I walked along the street, clinging somehow
involuntarily to the walls, like a blind man feeling his
way. And then suddenly appeared before me the face
of Renata, frightened, pale and with dilated pupils.
She wanted to ask me something, but I thrust her aside
with such force that she almost fell, striking the corner
of a house, and I ran on without saying a word.

Chapter the Eighth

Of my duel with Count Heinrich

WHEN I had traversed several streets and had grown freshened by the movement and the cold, I regained the ability to think clearly and form deductions, and I said to myself:

"Your duel with Count Heinrich is definitely decided. To retreat now would be unthinkable and ignoble. It remains, therefore, only to see that the affair is carried through as satisfactorily as possible."

Personally, I was never a supporter of duels, which have made such pernicious progress in France in recent times, and though I am familiar with the admirable words of Iohann Reuchlin: "Honour is the most beautiful of our possessions"—I have never been able to accept the view that honour leans upon the point of a sword, and is not based upon nobility in deeds and words. However, in days when even the wearers of crowns did not disdain to send each other challenges to single combat, I did not think it good to decline duels, and in my landsknecht time I appeared in them on more than one occasion. But now the position of affairs was complicated by the fact that, first of all, the challenger, and moreover without any real cause, was I, and, in the second instance, by the fact that the aim I placed before me was that of striking my opponent to death—and all this made my task heavy and hard, as if I were confronted with the duty of an executioner.

At this time I had no doubt whatever that the

balance of fortune in the combat would be mine, for, though I had had no occasion to exercise my arm for a considerable time past, I had been one of the best fighters in my ranks with the long sword, while Count Heinrich, being entirely devoted to book studies and philosophical reflections could have had no opportunity (it seemed so to me then) to attain a sufficient perfection in the art of Ponce and Torres. I was dismayed by yet another matter—the fact that, with the exception of old Glock, there was no one in the whole city with whom I was acquainted, and I could not think of anyone to whom I might entrust the parley with the opponent and the arrangements for the encounter with him, according to the custom of duels. After long hesitation, I decided to knock upon the door of one of my old companions of the University, Matthew Wissmann, whose family had resided in Köln for many generations, and whom, therefore, rather than anyone else, after the many years that had passed, I was more likely to find in the same dwelling place as before, at the same old *penates*.

My expectations were not deceived, for it turned out in truth that the Wissmanns still resided in their old dwelling, though it was not easy for me to search out their squat, old-fashioned house, composed of three stories overhanging each other, amidst the new, tall, altogether elaborate houses erected around it by our enterprising age. To my good fortune, Matthew happened to be at home, but I could scarcely recognise the youth who, though he was even then a trifle slow and clumsy, had been not void of parts and, indeed, had been my (though unsuccessful) rival in wooing the pretty wife of the baker—in the stout and staid overgrown tun, with sleepy eyes and a funny beard that left his chin bare, to whom I was led by the servant of the house. Of course he too could hardly recognise the scholar of those happy days, riotous and unbearded, in the man, scorched by the equatorial sun and bitten by the winds of the ocean, but when I told Matthew my name, and reminded him of our past friendship, he genuinely gladdened, his face creased in a good-natured smile, and through the layers of fat there shone the glint of something youthful, like a beam of light through a dull glass.

Embracing me cordially and kissing me with his oily lips, Matthew said to me:

"Do I remember Rupprecht! Brother—do I not remember you every time I get drunk! I swear by the pure blood of Christ that I miss you and no one else of all our former crowd. Well, crawl in, crawl into my den, make yourself seated and unloosen your tongue! And I shall bid them serve immediately two quarts of fair wine."

To Matthew's sorrow I refused the wine, but for a long time I found it difficult to approach the unfolding of my business. Reluctant though I might be, I had to relate to Matthew all my adventures: the years at Losheim, my service as a landsknecht, the wanderings in Italy, the journey to New Spain and my expeditions there. And then Matthew did not scruple to tell me how, forgetting all the pranks of his youth, he had succeeded in the laborious calling of a university scientist. More than five years he had spent, having first mastered a few "art" sciences and defended several "sophisms" in disputes, in obtaining the title of bachelor; an equal number of years it had taken him to conquer the books of Aristotle, show his worth in declamation, and become a licentiate; this year, at last, he hoped to achieve the *inceptia* and become a magister, after which access to all the highest faculties would be open to him. Matthew spoke with such self-satisfaction of the sessions in council with the doctors and the rector, so sincerely feared the great "*promotii*" that confronted him, and so naively thought himself a scientist, that I did not deem it necessary to revive the ancient dispute between the "poets" and the

193

"sophists," though I saw clearly that neither the "Letters of Obscure Men" nor the famed reforms of recent years had had much effect in stirring the Idol of Köln, beneath whose shade so long ago I had wearied of scholastics!

At last I succeeded in breaking through the stream of this narrative of a professor carried away by his glory, and somehow, concealing the true nature of affairs, in outlining my request. Matthew screwed up his face as if he had taken a dose of some bitter drug, but soon he found a cheerful aspect of my proposition to seize hold of, and once again was merry:

"This is not in my line, brother!"—he said to me—"Nowadays, it is true, students too draw swords, but I hold by the old order—that a scientist is like a monk—weapons to him are like spectacles to an ass. But, none the less, come what may, for an old friend! And, moreover, I have no patience with this nobility that lifts up its noses in front of us! We sweat the doctorates out of ourselves, and they get learned degrees granted them by the princes or the Emperor. I've no doubt your Count, too, is one of these doctor-by-virtue-of-a-bull fellows! If you'll undertake to stick him on a spit, I will do my best for you! . . ."

I indicated the place arranged for the meeting for parley, explained where I lived myself, then took my leave, and Matthew came to see me to the street door. As we were crossing the dining-room filled with heavy furniture of old-fashioned German workmanship, there ran unexpectedly out of the neighbouring room a young girl in a pink dress, greenish apron and golden girdle, who, on meeting us, became confused, and stopped and knew not what to do. The slimness and tenderness of her image, the oval childish face, with the irregular drooping shadow of her long eyelashes over her blue eyes, the flaxen, golden tresses gathered beneath a white bonnet, this whole vision, appeared to me, accustomed to sights of sorrow and despair, to features distorted with passion and anger, as the passing flight of an angel would appear to a condemned spirit at the moment of entering its hell. I stopped also in confusion, not knowing whether to pass by, or to bow or speak, and Matthew, roaring with laughter, surveyed our embarrassment.

"Sister, this is Rupprecht,"—he said—"a good fellow, whom sometimes we have recalled together. And this, Rupprecht, is my sister Agnes, whom you used to see then, thirteen years ago, as a baby girl, quite a tiny poppet. What are you staring at each other for, then, like a cat at a dog? Get acquainted! Maybe I shall match you together yet. Or you, brother, are perhaps married already, eh? Answer."

I cannot explain why, but I answered thus:

"I am not married, dearest Matthew, but you should not put both me and the young lady to the blush with such words. Excuse me, Mistress Agnes, it has given me great pleasure to see you again, but I am pressed now, by the urgency of some affairs."

And, bowing low, I hastened to leave the house.

I know not whether as result of the impression of this meeting, or independently of it, but, when I thought of returning home, I felt a feeling of revulsion, such as would inevitably be felt, were they endowed with sentience, by two magnets activated by similar poles. I felt it would be unbearable to be with Renata, to see her eyes, to hear her speech, to speak with her of Heinrich.

For quite a long time I wandered through the streets of the city, pausing, for some reason, at certain corners, and hastening rapidly, for some reason, through other squares, but at last fatigue and cold forced me to seek shelter, and I walked into the first tavern that presented itself, sat alone in a corner, and asked for beer and cheese to be brought before me. The tavern was full of countrymen and harlots, for the day was a market day, and all about rose shouts, quarrels, recriminations,

195

curses and abuse, backed up occasionally with a good
cuff; but I felt happy in the stale, cold air and amidst
the tumult of the drunken people. The coarse, brutal
faces, the uncouth, illiterate speech, the obscene pranks
somehow strangely blended with the turmoil within
my soul, as the screams of the drowning blend in
chorus with the howling of the tempest.

Then an ill-shaven body, in a gay holiday dress,
sat down beside me as if he had crawled out of an
etching by Sebaldus Beham—and began a long speech
about the poverty-stricken condition of the peasants, in
no sense new, but not devoid of truth. He bewailed
the burden of the discharges, of the service, of the dues,
of the fines and every kind of impost, of usury, and of
the prohibition upon engaging in artisanship in the
villages, recalled the riot that had occurred ten years
before, and all this with threats, as if directly concerning
me, as if I were responsible for it all. I tried to reply
that I considered myself rather as one of the peasants,
and that all I possessed had been earned by my own
two hands, but of course my words were wasted, and I
resigned myself to listening meekly—for it was all one
to me what I listened to—as my chance companion
threatened the knights and the burghers with flames
and hay forks and gallows. . . .

As it was I who treated my companion, he gradually,
little by little, became quite drunk, and I was once more
left alone in the general tumult of voices. Looking
round, I saw a repulsive picture; here and there lay
the forms of people, dead tipsy, in a corner two were
hammering away at each other, clutching at one
another's hair, everywhere stood splashes of spilt
beer and human vomit, and, in the midst of this,
others continued their carousal or obscenely joked with
the harlots, who were also tipsy and hideous, or tried
to gamble with dirty cards. I suddenly visualised two
images: the gloomy Renata and the radiant Agnes;
felt surprised at myself for sitting in this dark and evil-

smelling corner, and, paying the reckoning, I hastily walked out once more into the wintry cold. It was already twilight, and I listlessly stumbled home.

While I was knocking at our door, my soul felt empty like a baled out well, but in the house it was immediately filled with solemn silence, which restored me irresistibly into the familiar circle of both thoughts and emotions. I could almost physically feel how there slid off from my face the expressions that had distorted it during the day, and how my lips folded into that soft smile with which I always met Renata's eyes. With my heart beating fast in tremor, as on the first occasion I had ever done so, I opened the door into Renata's room, and immediately, seeing her in her habitual pose at the window with her face pressed against its cold little round panes, I rushed to her and fell to my knees before her.

Renata did not say a word about the rudeness with which I had thrust her away in the morning, did nôt reproach me for having returned so late, did not desire to know the substance of my conversation with Heinrich, but only, as if everything else were known to her, asked:

" Rupprecht, when is your duel ? "

Not surprised, at the moment, at that question, I answered simply:

" I do not know, it will be decided to-morrow. . . . "

Renata did not utter another word, and lowered her eyelashes, while I stayed at her feet, motionless, resting my head against the window-ledge, my eyes raised to the figure sitting there, to the beloved, cherished, though irregular features, sinking every moment once more deeper and deeper into their charm, as if deeper and deeper into the depths of a bottomless whirlpool. I gazed on this woman, whom only yesterday I had caressed with all the imaginable busses of a contented lover, and to whose hand, to-day, I dared not even touch my reverent lips, and felt radiate from her whole being a witching power, that locked all my desires within its spell. Like thin chaff before the winnow, all the riotous thoughts and chance temptations of the day flew off and dispersed in greyish smoke, and there fell directly upon the threshing floor of my soul the full-weighted grain of my love and my passion. I did not wish to think either of Heinrich or of myself; I was happy, softly touching Renata's hand; I was happy, that that was returning which had existed before, and that the minutes were passing, passing, passing unheeded.

Thus, in silence, not daring to break it by a careless word, I could have stayed until morn and thought myself at the gate of Eden, but suddenly Renata lifted her head, touched my hair with her hand and said tenderly, as if continuing a conversation:

" Dearest Rupprecht, but you must not kill him ! "

Startled, dragged out from beneath the spell, I asked :

" I must not kill Count Heinrich ? "

Renata confirmed her words :

" Yes, yes. He was not made for killing. He is light, he is beautiful, I love him ! I am guilty before him—not he before me. I was like a blade that cut through all his hopes. One must bow before him, kiss him, obey his every whim. Do you hear, Rupprecht ? If you as much as touch one hair of his head—his hair is of gold—if you shed but one drop of his blood, you will never hear more of me, never, never again ! "

I rose from my knees, folded my arms across my chest, and asked :

" Then why did you not think of all this before, Renata ? Why did you then force me to play the fool's part in this comedy of the duel ? May one dare to be light-hearted with matters of life and death ? "

My breath was cut short by my emotion, but Renata replied to me sharply :

" If you dare to scold me, I shall not listen ! But I

forbid you, do you hear, forbid you to touch my Heinrich! He is mine, and I desire for him only happiness. I will not yield him to you, I will not yield him to anyone in the world! . . ."

Making a last effort, I asked:

"Then you have forgotten how he insulted you?"

Renata exclaimed:

"Oh, that was good! Oh, how beautiful it was! He cursed me! He wanted to strike me! Oh, let him crush me with his feet! He is my beloved! Dearest! I love him!"

Then I said in a heavy voice:

"I will execute all as you wish, Renata. But there is nothing else for us to speak about. Farewell!"

I went away into my room, flung myself on to my bed, and it seemed to me as though I were being hunted down like an animal, chased into a circle of prickly hedge, which I had no power to break through, and as though I were fallen to the ground, waiting for the huntsmen to finish me off. I wanted either not to be, or to wake out of life as out of a dream, and for the first time I began to gain an inkling of the temptation—to lift one's hand against oneself. Thinking of my fate, I decided that I would not speak to Renata of anything else, and that on the morrow I should go into the combat with lowered sword, and rejoice at feeling the steel of another within my breast. And, in imagining my body prostrate, covered with blood, in snow-clad grass, I experienced a sympathy and tender compassion for myself, as a child does to whom are read the sufferings of the saints.

In the morning, however, in the sober rays of the sun, feeling somewhat reposed, I once more thought out my position and desired, all the same, to consult with Renata, finally and mercilessly, for her decisions were always as shifting as the outlines of a cloud and might easily have changed during the night; but it proved that Renata had risen before me and already left the house. I went then to Matthew, to suggest to him not to insist at the parley on decisively fatal terms, because for some instinctive reason I continued to endeavour to preserve my life, although at the time it seemed to me useful for no purpose; but Matthew, too, I did not happen to meet. Then, somehow deprived of volition, I returned home and gave everything into the hands of the Three Spinsters, like a man already condemned in any case to death, for whom the only choice yet open is either the axe or the gallows.

After noon came Matthew, and the appearance of the robust, good-natured, fat man in our apartment of gloom and despair was strange; strange was his roaring, care-free laughter amidst the walls accustomed to reverberate with the sound of weeping and sighs. Matthew greeted me with these words:

"Aha, brother, in vain did you yesterday assume the airs of a communicant. I've found out, I have, that you do not live alone here. Only, do not be alarmed, to my friends I am—a fish—mouth shut, for who is without sin? Only, it is not good to hide things from one's friends! I shan't take the pretty one away from you—I'm not one of those fellows."

And, when I interrupted Matthew's speech and asked him to give a report of his parleys, he said:

"All went like a ship sliding on butter. I'll never let down a friend, not I, no wolf will ever eat him through my doing! There came from your Count a gilded popinjay, curtsying like a lass, his hair all curled. But I set him in his place! Next time he won't boast of his knighthood in front of a good burgher. And your meeting is this very afternoon at three—why put it off?—in the wood near Lindenthal. Nobody will interfere with you there, and you can break every bone in the whipper-snapper!"

I listened to this, my sentence, without betraying any sign of emotion or dissatisfaction; in the most business-like manner I arranged with Matthew about the various details of the encounter and asked him to call for me when the time had come. After having seen Matthew off, I ordered Martha to serve me dinner, for I did not wish weakness on my part to influence the outcome of the affair, and then, taking hold of my long sword, I began to exercise my arm, trying to regain the necessary suppleness. It was at this occupation that Renata found me, appearing in the doorway, all wrapped in a cloak, like some ghost, and, piercing me with her searching and threatening glance:

"Rupprecht,"—she said—"you swore to me yesterday!"

I replied:

"I will fulfil what I have promised, Renata. But what if now Count Heinrich slay me?"

Thrusting her head back, Renata said firmly:

"And what of it, then?"

I bowed ceremoniously as two opponents bow before the commencement of the combat, sheathed my sword, and again, as yesterday, left the room: for to gainsay Renata I had no will, and I did not wish to be weakened by her influence.

The remaining time I spent in writing a letter to my mother, to whom I had sent no news of me all the seven years since secretly I left the parental roof. Shortly did I relate in this letter all my adventures, concealing, of course, those that had occurred since my return to Europe, and begged forgiveness for all the insults and troubles I had caused during my life. Further, I did not forget to write also my testament, addressed to Renata, in which I commissioned her to take out of the sum of money left to me such amount as she found necessary, and to send the remainder to my family at Losheim. In some remarkable way my relatives, father and mother, brothers and sisters, to whom I had scarcely given ever a thought, suddenly became extraordinarily dear to me, and I clearly remembered their faces, their voices, and longed terribly to embrace them, and tell them that I had not forgotten them. Probably, the threat of death softens even the firmest spirits, as strong heat softens metals, for I felt myself no longer like a hunted boar, but like a baby that has no breast on which to cry out its heart.

At half-past two, Matthew, still not downhearted, came for me, and began to hasten me in a friendly way, though all my preparations were limited to putting on a warm cloak and attaching my sword to my belt. Before my actual departure, I warned Matthew that I had a small matter to attend to, and he winked slyly, pointing to the room of Renata, into which, it was quite true, I could not refrain from going once more. For the third time, I made an effort to draw her attention to me, to drag from her, almost by force, at least one heartfelt word addressed to me, and finding her at the prie-dieu, as if in prayer, I said to her :

" Renata, I go, I have come to bid you farewell. Perhaps we shall never see each other again in this life, Renata. . . . "

Renata turned her pale face towards me, and I took it in with my glance, searching her features for the least hope, concealed somewhere in the fold of the lips, in some wrinkle near the eyes—but the expression of this face was like a sentence of execution to me, and the words that I now heard for the second time were unbending and merciless, like a stone that falls inevitably but without malice :

" Rupprecht, remember what you swore to me ! "

However, this cruelty of Renata rather added to my strength than shook me, as her caress probably would have done, for I felt that I had nothing dear to me to love, and therefore nothing to fear. I returned to Matthew with a countenance almost cheerful, and when, having come out, we seated ourselves on the horses he had obtained for us (for we had rather a long way to go) I even laughed not a little at the amusing figure the mounted professor cut. All the way Matthew entertained me with jokes and witticisms, with which he

desired to keep up my spirits, and I deliberately forced
myself to take them as near to heart as I could, so as
not to think that of which it was horrifying to think.
From outside, one might have taken us for two merchants who, having clinched a profitable deal in the
city, had drunk deep and well, and were returning to
their home village laden with presents for their wives.

Having accomplished rather a long distance along
the heavy, frozen road, we distinguished at last in the
distant haze of the rapidly diminishing winter's day, a
sloping hillock, and two horsemen, darkling before it
against the edge of the wood.

"Eigho, we are late, it seems!"—said Matthew—
"Master Knight is impatient, first he came, maybe he
is anxious to be carried away last!"

Approaching, we bowed in silence, and I saw again
Count Heinrich, wrapped in a dark cloak, and his
companion, a youth slim as a maiden, with a tender,
oblong face, in a biretta with a feather, like one of the
portraits of Hans Holbein. Then we alighted from
our horses, and while we two, Count Heinrich and I,
remained facing each other, our comrades walked
aside to arrange the final terms. Heinrich stood before
me motionless, half covering his face, leaning on the
hilt of his sword, as if welded with it from one piece of
metal, and I could not guess whether he were calm,
indignant, or weary of his fate like myself.

At last our comrades returned to us, and Matthew,
shrugging his shoulders and trying by all means to
make it clear he thought it superfluous, declared to us
that the Count's friend, Lucian Stein, desired to attempt
a reconciliation. If, then, I am to be truthful, and not
afraid to admit myself a coward, I must confess that
at this intelligence my heart began to beat in gladness,
and it seemed to me that this exquisite in a velvet cape
must be a messenger from Heaven.

But this was the speech of Lucian Stein which was
addressed to me:

The Fiery Angel

" From our parleys of this morning,"—he said—
" it has transpired that you, honourable sir, are by
descent not of knightly house, and therefore my friend,
Count Heinrich, could, in honour, disregard the insults
you have heaped on him, and not accept your challenge.
But, seeing in you a man of education and upbringing,
he does not reply to you with a refusal, and is ready,
with arms in his hands, to prove the flimsiness of your
assertions. However, before entering the combat, he
thinks it necessary to offer that, having thought better
of it, you should cease this quarrel peacefully. For,
except in extreme cases, man, a being made after the
image and pattern of God, must not threaten the life
of another man. If you, honourable sir, are prepared
to admit that you were led by someone into an error,
that you regret and apologise for your words of yesterday—my friend will willingly stretch out his hand to
you."

Despite the arrogance of these words, I would not
perhaps have shirked the ignominy of apologising, for
it was still the best door left open to me for a retreat,
but the first part of the speech made it impossible for
me to do so. Lucian's hint that yesterday I had falsely
called myself a knight made all the blood rush to my
face, and I was ready to strike the speaker, whose life
was not forbidden me, and to whom therefore, with
full freedom, I could show the strength of my unknightly
arm. And, still in the throes of this excitement, which
prevented me, like some mountainous sea-wave, from
seeing the goal upon the beach beyond, I replied :

" I do not withdraw any one of my words. I repeat,
that Count Heinrich von Otterheim—is a deceiver, a
hypocrite, and a dishonest man. May God be our
judge ! "

At my answer, Matthew sighed with relief like an ox
gathering breath, and Lucian, turning aside, walked
back to Heinrich.

We threw off our cloaks and unsheathed our swords,

while our comrades traced on the ground, barely whitened with hoar-frost, a circle out of which we were not to step. I studied Heinrich's expression, and saw that it was concentrated and manly, as though from behind his angelic features gazed an earthly man, and thought to myself that thus he had borne himself in those hours when, as a man, he answered Renata's caresses. Then, exchanging with him the customary bow, I noticed that he was supple as a boy, that all his movements were unstudied and beautiful as those of an ancient statue, and remembered the words of entrancement with which Renata had described him to me. But scarcely had our blades crossed, scarcely had steel clinked against steel, than in me started and woke the soul of a warrior: I forgot at once everything except the fight, and my life, bounded by the narrow distance between me and my opponent, and by those few short moments during which our combat would last. All the details of the struggle, fleeting, momentary—the effort of the lunge, the speed of the parry, the degree of suppleness of the opposing blade—at once became events containing in them each as much significance as a whole year of life.

I knew that I should not break the pledge I had given to Renata, for she had chained my will with almost supernatural force, but I had hoped that I should be able and contrive, without touching Count Heinrich, to knock the sword out of his hand, and thus end the combat with honour to myself. Soon, however, I was satisfied that I had quite baselessly misjudged the fencing art of my opponent, for beneath my blade I found a sword firm, fast and full of skill. To all my artifices Heinrich replied immediately with the ease of a master, and very soon himself took the offensive, forcing me to concentrate my whole attention upon beating off his dangerous lunges. As if handicapped by the fact that I could not strike myself, I parried the thrusts of my opponent with difficulty, and the point of his sword rushed every moment at me from the front,

from the side, and from below. Losing the hope of a
successful issue to the fight, I was losing at the same
time self-control : my fingers became blue from the
frost, my sword no longer obeyed me ; I saw before me,
as it were a wheel of whirling fiery blades, and in the
middle of them, also fiery, the image of Heinrich—
Madiël. And already it began to appear to me that
the eyes of Heinrich shone somewhere far above me,
that our fight was taking place in the untrammelled
supra-terrestrial spaces, that it was not I who was
repulsing the thrust of an enemy, but the dark spirit
Lucifer, hard pressed from the heights above the stars
by the Archistratcgus Michael, and pursued by him
into the darkness of Hell. . . .

And suddenly, at one of my untrue ripostes, Count
Heinrich with force flung off my sword, and I saw the
glitter of the hostile blade at my very breast. Immediately afterwards I felt a dull hit, and a piercing thrust,
as always when one is wounded by cold steel ; the sword
fell from my grasp, a crimson cloud rapidly obscured
my vision—and I fell.

Chapter the Ninth

How we spent the Month of December and the Festival of Christ's Birth

AS I learned later, there hastened to my assistance, while I lay prostrate and unconscious on the cold ground, not only Matthew but also my opponent and his friend. Count Heinrich showed all the signs of extreme despair, bitterly reproached himself for having accepted the challenge, and said that if I were to die he would know no rest all his life. Having bandaged my wound, all three constructed a kind of hurdle, and decided to carry me into the city on foot, for they feared to submit me to a shaking on horseback on a bad road. Meanwhile, I perceived scarcely anything of what was happening to me, and lay submerged in a confused, almost beatific, consciousness, that was interrupted by a hurtful pricking pain that forced me to open my eyes—but, seeing above me the blue skies, I imagined for some reason that I was floating in a boat and, comforted, let my mind and soul slide once more into delirium.

I have no recollection of how I was carried home or of how Renata greeted me, but Matthew told me afterwards that she met the circumstances with fortitude and efficiency. I passed the days that immediately followed also in unconsciousness, as always happens in cases of inflammation of a wound and loss of blood, and I cannot even relate here the apparitions of my fever, for words, created for matters of reason, have no correspondence to the phantasms of madness. I know only

that in some strange way the memory of Renata never
entered into this delirium : all the painful happenings
of the immediate past were erased from my memory as
chalk writing is erased from a slate by a sponge, and I
imagined myself as I was during the years of my life in
New Spain. When, in a rare moment of consciousness,
I saw before me the intent face of Renata, I imagined
that she was Angelica, the baptised Indian maid with
whom I lived for some time in Cempoalla, and from
whom, not without regret, I had to part, owing to her
unseemly behaviour. And therefore, in my delirium, I
always indignantly pushed away Renata's hands and
angrily said to her, in reply to all her solicitude :
" Why are you here ? Begone ! I would not have you
near me ! "—and Renata accepted this rough usage
from the invalid without a murmur.

My combat with Heinrich had taken place on a
Wednesday, and only on Saturday, at the hour of the
night mass, did I first recover my senses sufficiently to
recognise the room that bounded my horizon and the
days through which life carried me, and, finally, Renata,
in her pink blouse with the white and dark blue trimmings, in which I had seen her on the first day of our
acquaintance. She, who was watching my face attentively, suddenly guessed by my eyes that I had come to,
and flew towards me in a burst of joy and hope, crying :

" Rupprecht ! Rupprecht ! You know me ! "

My consciousness was as yet very unclear, like a
misty distance in which masts appear as towers, but
I already was able to recollect that I had fought with
swords against Count Heinrich, and, in trying to draw
breath, I distinctly felt a torturing pain through all
my chest. It came into my mind that I was dying of the
wound, and that this ray of memory must be the last,
that so often presages the coming end. And, by virtue
of that whimsicality of the human soul that enables the
criminal to crack jokes with the executioner on the
scaffold, I tried to say to Renata those words that seemed

to me most graceful for the occasion, though they came
not at all from my heart:

"See, Renata; here I am, dying—in order that
your Heinrich may live. . . ."

With a sob, Renata fell on her knees before the bed,
pressed her hand to my lips, and not so much spoke to
me as shouted, as if through some wall:

"Rupprecht, I love you! Do you not know that I
love you? For long I have loved you! You alone!
I do not want you to die without knowing!"

Renata's avowal was the last ray that then imprinted
itself on my consciousness, when once more it sank into
darkness, and on its surface, like the reflections of an
invisible fire, again danced red devils, waving their
voluminous sleeves and plaiting their long tails. But
a sound penetrated to me as though, in their monstrous
dance, they were continuing Renata's words in chorus,
and singing, and crying, and howling above me: "I
love you, Rupprecht! For long I have loved you!
You alone!" and throughout the labyrinth of delirium,
along its steep staircases and down its headlong abysses,
it was as though I bore these words, precious, yet
crushing as a burden upon my shoulders and my chest:
"I love you, Rupprecht!"

The second time I came to, it was from the sound of
the church bells at early Sunday Mass, and this time,
despite the weakness and pain of the wound, I felt
that an edge had been overpassed, that life was in me
and that I was in life. Renata was near me, and I made
a sign to her with my eyes that I recognised her, remembered the words she had spoken yesterday, was grateful
to her, and happy, and she, understanding, lowered
herself once more on her knees to the floor and bowed
her head against me, as one bows one's head in church
in prayer. The realisation that I had as if risen from
the grave, the touch of the tender eyelashes of Renata
upon my hand, the soft rays of the dawn and the
carillons of bells softly penetrating through the panes,

made the moment unspeakable and unearthly, as though, by some purpose, it combined in it everything that is most beautiful and most precious to man.

From that day began my recovery. Chained to the bed, almost without strength to move, I watched with astonishment how, smartly and efficiently, Renata ordered all the flow of domestic life, fussing over me, forcing Martha to perform her desires, not allowing visitors to bore and worry me. Visitors, during this time, knocked at our door far more frequently than one might have imagined, for Matthew came to me unceasingly every day, somewhat cast down by my failure, but of course not having lost his healthy cheerfulness and his gay animation, and nearly as often appeared Lucian Stein, insistently demanding news of the progress of my illness that he might carry it to Count Heinrich. And lastly, also every day, the doctor engaged by Matthew came to me, a man in a black cloak and a round hat, a pedant and an ignoramus, to whom I consider I am less indebted for my life than to all others.

Being not entirely ignorant of medical sciences, and having seen not a few wounds in the course of my service in New Spain, as soon as I had recovered the ability to reason sensibly, I ordered them immediately to throw away all the oily ointments of various repellent composition confected by this priest of Aesculapius, and began to treat my wound exclusively with warm water, to the great worry of Renata and the indignation of the black doctor. I, however, knowing that the question was one of life or death to me, now found in me sufficient strength to clothe my decision in armour impenetrable either to threats or entreaties, and later, pointed out day by day the success of my care, a vindication both of doctor and patient.

And when Renata and I were left alone, we forgot my illness, for she wanted only to repeat that she loved me, and it was sweet to me to listen to these admissions, oversweet, for my heart began to beat so fast that I felt

pain in my wound. I asked of Renata for the hundredth
and thousandth time: " So you love me ? But why
did you not tell me so before ? "—and she for the
hundredth and thousandth time answered:

" It is long that I have loved you, Rupprecht. How
is it that you did not remark it ? Often I would softly
whisper to you the words ' I love you.' Not hearing them,
you would ask me what I was saying and I would
answer thus: ' Nothing, no matter.' I admired your
face, stern and forbidding, your brows joined together,
your firm step, but when you chanced to catch my
loving glance I began to speak to you of Heinrich. How
many times, when you slept alone, have I crawled at
night on tiptoe into your room and kissed your hands,
your breast, your feet, trembling lest I might wake
you ! Even when you were not at home I would enter
your room and kiss your bedclothes, the pillows on
which you slept. But how could I admit my love to
you, after all that I had told you of my love for Heinrich?
I felt that you must despise me, that you would think
my love unworthy, if I threw it from one to another like
a ball. Ah, am I guilty in that you have conquered me,
with your tenderness, with your devotion, with the
strength of your love, unbending and mighty as a
mountain torrent ! "

I asked Renata:

" Notwithstanding this, you sent me to almost certain
death ? You forbade me to touch Heinrich and commanded me to offer my breast to his thrust ! He came
near to plunging it into my very heart ! "

Renata replied:

" That was the final trial, the Trial of God. Do you
remember that I was praying while you were on your
way to combat? I was asking the Lord whether He willed
that I should love you. If it were His will, He could
preserve your life even before the blade of an adversary.
And I also desired to test your love for the last time—
would it dare to look—eye to eye—at death ? And, had

you perished, know that, that very day, I should have
locked myself away in a convent cell, for I could not
have borne further to live—were it not by your side!"

I do not know how much truth there was in the words
of Renata! I am well prepared to admit that she did
not relate the whole of the matter as it had been in the
past, but as she now represented it to herself; however,
at that time I had no opportunity of judging the value
of her words, for I had barely the strength to drink them
in as a wilting flower drinks in the moisture of the rain.
I was like a pauper, who for many long years has
fruitlessly begged pitiful coppers on the church porch,
and before whom suddenly open all the riches of the
Lydian Crœsus, offering him to take gold, diamonds
and sapphires by handfuls. I, who had listened with a
face of stone to all the cruellest reproaches of Renata,
could not find strength in me now to bear her tenderness,
and often it was not her cheeks but mine that were now
moist with tears.

A painful sweetness was imparted to our intimacy
by the fact that my wound made it for many a day
impossible for us to give ourselves up to our passion in
full measure. At first I had barely strength enough to
approach, raising my head, my lips to Renata's lips,
as if to a burning coal, and, bereft of power by such an
effort, I would then fall back breathless into the pillows.
Later, when I could already sit up in bed, Renata had,
with meek insistence, to restrain me from mad enthusiasm, for I desired, taking her in my arms, to press her,
kiss her and caress her, and make her live through all
the tremors of the joy of love. But true, at the very
first attempt to trust myself to the hurricane of passion,
my forces betrayed me, blood oozed through my band-
ages, before my eyes began to whirl single-hued rings,
in my ears to whistle a monotoned wind, my hands
dropped, and Renata, smiling and forgiving, put me
into bed like a child and whispered to me:

"Precious, dearest! Please don't! We have the

whole of life before us yet! We have the whole of life before us yet!"

About the end of the first December week, I was at last sufficiently recovered to wander weakly round the room and, seated in the large armchair, I fingered with my thin hands the volumes of the magic works, now abandoned by us. Simultaneously with my recovery, the stream of our lives began to pour into a more familiar channel, as our visitors one by one disappeared: first Lucian Stein, who had nothing more to inquire after, then the black doctor, to whom I myself showed the door, and finally the good Matthew, who got on very badly with Renata. Around us there began to form a solitude to which we were used, but how different did it seem to me from that in which I had been plunged heretofore! One might have believed that above me was a new sky, and new stars, and that all the surrounding objects had been transformed by some magic power—so unlike was it all to the past I had lived through within these same walls, that formerly had oppressed me like an unrelenting nightmare!

And now, when I recall this December, that I lived through with Renata, like a newly-married couple, I am willing to go down upon my knees and give thanks to the Creator, if it came about by His will, for the moments I was permitted to experience. And during these days only one thought insistently occupied and tormented me: that my life had reached its peak, and that thereafter there must inevitably begin a descent into a depth, that I, like Phaeton, the driver of the chariot of the Sun, was now borne to the zenith, and being unable to check my father's steeds, must soon be hurled ignominiously along the steep decline back to earth. With agonising haste I strove with all my being to inhale the bliss of the heights, and wildly said to Renata that the most reasonable course for me would be to die, so that, happy and a conqueror, I might leave this life in which otherwise there undoubtedly still lay in wait for me, not for the first time, tragic masques of sorrow and defeat.

But Renata replied to all these speeches of mine:
" How unaccustomed you are to happiness! Believe me, dearest, we are only at the doors of it, we have not yet traversed the entrance hall. I have led you through the catacombs of torment, and I will lead you through the palaces of bliss. Only stay with me, only love me—and together we shall rise higher and higher! It is I who made you so aghast, but I want you to forget all that, I want to repay each moment of suffering with days, whole days of happiness; for you, by your love, have already repaid me for a whole lifetime of despair and ruin!"

As she said this, Renata assumed the air of one who all her life had been nourished upon happiness, as the birds of paradise are nourished upon air.

And just as she knew no limits in expressing her despair, so Renata knew no limits in the expression of her love. I was by no means a novice in sailing the ocean of sensuality in the galley with the banner of the goddess Venus at the masthead, but it was the first time I had encountered such a greed for passion, a greed before which all caresses seemed too weak, all unions too imperfect, all joys insufficient to fill the measure of desire. Moreover, as if eager to recompense me for the cruelty with which she had previously treated my love, Renata now sought to achieve, in passion, meekness and humility. I had to use no little opposition to prevent her from kissing my feet, as the Magdalen did those of Christ, and to restrain her almost by force from a great deal of which I cannot trust even a hint to this manuscript.

Our honeymoon lasted for about two weeks, a time during which my strength nearly returned to me, and, with it, that sober outlook innate in me, that I value more than any other of my abilities. At the same time, there passed in me also that tautness of all my feelings, in

which I had so long been held by the indefiniteness of my
relations with Renata, by our continuous searching for
something, our unremitting expectation of something,
and I began to feel as though a long drawn bow had
at last been discharged in my soul, and the arrow sped
to its mark. Naturally, even in the first days of our
unexpected intimacy, when Renata desired to transform
our lives, as it appeared, into the realised delirium of
two maniacs, I did not altogether lose my head and,
through all the frenzy of mutual oaths, avowals of love,
and caresses, following one another in an uninterrupted
chain, I was yet aware of stern reality, like the light
of day through thickly-growing lianas, and did not forget, even for a single hour, that we were only pilgrims
on an enchanted island. And when my being had at
last been satiated with unaccustomed, and by it forgotten joys, when the black and flaming nightmare of the
months of torture had been completely screened behind
the roseate veil of the present, I could not refrain
from thinking, soberly and clearly, about the future.

I was chiefly urged to do so by the knowledge that
of the money I had gathered beyond the Ocean, there
was left barely half, and that too was melting fairly
rapidly. Second, apart from the necessity to consider
earning money, I was visibly affected by my many
months of idleness, and often dreamed of business and
affairs, as noble joys. Lastly, I had never lost the
conviction that all thinking men arrive at in mature
judgment, that one cannot bale out one's life with
personal pleasures alone, any more than one can bale
out the sea with the tankards of a festive banquet.
True, in order to work it was necessary that our future
course should first definitely be decided, but I firmly
recollected that, in the days when she had still concealed her love under the mask of severity, Renata had
given agreement to be my wife, and I could not doubt
that she would consent now, when she had revealed
its face.

Choosing an appropriate hour, I said to Renata :

" Dearest mine, you know well enough from what I have told you that we cannot indefinitely lead together a care-free existence like the present, and I must, without question, devote myself to affairs of some kind. I should prefer a business of which I have long thought ; trading with the heathen in New Spain. And so to-day, Renata, now that you have given me many thousands of proofs of your affection, I repeat to you my prayer, that heretofore I have hardly dared to voice : that you become my wife, for I desire my sweetheart to be able to look without confusion into the eyes of all women. If you will now repeat once more your ' yes,' we shall repair straightway together to my native Losheim, and I am sure that my parents will not refuse us their blessing—otherwise, we shall do without it, for I have already long hewed my own way through the wilderness of life. And so, husband and wife, we shall set sail for the New World, to realise there those years of light and bliss you have foretold to me."

To my surprise, this offer, which I still believe to have been reasonable and natural, produced on Renata the worst possible impression, and there fell at once upon her face, as it were the shadow of some past swooping wing. I should mention, in this connection, that this shadow invariably darkened her face whenever I spoke of my parents and my home ; she herself never, not even in the moments of nearest intimacy of two passionately fond, mentioned to me anything of her own father and mother or her native lands. And then, with puckered brows, she answered me as follows :

" Dearest Rupprecht, I promised you to be your wife, if you killed Heinrich. This did not come to pass, perhaps by my fault, but thus I am not bound by that oath. Let us wait, therefore, to speak of the future. Can you not accept happiness without any foreign thought, take it as you would take a glass of wine, and drain it to the dregs ? When it becomes necessary to worry about the cares of life, then we too can take heed, and believe me, in me you will find a courageous helpmate. But now I give you all my love, and of you I ask only one thing : let your arms be strong enough to receive it to the full ! "

Having delivered this unexpected and unjust reply, Renata pressed herself tenderly against me, and tried to transport me into the garden of caresses, but, of course, she did not thereby dispel my doubts and, however strange it may be, this conversation proved to be the definite break in the flow of events, and that day must be regarded as the last day of our honeymoon. I could not but ascribe the failure of my offer to some secret cause, and my passionate feeling towards Renata somehow straightway became dimmed, and at the bottom of my soul began to gather an indefinite dissatisfaction, drop by drop, like a growing pillar in a cavern of stalactites. Simultaneously, like mice from the hat of a conjurer, there suddenly began to spread out fanwise through our life all kinds of misunderstandings, at times stupid and unworthy of us.

Came then the festival of the Holy Birth of Christ, and Renata, with the usual capriciousness of her fancies, desired by all means to spend it gaily, and amongst others. She suddenly required acquaintances, sights and a variety of songs, and I, remembering with what application Renata had previously immersed herself in Latin texts, was only puzzled to see with what childish simplicity she gave herself up to the various pleasures of the streets.

First of all, of course, we had to visit all the church services. On the night of the Eve of the Birth, we admired, in the Church of Saint Cecilia, the representation of the holy cradle with the kings kneeling before it, which reminded me vividly of the days of my childhood ; we did not miss Mass on the day of John the Evangelist, or on that of the Forty Thousand Innocents, or on the day of the Lord's Circumcision; and we walked

the city with all the church processions. Then it pleased
Renata to receive in our rooms children who came to
praise Christ with a manger made of little planks, to
listen to their singing, talk to them and give them sweet-
meats. Further, Renata led me through all the booths
built along the quay and on the market, in which were
displayed various curios, and only laughed when I
reminded her of her former saying regarding the un-
bearableness of the street crowds. And we spent whole
days amongst drunken and coarse yokels, watching
players on bandores and on bagpipes, acrobats walking
on their heads, conjurers who produced live snakes
from their nostrils, sword-swallowers and men who
released fountains from their mouths, women with
beards, ichneumons, rhinoceroses, dromedaries, and
other rarities by means of which the travelling men
contrive to rid the burghers of their hard-earned
coppers.

And lastly, to my surprise, there appeared in our
house two women, apparently of burgherly station,
whom Renata named as Katherina and Margarita,
and whom she introduced to me as neighbours of ours
and her acquaintances of long standing. The women
looked to me dense and uninteresting, and I could
never understand why they were supposed to be
necessary in our midst, after we two had so rejoiced
at having refound our solitude. Having spent a very
dull hour in conversation with the two visitors on the
relative merits of the paters of the various parishes, I
began thereafter to speak out rather bitterly to Renata
about this new acquaintanceship, and this served as
cause for our first quarrel. Renata replied to me with
unexpected hotness, I could not demand, could I, that
she should see nobody in the world, and asked whether,
in asking her to accompany me to the New World, I
had the intention on arriving there of locking her up
within four walls. I did not scruple to point out to
Renata how unreasonable were her words, but she had

no desire to listen to anything and, pouring out reproaches on me, threatened to walk out of the house,
on the spot, as she would out of a prison.

True, having exchanged these very cruel words like
sword thrusts, after a few minutes we both saw the
stupidity of our quarrel, and hastened to blow out the
flame of discord with the fierce wind of oaths and confessions, and pour over it the moisture of kisses and
caresses—but under the ashes there still lay glowing
coals. Some two days after this occurrence, Renata
suddenly declared to me that she intended to visit one
of the two neighbours during the afternoon hour, and
that I too was expected at this gathering. I replied
with indignation that I had no desire to pursue this
stupid acquaintanceship, and when Renata, none the
less, prepared herself for company and left the house,
to spite her I went to Matthew, whom I had been
wanting to visit for some time—and that was the first
time after my illness that I parted from Renata.

Matthew greeted me grumblingly but good-naturedly,
and Agnes, who, to judge by everything, was now
advised of the existence of Renata in my life—timidly
and cautiously. I tried to break the ice that covered
my relationship with Agnes, and entertained her for
some time with stories of New Spain, with which I
invariably produce an impression on all new acquaintances, again narrating of the temples of the Maya, and
the huge cacti, and the perilous hunts of the bear and
the ounce. We parted friends again, and when, on
my return home, I heard from Renata sly words about
some youth, the son of a merchant, who had shown her
especial attention at the house of the neighbour, I
hastened for my part to tell of Agnes, who had attracted
my attention in the house of Matthew. This new duel
of ours, in which the blades each endeavoured to prick
the jealousy of the adversary, ended in my favour, for
Renata, at first making believe to despise my confessions, soon changed over to plaintive reproaches,

219

and then was even unable to restrain her tears, so
that, comforting her, I had to swear that I felt no
inclination towards Agnes, while she confessed to me
that the son of the merchant had existed only in her
imagination.

This did not, however, prevent Renata from declaring
to me a few days later that she had accepted another
invitation from the neighbour, to which I replied
with a new visit to Matthew. And as these tourneys
had more such repetitions, I soon became a really
frequent visitor to the Wissmanns, and leaving Matthew
to his learned books, began to spend long hours with
Agnes. I liked very much this creature soft and mild,
a maiden with whom it was good to talk of anything
in the world, for everything was new to her, and she
believed it all with the trustfulness of a child. And,
in her own mind, grandmother's tales were fancifully
intermingled with university wisdom, with which her
brother had been accustomed to tease her common-
sense, and this brought her to the most absurd and
entertaining ideas and conclusions, with which I
delighted to amuse myself, as children play with toys.
Agnes asked me quite seriously whether it were
correct that on the faces of men is written in Latin
characters HOMO DEI, and that the two eyes are the two
letters O, the nose the letter M and so forth ;—that
Jesus Christ was crucified in the very centre of the
earth, for Jerusalem is the centre of the cosmos as the
heart is the centre of a body ;—that there are as many
kinds of plants on earth as there are stars in Heaven,
for the various kinds of plants appeared in obedience
to the stars at the union of cosmic matters ;—that
the emerald has been taken unto herself by the Most
Holy Virgin, and that that stone shatters of itself into
smithereens if near it is committed the sin of love—
and much more of this kind.

I must, however, declare here and now, and with all
definiteness, that in my relations with Agnes there was

nothing resembling even the inception of love, though, of course, the proximity of a tender and youthful maiden was sweet to me; as if completing the passion and experience of Renata. But I must also confess that, in truth, in those days, I did not find in the depth of my soul either that unquestioning loyalty which had first given me, swordless and armourless, into the hands of Renata, nor that intoxicating passion which had held me in its chains of roses in the first days of intimacy after my illness. There came the natural collapse of that wave of emotions, that had swelled for many months, raised its crest to the highest in our honeyed days, and scattered at last in impotent foam. My passion, having overwhelmed me for two weeks with a flood of bliss, recoiled as if in an ebbing tide from the shores of the soul, stripping the bottom, and leaving on the sand, sea-stars, cockles and seaweed.

I knew, if not consciously, by instinct, that the hour of a new rising tide would come, and therefore I continued to repeat to Renata the old words of love and to swear that I was as true to her as I was before. Many times, too, I repeated my prayer—that she should agree to our marriage and that we should leave the City of Köln, where we had endured so much and where it would be difficult to set our lives on a new course. But the change that had occurred in me could not be concealed from Renata's sharp sight. She asked me bitterly, whether it were not because she had admitted her passion for me and given me the proofs of her flame that I had cooled towards her. And to my pleading she answered that she yet loved me overmuch and not for anything in the world would she, as now, see the face on which she was accustomed to read torment for her, or happiness through her, unmoved and bored.

In this time of our shallowed love, Renata and I would not see each other for whole days, then again would fall upon each other in a gust of flaming-up desire, then would drop once more into abysms of enmity and anger. In the hours of quarrel, Renata would sometimes attain to extremest rage, and at times reproach me with things it is perhaps better even not to remember, then threaten that she would cut my throat in dead of night, or lie in wait for Agnes in the street, to slay her, then once more she would expend herself in tears, fall upon the floor and give herself up on my account to just such a paroxysm of despair as before for Count Heinrich. In contrast, on the days of reconciliation all the ecstasies of two happy lovers would be revived: once more we would be like Antonius and Cleopatra in their Egypt, or like Tristan and the beautiful Iseult in their cave, and our recent discords would seem to us but an absurd misunderstanding, caused by the pranks of the wicked house demons, those whom Renata herself called the " tiny ones."

There can be no argument that all these continuous alternations of joy and torture wearied me more than the former pains of love refused, and my longing for a life peaceful and occupied in work ever increased, like a slowly-brooding storm. But we had still some time to wait before the first lightning flashes, for Renata still preserved her sway over my soul, which, after a short excommunication, once more cleaved towards her, to her glance and to her kiss, as the root under the earth cleaves towards moisture. However, in the being of Renata herself there was a something that did not permit of a slow march of events and, carried away by a new inner upheaval towards a new road of thoughts and emotions, she suddenly turned herself, and the whole of our life, on to another tack.

Chapter the Tenth

How Renata left me

ONE evening, which I had spent, as usual, with dear Agnes, I returned home rather late, so that I had to obtain the right of way from the night-watchman with small presents. Approaching our house, I distinguished in the darkness someone sitting in the porch like a cat, and soon saw that it was Martha. She rushed to meet me, and related, not without simple horror, that something unexpected and terrifying had happened to-day to Mistress Renata, and that she, Martha, was afraid lest it might not be the interference of some unclean power. From the detailed description I soon gathered that Renata had been victim of another of those fits of possession, that I had already had opportunity to witness, when the spirit that was entered within her body cruelly tortured and insulted her. And now I remembered that Renata had been especially sad and restless during the last few days, to which I, however, had reacted with a disregard at once light-hearted and ignoble.

At this moment my feeling was as if someone had pricked me in the heart, and the stream of my love for Renata had suddenly burst in my soul into a flood strong and full. I hurried upstairs, already imagining to myself in every detail how I should plead for pardon and forgiveness from Renata, and kiss her hands and listen to her tender answering words. I found Renata in bed, where, as always after a seizure, she lay exhausted almost to death, and her face, feebly lit by a candle, was like a white wax mask. Seeing me, she

did not smile, rejoice or make a single movement that
would manifest emotion.

I kneeled at her bedside and began to speak thus :
" Renata, forgive me ! All this time I have been
behaving unpardonably. I am cruelly guilty in that I
left you. I do not know how or why I did so. But it
shall never be again, I swear to you."

Renata stopped my speech and said in a voice soft,
but clear and decisive :

" Rupprecht, it is I who must speak now, and you
who must listen. To-day there has happened to me
something so important that I cannot encompass it
within my reason. To-day my life was severed in two,
and that which awaits me in the future will not resemble
that which has been in the past."

After this solemn exordium, Renata, turning to me
her pale and serious face, related to me the following :

During the last week, when I had paid little attention
to Renata, she had suffered much from solitude and
wept for whole days, carefully concealing the fact
from me. But, when a person is in weariness, he
becomes defenceless against the assault of inimical
demons, and so the long-standing enemy of Renata,
who had persecuted her ever since the castle of Count
Heinrich, had once more vanquished her, entered into
her, and, torturing her, felled her to the floor. However, as she lay, prostrate and scarcely aware of anything, suddenly there rose before her a brilliant radiance,
and in it appeared the image of the fiery angel, whom
she had not seen since the very days of her childhood.
Renata at once recognised her Madiël, for he was now
as he had ever been : his face shone, his eyes were blue
as the skies, his hair as if of threads of gold, his robe
as if spun from flaming yarn. An inexpressible ecstasy
seized Renata, like that which possessed the apostles
on Mount Tabor in the hour of the Transfiguration
of our Lord, but Madiël's face was stern, and speaking,
he said thus :

224

The Fiery Angel

" Renata ! From that selfsame day on which you, succumbing to the temptations of the flesh, desired by deceit and cunning to bend me to passion, I left you, and whenever after you imagined that you saw me, it was not I you saw. And that Count Heinrich, in whom you supposed you recognised my incarnation, was sent to you by none other than the Tempter, to seduce and kill your soul utterly. In the gardens of bliss, before the face of the One in Whose Hands is All, where soar the angels, oft-times and many did I shed tears of sorrow at seeing you perish and beholding the evil triumph of the enemies of you and ourselves. Oft-times and many did I raise, like the smoke of an incense-burner, my voice in prayer to the All Highest, that He might grant me to put my hand on your shoulder and withhold you from the abyss, but ever the Voice restrained me, saying : ' She must yet cross, even this step.' Now it is given unto me, at last, to reveal to you all the truth, and know, that heavy are your sinnings on the scales of Justice, and your soul is already half submerged into the fires of Hell. Not of the crown of Saint Amalia of Löthringen does it behove you to dream now, but only of a crown of martyrdom, with blood washing away the uncleanness of your crimes ! Sister of mine beloved ! Prostrate yourself in horror, repent, pray unceasingly unto the Lord, and it will be permitted to me again to protect and fortify you ! "

While Madiël was speaking all his words were revealed to Renata in vivid pictures. Thus she saw—first the gardens of Paradise in which the angels sing hymns to the Creator, and fly up like birds, forming in their flight the mystic letters, D, J, L; then the steps of a staircase, portraying to her her earthly life, as she descended it amidst serpents, basilisks, dragons and other monsters ; then herself submerged waist-deep in the fire of Hell, and the devils dancing round in jollification. And when Madiël ended his speech of wrath, Renata was in the last despair, and it seemed as

225

if the breath of life were leaving her. Then, seeing his companion in this terrible state, Madiël suddenly changed, his face assumed an expression mild and tender, and he became like an affectionate elder brother, as he had been in the days when he played with her as a child ; approaching, he bent over the swooning Renata, and tenderly kissed her on the lips, fanning her with a sweet and not burning fieriness. With a cry of joy, Renata desired to embrace him, but her outstretched arms encountered only old Martha, who had run in attracted by the noise of her fall and her pitiful moans.

This was what Renata related to me, leaving me, as ever after her confessions, in doubt : what part in her words was reality, and what part the vision of her delirium or the invention of her mind, fatally inclined to lying. That day I took care only to comfort and quieten the ailing one, persuading her not to think as yet about what had happened, and trying to console her with the promise of better days in which I should consecrate to her all my hours and all my minutes. But Renata only shook her head to all my words, or smiled indulgently, as a mother smiles to her child when it tries to cheer her weariness away with its toys. Lulled by my tender words, however, she soon fell asleep, into the sleep of one tired and tormented, and I fell asleep near her, as in the old days, before we were yet intimate.

That same night, however, I was able to convince myself that Renata had not spoken light-heartedly when she spoke of a severance of her life in two : at the first streaks of dawn, Renata woke me, and her face was strangely solemn as she asked me to help her rise and escort her to early Mass. I obeyed, involuntarily awed by the sternness of her voice and the silence of the morning hour, and Renata, dressing hastily, made me take her, though she was so weak that she could hardly step, to the Church of Saint Cecilia. There,

falling at a prie-dieu, in the bluish twilight of the
temple, Renata prayed insatiably and shed copious
tears until the very end of the service, like the last of
sinners, seeking liberation from her sins. And, as I
watched her zeal, I began to understand that there had
taken place in Renata not a temporary change, but
some great upheaval, that had transformed all her
thoughts, feelings, and desires with lasting effect, as
if it had rebuilt on a new plan all her being.

In truth, from now onwards began an entirely new
life for Renata, and for me together with her, and at
times I felt that, even if it had been possible to have
found a unity in all the various aspects of Renata which
she had previously shown me, yet her new image was
that of quite another woman. Not only did Renata
express quite other ideas than before, not only did
she begin to lead an entirely new mode of life, but I
could scarcely recognise her very manner of speech,
acts, mode of behaviour toward people ; the sound of
her voice itself, her walk, even perhaps her face hardly
seemed familiar to me. But when I reminded myself
of what Renata had told me of her childhood, how
she had spent whole nights in prayer, how she had
gone out naked into the frost, how she had flagellated
herself and torn her breasts with sharp points ; or,
also, of those words she had said to me on the barge
when we were voyaging together towards Köln : " We
should all of us feel horrified and, like a stag from the
huntsman, flee into a monastic cell "—I then realised
that all this had actually been in Renata before, but
only hidden, like a body beneath chance garments.

In order to depict, even if only in a very general
way, this last period of our life together, I must say
first of all that Renata instilled into her repentance
that same fierceness that she had first into her sorrow
and, later, into her passion. On one of the first days
following her vision she desired to go to confession
and, however strongly I warned her of the dangers to

which it might lead, she actually fulfilled her intention
in our parish church. I do not know whether Renata
did frankly confess all her sins before our parish pater,
sins the least of which, had it been made publicly known,
would have led her to the stake as a witch, but, in any
case, on returning home, overcome and all in tears, she
told me of the *epithimia* that had been imposed on
her. And from that day forth, she fulfilled it, never
missing a morning without being present at a Mass,
greeting each church with a prayer, praying till exhaustion each evening at the prie-dieu, keeping all the
fasts prescribed for the faithful, on Wednesdays, Fridays
and Saturdays, and at times she would even fly out
of bed at night in order, wringing her hands and weeping bitterly, to implore absolution from her sins.
Unsatisfied with the penances suggested to her, Renata
thirsted to reinforce her exploits, to express still more
fully her repentance, and perhaps thereby to supplicate
a more rapid pardon for herself. More than once I
had to restrain her as she furiously beat her head
against the floor, more than once I had to raise her,
unconscious from the fatigue of her prayers, and once
I tore away from her a dagger with which she had
already traced upon her breasts a bloody cross. At
such moments, Renata's face was always happy and
child-like, and she begged me humbly :

" Rupprecht, leave me, I am happy, I am happy ! "
In these first days of her penitence, Renata was calm
and kind to me, as a sister to a brother in a Brigittian
monastery, not replying sharply to me, obeying me in
small matters, but in the substantial firmly holding to
her road. But of course Renata had renounced all the
temptations of passion, and she did not allow me even
to touch her, speaking of earthly love with that same
coldness as would a scholastic like Vincent of Beauvais.
Insistently, Renata pleaded with me to join her in
her repentance, begging me on her knees and with
tears like some good sister, or exhorting me with

228

threats like a preacher—but in my soul, where Iacob Wimpfeling had flung his seed, these appeals could find no echo. All my life I have preserved in the depths of my heart a live faith in my Creator, the Defender of the World, in His Sanctifying Grace and in the expiatory sacrifice of Christ our Saviour, but never have I agreed that true religion demands outward manifestations. If the Lord God has given into the possession of mankind the earth, where only by struggle and toil can we fulfil our duty, and where only passionate feelings can bring true joy—then, in His Justice, He cannot demand that we renounce toil, struggle and passion. And, besides, the example of the monks, those true wolves in sheep's clothing, who have long since become a broad target pierced by all the arrows of satire, shows sufficiently how little a life of idleness and dependence may approach to saintliness, though it be conducted in the proximity of altars and the presence of daily Masses.

However, the sincerity and abandon with which Renata gave herself up to her repentance revived in me my feeling for her to such an extent that, during a week, or perhaps even for a whole ten days, I made belief that I also experienced what she did, for I desired so much not to be parted from her, to share with her her every minute. Together with Renata I visited the churches; again, leaning against a pillar, did I watch her bent over her prayer book; listened to the rhythmic swelling of the organ and dreamed hopelessly that it was the Mexican forests that rustled around us. I also did not refuse Renata when she called on me to pray with her, affectionately made me kneel by her side, and tenderly begged me to repeat after her the words of psalms and canticles. I yielded myself wholly to Renata's will, and when she desired to repent all that she had committed in her life, then, kneeling before me and pouring out her tears, for whole hours she would curse herself and her acts, relating to me of her shameful past, and appearing to me to find especial sweetness therein in accusing herself of the darkest crimes, of which she had never been guilty, in piling upon herself the most shameful untruths.

In these stories, she depicted her life with Count Heinrich as having been a complete horror, for she now declared that the secret society of which Heinrich had dreamed of being Grand Master was a society of the very lowest magi, which celebrated the Black Mass and prepared witches' brews. According to Renata's words it was in those very days that the ways to the Sabbath and the secrets of magic had been shown to her, so that she had only been pretending when she had made belief to be learning them with me. But even of our own life together, with no less emotion, did Renata relate such things as I could on no account believe, and which showed the events I had experienced personally as though reflected in a crooked mirror. Thus Renata assured me that, before meeting me, she had had no other desire than to shut herself up in a nunnery. But then some voice, belonging most certainly to the Enemy of Mankind, had spoken in her ear, saying, that the demons would give her back Heinrich, if, in his stead, she would help them to catch some other soul in their nets. After that, our whole life, it seemed, had consisted only in Renata using lies and hypocrisy that she might drag me into deadly sin, despising no form of deceit. If Renata were to be believed, one would have to suppose that she had played the part of the knocking demons herself, to tempt me into the sphere of demonomancy, that my visions of the Sabbath were those she had inspired in me, that Iohann Weier had been right in asserting that it had been Renata who had smashed the lamps at our experiment in magic, and so forth.

Meanwhile, Renata demanded firmly that all the magic books still lying about on the lectern in her room should either be destroyed or thrown away, and however much I protested against such an undeserved execution of the books of Agrippa of Nettesheim, Peter of Apponia, Rogerius Bacon, Anselm of Parma and others, she remained unbending. Taking away the pile of tomes, I hid them in the far corner of my room, for I should have considered it sacrilege to behave like that Pope who burned Titus Livius, and raise my hand against a book, the highest treasure of mankind. But, in place of the tomes which had vanished from Renata's desk, there soon appeared others, just as excellently bound in parchment and with no less glittering clasps, and perchance with a content that differed from theirs no more than an apple from a pear, for they too treated of demons and spirits. And, as the majority of these new compositions towards which the thirsty soul of Renata now strove were written in Latin, I had once again to be interpreter, and there repeated themselves for me and Renata those hours of joint study, during which, seated side by side at the desk and together bending over the pages, we had explored together the words of the writers.

It was once more my task to procure the books, so that I resumed my visits to Jacob Glock and once more became a digger in his rich mines; but Renata sharply forbade me to bring the works of Martin Luther and all his henchmen and imitators, and I would on no account allow upon our desk even one book by "the Obscure Men" by some Pfefferkorn or Hochstraten, so that, excluding all the contemporary literature of both warring camps, I had to limit my choice to the theologians of an older cut, to the treatises of the old and new scholastics. However, the first we chanced upon was that noble and interesting book by Thomas à Kempis "On the Imitation of Christ"; but then followed immediately various "Handbooks of the Exposition of Faith"; an "*Enchiridion*" on which was marked: "*eyn Handbuchlein eynem yetzlichen Christenfast nutzlich bey sich zuhaben*"

further, books such as "*Die Hijmelstrasse*" of
Lanzkranna or "Of Prayer" by Leander of Seville;
tempting by their titles and far-famed, but their fame
not deserving of treatises; and still further—the lives
of the saints, such as: Bernard of Clairvaux, Norbert
of Magdeburg, Franciscus of Assisi, Elisabeth of
Thuringen, Catherine of Sienna and others; and,
lastly, the works of the two suns of this particular
sphere—two folios, one slightly smaller and the other
disproportionately large, for which I did not grudge
my thalers, but through which we only made slow
progress: the works of the seraphic doctor Iohann
Bonaventura, the "*Itinerium mentis*," in places not
devoid of entrancement, and that of the universal
doctor Thomas Aquinas, the "*Summa Theologiæ*,"
a book of quite dead learnedness, incapable of being
brought to life.

Renata clutched at one work after another as at an
anchor of salvation, and hurried me on now to translate
for her a page from the lives of the saints, now to explain
a theological dispute, admiring the miracles described,
terrorised by the threats of hell tortures, and, with a
simplicity not characteristic of her, accepting as gospel
every incongruous invention of the scholastic doctors.

I cannot now remember the sum total of the extrava-
gances and incongruities that it was our lot to read in
these diligent studies, worthy of a more prudent application, but I will give here a few examples of the stories
that shook Renata with especial force, causing tears
to appear on her eyelashes. For example, Renata
read with real horror the description of Hell in Thomas
Aquinas, more detailed than that of the poet Dante
Alighieri, with an exact distribution of where the various
sinners will be housed and to what tortures they will
be submitted: the forefathers who died before the
advent of Christ, children who died before baptism,
thieves, murderers, adulterers, and blasphemers.
Touched, and with becoming sighs, Renata listened

to the enumeration of the number of lashes received by the Saviour after His betrayal, and it appeared that there were 1,667 lashings with whips, 800 slappings with hands, of which 110 were definitely buffets on the ear; and it was stated also that He shed 62,200 tears on the Mount of Olives and that the drops of His bloody sweat amounted to 87,307; that the crown of thorns inflicted on His immaculate forehead 303 wounds, that He emitted 900 moans and sighs, and so forth. Deeply affected was Renata by the story of how the Mother of God appeared to Saint Catherine of Sienna, and led her to Her Son, who then gave to the saint a ring set with a diamond and four pearls in token of betrothal, to the sound of a harp played by King David; or of how Christ Himself appeared to Saint Iutta at Thüringen, suffered her to press her lips to His pierced rib and to suck His immaculate blood. No less seriously did Renata accept the story of how, as it appears, from the grave of Saint Adalbert in Bohemia, when it was opened by the Bishop of Prague, there flew so strengthening an aroma that all those present required no food for three days after, and of how, so it was said, in a Cistercian convent in France the saintliness of life was so high that, by a special benediction of God, in order not to have to introduce anyone into the convent from without, and yet continue its population, each nun, without knowing a husband, contrived to bear a girl who should be her successor. I do not know whether faith always wars with reason, and whether it be true that the study of theology softens the brain, but as I watched how trustfully listened to these stories Renata, who in other days knew how to use logic, I could only repeat to myself the words of Saint Bernard of Clairvaux: " all the sins derive from the sin of disbelief."

As far as I was concerned, these scholastic mumblings only amused me as a novelty for the first few days, for all theological compositions have one bad peculiarity:

they are all very similar to one another—so that soon these hours of reading with Renata became an unpleasant duty to me. Equally too, my feeling for Renata, which had suddenly revived under the influence of her vision, began to die down again, like a ball that someone pushes suddenly, but which nevertheless cannot roll freely along a stony path. And very soon the monastic mode of life that Renata had introduced into our house with prayers, genuflexions, sighs and fastings began to seem like some incongruous masque. I began to avoid escorting Renata to church, made various pretexts to leave the house during those hours when we should have undertaken our readings, sharply interrupted the pious discourses, and at nights, when I heard the strangled weepings of Renata I did not hasten to her side. And then came a day when I could not, and had no desire to, master my impulse to return to Agnes, as if to the clear air above green pastures, after the blue and flaming rays that shine criss-cross into cathedrals through stained-glass windows.

That day, though I had no means of foreseeing the fact, if it did not determine, at least foretold our fate. Renata had then been at the Cathedral since the morning, and, having waited for her till noon, suddenly and almost unexpectedly to myself, I walked out into the street, turned my steps not without embarrassment to the well-known house of the Wissmans and knocked at the door like one deeply guilty. Agnes received me with unaltered kindness, and said to me only:

" You have not been with us for so long, Master Rupprecht, I began to think something unpleasant must have happened to you again. My brother forbade me to question you, saying that you might have reasons it is not for an honest maiden to know—is that true ? "

I replied :

" Your brother was joking at your expense. It was simply that unhappy days came into my life, and I did

not wish to sadden you with the sight of my face full of
sorrow. But to-day I felt too gloomy, and have come
to be silent with you, and to hear your voice."

I really was silent nearly all the time I spent with
Agnes, but she, soon getting used to me again, chirruped
like a swallow under the eaves, about all the petty
gossip of the last few days : of the demise of a neighbour's lap dog, of a comical incident at Mass on Sunday,
of a professional carouse that had taken place recently
at her brother's, of some remarkable silk shot with three
colours sent to her from France, of a great many other
matters that made me smile. Agnes' speech flowed like
a rivulet in a wood, it was easy for her to talk, for all
the impressions of life she described and all the words
she said glided through her without touching anything
within her, and for me it was easy to listen, for I had
neither to be attentive nor to think, but could just drop
the reins of my soul, which so often I had to pull taut.
Again, as always, I departed from Agnes refreshed, as
though by a light breeze from the sea, comforted, as
though by long contemplation of a yellow cornfield set
with blue cornflowers.

At home I found Renata at her books, carefully
studying some sermon of Bertold of Regensburg,
written in a difficult and antiquated style. The stern,
concentrated face of Renata, her calm, cold glance,
her meek, restrained voice—all this was such a contrast
to the childlike carefreedom of Agnes, that my heart
felt as if clutched by a pincers. And then, suddenly,
with extreme invincibility, I desired the old Renata,
the Renata of so little while ago, her passionate eyes,
her frantic movements, her unrestrained caresses, her
tender words—and the desire was so acute, I was ready
to sacrifice my all to satisfy it. At this moment, without
hesitation, I would have given my whole future life
for one instant of caress, the more so since it seemed to
me unattainable.

I rushed to Renata and, kneeling before her, as in

the good time that was gone, I began to kiss her hands and tell her how fathomless was my love, how mortally I had suffered all these days from her stern inaccessibility. I said that, from the darkness of Hell, I had almost entered into the radiance of Eden, that, like Adam, I had not known how to use my blissfulness, and that now I was standing at the gates of Paradise and a guard with a flaming sword was barring my return—that I was ready to die straightway, if only once more it might be given to me to inhale the aroma of Eden's lilies. I knew, even at that very moment, that I was telling falsehoods, that I was repeating words true once but no longer, but a lie was the high price with which I hoped to buy a loving glance and tender touch from Renata. I did not even stop at other, yet more ignoble means of temptation, trying to cloud Renata's consciousness, trying to wake in her once more a feeling of sensuality, for her passion was necessary to me at all costs.

I do not know whether it was the art of my speech that conquered, or whether there was then in me myself so much fire that it could not fail to transfer itself to the being of Renata and set her aflame, or lastly, whether in her herself the violence of passion, forcibly overlain by the stones of reason, burst forth into the open—only was it certain that the Goddess of Love triumphed that evening, and her winged son was able to blow out his night torch. With such fieriness did we press against each other, with such tender fury did we seek to kiss and embrace, that it might have been our first fusion, and in the drunkenness of happiness it seemed to me as though we were not in our familiar room, but somewhere in a desert, amidst wild rocks, in a cave, and the lightnings of the skies and the nymphs of the woods acclaimed our union, as once that of Aeneas and Dido:

fulsere ignes et conscius æther
Connubiis, summoque ulularunt vertice Nymphæ.

And Renata, discarding the stern appearance of a nun, repeated to me these words of caress, that were sweeter to me than the sound of violas and flutes:

"Rupprecht! Rupprecht! I have no other desire, only love me; I want neither bliss, nor Paradise, I want you to be with me, to be mine—and I thine. I love you, Rupprecht!"

But then, when the gust of passion was past, when, as if from some limbo, the walls of our room and all its furnishings began to stand out, and there gradually became visible the books strewn about on the desk, the volume of the sermons of Bertold of Regensburg which had fallen on the floor, and we two, prostrate in exhaustion on the crumpled bed—despair immediately seized Renata. Jumping up she ran to the prie-dieu, flung herself on her knees, whispering a prayer, and then rose again as quickly, and, pale and angry, began to fling reproaches at me:

"Rupprecht! Rupprecht! What have you done! I know this is the only thing you need of me! I know you do not seek or desire anything else of me! But why of me? Go to a brothel—there for little payment you will find women for yourself. Offer yourself to any maiden, and you will easily obtain a wife who will do service with you every night. No, you must be pleased to tempt me, me alone, just because I have given my soul and body to the Lord!"

To this I replied:

"Renata, be merciful and just! Remember that I lived for long months at your side not pressing for your caresses when I thought that you were pledged to another, making then no complaint of your coldness. But how can you desire that I should suffer it in quietness now that I know that you love me, now that I feel the nearness of your love? I do not believe that the caresses of two lovers are displeasing in the sight of the Lord God, and you yourself, only a few moments ago, said that you were ready to sacrifice for them all the bliss of after-life."

But, instead of answering, Renata began to weep, as she always did, without restraint and without consolation, so that in vain did I try to soothe her and comfort her, beseeching her pardon, blaming myself and promising that nothing of the kind that had happened that day would ever be repeated. Not heeding me, Renata wept as if for something lost beyond recovery, as might weep, perhaps, a virginal maiden dishonestly debauched by a seducer, or as maybe wept our fore-mother Eve, when she realised the hypocrisy of the Serpent. And I, seeing these tears and this agony, swore to myself solemn oaths that never again would I succumb to temptation, better I leave Renata, than show myself in her eyes once more as a man seeking coarse delights, for not for these but for tender glances and soft words did I thirst.

However, despite all these promises which I gave to Renata, and to myself, this day served as a pattern for many others, modelled, if of a different clay, yet in the same mould, and moreover with such exactitude that in each of them Agnes occupied her appointed niche. It invariably happened as follows, I would go during the day to Agnes, listen to her soft speeches, gaze at her flaxen tresses, and with my soul quietened like a becalmed sea, return to Renata reminding myself on the way that to-day I must firmly restrain myself. At home we would always begin the reading of some improving composition, while I, mastering my feeling of boredom, strove to penetrate the discourses that aroused the interest of Renata, but, little by little, the nearness of her body would begin to carry me away like some love potion, and, almost without noticing it myself, I would either glue my lips to her hair or press her hand closer to my own. Recalling now these moments, I think that it may not always have been I who made the first movement, but that a feeling similar to mine was felt also by Renata, who likewise was attracted, against her will, to passion, or perhaps the whole may have been influenced by beings invisible and inimical to us In any case, without one single exception, all our readings after the first sinful fall began to end in the same way : with, first of all, furious caress and mutual vows, followed by Renata's despair, her tears and cruel reproaches, and my belated remorse. And the number of images as like to each other as the leaves of one tree increased in our memory each day by one.

Thus our life, as if swirling round the narrowing ring of an eddy, now locked in a very tight circle what formerly it had embraced in a wide round. The first months of my life with Renata we had been strangers to each other ; then, during the two weeks following my duel with Count Heinrich, we had been, on the contrary, as near as only human beings can be. In the period immediately following, and lasting till Renata's vision, these changes of animosity and intimacy had occurred at intervals of several days, and at times we had managed within one week to be both cruel enemies and passionate lovers. And now the same cycle was locked into the shortness of four-and-twenty hours. From the space of morning to evening we contrived each day to ascend the tall staircase from brotherly nearness, through friendly trustfulness, to the most burning, self-forgetful love, and thence, to hatred, sharpened like a dagger. Each day our souls, like blades, first burned to white heat on the forge of passion, then suddenly plunged into icy coldness, and it could easily be foreseen that, unable to withstand such alternations, at the last they must sunder.

I felt myself completely worn out by all my life with Renata, and once more I secretly contemplated leaving her and fleeing to other lands, yet at the same time the thought of losing her and her caresses was so fearful to me that I simply did not dare to imagine myself again alone in the world. And, at this time

also, Renata more and more often found the courage
to say to me, in the hours of our quarrels, that she could
not remain with me, that the Devil inhabited me, to
tempt her, that it were better for her to die of her longing
for me than to commit deadly sins for the sake of
nearness to me, and that the only harbour that was now
a fit place for her was a nunnery. I did not then attach
much importance to these words, but even to me our
life together then seemed a room from which there
was no egress, a room all the doors of which we had
ourselves walled in, and in which we now flung ourselves about, hopelessly beating against its stony limits.

But the catastrophe that was to shatter these limits
into dust, that was to fling us into the depths of other
abysses, on to the points of other sharp rocks, still
approached somehow unnoticed, as if fate crawled
upon us, in a mask and on tip-toe, and seized us both
from behind.

The day remains in my memory perhaps more vividly
than any other day, and therefore I know that it was
the fourteenth day of February precisely, a Sunday,
the day of Saint Valentine. That day I was especially
comforted by the tenderness of Agnes, and Matthew
too was present, all three of us made more than a few
jokes about the signs and customs associated with the
holiday. Returning home, I was once more in a kind
benignant mood, and was saying to myself: " The
soul of Renata has been wounded by all that she has
lived through. She must be given soothing quiet, as
an invalid is given medicine. Who knows, perhaps
after several months of clear and peaceful life, her love
and her repentance will flow together into an even
channel—and then will become possible for us that
happy and busy life as husband and wife, of which,
already, I am beginning to cease to dream."

Armed with such good intentions, I entered Renata's
room and found her as usual amongst her books, poring
over Latin folios, the sense of which she tried in vain

to fathom. She was so interested by the content of the book, which remained dark to her, that she did not hear me as I approached, and, starting, she turned her clear eyes upon me only when I softly kissed her shoulder.

As if having forgotten all her cruel reproaches and plaints of yesterday, Renata said welcomingly to me:

" Rupprecht, how long I have waited for you to-day ! Help me, I can see that this book is of great importance but I understand it ill. There are revelations here which, if we bear them in mind, will restrain us from many evils."

I sat down at Renata's side and saw that it was a book I had only recently unearthed at Glock's, for it had long been out of print : a beautiful volume, printed in the town of Lübeck as late as the last century, under the title " *Sanctæ Brigittæ revelationis ex recensione cardinalis de Turrecremata.*" The book was open at the description of the journey of Saint Brigitta of Sweden across Purgatory, and of the kinds of tortures that she there observed. We immediately began to read of some sinful soul whose head was so tightly strapped by a heavy chain that his eyes, pressed out of their sockets, depended on their roots right down to his very knees, and so that his brain had burst and oozed through his ears and nose ; further on was depicted the tortures of another soul, whose tongue was drawn through his open nostrils and hung down to his teeth ; and yet further followed other forms of various tortures, flaying, complicated whippings, tortures with fire, boiling oil, nails and saws.

I never had the opportunity to read in this book the description of the agonies of Hell proper, but in the description of Purgatory I was interested merely by the power of the untrammelled fantasy, a great deal of which was lost however, owing to the bad exposition of the Cardinal, who was not quite firm in his Latin style. None the less, on Renata the visions of Saint Brigitta made a terrible impression, and, pushing away the fearsome book, she huddled against me, all atremble,

241

evidently visualising to herself all the torments of after death ; which must have opened before her eyes with all the vividness of things seen. With a feeling of genuine terror, like a child left alone in a dark room, she exclaimed at last :

" I'm afraid ! I'm afraid ! And they threaten all of us, every one, you and me also ! Let us go and pray, Rupprecht, and may the Lord grant us life long enough to expiate all our sins ! "

At this moment Renata in her simplicity and timidity was like some tiny baby village girl, whom a travelling monk frightens, hoping with her aid to sell the more *indulgentiæ*, and she was beloved and dear to me as words cannot express. I willingly followed her to the small altar that was in her room, and we kneeled, repeating the holy words : *Placare Christe servulis. . . .* This common prayer, spoken as we stood side by side like two statues in a church, and with our voices mingled like the scent of two adjacent growing flowers, decided our fate, for neither of us mastered the desires that suddenly rose from the bottom of our souls, as the snake rises from the basket in answer to the whistle of its charmer.

I do not wish to accuse Renata of responsibility for this last act, but I cannot take all the guilt of it upon myself, so let Him judge us in His good time Whom it behoves to judge and to forgive, in Whose hands the scales never falter, and from Whom the faces are concealed. But whichever of us may have been guilty of this last fall, the sorrow that overpowered Renata, as soon as the giddiness of passion was past, had not its equal in all the days that had gone before. Renata shrank from me with such astonishment and such trembling as if I had possessed her clandestinely in her sleep, or by rape, as Tarquinius took Lucretia, and the first two words she spoke cut my heart with their whip-lash more than all her former curses. These two words, full of fathomless agony, were :

The Fiery Angel

"Rupprecht! Again!"

I seized Renata's hands, desired to kiss them, spoke hurriedly:

"Renata, I swear by God, I swear by the salvation of my soul, I do not know myself how it happened! It is all only because I love you too much, because I am ready to face all the tortures of Brigitta only to kiss your lips!"

But Renata freed her fingers, ran into the middle of the room as if to be farther from me, and shouted at me, beside herself:

"You lie! You pretend! Again you lie! Dastard! Dastard! You are Satan! The Devil is in you! Lord Jesus Christ, shield me from this man!"

I tried to catch Renata, stretched out my arms to her, repeated to her some useless excuses and fruitless vows, but she shrank from me, shouting at me:

"Away from me! You are hateful to me! You are loathsome to me! It was in madness that I said I loved you, in madness and despair, for there was no other course left to me! But I trembled with repugnance when you embraced me! I hate you, accursed one!"

At last I said:

"Renata, why do you accuse only me, and not yourself? Are you not as guilty in giving in to my temptation, as I in yielding to yours? Or rather, is not God the guilty one, in that he created human beings a prey to weakness, and did not endow them with strength to combat sin?"

At this Renata stopped, as if terrified by my blasphemies, began to look round wildly, and, seeing a knife lying on the lectern, clutched it to her like a weapon of liberation:

"Here, here, look!"—she shouted at me in a hoarse voice—"Here is the weapon bequeathed to us by Christ Himself against the temptations of the flesh!"

Speaking thus, Renata struck herself in the shoulder with the blade, and blood stained the place of the wound,

243

and in a moment streamed also from the sleeve of her robe. The thought that this paroxysm must be the last, and that after it would come complete loss of strength, flashed through my brain, and I made as if to catch Renata in my arms in anticipation of her fall. But, against my expectation, the wound only gave her new fury, and with redoubled indignation she pushed me away, threw herself to one side, and shouted at me again :

"Begone! Begone! I do not want you to touch me!"

Then, quite out of her mind. and perhaps having fallen under the sway of an evil spirit, Renata made a swing and threw the knife she still held in her hand at me, so that I was barely able to escape the dangerous thrust. She then lifted some heavy volumes off the desk and began to throw them at me, like projectiles from a ballister, and after them all manner of small objects that were in the room.

Defending myself as best I could from this hailstorm, I desired to speak to her and bring her to her senses, but each new word of mine threw her into still greater irritation, each movement of mine infuriated her more and more. I saw her face, pale as never before and distorted with convulsions until it was unrecognisable, I saw her eyes, the pupils of which were dilated to double their normal size—and her whole figure, her whole body that trembled unceasingly, proved to me that she no longer ruled herself, that someone else was governing her body and her will. And then in that moment, listening to Renata's repeated shouts: "begone! begone!" seeing into what fury my presence threw her, I came to a decision, precipitate perhaps, yet for which even to-day I dare not reproach myself : I decided really to leave the house, thinking that, without me, Renata would the sooner gain control over herself and quieten down. Moreover, I was unable to remain firm indefinitely, like a Marpessan

rock, listening to ceaseless insults being hurled at me,
and although my reason enabled me to realise that
Renata was not responsible for them, yet it was not
without difficulty that I restrained myself from shouting
at her, in reply, accusations of my own.

Accordingly, I preferred to turn round and walk
quickly out of the room, and I heard behind me the
unrestrained rampaging laughter of Renata, as if she
triumphed with some long-awaited victory. Bidding
Martha go up and await the orders of her mistress, I
threw on my cape and walked into the spring air, into
the twilight of the approaching evening—and the
narrow street, the tall Kölnish houses, and still more the
white moon above them, seemed strange to me after
the madhouse in which I had just been hearing screams,
the gnashing of teeth, and laughter. I walked on,
not thinking of anything, only taking in with my eyes
the darkening blue of the skies, and suddenly I was
startled to discover myself at the door of the house of
the Wissmanns, whither my legs had carried me of
their own accord. Of course I did not call on them a
second time, but, crossing to the other side of the
street, I peered at the windows, and it seemed to me
that I recognised the dear and tender silhouette of
Agnes. Comforted merely by this, and perhaps by
my walk also, I turned slowly homewards.

But at our house I found Martha in confusion, and
Renata's room empty, and the floor strewn with her
things, various parts of her garments, some rags,
sundry pieces of string—everything betrayed the fact
that here someone had been preparing a hasty departure.
Of course I guessed at once what had happened, and
extreme terror seized me, like an inexperienced magus
who secretly invokes a demon to appear, and then falls
incontinently face downwards at his horrible apparition.
In excitement I began to question Martha, but she
could explain to me but little :

" Mistress Renata"—thus mumbled Martha—" told

me that you had bidden her farewell, and that she was
going away for a few days. She ordered me help
gather her things and pack, but forbade me to follow
her. And I, I never contradict my masters, I don't,
and do all as they bid. I was only surprised that the
arm of Mistress Renata was all smeared with blood,
but I bandaged it with clean linen."

To argue with the stupid old woman or to curse her
was useless, and I ran, without response to her mutterings, with head uncovered into the street. It seemed
to me that Renata could not have gone far, and I
hoped to catch up with her, to beg her, supplicate her
to return, make her listen to my prayers. I pushed into
the rare evening passers-by, stumbled of my own accord
into walls, and, heedless, with my heart beating like
the hammer of a blacksmith, rushed through street
after street, until the tinkle of the street chains began
to be heard, and here and there flickered hand lanterns.
Then I realised the hopelessness of my search, and
returned home, shaken and lost.

Though I consoled myself with the thought that
Renata had surely not had time enough to leave the
city before the locking of the gates, nevertheless this
first night that I spent without her was in truth horrible.
First I threw myself upon my bed and waited in anguish,
believing against all probability that, hark, a knock
would sound at the door and Renata would return—
greeting each rustle as a hope, as an omen. Then,
leaping from the bed, I knelt and began to pray with
the same fervour as that with which prayed Renata
herself, imploring the All Highest to return her to me,
to give her back to me cost what it may. I made a
hundred vows, of which I pledged accomplishment if
only Renata would return ; swore to order a thousand
Masses, swore to make ten thousand genuflexions,
swore to set out on a pilgrimage to the tomb of God,
agreed to give up in return every other joy of life that
might yet be in store for me in the future—saw, myself,

246

all the stupidity of these vows, and yet uttered them, compressing my hands together. Then I rushed into the vacated room of Renata, where all was yet alive with her, lay down on her bed, on that sheet to which only yesterday she had pressed her body, kissed her pillows and ground my teeth in them with agony, imagined Renata in my embraces, spoke to her all the passionate, all the tender words that I had omitted to utter during the days of our intimacy, and beat my head against the wall to restore awareness with the sensation of the pain. I do not know how I failed to lose my reason that night.

Dawn broke, and I was already up on my feet, already searching for Renata, already lying in wait for her at the town gates and on the quays from whence the barges sailed. But I did not find Renata anywhere, I did not find her at home—she did not return to me either that day, or the next, or on any of a long ladder of days—she did not come back to her room, evermore.

Chapter the Eleventh

How I lived without Renata and how I met with Doctor Faustus

J SHOULD probably be unable to describe in detail how I passed the first days after Renata's departure, for they are swamped in my memory into one blurred smudge, as, in a fog, the docks, the surrounding houses, and the people moving to and fro upon the quays merge all into one. And never before, even when I had imagined the consequences of parting with Renata, had I conceived that despair would so invincibly seize me in its talons, as a mountain eagle a small lamb, and that I should feel so helpless and unprotected before the assaults of mad, insatiable desires. In those days all my soul was filled to the brim, over the brim, with the consciousness that the happiness of my life consisted in Renata alone, and that, without her, neither the sight of each day, nor the oncoming of each evening, had any purpose for me. The months I had spent with Renata represented themselves to me as a time of Eden happiness, and at the thought that I had hazarded them so lightly, I was ready to shout curses at myself in fury, and to strike myself in the face, as the most despicable of blackguards.

Of course I did everything within the limits of my power to find Renata. I questioned minutely the guards at each city gate, not grudging douceurs, demanding whether there had walked through, or ridden through, that gate any woman resembling Renata. I made every possible enquiry in hostelries and nunneries and other places in which she might have found asylum, and, I must confess, in this madness of mine I even addressed questions to houses of ill repute. I was not ashamed to carry my troubles into the street, and I went with my sorrows and enquiries to those neighbours of ours—Katherina and Margarita, with whom, at one time, Renata had a peculiar friendship. But in reply to all my enquiries I received only a shrugging of the shoulders, and, in some cases, when I questioned with undue excitement and with too passionate insistence —I received in return even cruel ridicule or simply oaths.

None the less, clutching to the baseless hope that I might meet Renata somewhere at a cross roads, I ran tirelessly about the streets and squares of the city, stood for hours upon the quays and markets, entered all the churches in which Renata had loved to pray, searching with inflamed gaze among the faces of the kneeling congregation, dreaming that in its midst I might distinguish the figure I knew only too well. A thousand times did I imagine how, coming face to face with Renata in some narrow passage, I should seize her by the cape if she strove to hasten away, fall upon my knees in the mud of the street, and say to her : " Renata, I am yours, yours again, for ever and utterly ! Accept me as your slave, as a plaything, accept me as the Lord accepts a soul ! Do with me what you will : crumble me as the potter crumbles his clay, command me—happy shall I be, to die for you ! " In short, I myself suffered, with perfect exactitude, all that Renata before had suffered, seeking her Heinrich wildly through the streets of Köln, and, methinks, my feelings now in no way differed from the fiery madness of her days before.

The evening hours, which I spent at home, opened to me unlimited breadths of despair, and the time till the breaking of dawn was a period during which I submitted myself to merciless torture. Despite this, I

The Fiery Angel

held it would have demeaned me to have recourse to
any soporific means, and I desired to drink not even
one glass of wine, preferring to meet sorrow face to
face, my visor up, like an honourable knight in a
tournament, rather than purchase temporary quietude,
at the price of forgetfulness of Renata. Again, as on
that first night without Renata, I would pass from one
room to the other, now locking myself in my own, that
I might not see, that I might not be reminded of the
objects that Renata touched and on which it was
unbearable for me to look, now throwing myself once
more on to that very bed in which she had slept, kissing
the pillows that her cheeks had pressed, striving to
recall all the tender words she had pronounced. Exhaustion would at last close my eyes, and then, in my
sleep, she would droop into my embrace, snuggle to
my bosom with her small, frail body, or walk to me
through mirror-panelled halls, triumphant as a queen
conferring upon me a crown, or, on the contrary, she
would enter pale, ailing, exhausted, holding out her
hands to me, pleading for protection . . . I would
wake, as if falling from a tall tower of happiness,
into the darkness and coldness of my dejection.

Thus, in dreams, I passed three or four days, and
after that a last despair and a hopelessness unbounded
possessed me so that I had not strength enough even
to prosecute my searchings. The clock round I stayed
in my rooms, alone in my despair, like a criminal locked
in a cell with a savage ape that every moment hurls
itself at him again and again, clutching at his throat
with its strangling hands. At times I would summon
Martha, and begin for the hundred and first time to
question her concerning the circumstances attending
Renata's departure, especially stubbornly repeating
the question : " So she said that she was leaving only
for a few days ? "—and torment the poor old woman
till, shaking her head, she too would leave me, returning
to the floor below. Then I would give myself up to

reminiscences of Renata, poring in my mind over all the days and hours we had spent together, as a miser pours from one palm to the other the coins he has gathered, and sometimes laughing like an idiot, when there swam past in my memory some forgotten word, some forgotten glance of Renata. And again, I would invent various signs, each more senseless than the other, which did not so much deceive me, as somehow amuse me. So, looking through the window, I would say to myself:—" If that man should pass along the right of the street, Renata will return to me." Or thus:— " If I can count up to a million, without getting confused, then she is still in Köln." Or yet again:— " If I can remember by their names all my comrades of the University, then I shall meet her to-morrow." And days passed in such a state of impotence and lack of volition, and it became more and more strange for me to think that I might ever return to mankind, while the image of Renata already began to seem to me not as the memory of a person of flesh and blood, but as some holy symbol.

Once I invented a new game, as follows: seated in the armchair I shut my eyes and imagined that Renata was there, in the room, that she was walking from the window to the table, to the bed, to the altar, that she approached me, touched my hair. In my enthusiasm, I as if in reality heard steps, the rustling of a dress, as if felt the touch of tender fingers, and the self-deception was painful and sweet. Thus I drank for whole hours the waters of fantasy, and tears not once filled my eyes, but suddenly my heart stopped and began at once to pulsate riotously, while my hands grew cold: I heard the real rustle of a dress, and distinct feminine steps in the room.

I opened my eyes: Agnes was before me.

With a slow, as if unconscious movement, Agnes approached me, knelt before me, as I had knelt before Renata, took my hand and whispered:

" Master Rupprecht, why did you not tell me of it long ago ? "

And such was the compassion of her voice, and so heedfully did it touch the wounds of my heart, that I was not ashamed of my sorrow, nor alarmed at the presence of a stranger in this room. I pressed Agnes' hand in turn, and said in reply to her, speaking as softly as she :

" Stay with me, Agnes, I thank you for having come."

And at once, for nothing else filled my thoughts at that hour, I began to speak to Agnes of Renata, of our love, of my despair. At last there found satisfaction my thirst, that for long had tortured me, to describe aloud, loudly, my emotion, to determine, with exact details and mercilessly, my position—and words somehow escaped me against my will, without restraint, sometimes without any sequence, like those of a madman. I saw how Agnes grew paler at my avowals, how her clear and ever care-free eyes became veiled with tears, but already I had no power to curb myself, for the sight of another's sorrow somehow lightened my own. And if Agnes tried to put in a word, to say something consoling, I forcibly interrupted her speech and continued my own with yet greater frenzy, as if some demon were carrying me on his wings into an abyss.

My mad outburst lasted probably about an hour, and at last Agnes, unable to bear longer the torture to which I was submitting her, suddenly fell upon the floor crying and repeating : " And of me, of me, you never even thought ! " Here I came to my senses, lifted Agnes up, made her comfortable in the armchair, said that I was unboundedly grateful to her for her kindness, and truly, at that moment, I felt for her all the tenderness of an affectionate brother. And when Agnes had grown comforted, dried her reddened eyes and set in order her ruffled hair, and was about to hasten home so that her absence should not be noted, I, on my knees, implored her to come again on the morrow, if only for a minute. And after Agnes' departure I experienced a strange peacefulness, like a wounded man who, having lain for long on the field of battle without succour, comes at last into the hands of a careful and attentive physician, who washes his deep wounds, not without a certain agonising pain, and dresses them with clean linen.

Agnes returned to me the next day, and then came on the third and the fourth, and began to appear in my rooms daily, finding some means to deceive the vigilant eye of her brother, and the argus glances of the neighbouring gossips. I certainly could not fail to guess why she came to me, and, still more, her tremblings when I chanced to touch her, the submissiveness of her glance, the timidity of her words, sufficiently explained to me that she felt towards me the whole tenderness of a first emotion. But that did not prevent me from torturing her with my confessions, for I needed Agnes only as a listener before whom I could freely speak of that which inhabited my soul, and in front of whom I could pronounce the name of Renata, so sweet to me. Thus, reflected in reverse, were repeated for me those hours during which myself I had had to listen to the stories of Renata about Heinrich, for now I was not the victim, but the executioner. And, looking at little Agnes, who came daily to me for tortures, I reflected that we four: Count Heinrich, Renata, myself and Agnes—were clamped together like cogwheels in the mechanism of a clock, so that each bites into the other with its sharp points.

I will say that Agnes bore these trials with a fortitude unexpected in her, for love, evidently, endows all, even the weakest, with the strength of a Titan. Forgetting her maidenly modesty, she listened humbly to my recital of the days of my happiness with Renata—in which it pleased me to recall even the most intimate details. Overpowering her youthful jealousy, she followed me into Renata's room, and allowed me to

253

show her the corners favoured by Renata, the armchair
in which she often sat, the prie-dieu at which she
prayed, the bed at the foot of which I used to sleep,
at times not daring to raise my eyes higher. I also
made Agnes discuss with me the question of my best
future course, and, in a timid, hesitating voice, she
tried to convince me that it was absurd to go searching
for Renata through all the cities of the German lands,
especially as I did not even know the whereabouts of
the birthplace of Renata, nor where lived her relatives.

However, it would not seldom happen that I omitted
to temper my blows to the strength of the victim, and
then Agnes, suddenly dropping her hands, would
whisper to me: "I cannot endure any more!" and
her whole body would somehow droop, as she either
lowered herself in soft tears on to the floor, or prudishly
pressed her face against the armchair. Then a true
tenderness for the poor child would arise in me, and I
would embrace her caressingly, so that our hair would
mix and tangle, and our lips approach into a kiss, which
to me, however, did not mean anything except friendship. It was perhaps for these short minutes that Agnes
came to me, and, waiting for them, she was ready to
accept all my insults.

More than a week went by in this way, and still I
tarried in Köln, first, because in truth I had nowhere
else to go, and, second, because my lack of will power
still held me enmeshed as though in a thick net, and I
was afraid to part from the last anchorage still left
me upon earth—my attachment to Agnes. My soul in
those days was so softened by all that I had lived
through, that no one could have recognised in me a
stern follower of the great conquistadors, who had led
expeditions through the virgin forests of New Spain,
but, on the contrary, wholy wrapped up in the alternations of my feelings, I resembled rather some
"*cortegiano*," so neatly described by the witty
Baldassare Castiglione. And perhaps, not having the

will to make a decisive step, I should have prolonged my strange mode of life yet for many a day, if an end had not been put to it by an incident that it would be more correct to regard as the natural consequence of all that had happened, rather than a chance.

One day, at the decline of the afternoon, to wit on Saturday the 6th of March, when Agnes, not having been able to bear the trials to which I had subjected her, was lying powerless on my knees, and I, again repenting of my cruelty, was softly kissing her—the door of the room we were in suddenly flew open, and on the threshold appeared Matthew, who, on seeing this unexpected picture, was as if stupefied by his surprise. At the appearance of her brother, Agnes jumped up with a cry, and flung herself confused against the wall, pressing her face against it, while I, feeling guilty, also did not know what to say—and for the course probably of a whole minute we represented, as it were, a dumb scene from the pantomime of a street theatre. At last, having recovered the gift of speech, Matthew spoke thus, in anger :

" This, brother, I had not expected of you ! I thought anything you like about you—but of one thing I was certain—I thought you an honest fellow ! And I wondering that he had ceased to call on me ! Once it was every day, every day—and now—for two weeks he had not shown his face ! So he has been tempting the chicken ! And thought : now she will fly to me herself ! No, brother, no, you're mistaken, you won't get out of this so easily ! "

Speaking thus, and inflaming himself by his own words, Matthew advanced towards me with his fists almost uplifted, and in vain I attempted to bring him to reason. Later, remarking Agnes, Matthew hurled himself at her, and, panting still harder, began raining upon her obscene oaths and curses that I should never have dared to utter in the presence of a woman. Agnes wept still more frantically, on hearing these cruel accusations, trembled all over like a butterfly that has singed its wings in the fire, and fell to the floor half-unconscious. Here I definitely interfered in the matter and, shielding Agnes, said firmly to Matthew:

"My very dear Matthew! I am indeed guilty towards you, but perhaps not so heinously as you think. But your sister is not guilty of anything, and you must leave her in peace until you have heard my explanations. Let Mistress Agnes go home, while do you sit down and allow me to speak."

The confidence of my tone acted on Matthew; he stopped cursing, and, grumbling heavily, lowered himself into the armchair.

"Well then, let's hear your dialectics!"

I helped Agnes to rise from the floor, as she scarcely knew what she was doing, accompanied her to the door, and immediately locked it, pushing home the bolt. Then, returning to Matthew, I sat down opposite him, and began to speak, in as calm a voice as I could muster. As invariably happens with me at a moment when action is necessary—there now returned to me clearness of thought and firmness of will.

I explained to Matthew, as far as it was possible to do so to a coarse and rather simple man, what circumstances of life had brought me to the verge of despair, and I depicted the visits of Agnes as a deed of charity, akin to the visitation of hospitals and prisons, which is blessed even by the Church. I insisted that neither on my part nor on the part of Agnes had there been one word of love, without even mentioning baser impulses, and that our relations had not overstepped those that are permissible between brother and sister. That picture of which Matthew had been a witness I explained as due solely to the kindness of Agnes, who had wept over my sufferings and been moved by my inconsolable sorrow. I tried, moreover, to speak with all the air of persuasion I was able to summon, and I fancy that Marcus Tullius Cicero himself, the father of orators and hypocrites, would, after listening to my sanctimonious speech, have slapped me on the shoulder kindly and approvingly.

In the course of my speech, Matthew grew somewhat calmer, and at its conclusion he demanded in reply:

"Look here, brother. Swear to me by the immaculate body of Christ and the bliss of the Holy Virgin in Heaven that nothing evil has taken place between you and Agnes."

I willingly gave this oath with all solemnity, and then Matthew said to me:

"And now this is what I will say to you. Into the fineness of your feelings I cannot, and have no desire to penetrate, but of Agnes you must cease even to think. Had you asked her in marriage, I should perhaps not have refused you, but all these compassions and tendernesses are not for her—she needs a husband, not a friend. It will be better for you not even to think of showing yourself to her, and, more, do not secretly send her any letters—no good would come of it!"

Having delivered his decision, Matthew got up from the armchair, ready to go, but then, changing his mind, he walked up to me and, in a voice that had already become more kind, said:

"And, moreover, I should like to add, Rupprecht: travel away from here while you yet may. This is what I came to see you about, to warn you. Yesterday I heard such talk about you that it made me feel anxious. People declare that you, together with your runaway wench, have been engaging not only in the Black Arts, but in other things much worse. I, of course, don't give them much credit, but you know yourself that, under torture, anyone will confess anything. And there is talk about it being time to call you to answer. True, our Archbishop Heinrich is a kind man and cultured, but one must not be lenient to practitioners of Black Magic. In short, do harken to me—from my very heart I say to you—go away and the sooner the better!"

After these words, Matthew, still not offering me his hand, turned and walked away, and I was left alone. It is remarkable that this incident, which happened extraordinarily quickly, within the space of ten or fifteen minutes, and in which tragedy mingled with light comedy, influenced me in a most stimulating way. I felt a sensation as though, while I slept, someone had drenched me with ice cold water, and I wildly looked around me, shivering yet alert. As my excitement gradually subsided, I said to myself:

" Is it not apparent that this incident has been sent you by Fate to summon you from the swamp of inactivity in which your soul was bogged. A little more, and the better part of your feelings would have been overgrown with marsh reeds. It is necessary to make a choice—either life or death: if you cannot endure to live, then die without delay; if, however, you desire to live, live then, but do not resemble a snail! To weep your days through, be touched by the compassion of another for you—this is unworthy of man, who is placed, in the words of Pico della Mirandola, at the apex of the world, to survey the whole of existence!"

These simple considerations, that most certainly ought to have come into my mind even without the preaching of Matthew, sobered me, and I began to examine my position with the eyes of reason. It was clear that the time was come for me to leave the City of Köln, where I had no reason to remain, and where, as Matthew told me, I might be threatened with exceeding unpleasantnesses. Immediately, without postponing the matter, I set about making ready for departure, going through the bulk of objects that had accumulated during the months of living in one place, and counting my money, of which I had left more than 100 Rhine florins—a sum that enabled me to regard myself as not yet a pauper. Whither to go, I had at that time made no definite decision, of only one thing I was firmly certain, and that was that I should not go to my home town of Losheim, to my parents; for even then it seemed to me unendurable that I should come to them as a failure, without wealth, without prospects, so that my father would have the right to tell me to my face: " A good-for-nothing you were, and a good-for-nothing you remain."

The next day was a Sunday, and that day I determined to set aside for saying farewell to Köln, for too much that was dear to me had taken place in that city to allow me to take leave of it as of a hamlet in which one has spent a chance night. To the ringing of church bells, I donned my best clothes, sadly remembering how Renata and I had formerly gone together on holidays to Mass, and made my way alone to our parish church of Saint Cecilia, which was filled with a gaily-dressed crowd. There, leaning against a pillar and listening to the swelling of the organ, I strove to imbue my soul with a feeling of prayer, so that, if only by that means, I might unite with Renata, who at the same hour, certainly, was praying too, somewhere in some other church, unknown to me—and thus commune as two lovers commune, divided by the Ocean, and yet gazing in the evening at one and the same star.

Afterwards, when the Mass was ended, I wandered long from street to street, reviving in my memory the events of the last months, for it seemed as though there were not one stone in the city with which some memory was not connected. There, behind the Hanseatic quay, Renata and I had used to sit together, silently gazing at the dark waters of the Rhine; here, in the church of Saint Peter, she had had a favourite pew; there, at the tower of Saint Martin, Renata had waited long and confidently for her Heinrich to appear; through this street I had ridden with Matthew to the duel with Heinrich; in that tavern, once, I had passed stupid hours in dreaming of Renata and Agnes. And, endlessly, many memories rose towards me from the walls, mounted from the earth of the cross roads, nodded to me from the windows of houses, peeped at me from behind the counters of the shops, stooped towards me from the spires of the church towers. It began to seem to me as though Renata and I had peopled the whole City of Köln with the shadows of our love, and I became as reluctant to part from the place, as from a promised land.

And it was in this way, in the course of my moody and dreamy wanderings, that I came to the Cathedral, not for the first time, and without any definite reason paused in its shadow, near the colossal south windows, when, from among the crowd, there suddenly stepped forth two men, who, apparently, had even before been watching me, and they approached me. I looked at them in surprise, and I must confess that from an even very perfunctory scrutiny, they appeared to me to be very remarkable. One of them, a man of about thirty-five, dressed as doctors are usually dressed, and with a small curly beard—made the impression of being a king in disguise. His bearing was noble, his movements self-assured, and in the expression of his face was a melancholy, as of a man weary of ruling. His companion was attired in the habit of a monk; he was tall and thin, but all his person every instant changed its external appearance, in correspondence with the changes of expression of his face. At first it appeared to me that the monk walking towards me could hardly restrain his laughter, as if preparing to relate some witty quip to me, in a moment I felt convinced he had some evil design, so that I inwardly prepared myself for defence, but when he came near enough to me, I saw on his face only a deferential smile.

With elegant politeness the monk addressed me:

" Kind sir, as far as we observe, you are engaged in looking round this handsome city, and moreover, it seems that you are well acquainted with it. Whereas

we are travellers, here visiting for the first time, and
would be very glad of someone to show us the sights
of Köln. Will you not grant us your attention, and,
for to-day, agree to be our guide ? "

There was a remarkable wheedling quality in the
voice of the monk, or, more correctly, there was in him
some magical power over the soul, for I felt as if straightway entangled in the net of his words, and, instead of
breaking off the conversation with a curt refusal, I
answered thus :

" Forgive me, kind sirs, but I am surprised that you
should address such a request to one who does not know
you, and who, perhaps, has more important business
on hand than to conduct two newly-arrived travellers
through the city."

With redoubled politeness, under which may also
have been concealed sarcasm, the monk countered me :

" We had no desire whatever to offend you. But it
occurred to us that you were far from being gay, while
we are merry fellows, live for every minute without
thinking of the next, and perhaps, if you agreed to
join us, we should be rendering you a service no less
than you would render us. But, if you are deterred
by your lack of our acquaintance, that can easily be
remedied, for each being and each object has a name.
This is my friend and protector, a most worthy and
learned man, doctor of philosophy and medicine,
investigator of elements, Iohann Faustus, a name of
which you have perchance heard. And I—a modest
scholar, for many years a student of the lining of
things, and prevented from becoming a good theologian
by a superfluity of pyrrhonism. In my childhood they
called me Iohann Mullin, but I am more accustomed
to my nickname in jest—Mephistophilis, by which—
please like me."

At the time both the strangers appeared to me to be
persons of merit, and I thought it no harm if I were to
spend a while in the company of two wayfarers, and

seek to drown my heavy sadness in their healthy cheerfulness. Preserving my dignity, I replied that I was
prepared to come to their assistance, and that, as I
had long loved the City of Köln, I should be glad to
acquaint visitors with its riches. Thus a pact was
concluded and I entered on the spot upon my duties
as guide, suggesting that we should begin our inspection
with the Cathedral near which we were standing.

All those who have visited Köln are familiar with
this Cathedral, of which I have many times made
mention in my narrative, but even those who have not
visited the town of course have heard of the huge structure, undertaken three centuries ago, and in its present
form eloquently testifying to the weakness of the performance of man contrasted with the might of his
imagination. I related to my companions all that I
knew of the building of this temple, of which the choir
was consecrated a century after the commencement of
the work, the nave dedicated for service fifty years
later, the towers, although not having yet attained to
their full height, equipped with bells after another
eighty years—and which still stands in the midst of
the City like a Noah's Ark being prepared for some
future deluge, pointing menacingly from its roof, as
if with a stern finger, by means of its gigantic crane
for the uplifting of stones. When I had ended my
account, Mephistophilis said :

" How small mankind has grown ! Solomon's
temple was no smaller than this, and that was built
in only seven years and a half. Though I must admit
in truth : not only slaves, but the spirits of the universe
used to work for the old man. Often he would threaten
them with his ring, and they used to tremble in terror,
like autumn leaves."

I gazed with astonishment at one who referred to
the King-Psalmist as to one whom he had known
personally, but then I thought it must have been a
joke, and advised my companions to enter the temple

and see the seven chapels that surround the choir.
When I showed them the chapel of the Three Magi,
where, according to legend, lie the bodies of the three
magi of the Evangels, handed over to Köln after the
sack of the Italian city of Milan, Doctor Faustus, who
had hitherto been silent almost all the time, said:

" Good people! Haven't you lost your way a little,
since you have arrived here instead of at Bethlehem in
Palestine! Or perhaps were you flung after death into
the sea, and swam to Köln along the Rhine, that you
might find tombs for yourselves here!"

We all laughed at this conceit, while Mephistophilis
added, in the same vein:

" Poor Melchior, Balthazar and Kaspar, you haven't
been too lucky! During your life you were baptised
by the apostle Thomas, who himself didn't believe
too well in Jesus Christ, and after your death you
have been placed to rest in a temple that knows no
rest itself!"

Having inspected the Cathedral, we went to the
ancient church of Saint Cunibert, then to Saint Ursula,
then to Saint Gereon, to the remains of the Roman
wall, and so forth—to all the noteworthy places of the
City of Köln. Everywhere my companions found
something witty or comical to say, but whereas in the
words of Doctor Faustus there was more a kindly
humour, Mephistophilis preferred pungent sarcasm.
In general this new turn over the well-known scenes
with my two indefatigable companions somewhat dispersed the black cloud of despondency, that had again
enveloped the horizons of my soul, and when, after a
prolonged walk, we all became very tired, I accepted
with pleasure the suggestion of Mephistophilis to
step into the nearest tavern and drink a quart of
wine.

In the tavern we took a place in the corner, near a
window, and, while the host and his servants roasted a
goose for us and served the wine, I began to question

my new friends in more detail, as to who they were and whither bound. Mephistophilis answered me thus:

" My friend and protector, Doctor Faustus, having grown weary of the burden of hearsay knowledge—for he is of the most learned—desired to put personally to the proof the question whether the world be organised according to the principles of science, or no. And on our way, journeying through countries and inspecting towns, we have at the same time had proof that everywhere wine makes men drunk, and everywhere men run after women."

Doctor Faustus added sadly:

" You would do better to say that, in all latitudes, happiness cannot be bought with money, nor love obtained by force."

I asked in what countries they had been, and Mephistophilis readily gave me a long list:

" First of all "—he said—" we visited Italy, saw Milan, Venice, Padua, Florence, Naples and Rome. In Rome, my friend was powerfully envious of His Holiness, and strongly reproached me with not having made him Pope. Then we went to Pannonia and Greece. In Greece, my friend deplored the fact that he had not lived in the times of Achilles and Hector. Then by sea we crossed to Egypt, where I showed the doctor the pyramids, and he at all costs desired to be a Pharaoh. From Egypt we journeyed to Palestine, but I am not too fond of that country, and we migrated to Constantinople, to the Sultan Soliman, the most glorious of all the rulers of the world, and had I not restrained the doctor he would undoubtedly have adopted the faith of Mahomet. From Constantinople we proceeded to Muscovy; and Doctor Faustus demonstrated his learning at the court of Princess Helena, but did not want to stay there on account of the fierce frosts. Now we are travelling the cities of the German lands: we have been to Vienna, Munich, Augsburg, Prague, Leipzig, Nürnberg and Strassburg. Further, we are going on to Trier, and afterwards we shall travel to France and England."

While Mephistophilis was rendering me all this *itinerarius*, wine was brought for us, and at the glasses of Rheinwein our conversation livened. I still endeavoured to worm out of my new acquaintances to what extent they were making game of me, and to what extent speaking the truth, but they were both very evasive in their answers. Mephistophilis continually cracked jokes, and slipped out of all questions like a snake, but Doctor Faustus spoke little, as if nothing in the world interested him, he denied nothing, but also he confirmed nothing. However, when, having learned that Doctor Faustus was not a stranger to practising magic, I described to him my journey to Agrippa of Nettesheim, the doctor listened to my narrative with apparent curiosity, and in reply spoke as follows:

"I have read the compositions of Agrippa, and he seems to me a very painstaking, but not gifted man. He occupied himself with magic, just as he might have concerned himself with history, or any other science. It is the same as if a man sought by taking pains to achieve the perfection of Homer or the profundity of Plato. All the compositions of Agrippa are based not on experiment in magic, which alone opens the door to this science, but only on a thorough study of various books—nothing more."

As best I could, I defended the importance of Agrippa, for in truth I consider the "*De Occulta Philosophia*" a triumph of the human intellect, but Mephistophilis, interrupting, put an end to our discussion with these words:

"Perspire though you may, gentlemen, over formulae, and however much you may exercise yourselves over experiments in magic, you will none the less be able to catch in your toils only some pitiable denizen of the world of demons, for whose sake it was not even worth while to labour. For, as far as the more powerful ones are concerned, it is not for you to measure forces with them if not Adam, nor Solomon, nor Albertus Magnus was able to shackle them! Well, let us stop philosophising and systematising: truly I cannot bear a learned mien any longer; let us be gay: have we not promised it to our guest!"

The frequenters in the tavern were fairly numerous, and Mephistophilis, suddenly transforming his serious air to the appearance of a real saltimbanco, addressed himself to those present with some quip, offering to sing a song. A few approached us, while Mephistophilis, seating himself on the table and in a ringing and tolerably pleasant voice, began to sing rollicking couplets of which I remember only the refrain, in which the whole hall soon joined:

> " *Wein! Wein!*
> *Von dem Rhein!* "

Having finished the song, Mephistophilis turned to his listeners with this proposal:

" Gentle sirs, we have visited your city on our travels, and are very pleased with its situation, and now we should like to express our gratitude to you in some way. Please permit us to treat each of you to a fair bunch of young grapes!"

Everyone took his words for a joke, for the spring was just beginning, and there could not have been even one green leaf on the vines, but Mephistophilis, with a half-jesting, half-serious air, set himself to the execution of his promise. He took in his hands two trays, lifting them up as high as the window, which, owing to the closeness of the room, was slightly open, and now said, with a comically mysterious air, some meaningless words that sounded like incantations. The spectators roared with laughter at seeing these antics—as if they had been part of the patter of an amusing haukler, but in a few moments Mephistophilis placed the trays on the table and they proved to be filled with bunches of white and purple grapes.

I, of course, never doubted that in this miracle was concealed only the cunning of a dexterous conjurer, but at the same time I was astonished no less than the others and an exclamation of surprise escaped us all involuntarily. Mephistophilis invited everyone to try his fare, and those who dared to do so were able to convince themselves that the grapes gave the impression of being quite fresh. For some time Mephistophilis was the object of general admiration, for he was looked on not without a sort of sacred awe, as a sorcerer or miracle worker, and, folding his arms on his breast, he stood amidst the crowding burghers like an idol, with the proud face of a Lucifer.

When, however, the first surprise had passed, someone remarked that such a deed could not have been accomplished without the aid of the Powers of Darkness, and this opinion was supported by the tavern attendant, for it was by no means to his taste that the guests should regale themselves with magically obtained victuals. A drunken yokel even advanced towards Mephistophilis with clenched fists, and began to demand with oaths that he should at once kiss the cross, and confirm himself a good Christian. A third fellow, apparently a student from the Bursary, began to warn everyone that the grapes might prove poisoned.

Mephistophilis listened for some time to the swearing and abuse with a proud air, but then suddenly answered everyone thus:

" If, you drunkards, you do not find my grapes to your taste, then you shall have none of them ! "

Having said this, he threw the corner of his cloak over the trays, and, when he lifted it—the grapes were gone, utterly, and we might all have thought we had seen and tasted their fruit only in our imagination.

Then there arose an indescribable tumult, for everyone flew into a rage at once, and threw themselves upon

us to thrash us. They howled in our faces that we were
swindlers, and that we should be handed over to the
city authorities, while fists were raised already even
above our heads, and we bade fair to fare badly, for
we were hunted into a corner. I had already gripped the
hilt of my sword, thinking that I should have to defend
my dignity with arms, but the intervention of the innkeeper, who did not wish this establishment to become
an arena of murder, somehow quietened the brawl.
Mephistophilis threw a large coin on the table, and we
reached the door escorted by the attendant, to the
accompaniment of very unflattering shouts.

When we were already in the street, Doctor Faustus
said severely to Mephistophilis :

" How is it that you are not bored with repeating
ever one and the same jokes ! There is an imp in you
that cannot live an hour without some prank. Your
face probably gets tired of remaining serious, and has
to screw of itself into a grimace from time to time. To
remember all your urchin's tricks fills me with shame ! "

Mephistophilis answered with exaggerated respect :

" What is there to be done, kind doctor, we can't all
be investigators of elements like you, and besides, did
we not promise to amuse our comrade ! "

Faustus resumed :

" And what if the host had not interceded for us,
we should have made acquaintance with Kölnish fists ! "

Mephistophilis opposed :

" Rubbish ! I should have played on them the same
joke as I did on the drunkards in the Auerbach cellar
in Leipzig, and we should have doubled the fun."

In order to change the subject, I asked Mephistophilis
how one should regard the trick he had shown : was
it the quickness of the hand, or the deceit of the eye—
but he replied to me :

" You are mistaken, it is neither the one nor the other,
but a knowledge of how to use the laws of nature. It
is probably known to you that the year is divided

between two parts of the earth, so that while we have winter here, there is summer in the Sabaean Indies—and vice versa. All that remains further is to have at one's disposal a small spirit capable of flying fast, and, without difficulty, during any month, he will fetch any fruit, from thence where it ripens at the other end of the world."

As always when Mephistophilis was speaking, one could not tell whether he spoke to make fun of one, or whether the words came from his heart, but I did not insist on explanations. By that time we had reached the cross-roads where we were to part, and, obeying a sudden impulse, for my new acquaintances occupied my curiosity in great degree, I spoke thus, addressing myself to Doctor Faustus :

" Dear doctor ! This morning I willingly performed your request—not one I was quite accustomed to receiving—that I should serve you as guide. This evening, in my turn I should like to make you a request, perhaps an indiscreet one. You tell me that you intend to continue your journey, and are travelling to the City of Trier. But I too must travel thither. Will you not allow me to join you, though, of course, I shall bear all my expenses myself ? A fair sword will never be a hindrance on the road, and my melancholy should be compensated for by the continual gaiety of your companion."

As soon as I delivered this speech, the face of Mephistophilis, which was capable of changing its expression as a chameleon changes its skin, became haughty and contemptuous, as that of a ruler speaking to some flatterer of the court, and he said to me :

" Excuse us, Master Rupprecht, we need neither coin nor sword. We travel two, and have no place for a third. You will do better to arrange yourself with a caravan of traders."

I had not had time to answer this insult when Faustus, who hitherto had displayed only the extremest gentleness, flew into a violent rage, and shouted at his friend angrily, as only a master might, at his dog :

" Be silent, and allow me to choose my companions myself ! Do you think it is pleasant to me to see ever near me only your grimacing face ? My God, it will be happiness to hear near one a live human voice ! "

Mephistophilis laughed at these angry words of Doctor Faustus, as if they had been some merry jest, and replied :

" Your duty, doctor, is to give orders, mine to obey, and I am your obedient servant until a certain change occurs in our relationship. If I refused the gentleman, it was only because I was afraid of disturbing you, for I, personally, am glad to have a comrade—a fair bottle companion and an ardent arguer. For wine and logic are my weaknesses, without them life is no life for me."

Then, turning to me, Mephistophilis added :

" We start our journey to-morrow at dawn, and you will find us at the hostelry of ' The Three Kings '."

After that we politely took leave of one another, and walked off in opposite directions.

It was still early, and it came into my mind to walk to the house of the Wissmanns, and to steal, though even secretly, a glance through their window, but I noticed at once that my yesterday's decision to leave, and my adventures of the day, had completely fogged the image of Agnes within my soul, and in vain I sought in my heart the traces of my former friendly feelings towards her, as one seeks the trace of light drawings in the sand, effaced by the powerful waves of the tide. So that I was not curious enough even to find out the fate of Agnes, and to this day I do not know whether her brother sent her to a nunnery for her sins, or limited himself to a domestic punishment, or, believing my story, forgave her altogether. I never saw Agnes again, and never spoke of her with anyone, and only, in beginning these notes, brought once more to life her image, which was resting peacefully in one of the coffins in a dark corner of my memory.

Arriving home, I paid off Martha, who did not let slip the opportunity to shed a few tears, gave her for safe keeping various heavy articles such as books, packed the others finally and threw myself into bed, after a day full of curious adventures. I was up at the appointed hour, in the early morning, and, throwing my travelling bag over my shoulder, I hastened to " The Three Kings," one of the best hostelries in the town. At the gate stood a strong, covered coach, harnessed with four good horses, and Doctor Faustus and Mephistophilis were standing on the porch, ordering the disposition of the last packages.

The doctor greeted me kindly, and Mephistophilis slyly, but he could never manage without his sly joke. My modest bundle we hung behind the body of the coach, then Doctor Faustus and I got inside, and Mephistophilis on to the box, next to the driver. Soon was heard the cracking of the whip, the horses pulled, and the coach rolled along the Bonn road towards the Severin gates, carrying me away, perhaps for ever, from the City of Köln, where I had passed the most remarkable days of my life.

Chapter the Twelfth

*How I journeyed with Doctor Faustus and how I
sojourned at the Castle of the Count von Wellen*

ONLY when the walls of the town had long been
left behind, and my glance involuntarily began
to drink in the distant spring fields—did I
suddenly realise the incongruity of my position,
and, surveying myself as if from outside, in a coach
belonging to strangers, in the company of strangers,
for some strange reason journeying to Trier—I inwardly
laughed. In truth, pace after pace, step after step,
Fate had forced me to descend into depths so far
removed from all my previous plans and intentions, that
my former life now appeared to me as a snowy peak
behind clouds.

However, having long ago made it a rule never to
regret any action once committed, I tried to turn also
this journey with Doctor Faustus so that its most profitable side should be towards me. Little by little, despite
the shaking of the coach, for its body was not hung on
leather straps as is nowadays contrived for the comfort
of travellers, I succeeded in drawing my companion
into animated conversation. And soon I was able to
discard any thought of regret that I had undertaken the
journey, for Doctor Faustus proved a most remarkable
conversationalist. We talked together *de omni re
scibili*, if one may use the favourite expression of
Pico di Mirandola, and I had opportunity to discover
that the spheres of grammatica and natural philosophy,

mathematics and physics, astronomy and judiciary astrology, the sciences appertaining to medicine and to law, theology, magic, political economy and other arts were all equally well-known to my companion, as an orchard is known to a good husbandman. At first I disputed some of the remarks of the doctor, then interrupted his speech with occasional interjections, but finally our conversation transformed itself into a monologue, in which I preferred the part of a respectful listener. Thus it continued until Mephistophilis, turning his grimacing face to us from the box, cut through my attention with the spear point of some stupid joke.

This happened as we were nearing the hamlet of Brühl, where we rested our horses and spent a few hours in some bad hostelry. Here we met with some Lollards, who, entering into conversation with us, started to praise the headway made by Lutheranism and such-like teachings, pointing to the growing strength of the Schmalkalden Union of the Protestants, now scarcely less powerful in Germany than the Emperor himself, to the daring of the English king, who had declared himself holy head of the body temporal of the Church in place of the Pope, to the deeds of the Swedish and Danish kings, who had confiscated from the clergy all their age-old properties, and, lastly, to the stubborn resistance against the Catholic army set up by the new prophet Iohann Buckholdt at Münster. Mephisto-philis, joining in the discussion, hotly defended the dignity of the Holy Church, and said, among other things :

" These new heresies make progress only because the princes sense gain in them, as dogs sense roast meat, and, as for Luther himself, a merry fellow of a devil leads him by the nose. In the end, after all these new faiths and new catechisms, Christianity will become so shallow that the Prince of Hell will find it far easier to fish his fish from the shore."

273

The patient reader will soon see why I have thought it necessary to record here these words of Mephistophilis.

From Brühl we went on by road to Euskirchen, but both Doctor Faustus and I were considerably tired, so that we passed this stage of the journey almost in silence, and in vain did Mephistophilis seek to make us gay, either with his quips, or by making our driver, who was gloomy in appearance, reminding one of a robber or of some denizen of Hell, join with him in singing songs. It was already twilight when we arrived at Euskirchen, each dreaming only of his comfortable bed, but here an adventure awaited us, the hero of which was once more to be that same untiring practical joker, Mephistophilis.

The matter was, that there happened to be many travellers in the town, and it was only after long disputes that we were able to obtain from the hostelry under the sign "*Im Schlüssel*" leave to spend the night in the general room, after all the visitors had left. We had to be grateful even for that, and in the large room on the upper floor, packed like the hold of a merchantman, we arranged ourselves, for lack of free space, to sup in a corner, at some planks placed on two empty barrels. Amongst the carousing guests, the majority of whom were already completely drunk, flitted the owner of the hostelry and his servant along every diagonal, their senses gone with exhaustion, unable to feel their feet under them. After we had tried for a long time to get something served for supper, Mephistophilis at last caught the servant by the throat, and, pulling a terrible grimace, shouted into his face that he should at once bring us wine and mutton.

Some time later the lad reappeared before us, with his hair stuck to his forehead with weariness, in appearance a perfect imbecile, and shoved towards us a quart of wine and three glasses.

At once we asked him where was the mutton, but,

angered, it must have been, by the general reproaches,
he answered us rudely :
"Be patient, better than you have to wait!"
On hearing this rebuke to us, some of the guests
roared with drunken laughter, and someone at a far
table even shouted : "That's the way to treat the fops!"
though none of us was parading smart clothes. To be
irritated by the words of an idiot *karsthans* was certainly not clever, but, on an involuntary impulse, as
one involuntarily raises one's hand at a threat, I
shouted something at the brute. I was, however,
forestalled by Mephistophilis, who, posturing like a
travelling buffoon, seized the lad's shoulder with his
hand and shouted at him in an exaggeratedly loud
voice:
"Ah, blackguard! Think you that we shall drink
without a snack to go with it! A good glass of wine
requires a good morsel! And if you will not serve
mutton to my wine, then I shall eat you!"
Those who heard this speech began to roar still more
heartily, while Mephistophilis, quickly emptying his
full glass of wine, then opened his mouth to an unnatural
width, till it became like the mouth of a serpent, making
as if he really were about to devour the poor lad. And,
however strange and incredible it may appear, yet I
must testify that at that very moment the servant
disappeared from before our eyes, as if he had never
been there at all, while Mephistophilis, shutting his
mouth, as if after a hearty gulp, sat down again at the
table and asked for another glass of wine to be poured
out for him.
All those present were aghast at such a miracle :
some remained, literally, with mouths agape, and for
some time the drunken noise of the hall was replaced by
a quiet such as one hears only at sea in an hour of
completest calm, when the water is like a green mirror.
Amidst this silence Doctor Faustus said to his
henchman under his breath:

The Fiery Angel

" Is it really possible that it amuses you to play the part of a magus before all these dullards ? "

Mephistophilis replied, also in a whisper:

" Dear Doctor ! We all play some part or other, I— the magus, you—the scientist, whom nothing amuses and nothing attracts. Every man, according to Moses, is but an image of God. And I should like to know, what indeed in general can be perceived, except images ? "

In the meantime the owner of the hostelry had run to us, bewildered and frightened, hat in hand, and, flinging himself on his knees, as if before ruling princes, he began to plead, speaking thus :

" Kind and merciful Masters ! Do not allow yourself to be angered by my poor zany : he has suffered from melancholy since childhood. We shall serve you of our best, and I shall give up my own room to you for the night. But only return to me my kellner, for to-day there is more than I can do. Another time I should not have troubled your lordships with my stupid request, but, see for yourselves : alone I cannot manage ! . . ."

Mephistophilis laughed, with a laugh that was raucous and in no way merry, and said :

" Well, friend, as it was the first time, I shall pardon him ! Go down, there under the stairs you will find your servant."

The host and all the revellers, and I in their number, ran down, and, in truth, there under the staircase, where logs were stored, sat the poor lad, trembling like a new born calf, as if he had a cruel fever. The host dragged him into the light, and we all, interrupting one another, began to question him as to what exactly had happened to him, but we could not get a word out of him, for fear had probably struck away his power of memory. Returning upstairs, I refrained this time from questioning Mephistophilis, knowing already his habit of answering with meaningless jests.

As to the host, he kept his promise, and in truth

276

placed at our disposal for the night his room with a huge wooden double bed, himself and his wife migrating to some garret. On this very marital couch we spent the hours till dawn, side by side, the two of us—Doctor Faustus and I, Mephistophilis preferring to pass the night somewhere else. Before going off to sleep, I said to the doctor, as if with no ulterior thought:

"I suppose the ingenuity of your friend frees you from many of the misfortunes of travel."

Doctor Faustus replied to me:

"I would I might experience, both in travel and in life, an infinite number of misfortunes, both large and small, for then I might know joys also."

These words were spoken much more seriously than my question demanded, and immediately afterwards the doctor, closing his eyes, made belief that he had fallen asleep, and soon afterwards weariness also broke the entangled thread of my reflections on the day's adventures.

The next day, early in the morning, to the accompaniment of low bows from the host, we set off further along our road, heading for Münstereifel, a pretty place on the banks of the Erft, with an old church; there we took our rest without, this time, any special incidents. From thence we turned somewhat towards the east, holding our road towards the Ahr Mountains, across the lands of the Archbishop of Trier, where at each step we sensed the fullness of life fostered by the wise government of the late Archbishop, Richard von Greiffenklau. That day I tried once more persistently to draw out Doctor Faustus into discussions and monologues, for it was necessary for me continuously to preoccupy my attention, that I might smother in my soul the burden of my craving for Renata and the lost days of happiness, which, despite all the vagaries of travel, rose in my spirit ever and again, as the heated water at its appointed hour rises in Iceland springs.

At the decline of the day, having passed through

Freisheim, we began to bethink ourselves where we should spend the night, when a sudden happening transformed all our anticipations, and led me, by a path unforeseen and tortuous, to the fatal outcome of that sorrowful history that I have related in these pages. This happening has its place, like a link, in that sequence of chance happenings, which, by the very calculated nature of its regularity, forces me to consider life not as the plaything of blind cosmic forces, but as the creation of a skilled artist, hewn according to some definite and miraculously perfect plan.

For some time, already, our curiosity had been attracted by a handsome castle standing on the high bank of the Wischel, through the valley of which we were passing, and dominating the whole horizon with its square towers of ancient build. When, after a bend of the river, we came near to it, we noticed that a horseman was rapidly approaching us, waving his hat, and obviously making signs to us. Mephistophilis now ordered the horses to stop, while the messenger, attired like a herald at a tournament, rode up and said, bowing politely:

" My master, Count Adalbert von Wellen, the owner of this castle, bade me enquire: whether you are not the famous doctor of theology, philosophy, medicine and law, Iohann Faustus of Wittenberg, journeying through our lands on his way to the City of Trier ? "

The doctor admitted that it was he, and the messenger then proceeded:

" My master very humbly begs you and your companions to visit our castle and make use of our hospitality for the night, or longer, if it please you."

Hearing these words, Mephistophilis exclaimed:

" Dear Doctor ! Remark, what all popular fame *we* have already achieved ! As far as I am concerned, I am not averse to the countly invitation. I had rather luxuriate on an aristocratic couch, than toss about with the bugs in a country inn, or spend the night on the host's double-bed in Florentine fashion."

This last remark is explained by the fact that the Florentines have the reputation of being confirmed sodomites.

As the doctor and I had no reason to refuse the asylum so kindly offered us, we hastened to answer the messenger in the affirmative and then turned our horses towards the castle.

We first passed across a draw-bridge, thrown over a moat filled with water, through the first court, where we gave our horses and our coach into the charge of the servants, then passed on foot through the second gate into the main courtyard of the castle, transformed by the care of the owner into a small garden in the Italian style. Here, in front of a staircase leading into the interior of the castle, we were met by Count Wellen himself, surrounded by a small suite; he was a man young and pleasing, with one of those open faces trimmed by a small beard that the Venetian master, Tiziano Veccelli, loves to paint. The Count greeted Doctor Faustus with a ceremonial speech, in which mention was made of Hermes Trismegistus and Albertus Magnus, the gods of Olympus and the prophets of the Bible, and the exaggerated pomposity of which I only later understood. The doctor answered him shortly and with dignity, and then, at a sign from the Count, pages invited us to follow them into the guest rooms, where we could put ourselves and our clothes in order after the day's journey.

Even in only passing through the rooms, I was yet able to notice that the castle of the Wellens presented a noble exception to those knightly nests that more and more often become transformed into veritable robbers' dens. As is well known, in these our severe sober times, when in war is required not so much personal valour, as discipline among the soldiery and quantity in the supply of cannons, flint-guns and muskets, and when

in life the main rôle is played not by descent from noble
ancestors but by the power of coin, so that bankers
dispute influence with kings, knighthood has fallen
into decay, and the former paladins, say what Ulrich
von Hutten may in their defence, have come to repre-
sent the most backward element in present day society.
None the less, in the castle of von Wellen, at every step
were to be seen traces of good taste and enlightenment,
and, what is more important, of a refined mode of life,
and it was easy at once to perceive that its master desired
to march in step with the age, of which that same
Hutten exclaimed : " What a joy it is to be alive in
such a time ! " Elegant Italian furniture in some of
the rooms, pictures that one could attribute to the
school of the renowned colourist, Mathias Grunewald,
statues that might have been cast by Peter Fischer
himself, and many other details, all seemed like a fresh
pattern on the sumptuous tissue of the background of
antique furniture from the time of the campaigns in
Palestine, heavy but not devoid of grandeur. Lastly,
in the rooms appointed to us, we found the most elegant
of toilet accessories, scents, ointments, combs, brushes,
nail files, as if we had been women of pleasure, or
Roman courtesans.

Washing in aromatic water, and changing, with the
help of a servant, my travelling coat for one of blue silk
provided by the Count, I felt myself, not without
unworthy vanity, flattered at being received in such a
place as a guest of honour, forgetting that I had been
invited only as the chance companion of Doctor
Faustus. This empty vanity had not yet left me, when
we were conducted downstairs into the banqueting
room, where was set out a spacious table, laden with all
manner of dishes and wines as the booth of a street
vendor is laden with goods, and where was assembled
the whole company of the castle, with the Count and
his consort. In that spacious hall, which had certainly
served in days gone by as the chamber wherein the

seigneur received his vassals, the walls of which were
decorated with paintings on the theme of the Trojan
war, and which was brilliantly illuminated with torches
and wax candles, as I stood in the midst of a small
company of elegant cavaliers rustling with silk and
satin, in hats trimmed with ostrich plumes, and surrounded by ladies sparkling with golden ornaments,
with lace and remarkably rosy complexions—for a
moment I felt myself—how petty is man!—almost
happy.

But very soon there awaited me a merited disappointment. First, I was soon able to satisfy myself
that no one was likely to notice me personally, while
for my own part, more accustomed as I was to cam-
paigning or gentle conference eye to eye, I had no idea
how of my own accord to wedge myself into the general
animation. Second, I could not but distinguish that
in all the signs of respect that the Count and his courtiers showered on Doctor Faustus, in their treatment of
him and of all three of us, there was a concealed
particle of derision. The thought arose in my soul that
we had been invited by the Count only as some rare
jesters, with whom one might sport in the tedious
spring weeks—and this tiny twig of suspicion was
fated to grow into a whole tree.

When we took our places at the table, I contrived to
seat myself at the very end, where sat the chaplain of
the castle and a very silent gentleman in a velvet doublet,
both of whom were more concerned with their cups
than with me—and this gave me the opportunity to
make my observations untrammelled. I saw that the
attention of the whole company was centred on Doctor
Faustus, who was placed near the Countess; to him
the Count uninterruptedly addressed himself, offering
him dishes, spreading before him compliments to his
learning, or putting to him various, apparently very
serious questions; when Faustus began to speak the
Count made signs calling everyone to silence, as if

preparing them each time to hear revelations of wisdom. But this universal attention itself, and the rhetorical praises of the Count, and especially the quasi-scientific problems put to the doctor, all were strongly reminiscent of parody and satire, and I even noticed twice or thrice the imperfectly muffled laughter of some of those present, which showed me that the whole company partook of the plot. When I became convinced that my discovery was correct, I felt so ashamed for myself, and so hurt for the doctor, that I was even ready to get up at once, and, delivering myself of some cutting words, depart from the castle, but I was restrained by the thought that it was not for me to take the step first, but for my companions.

However, Doctor Faustus, it seemed, had guessed his position even before I did, for he who not so long ago had willingly opened the treasury of his mind to me, a chance companion, now became as chary of his words as a hero of Maccius Plautus. All the ardent flattery of the Count was extinguished by his cold politeness, and for the major part he shirked answers to the sly questions that were every minute addressed to him, as to an oracle, by those present. Mephistophilis, on the contrary, not to be taken aback by anything, eagerly seized all these questions on the wing, like balls, and threw back arrows in answer, that sometimes struck the very eyes of the hypocritical questioners.

Thus, with a very serious mien, the young cousin of the Count, knight Robert, addressed this speech to Faustus :

" I would like to question you, most learned doctor, as to the means of rendering oneself invisible. Some maintain that it is enough for this purpose to wear under the armpit of the right arm an amulet containing the hearts of a bat, a black hen, and a frog. But the majority of those who have experimented with this method declare that it does not well succeed. Others recommend a far more complicated method. One

282

must take on a Wednesday, before the sun rises, the head of a dead man, and placing a black bean on each of its eyes, ears and nostrils, make upon it the sign of a triangle and bury it in the ground, visiting and watering the grave on each of the next eight days ; on the eighth day a demon will arise before you and will ask of you, what you are doing ; you must answer : ' I water my flower '; the demon will then ask you for your watering-can, holding out his hand to you ; if on his hand is the same sign that you traced on the dead man's head, then you give up the watering-can and the demon himself will water the planted head ; on the ninth day a beanstalk will grow, and it is sufficient to put only one bean from this into one's mouth to become invisible. But this method is too complex. A third group, finally, asserts that there has been only one means of becoming invisible ; that is, the ring of Gyges of which Plato and Cicero tell, but this has been lost irretrievably."

Hardly had the knight finished speaking when Mephistophilis exclaimed :

" To me, gracious knight, is known a more simple method of becoming invisible ! "

Naturally at these words every glance turned to Mephistophilis, as if he had been Æneas, about to relate to the Carthaginians of the fall of Ilium, but amidst general silence he said :

" In order to become invisible it is sufficient to hide behind an object that is not transparent, a wall for example."

This quip of Mephistophilis caused general disappointment. However, a little while later, the seneschal of the castle turned to the doctor with the following question :

" You, highly esteemed doctor, have travelled far. Do then explain to us, is it indeed a truth that the ashes of that she-ass on which Jesus Christ made his journey to Jerusalem rest in the town of Verona ? And that the other she-ass, on which once rode the prophet

Balaam, is still living, and is preserved in a secret place in Palestine to bring back from Heaven the prophet Elijah on the day of the Second Advent?"

Again Mephistophilis took it upon himself to provide the answer, saying:

"We, kind sir, have not verified the facts of which you speak, but why should the ass of Balaam not be immortal, since amongst mankind *asses* have not ceased to exist during thousands of years?"

This joke had no mean success with the company, but ever new and new questions were addressed from all ends of the table to Doctor Faustus, while the more flushed became the banquet, so that all grew more tipsy, the more these questions grew impertinent, at whiles closely bordering on insults. At the same time, from my post of observation, I could observe how the drunken cavaliers began to conduct themselves more loosely than was becoming, how some secretly pressed the hands and bosoms of their neighbours, while others, burdened with wine, unfastened unnoticed the buttons that oppressed them. Then the Count, who had borne himself the whole evening with great adroitness, interrupted the orgy that was beginning with the following speech:

"It seems to me, friends, that it is time to allow our guests to repose. We have given honour to Bacchus, and to Comus, and to Minerva; it is time to make an offering to Morpheus. Let us thank our guests for all their sage explanations, and let us commend them to the good counsels of the god Phantas."

The clear and composed voice of the seigneur impelled all those present to master themselves, and, rising from the tables, they all began to take leave of us, once more displaying the utmost courtesy. We all three bowed to the Count and Countess, thanking them for the feast, and pages conducted us to our rooms, where already every comfort was prepared for us: soft beds, night gowns, slippers, night caps, and even chamber

284

pots. The bounty of the courteous Count was only
incomplete in that he failed to offer to his guests a woman
of light conduct each, as once the inhabitants of the
City of Ulm provided to the Emperor Sigismund and
his suite.

For my part, as I fell asleep in this room where
perhaps had rested some companion of Godfrey de
Bouillon, I gave myself the promise that I should leave
the castle the next morning, even if without my companions. I decided this, however, without the Lord's
consent, as the saying goes, and everything turned out
differently, for Fate, which had led me to Count
Adalbert, had objects far more remote than merely
to have shown me—this banquet of noble malaperts.

As is my custom, I woke the next day very early, and,
not wishing to disturb anyone, quietly went down and
walked out upon the terrace, a kind of Italian loggia
not infrequently to be seen in our old knightly castles.
There, leaning against a column, inhaling the freshness
of the March morning and resting my eyes upon the
beautiful, far away fields, I involuntarily began to think
of my sorrows, and all my sad thoughts, breaking
through the dam of my consciousness, came flooding
into my soul. In imagination I saw Renata, somewhere,
in a town unknown to me, passing hours of joy with
another, and not with me, or perhaps pining after me,
repenting of her flight, but deprived of the possibility
of finding me, torn from me for ever ; or, yet again,
stricken with illness. in her customary despair, surrounded by strangers, coarse persons who jeered at her
sufferings and at her strange speech—and none to
approach her, none like myself, to lighten her misery
with the kindness of a word or the tenderness of a
touch. . . . And another access of the old sorrow gained
mastery over me with such violence that I could not
restrain myself, and, dropping my face on the stone of
the parapet, gave freedom to my tears, helpless and
uncontrolled.

While I was thus weeping, thinking myself in solitude, on the terrace of the Castle of von Wellen, a hand touched my shoulder, and, raising my head, I saw that it was the Count himself who had approached me. Though he was younger than I, none the less, with an almost paternal solicitude, he embraced my waist and led me along the gallery, gently and in friendship asking me the reason for my sorrow, whether I had been offended by any of his retainers, whether I had met with a reverse in my private life. Confused and ashamed, I overpowered my emotion and answered the Count that I had brought my sorrows with me in my baggage, and that I had experienced nothing whatever to complain of in the castle. The Count, however, would not leave me, and we continued in conversation walking up and down the terrace.

It soon came out that I did not belong to the suite of Doctor Faustus, but had made his acquaintance only three days before, and this very much disposed the Count in my favour. At the same time, the speech of the Count, in which the good education he had received bubbled with an effervescent, almost mercurial liveliness, persuaded me to forget the part he had played yesterday in the jokes at our expense, and enabled me to regard him with confidence. And when, word by word, it came to light that we had common favourites in the world of books and authors, and he offered straightway to show me his library, I saw neither reasons nor causes to refuse.

In the study of the Count, I once more convinced myself that my first impressions had been just, and that the Count belonged to the best men of his estate, for his collection would have done honour to any learned man. He led me past whole rows of shelves with books, showed me precious bindings of parchment, wood, leather, red, green, black and various rare editions from the finest presses, also the landmarks of our time, that he had lovingly assembled, such as the " *Epistolæ obscurorum virorum,*" the "*Laus Stultitiæ,*" the "*Œstrus,*" which I greeted as good friends whom for long I had not seen. Then the Count showed me various scientific appliances, of which he had a multitude : globes, astral and terrestrial, astrolabes, armillaries, torquets and yet others unknown to me, and there and then he related to me the daring and remarkable theory of Nicolaus Koppernigk of Frauenburg about the construction of the heavens, which then I heard for the first time, for the compositions of that astronomer are as yet unpublished. Lastly the Count opened me his desks, and took out some manuscript codices of Latin authors obtained by him from the neighbouring monasteries, a collection of beautiful antique intaglios he had brought back from his travels in Italy, and finally, in a special casket, a bundle of letters from the famous Ulrich Zasius, with whom he was in personal correspondence.

It was easy to perceive that the Count was displaying his collection not without a childish ostentation, but nevertheless his love for science and the arts quite reconciled me to him, and, wishing to be pleasant, I told him that his riches might be envied by the Vatican itself. Quite carried away by my flattery, the Count sat me down opposite him and spoke to me thus :

" I can no longer consider you a stranger, for, like myself, you belong to the ranks of the modernists, and —I swear it by Hyperion !—I should be ashamed to deceive you. Therefore I must ask you first of all to tell me frankly what you think of Doctor Faustus."

I replied that I considered Faustus a man of the old school, but extraordinarily learned and clever, and I could not prevent myself from adding that Faustus was worthy of greater respect than that accorded to him in the castle.

Then the Count said to me as follows :

" And do you know what rumours are current of Faustus and his crony ? It is said that this Mephistophilis is none other than the Devil, bound to serve the doctor for four-and-twenty years, that he may then obtain his soul into his power. I, it is of course understood, attach no credence to such a rigmarole, for in general I do not believe in pacts with the Devil, and I consider that the Devil would make a bad bargain if he were to receive only a mere soul in payment for tangible services. To me the matter appears far simpler, and that is, that your companions, and my guests—are nothing more than impostors who employ not the powers of Hell but the methods of cunning charlatans. They travel from castle to castle, from town to town, everywhere posing as magi and performing tricks, and collecting in exchange money that enables them to live without poverty."

These words confused me greatly, for until then I had thought Doctor Faustus an entirely noble character, and I began to defend him with all the fervour in my power, so that there finally ensued between us an even quite obstinate dispute. In the end the Count confessed frankly to me that he had invited the passing Doctor Faustus with the sole object of unmasking his doings and bringing him into the light of day, and on the spot he proposed to me that I should take part in the common plot and help him in this matter. Thus it suddenly happened to me to be confronted with a difficult choice, like Hercules at the cross-roads, only with this difference, that to me it was not so clear on which side lay Virtue and on which Sin, for the image of the Count had emerged from our conversation as a very attractive one, while of Doctor Faustus I had formed the most flattering opinion. For some time the scales of my soul swung rather undecidedly, but then I found the point of equilibrium, and said to the Count:

" In no event shall I agree to take part in a plot against a man who has never done me any evil and whom I consider to be very erudite. But out of respect for you, Count, I shall undertake nothing against your plan, and I promise you not to say a word to my companions about our conversation."

When the Count accepted my decision, I felt it would have been unseemly to speak at once of my departure, and I decided to spend one more day at the castle, but I confess that I met Mephistophilis and Faustus not without embarrassment, like one guilty. And feeling myself neither landed on one shore or the other, as if in the field between two warring camps, I was yet less able than on the eve to show myself a gay companion, and from that very time was reputed in the castle as a gloomy and misanthropical man. However, I have noticed that in any given company we ever bear that selfsame mask that by chance we wore on our first time there, and thus it comes that each and every one of us bears a multitude of various masks, each in a different company.

The whole of the second day that we passed at the castle was spent in a hunt, given by the Count in honour of his guests, but which I shall not describe lest I wander too far into the by-ways in the course of my narrative. I will only say that, despite the early time of the year, the hunt might be considered an unqualified success, as it provided no little gaiety to its participants, and as a boar, an animal rare in those parts, was run to bay. Faustus, as yesterday, was the butt of various attacks, to which, again, reply was for the most part made by Mephistophilis, sometimes well-aimed, sometimes rather coarse, and in doing so he exhibited himself as what the Spaniards call *chocarrero*, and gained the undoubted favour of the ladies.

It was already late when we returned to the castle, with that brisk and fiery tiredness conferred by exercise in the open air, and again a generous supper awaited us, prepared in the same hall as yesterday. However, the Count did not wish to postpone his scheme, and hardly was hunger appeased when himself he turned to the doctor with the following speech:

The Fiery Angel

"It is known unto us, respected doctor, that you have achieved such brilliant successes in the sphere of magic, that it would be misplaced to rank you only equal to any contemporary magician, even to the Spaniard Torralba (may it be light for his soul in the kingdom of Pluto), or the young Nostradamus, of whom so much noise is made nowadays. It is also known unto us that you have not denied the requests of others to show your skill, and that, for example, you enabled the Prince of Anhalt to see with his own eyes Alexander the Great of Macedonia and his consort, returned by your invocations from the shadows of Orcus to the light of Helios. Those assembled now add their prayers to mine, beseeching you to show us if only a particle of your wonder-working art."

With strained attention I waited to hear what Doctor Faustus would reply, for in the request of the Count I saw clearly the springs and discs of the trap, and I longed that the doctor might check with sharp words this hypocritical speech. But, to my surprise, Doctor Faustus, who had behaved hitherto with extraordinary restraint, now replied thus, with some haughtiness:

"Gracious Count, in gratitude for your hospitality I may be agreeable to show you that little that my modest knowledge will permit me, and I trust that thereafter the Prince of Anhalt will have nothing to boast of before you."

As I now interpret it, Faustus, offended by the attitude towards him of the Count and his courtiers, desired to prove to all of them that he did, in reality, possess powers unknown to them, and for the sake of this not altogether unworthy vanity, he resolved to lower magic to the level of a public experiment. But at that hour, under the influence of the Count's suspicions, it seemed to me that the doctor had exposed himself as a hired charlatan in agreeing to the Count's request, for only such are capable of invoking ghosts

at any hour and in any place—so that I was ready to
set him on a level with common quacks travelling the
villages for the sale of various amulets, healing plasters,
magic pills, thalers that always return, and the like.
In the meantime Mephistophilis, rising, approached
Faustus and began to speak persuasively in his ear,
but the latter angrily shrugged his shoulders, as if
saying " I will have it so," and Mephistophilis walked
away, annoyed.

As all had by now left the table, and were surrounding the doctor, expressing to him their gratitude
for his decision, I made use of the general movement
to leave the room, and went for a stroll in the deserted
gallery, angry with myself for not having put into
execution my resolution of yesterday, and, in general,
with my soul feeling like an untuned viola. Curiosity,
however, or, more exactly, a thirst for investigation
of which I am not in the least ashamed, did not allow
me to spend the evening away from the company, so
that within half an hour I had returned to the hall, and
was thus none the less a witness of the experiment in
magic performed by Doctor Faustus, and which I
shall describe here with impartiality, as I have hitherto
described everything else, endeavouring not to add a
single line to that which has imprinted itself in my
memory.

In the hall the table and the chairs had been pushed
aside into a corner, and all the company was seated on
benches placed across the room, and, whispering and
laughing, awaiting the beginning of the experiment as
if it had been the representation of some gay pastoral.
For the Count and Countess two chairs had been
moved forward, and Mephistophilis, standing by them,
was giving some kind of explanation, while Doctor
Faustus, very pale, some distance away, was giving
final directions to the servants. I placed myself at
the very edge of the bench in the second row, whence
it was convenient to observe all that took place.

When those present had quietened down in a measure, Doctor Faustus said:

"Gracious Count and Countess, kind ladies and famed knights! I shall now cause to appear before your very eyes the Queen Helena, consort of King Menelaus, daughter of Tyndareus Leda, sister of Castor and Pollux—she who in Greece was named ' the Fair.' The Queen will appear before you in that same image and appearance she bore in life, and will walk your ranks, allowing you to look at her, and will remain in your company about five minutes, after which time she will have once more to disappear."

Doctor Faustus spoke these words firmly, but I seemed to detect and hear in his voice a tension, and the look in his eyes was sharp set, so that one might have thought that he himself did not believe overmuch in the success of the enterprise he had undertaken. But, as soon as he had finished speaking, Mephistophilis added, sternly and commandingly:

"I must sincerely warn you, kind sirs, that so long as the Apparition be in our midst you must not pronounce a word, and still more, you must not address your speech to it, must not touch it, and, in general, not leave your seats—and to this you must give me your promise."

The Count answered for everyone that they were agreeable to these terms, and then Mephistophilis gave an order to extinguish all the torches and candles that were in the room, except one far away candle, so that almost complete darkness fell. Gradually in the eeriness of this darkness and in the excitement of waiting began to die down all the whispers that still sounded and the rustlings of the dresses, until the whole company sank into darkness as into a black depth. Then, suddenly, in various corners of the room, were heard those same crackings and knockings that I had had occasion to hear with Renata, and my heart met these with mournful throbbing. Next swam slowly through the whole room shining stars, disappearing suddenly, and despite the fact that I was by then already no novice in magic manifestations, an involuntary trembling took possession of me.

At last, from the far away corner, a whitish cloud separated itself from the floor, and, rolling and swaying, began to rise, grow and expand, taking the shape of a human figure. A few moments thence there showed itself through the cloud a human face, the wisps of the mist folded themselves into the folds of a robe, and it was as if a live woman were floating towards us, indistinctly visible in the deep twilight of the room. At first the apparition approached the Count, and stood for some time before him, swaying, not advancing, then, still as slowly, as if of air, moved to the left and began to approach me. And, however much I was shaken by the sight, I did not forget to collect all my attention that I might study the apparition in all its details.

Helena, as far as I can remember, was not tall in stature, and was dressed in a mantle of royal purple, of the kind beloved by the painter, Andrea Mantegna ; her hair, of golden colour, was loose, and so long that it fell to her very knees ; she had eyes as black as coals, very vivid lips of a very tiny mouth, and a white neck, slender as a swan's, and her whole appearance was not in any sense queenly, but seductive in the extreme. She glided past me extraordinarily rapidly and, continuing her path through the spectators, she approached Doctor Faustus, who, as far as could be seen in the half-darkness, rushed forward in extreme excitement and stretched out his arms towards the apparition. This movement surprised me very much, for it inclined me to suppose that the apparition was unexpected to Faustus himself.

But I had no time to think out the implications of this consideration, for there suddenly happened something of such a nature that it immediately interrupted our experiment, so tantalisingly begun. This was, when Helena, drawing away from the doctor, approached the cousin of the Count, who sat at the left end of the second row, the latter suddenly jumped up, courageously took the apparition in his arms, and in a loud voice shouted: " Lights ! " Faustus at once rushed at him with an exclamation of sorrow and indignation, everyone else rose impetuously from their seats, and the servants, beforehand prepared for this, seized torches that they had until now held hidden somewhere, and all the hall was lit with their yellow light.

For some time nothing could be discerned in the tumult, which was as if here, among the elegant guests, a battle was being engaged, but the decisive intervention of the Count quickly induced everyone to calm down. We saw knight Robert, in whose hands was a silken rag of dark purple stuff, and who repeated stubbornly:

" She escaped out of my hands, search for her in the hall, she must be here ! "

It was, however, evident to all that it would have been impossible for a live thing to have escaped from so many eyes, and it had to be admitted that the ghost of Helena the Greek had melted in the hands of the knight who had seized it, reverting to that same cloud from which it had been formed. Doctor Faustus complained bitterly to the Count that the promise that had been given had not been fulfilled, but Mephistophilis extinguished the discussion with these cold words:

" We should all be happy "—said he—" the doctor, that he invoked an apparition so seductive that the knight was unable to restrain his impulses, and the knight, that he did not suffer for his attempt to possess Helena the Greek ; Deiphobus, as you know, was less fortunate : for that very same offence his nose and ears were hacked off."

Certainly, such a speech was impertinent, and Mephistophilis might have had to answer for it, if the knight and the Count himself had not themselves felt somewhat ashamed, and been glad to settle the whole misunderstanding. The Count began some confused speech, half-apologetic and half-grateful to Faustus, and, under cover of the general conversation, I softly left the hall and retired to my room, as I felt suddenly ashamed of having taken part in the whole stupid affair. Whatever might have been the apparition I had witnessed, a real, magical resurrection of a person who lived in times immemorial, or a novel trick, such as those of which Mephistophilis had shown himself such a master—it seemed to me that we, the spectators, had played a contemptible part in it, and I desired as soon as possible to shake off from myself, as rain-water from a cape, all the heavy impressions of that evening.

I threw myself into bed, and when, some time later, Doctor Faustus knocked at my door in passing, I purposely did not answer, pretending to be already asleep.

Chapter the Thirteenth

*How I accepted Service with the Count von Wellen,
how the Archbishop of Trier arrived at the Castle,
and how we went with him to the Convent of Saint Ulf*

THE invocation of Helena the Greek was the
last adventure in my life that I shared with
Doctor Faustus, for I parted from him on the
very next day, being moved to it not only by
the general attitude of my companions to me, but by
yet another special circumstance.

As follows, waking up suddenly in the middle of the
night, I heard indistinct talk coming from the neighbouring room, which had been allotted to my two
companions of the road, and, involuntarily straining
my attention, I distinguished the voice of Mephistophilis, who was saying :

" Thank Saint George and me that you succeeded
with your experiment to-day, for there are matters
to which one should not aspire twice. Do not imagine
that all the universe, all the past and future, are your
playthings."

The voice of Faustus, raised and angry, replied :

" Argument is superfluous ! I desire to see her once
more, and you shall help me do so. And, if I be fated
to break my neck in the attempt, what is the misfortune ? "

The mocking voice of Mephistophilis retaliated :

" Mortals love to stake their lives, as a pauper to
hazard his last thaler. Yet any fool can break his

neck, it is for a wise man to consider whether an undertaking be worth the sweat."

The angry voice of Faustus spoke:

" If you refuse to help me, we part to-morrow ! "

The laughter of Mephistophilis was heard, strange and unpleasant, then his reply :

" All your dates are in terms of ' to-morrow ' ! It were better for you first to think how to rid us of this youngster from Köln, who so meekly blinks his eyes at all your tales. I noticed yesterday that he was whispering with the Count for a whole hour, and I think we might expect from him any treachery."

I was not at the time in any way affected by the insolent reference of Mephistophilis, for I expected nothing better from him, but on the contrary, I listened with deepest curiosity, waiting for the disputants, in the heat of their discussion, to expose the mystery of their strange relationship. Suddenly, how I myself have no idea, an insurmountable sleep seized me, and tight closed my hearing, as if Mephistophilis, instinctively guessing that I was eavesdropping, had placed the weakness upon me by means of a spell. What I had heard, however, was enough, so that in the morning, as soon as the impressions of the night had straightened themselves in my memory, I put the question to myself whether it were becoming for me to remain with Doctor Faustus, to whom I was evidently a burden, and accordingly I decided, after a short deliberation, that it would be more decent for me to part with my companions.

Knowing that our departure was fixed for that day, in the hours of the afternoon, I immediately went to find the Count, that I might ask his permission to spend at least another four-and-twenty hours in the castle, and I succeeded at last, not without difficulty, in obtaining an audience.

The Count met me very ungraciously, which was a striking contradiction to his behaviour of yesterday, but which immediately explained itself, for, as soon as I had unfolded the object of my visit, he changed in an instant, jumped from his arm-chair, shook me by the hand, and exclaimed :

" And so you are parting from your companions, dear Rupprecht ! But that puts a different complexion on matters altogether ! Of course you may not only ask, you may command my hospitality, in the name of Pallas Athene. We moderns form a sort of brotherhood, though the Parcæ may have spun for us different threads of fate, and we are bound to be of service to one another."

But when, surprised, I asked the Count why he was so glad of my decision, he informed me, after some hesitation that Mephistophilis had preceded me to him, and had asked, announcing his departure, for one hundred Rhine guldens as fee for the magic experiment of the previous day, and the Count had been indignant at my conduct, for he thought me a participant in the sharing of the money. I must confess that the news struck me as the blow of a bludgeon upon my head, for, though I realised that magic has nothing in common with alchymy, and that the most skilful necromancers are none the less in need of roof and food, yet, all the same, the action of Mephistophilis appeared to me most unknightly. Even had I had any doubts before, whether I were behaving well in parting from Doctor Faustus, the intelligence conveyed by the Count now blew them away, as the wind disperses a fog, and in the most polite words I expressed my gratitude to the Count for his hospitality.

The Count, evidently himself affected by his own kindness, spoke to me as follows :

" Why, in any case, hasten your departure from my castle ? Have you then business in Trier that you cannot postpone ? Stay in my castle, and I shall see to it that you shall not find it ill. And, moreover, I require someone who can write Latin, for I intend to write a treatise on the stars."

This offer was extremely unexpected to me, and even seemed to me, who had long been accustomed to independence, a trifle impertinent, but quickly casting a mental glance over my position, I decided that I had no reason to refuse it. On the one hand I had no definite plans determining my further path of life, and on the other—I have never looked askance at any office, having been, in the course of my life, both a simple landsknecht and an agent of merchant houses. So I gave my consent, thus obeying a new whim of that flow of life that was dragging me along a winding river, past islands and shoals—and I was transformed thus suddenly from the companion of a dubious magician to the scribe of a doubtful humanist.

That very day Doctor Faustus and Mephistophilis did indeed leave the castle.

Before their departure I called on Doctor Faustus to take my leave, and had a conversation with him, some parts of which I should like to give here. It was natural that we should discuss the experiment in magic of the previous day, and Doctor Faustus delivered himself of such a whole-hearted panegyric upon the beauty of Helena the Greek, in such exalted terms, that scarcely with greater passion was she acclaimed in Ilium before his father and brothers by Paris, the abductor, himself. Later, we talked of necromancy in general, and Doctor Faustus, as parallel to his own efforts, pointed out to me the invocation of the shade of the seer Teiresias by Ulysses, and of the prophet Samuel by the witch of Endor. At the end of our conversation, I brought up in very tortuous phrases, and hinted to Doctor Faustus, the real reason of my parting with him, in other words the popular fable that ascribed to him unworthy acts, and accounted for his power by most unworthy means. Doctor Faustus evidently understood my cautious hints, and, after a silence, thus replied to me :

" Never believe it, dear Rupprecht, if anyone tells

you that a true magus has made a pact with a demon. Perhaps some unfortunate unlearned fool may sometimes renounce eternal bliss in exchange for a few handfuls of stolen coins offered him by one of the smaller devils, but God's justice would certainly not punish such a contract, in which there must be more ignorance than sin! And what means have the demons to tempt a man who comprehends their nature and the limits of their powers? It is true that the demons possess certain faculties with which man is not endowed : they can fly fast from place to place, dissolve their substance to a light mist or condense it to any image, can rise to the aerial and other spheres. But are the desires of man limited to those that can be satisfied by the help of such means? Does not man thirst to comprehend all the mysteries of the universe, to its uttermost end, and to possess all its treasures, without limit or measure? A true magus always regards the demons as forces of a lower order, of whom he can make use, but to whom it would be an act of foolishness to submit. Do not forget that man is created in the image and similitude of the Creator Himself, and therefore there are elements in him incomprehensible not only to demons, but to angels as well. Angels and demons can strive only for their own bliss, the first—to the glory of God, the second—to the glory of Evil, but a man can seek sorrow and suffering, and even death itself. Just as God Omnipotent sacrificed His First-born Son for the world He had created, so we at times can sacrifice our immortal souls, and thus resemble the Creator. And remember the words of the Evangels : he that will save his life shall lose it, and he that shall lose it shall find it !"

This parting and as if monitory speech Doctor Faustus addressed to me with great enthusiasm, and I was sincerely moved, for much of it was in words that I myself might have expressed, so that my soul, listening to them, trembled as a string trembles at the sound of another attuned to it. When, however, I was just getting ready to reply to the doctor, there came the voice of Mephistophilis, who had crept up unheard during our conversation, and suddenly exclaimed :

" Excellent, doctor, excellent ! You were born to move all the smug lady parishioners to tears with your sermons from a church pulpit. There is yet time, I have many good friends in the papal curia, I can get you a profitable living· as a prelate ! Especially do I love it when you bring in texts from the Holy Scriptures to strengthen your arguments—this is the best method of proving anything. For it is only stupidity that is one-sided, truth can be turned with any facet outwards ! "

The presence of Mephistophilis always as if bound my movements by strong ropes, and in my confusion I really did not know what to say, while, turning to me, he added :

" 'And you, Master Rupprecht, probably find that we eclipse your qualities, and that without us it will be easier for you to get on. We shall be magnanimous and will cede you the field."

To engage in single combat with the lances of wit I had no desire whatever, and I bowed silently to the doctor, turned round and walked out of the room, which was of course not at all polite and might have been interpreted as an insult. Therefore, should these notes happen to fall into the hands of Doctor Faustus himself or of any of his friends, I hasten to testify here that all the evil in the deeds of my two companions I place entirely to the account of Mephistophilis alone. As regards Doctor Faustus, I thought differently of him at different times, but I must finally confess that my log-line did not fathom all the depths of his life and his soul, and that his image still bulks on the horizon of my memory as the shadow of Goliath.

At the departure itself of the doctor I was present as a mere spectator, already amongst the inhabitants of the castle, and once more there was permitted in that

scene much mountebankery in respect to the departing
guests. Knight Robert delivered a mock oration,
thanking the doctor for his visit, and the ladies crowned
Mephistophilis with a wreath of flowers grown in the
forcing rooms, and it must be confessed that the monk
looked quite comical in this unseemly decoration. For
my part I studied my erstwhile companions, trying to
distinguish in them those traits that had given rise to
the popular rumours about them, and I must confess
that they provided not a little food for various speculations. The weary repose of the doctor could without
difficulty have been taken for the indifference of one
who knows his fate beforehand ; in the quick movements of Mephistophilis the imagination might easily
have discerned something inhuman, devilish, and even
our gloomy, black-bearded coachman might easily
have been taken, if one so desired, for a common devil,
bronzed by hell fire, and accustomed rather to a poker
for shovelling coal in the fires of hell, than to reins.
And as the coach, all the jolts of which had, but so
short a while ago, been transmitted to my ribs, rattled
along the cobbled court of the castle, slowly rolled
over the draw-bridge and quickly twinkled along beside
the Wischel, I almost expected, carried away by the train
of my thought, that at any moment, on some bend of
the road, it would be transformed, as the fairy tales
tell, into a nut-shell, and the four goodly horses into
white mice.

On the same day, about evening, the remaining guests
of the Count, the knights and ladies, departed also,
so that there remained in the castle only its customary
inhabitants, of whom, however, there were not a few.
On the one hand there was the castle society : the
Count himself, Countess Louisa, her two ladies-in-
waiting, knight Robert, the seneschal, the chaplain
and such-like persons, and on the other hand the
numerous retainers, beginning with bowmen and huntsmen and ending with ordinary servants. I, of course,

remained in that company to which my education
entitled me, even if one does not take into consideration
the weighty reflections on *nobilita* of Poggio Braccolini,
and was invited to the general table, as well as to all
the evening conversations in the Countess's chamber,
but I must admit that my position at the castle began
none the less to assume an ambiguous character. The
Count alone treated me with unchanging friendliness,
and also the chaplain would at times engage me in
cordial discussion, but the Countess and knight Robert
tried to appear not to notice me at all. For my part,
I too sought intimacy with no one, outwardly preserved
that mask of sternness in which I had first appeared at
the castle, and even at dinner preferred to keep silence,
especially as the Count and his cousin loved to argue
on political questions little known to me, for example,
on the state of affairs at Württemburg on the return
there of Duke Ulrich, on the desires and attempts of
the Emperor to renew the Schwabian Union, on the
Seim to be held at Worms the following month, on the
matter of the siege of the City of Münster, and the like.

Recalling now the days that I spent in the castle in
this position of half-friend, half-servant, I am not overmuch surprised that I felt their burden so little at the
time, explaining it by the fact that, after spending half
a year of my life in torment with Renata, after the
passionate intensity of my short communion with Agnes,
and after the exceedingly varied adventures of my four
days' travelling with Doctor Faustus—my soul fell
into a somnolent swoon, as, during winter, fall certain
caterpillars.

After the departure of Doctor Faustus, I was placed
in another room, also very convenient and handsome,
in the west tower of the castle, with windows giving
on the far distant lines of the Ahr heights, and, as the
Count gave me leave to use the books from his library,
I was wont to spend the greater part of the day in this
retreat, at the window, book in hand, immediately

forcing my attention back upon the page almost as soon as chance dreams swept my imagination far away. Thus I read many remarkable compositions, previously unknown to me, mostly books of travel, and amongst them the beautiful opus of Petrus Martyr Anglerius, who describes so vividly and engagingly in his decades the discovery of the New World and the first conquests in New Spain. But, despite the wide leisure that I enjoyed, almost never did I give myself up to thoughts of my love, for I was afraid of exacerbating the wounds of my heart, which it seemed to me were healing, and I preferred to shield myself from my memories as if from poisoned arrows, by a shield of incogitancy.

Those of my duties which I took upon myself to execute did not prove to be burdensome, for the Count loved more to dream of his treatise, than really to work upon its composition. Every day he would invite me into his study, and, having whittled a new pen in order to write to his dictation, I would unfold a sheet of paper, but seldom did I have occasion to mar its white with the black of more than one or two lines, for the Count would either begin, transported, to explain to me the further chapters of his treatise, or simply to engage me in conversation on subjects foreign to it, and, moreover, these digressions were in no way irksome to me, but often, on the contrary, very instructive to me. As regards that little which, notwithstanding, I did take down, following the very promising heading: " *Tractatus mathematicus de firmamento septentrionali*," I shall keep silence about its content, for the Count did, in many ways, render me invaluable services, and proved himself, in many other spheres, to be a man of education and acute intelligence.

Of the Count himself I shall have yet to speak in more detail, here I will only say that he loved to pride himself on his extreme lack of faith, and often mocked me for my conviction, based on experiment, of the reality of magic manifestations. Thus, in the course of one of our conversations, he asked me, among other things, what I thought of the experiment of the invocation of Helena the Greek, of which we had both been a witness. I frankly declared that the experiment had appeared to me to be very remarkable, and that I had deplored it when knight Robert had prevented it from being brought to its proper conclusion. The Count, laughing, said to me:

"You are very easily credulous, Rupprecht! Would it have been difficult to find an accomplice among the maids of the castle? For two guldens any one of them would have been willing to play the part of Queen Helena, and equally unskilfully into the bargain! Indeed, I am even almost certain which of them we have to suspect."

Remembering well that there are none so blind as those who shut their eyes, I made no effort to bring the Count to reason, and kept silence.

On another occasion the Count asked me what I thought of astrology, and I quoted in reply the words familiar to everyone: "*Astra non mentiuntur sed astrologi bene mentiuntur de astris.*"

The Count, however, replied with indignation:

"*Me hercule!* I did not expect such an argument from an admirer of Pico di Mirandola! To search for predictions in the disposition of the planets, is the same as to deduce one's fate from the change of summer into autumn, for as one, so the other, obeys the laws of physics."

It is fitting to mention here that the Count, though he discoursed of the "brotherhood" of all "moderns," and though he considered himself a pupil of Æneas Silvius, began none the less familiarly to address me as "thou" as soon as I became to some extent dependent on him, a fact to which I did not think it necessary to pay attention.

However, my service with Count Adalbert did not last long, about ten days, and in all I spent in the castle

not more than two weeks, though at the end of that time
I began already definitely to feel the burden of my
position, and that faint thirst for change which has always
governed my life.   But, in correspondence with my
hidden desires, my fate too did not tarry, for the time had
come for it to lead me to the concluding and horrible
events of this history I have lived through.   Once,
when I was on duty at the desk in the room of the
Count, and listening to a lengthy explanation from him
regarding the distance between the sun and the sphere
of the stars, a messenger suddenly entered the room,
being admitted without announcement in view of the
importance of the letter he brought with him.   This
was an advice from the Archbishop of Trier, Iohann,
that he had embarked upon a journey to the convent of
Saint Ulf, where a new heresy had made its appearance,
and that he would spend the nearest night in the castle
of von Wellen.

The Count dismissed the messenger with courteous
phrases, but, when we were left alone, I had to listen
to a whole torrent of complaints and reproaches.

" *Hei mihi !* "—said the Count—" Ended are my
days of freedom, in which I could delight myself without
stint in the service of the Muses !   Ah, why am I not a
simple poet who knows no other duties than sacrifices
to Apollo, or a beggarly scientist who knows only his
books ! "

Continuing, the Count showered bitter accusations
upon his suzerain, comparing him in mockery to
another prince of the Church, our noble contemporary,
the Archbishop of Mainz, Albrecht, whom he lauded as
almost a paragon among mankind.   The Count was
especially upset by the fact that, having the estate of
Counsellor, he must inevitably accompany the Archbishop for at least the distance of a few days' march,
and he declared to me there and then that I should have
to go with him, for he desired on no account to interrupt
his work on the treatise.   I, of course, consented very

willingly, for the prospect of remaining in the castle during the absence of the Count did not attract me in the least, but I did not then suspect the fatal issue to this journey, nor the fact that the arrival of the Archbishop was itself but a chess move in the hands of Fate, who plays even with a Prince-Kurfürst of the Empire as with a pawn, to attain her mysterious ends.

At this very hour preparations were beginning in the castle for the reception of the eminent guest, and servants and serving-women fussed along all the corridors and passages like ants in a disturbed ant heap. I, of course, took no part in the flurry, preferring to remain in my customary solitude, so that even when, towards the decline of day, a second messenger brought information that the train of the Archbishop was approaching, I took no part in his reception, and am thus unable to describe its details. As a matter of fact, sitting in my room, I occupied myself with a childish game: from the sounds that faintly reached me I tried to guess what was happening in the courtyard, at the entrance, in the great hall, what speeches were being delivered, in what respects the reception of the suzerain differed from the mocking reception accorded to Doctor Faustus—but these idle speculations can have no claim upon the indulgence of the gentle reader.

In the state of inactivity in which I then was, I should perhaps have spent, without leaving the room, all the time until nightfall, had not the Count himself sent for me, bidding me to supper, and making myself as smart as I could, I descended into the Trojan hall. This time it was decorated with veritable pomp, for the number of lit wax candles and long torches was enormous, and in the depths of the hall was erected a gallery for musicians, who, with trumpets and fifes in their hands, were awaiting a signal. I at once distinguished amongst the arrivals the Archbishop, who seemed to me of goodish port, in a robe of deep purple, with a golden, gem-encrusted buckle on his breast, and with a ceremonial infula. But the men of his suite, prelates, canons and others, all made the most revolting impression on me, and as I gazed at all these obese bellies and fat, smug, self-satisfied faces I involuntarily recalled the unforgettable pages of the immortal satire of Sebastian Brant.

In all, I think, there were gathered in that hall more than thirty persons, for the regaling of whom were made ready three separate tables, so that each might be seated in accordance with his rights and dignities. At the main table sat down, with the Archbishop and his immediate suite, the Count, his consort and knight Robert, while to all others were exactly indicated their places, and at once they were conducted thither by pages dressed in gay costumes, with napkins hung about their necks, in ancient custom. I was appointed a cover at a small table to one side, where was placed also our chaplain, the seneschal of the castle, and about ten persons from the suite of our guest, and I was very glad that in that circle I was able to conceal myself, as it were, unnoticed.

I do not know what happened at the Archbishop's table, for on this occasion I had lost my zeal for observation, but at our table all flung themselves with veritable greed upon the viands with which our cooks had sought to display their skill, and while there circulated all manner of dishes, among which of course predominated fish—pike, carp, tench, eels, crayfish, trout, lampreys, salmon, while the pages diligently poured out all kinds of Rhine wines—there was heard only the champing of jaws, and seen only cheeks distended with rumination. Only towards the end of the supper did a sort of conversation arise between me, our chaplain, and my neighbour at table, a smallish and fattish Dominican monk—which discussion I at first conducted negligently, but later applied all my energy to it, which stood me later in good stead.

The Dominican began with complaints of the persecution to which, in this age, the Holy Catholic Church is subjected in Germany, and throughout the whole world, for, according to his words, the Protestants were comparable in the cruelty of their persecutions to the Goths and the Getts in Europe, the Vandals in Africa, the Arians in both the former and the latter, and even surpassed them. He went on to relate to us several cases in which Protestants had seized devout Catholics, both secular and clergy, forcing them to abjure the true faith, while those who were obdurate they slew with the sword, suspended above bonfires, crucified in churches on holy crucifixes, drowned in rivers and wells, submitted to various tortures, unendurable and shameful, for example, making horses eat their intestines while they yet lived, or stuffing the shameful parts of women with powder, and lighting the mines thus formed. Father Philip, our chaplain, expressed his indignation at such stories ; while I, surprised at the lustful exaltation with which our companion related these cases, which, if not quite impossible, for I myself had witnessed similar instances at the sack of Rome, must at least be rare and exceptional—enquired with whom we had the honour to be conversing. Then the Dominican, with a kind smile, named himself :

" I—a humble servant of the altar "—he said—" am Brother Thomas, known in the world as Peter Teibener, inquisitor of His Holiness, having authority to seek out and uproot the pernicious errors of heretics in all the lands bordering upon the Rhine : Baden, Speier, Pfalz, Mainz, Trier and others."

I confess that at the word " inquisitor " something like a perceptible shiver ran down all my body, from neck to ankles, especially at the coincidence of the name of our new acquaintance with the name of the famous Thomas de Torquemada, who shook Castile and Aragon with his persecutions half a century ago. I knew that inquisitors, ever since the Papal bull " *Summis desiderantes*," had been visiting towns and hamlets, seeking out those guilty of connection with the Devil, fixing upon the doors of churches and town halls notices demanding under threat of excommunication report of all suspicious characters, seizing their persons, enjoying the right to subject them to torments and to shameful execution. Very rapidly, as at the moment when one is about to drown, there passed through my mind, in consecutive order, the kiss given by me to Master Leonard, my invocation of the demon Anaël, my commerce with that master of the Black Arts, Agrippa, and my recent friendship with Doctor Faustus, and I immediately decided to be as polite as possible to my table companion, and to disarm in him any suspicion he might entertain as to the purity of my faith.

Accordingly, first naming myself, I began to denounce all the damned Lutherans and Martin Luther himself with such fury that our chaplain, who had previously heard me reason in quite another sense, nearly became dumb with surprise, but then joined me straightway with all his soul. The end of our supper was actually spent thus, emptying one glass of Bacharach after another, we vied with each other in merciless curses addressed to the prophet of Wittenberg:

" And what manner of philosopher be he ? "—fiercely asked the Brother Inquisitor—" He is neither a Scotist nor an Albertist, nor a Thomist, nor an Occamist. How can one fail to remember what was foretold by Jesus Christ : there shall arise false prophets; and they shall show great signs, to seduce even the elect ! "

" It is obvious that the Devil has abetted him "—intoned our chaplain—" It is not by chance that in the catechism of Luther the name of Christ is mentioned sixty-five times, but the name of the Unclean One—sixty-seven times."

" Of what use to discuss it ! "—I bravely declared—" The good Thomas Murner was right when he called Martin Luther just a great fool ! "

The Fiery Angel

Despite this accord I was very glad when the time came for dessert, lemon juice and cherries in sugar, and His Reverend Eminence had voiced the thanksgiving prayer.: *"Agimus tibi gratias, omnipotens Deus "*; so that one could at last rise from table and take one's leave. In any case I had not aimed amiss in flinging handfuls of seed into the soul of my table companion, for later, with horror and despair, I was forced to recognise the power of this Brother Thomas, who, as a result of our first acquaintance, now diligently pressed my hand and even asked me whether I was not secretly in the service of the Holy Inquisition.

The next day I awoke with the happy realisation that to-day I was leaving the castle, involuntarily comparing myself to a fish for which a gap out of the net has suddenly opened into the streams of the river, and in truth, on walking into the inner courtyard, I found the preparations all advanced for our departure. As I watched the horses being harnessed and saddled, the mules being burdened, bales being placed in carts and waggons, everything—at this sight of active human animation I felt a feeling of briskness to which I had long been a stranger. Gone also was the stubborn silence that had held me in its claws during the last week, and I more readily spoke to strangers, gave advice and helped in the preparations. There was in me a feeling that I was fitting out some caravan, in the train of which I should depart to search for a new world and a new life.

The preparations did not take less than two hours, for there was no less pother than if a small army had been starting on the march. Without reckoning the Count, who now commenced his journey with a few men from the castle, the Archbishop was accompanied by a suite, by no means small, of monks and prelates, as well as his field chancellery and several scribes, a medicus, an apothecary with a pharmacy, a barber and several servants. Yet more, separate carts were

laden with food-stuffs, wines, plate, crockery, sleeping
accoutrements, linen, a field library, and still many
more bales stuffed with things unknown to me. Methinks that when Moses led the Hebrew people from
Egypt, they carried with them not many more objects
and victuals for their many-year-long wandering in the
wilderness, than the Archbishop of Trier took with
himself for his journey, every night of which he could
spend under the roof either of a castle or a monastery.

At last, at midday, our seneschal gave a signal on a
military horn, and all began to take hastily the stations
allotted to them, and I in their number, astride a fair
horse given me by the Count, took my place in the
rearguard, where were all the other people from the
castle. Then on the balcony appeared two figures :
the Archbishop and the Count, and with ceremonial
slowness they descended down the staircase to where
they were awaited : the first by a closed-in, roomy
coach, harnessed with eight horses, the second by a
magnificent steed, richly caparisoned, with ribbons and
feathers, as if decked for a lists. A second signal was
given—and at once everything was set in motion :
horses' hooves began to lift, wheels to revolve, carts to
move, and as if one single many-members serpent,
elongating and contracting, the long train of the
Archbishop crawled off, carrying me with it beyond the
gate of the castle. Having crossed the draw-bridge,
which bent noticeably under so great a weight, we
spread out like a broad wave on that same road by
which, two weeks before, I had come to the castle, and
thus my interrupted journey was resumed, but in circumstances as if transformed by Archelaus the sorcerer,
for instead of the Doctor and his friend there was with
me now a whole cavalcade, noisy and glittering.

When we rode at last into the fields, I experienced an
entirely child-like joy : inhaled the soft, spring air like
some miracle-working balsam, admired the many-hued
greens of the far away woods and trees, caught on my

face, neck and bosom the warm rays of the sun, and all my being rejoiced like an animal awakened from its winter sleep. Without soul-ache I remembered in that hour Renata, with whom, only eight months ago, I had ridden side by side for the first time through deserted fields of exactly similar appearance, and I even experienced a sort of feeling of surprise, at recalling the forlorn abysms of despair into which I had fallen after my parting with her, and my tears, still so recent, on the terrace of the castle. I wanted mayhap to sing, mayhap to gambol, like a scholar playing truant from his school beyond the town, mayhap to challenge someone to combat, and fight sword to sword, suddenly pouring bluish sparkles from the shivering blades.

This cheerful state of mind lasted in me for nearly the whole day, and only towards evening was it replaced by a certain weariness, principally because we rode too slowly with many halts for rest and refreshments. Only in twilight did we at last achieve the goal of all our travel : the convent of Saint Ulf, though a smart rider could have galloped there from the castle of von Wellen in two, or two and a half hours at most. When before me rose the quadrangular wall of the nunnery, circled by a moat like a knightly castle, I had no other thought but that the rest of night was near, and no prophetic excitement warned me of what was awaiting me behind those walls. Without paying any attention I listened to one of the monks, who explained that the convent was founded three centuries before by the pious Elisabeth of Löthringen, who vied with Saint Clara in sanctity, that unique holy relics were preserved in its sacristies, such as the cloth with which the loins of the Saviour were wound as He hung on the cross—and never could I have imagined to myself that, for ever, with chains of remembrance that will never rust, my soul was to be bound to one of the cells of this retreat.

As here also the messengers had given warning of the approach of the Archbishop, so everything was prepared even before our arrival, so that those arriving were able to spend the night not without comfort. The Archbishop himself, and some of his suite, rode straight to the nunnery ; for the majority of his train the houses of the nearest village, Altdorf, were cleaned and adorned, and for Count Adalbert our men began to pitch a camp tent, as if we had been on a military march. Here and there were fired large tar barrels, which made the country round blaze strangely light, and the black images of men and horses swaying in this unruly glare seemed monstrous spirits fresh from Hell, assembled in some fairy valley.

When, having executed various commissions, I found the Count's tent, he was already there and rested, lying on the spread skin of a bear. Seeing me, he asked :

" Well, Rupprecht, are you much tired from the march ? "

I replied that I was as much a landsknecht as a humanist, and that if all marches were executed with as many conveniences as this one, there would be no more pleasant craft than the military.

The Count gave orders that I should always have ink and pens in readiness, in case he, like Julius Cæsar, should take it into his head to dictate during the expedition, and then he mentioned casually :

" By the way, this will interest you, Rupprecht, for you love everything that relates to the Devil or any kind of magic. Do you know what heresy has manifested itself in this convent before which we have just arrived with such a host ? I have only just been told myself. The trouble is that a new sister has entered the convent, with whom is present without respite some say an angel, some a demon. Certain of the sisters worship her as a saint, others curse her as one possessed and an ally of the Devil. The whole convent is divided into two parties, like the Blues and Greens of Byzantium, and all the district has taken sides in the squabble, the knights of the neighbouring castles, the yokels of the near-by villages, clergymen, monks. The Mother Abbess has lost all hope of mastering the upheaval, and now it is for the Archbishop and ourselves to decide whose agency is here : angel or demon ? or simply the general ignorance."

Only when this narrative was ended did a first foreboding startle me in my heart, and at once a confused excitement wrapped my soul, as objects are enveloped by black smoke. Something familiar breathed upon me from the words of the Count, and with a sinking in my voice I asked whether the name of that new nun had been mentioned, with whose advent in the convent these miracles had begun.

Having thought a little the Count answered :

" I have remembered : she is called Maria."

This reply quietened me on the surface, but somewhere, in the depths of my spirit, the secret alarm continued. And falling asleep upon my outspread cloak, I was unable to rid myself of the memories of that day when, in a wayside inn, I had been awakened by the pleading voice of a woman, penetrating from the neighbouring room. By reflections of the mind I tried to bring myself to reason, arguing that there was none around me but monks and warriors, but still, as I dropped off to sleep, it seemed to me as though soon I should hear the summons of Renata.

And this foreboding did not deceive me, for the very next day I was once more to see her, whom already I thought lost for ever.

Chapter the Fourteenth

*How the Archbishop strove with Exorcisms against
the Demons in the Convent of Saint Ulf*

THE morning of the following day was
bright and clear, and, walking out early in the
fields, I sat down on an eminence that sloped
gently downwards to a small stream that
separated our camp from the convent, which I began
to study diligently. It was a very ordinary convent,
of a type of which many examples were erected in olden
days, without any regard for beauty of construction,
and surrounded by thick walls that enclosed the rude
buildings of the cells and a chapel, of primitive pointed
architecture, within their quadrangle. Though I
could see, from my height, not only the yard, which was
very tidily and cleanly kept, and the cemetery with its
sand-strewn paths round the graves, but also the porches
of the separate dwellings, yet the hour was so early
that all was deserted and the first Mass not yet begun.
And I sat thus for a considerable time, like a spy
studying the way into an enemy city, but all the while
wrapped in thoughts nebulous and inexpressible, like
the impressions of a forgotten dream.

My musings were interrupted by Brother Thomas,
who had approached unheard, and who greeted me
like an old friend, and, however I might have regretted
the thought of my solitude being thus disturbed, I was
almost glad of the occasion, for it at once occurred to
me that I should be able to learn details of Sister Maria
from the inquisitor : for, indeed, that dark uneasiness

had not quitted my soul. Brother Thomas, however, instead of answering any of my questions, embarked upon a long and hypocritical sermon on the dissipation of the age, and began verbosely to complain that the Protestants were being encouraged by the Princes of the Church themselves. Thus, dropping his voice as though someone might overhear us, he informed me that the Archbishop of Köln, Herman, maintained a friendship with Erasmus, and yet more, had for long been lenient to the heretics of Paderborn, and that even our own Archbishop Iohann, in whose suite we now both were, had not disdained to conclude an alliance with Philip of Hessen, an avowed Lutheran. It is quite possible that all these calumnies and reports were motivated by the hope of hearing reports on others, on our Count for instance, from me in my turn, but I was very careful with my answers, and continually strove to change the matter of our conversation, wheeling it round to the events for the sake of which all our journey had been undertaken.

At last Brother Thomas said to me:

" Many praise Sister Maria as a saint, and assert that she possesses the gift of healing the sick by an imposition of her hands, like the most holy king of France. My modest experience whispers to me, however, that the sister is in league with the Devil, who has gained her confidence by appearing to her at nights in the shape of an incubus. This sin, to my regret, penetrates more and more frequently into holy communities, and not for nothing is it said, in the Scriptures, of the sinner : Behold, thou restest in the law and makest thy boast of God." The Prince-Archbishop hopes to expel the evil spirit by the power of prayers and exorcisms, but I fear, to my regret, that it may be necessary to have recourse to questioning and torture to expose the sinful soul and find the accessories to her crime."

I could extract no more from the inquisitor, and our

conversation soon ended, for the ringing of bells
sounded from the nunnery, calling to prayer. From our
height it was possible to perceive the sisters emerging
from the doors of the separate buildings, and making
their way in long files across the courtyard to the
chapel ; but in vain did I peer at the tiny figures,
which, owing to the distance and the fact that they were
clad in the similar all-grey habits of the Clarissian
order, looked all alike each other, and resembled the
marionettes of a street theatre. When the last of them
had been swallowed by the gaping mouth of the
chapel doors, and the sounds of the organ were floating
towards us, Brother Thomas and I took leave of
each other : he went to hear the Mass, I to seek the
Count.

I found the Count already fully dressed and in the
gayest of humours, which I tried artfully to exploit in
order to penetrate with his connivance into the nunnery.
Knowing with what bait it was easiest to hook him, I
reminded him of the views upon demons of the most
illustrious and celebrated Hemistus Pleton, who believed
in their reality, holding that they were gods of the third
degree, who, having obtained grace of Zeus, used it to
protect, strengthen and uplift mankind. I also pointed
out to the Count the possibility that certain of the gods
of antiquity, having survived the passage of centuries,
might have reached to our days, no other than Poggio
Braccolino, for example, having related of the ancient
god Triton being caught upon the shores of Dalmatia,
where the local washerwomen beat him to death with
drubbers. With this and kindred considerations I
tried to rouse in the Count an interest in the events at
the convent, and at last, for in any case, even, it behoved
him to be in attendance on the Archbishop, he declared
to me, half-laughingly :

" Very well then, Rupprecht ! If you are so taken up
with these angels and demons who inhabit the poor
nuns, let us go and investigate the matter on the very

spot. Only, mark you, neither Cicero nor Horace has ever narrated of anything like it."

Without delay we walked out of the tent, made our way down to the valley of the rivulet, crossed it, dancing about like hauklers, across two wobbling logs, and soon we were already at the convent gates, where the portress nun respectfully rose at our approach, and bowed low to the noble knight, almost to the earth. The Count ordered that we be brought to the Mother Superior of the convent, with whom he was slightly acquainted, and the portress conducted us across the yard and across a small garden, to a wooden dwelling standing by itself, up a rickety staircase leading to its upper floor, and, slipping first through a door, then held it open, bowing low and once more inviting us to enter. This short journey, the passage from the tent of the Count to the cell of the Mother Superior, has for some reason engraved itself in my memory in a remarkable way, as if some etcher had etched its image into my memory, so that now there stands out clearly before me every twist and turn of the path, each prospect changing as it twisted, the shrubbery on its flanks.

The cell of the Mother Superior was not spacious, and was all occupied with furniture, antique and heavy, with a multitude of sacred images everywhere : statues of the Virgin Mary, crucifixes, rosaries, various pious pictures hanging on the wall. When we entered, the Mother Superior, a woman of already exceedingly advanced age, whose name in her holy order was Martha, but who was sprung from a wealthy and noble house, was seated, as if weakened, in a deep arm-chair, at her side stood only her sister attendant, but opposite her stood Brother Thomas like a promoter, having found time to squeeze even into here. The Count very respectfully named himself, recalling to memory their former acquaintanceship, and the Mother Superior, despite her declining years, also greeted him, probably in accordance with the statutes of the convent, by a profound obeisance.

At last, after the many other politenesses required by what the Italians call *bel parlare*, we all took our places, the Count seated himself in another chair opposite the Mother Superior, and Brother Thomas and I stood behind him, as if of his suite. Only then, after all was done, did the conversation turn to its true focus, and the Count begin to question Mother Martha about Sister Maria.

"Ah, much honoured Count!"—replied Mother Martha—"That which I have lived through in the past two weeks is that which, with the mercy of God, I never expected to live through in the convent entrusted to my care. It is now for nigh on fifteen years that, to the measure of my feeble forces, I have been tending the flock of my sheep, and during all that time our convent has been the pride and ornament of the countryside, yet it is now become an infection and a cause of strife. Let me tell you, even now there are persons who fear to approach the walls of our convent, affirming that the Devil, or more, a host of evil spirits, inhabits it."

On hearing these words, the Count began to insist politely that the Mother Superior should relate all the recent events to us in detail, and not at once; and not willingly, she came at last to a minute narration, that I render here in my own phrases, for her speech was too long-winded and not altogether skilful.

About a month and a half before, as Mother Martha told us, there had come to her an unknown maiden, calling herself Maria and begging of her to be allowed to stay in the convent, if only in the position of the least among the servants. The stranger had pleased the Mother Superior by her modesty and by the reasonableness of her speech, so, taking pity on the homeless wanderer, who had brought with her no chattels whatever, she had permitted her to live in the nunnery. From the very first days the new novice, Maria, had shown an unusual zeal in her attendance at all the

church services, and a frenzied ecstasy in prayer, after
spending the whole night until the first Mass on her
knees before the Crucifix. At the same time, it had soon
been observed that a multitude of miraculous manifestations surrounded Maria; for now beneath her fingers
flowers would untimely open on winter stems, now she
would be seen in the darkness, radiant with some light
as if with a halo, now, when she prayed in church, there
would sound at her side a soft voice coming from
invisible lips and singing a holy canticle, now on her
palms would appear holy stigmata, as if she had been
nailed to a cross. At the same time the gift of miracles
had manifested itself in Maria, and she had begun to
cure all the ailing by her touch alone, so that the
diseased had begun to flock to the convent from the surrounding villages in ever greater and greater numbers.
Then the Mother Superior had questioned Maria,
asking by what power she performed these miracles,
and the latter had revealed that she was unceasingly
followed by an angel, who advised her and instructed
her in the performance of her labours of faith, and
she had explained it all so sincerely and openly that it
had been difficult to doubt her confession. And the sisters
of the convent, made enthusiastic by her miraculous
abilities, with which were coupled extreme modesty
and respect towards all, had become filled with burning
love for her, rejoicing that so holy a maiden had entered
into their community, and already thinking of her, of
course, not as a novice, but as their equal, or even as
the first among them.

All this had continued for about three weeks, and
during that time the fame of Sister Maria had grown
and grown throughout the surrounding neighbourhood,
as well as in the convent itself, in which latter she had
acquired the most faithful of admirers, who never
quitted her for a step, were loud in praise of her virtues,
and almost reverenced her as a new saint. But amongst
the other sisters had been some who, little by little, had

become ill-wishers, and who had begun to express doubts whether it were by true inspiration of God that Sister Maria was performing her healing acts, or whether all that was now taking place in the nunnery were not perhaps just a new device of the ancient Enemy of Mankind—the Devil ? It had been remarked that the manifestations constantly accompanying Sister Maria were not always becoming to angelic will, for at times had been heard near her knockings as if by an invisible fist upon the wall, and in her presence certain objects had fallen of themselves, as if thrown about, and so forth. Then some of the sisters closest to Sister Maria had repeated to the confessor at confession that they were being assailed by strange temptations, for example, at nights there had begun to appear to them in their cells visions of handsome youths, having the from of shining angels, who sought to persuade them to enter with them into fleshly love. When Sister Maria had been told of this, she had sorrowed much, and asked that the prayers be redoubled, the fasts and the rigours of the other conventual labours reinforced, saying that wherever holiness is near, there always prowls also the Spirit of Deceit, seeking to destroy the seeds of goodness.

However, though Sister Maria and her supporters had indeed prayed unceasingly and submitted themselves to all manner of pious trials, the manifestation of evil power in the convent had begun to increase in strength with the passing of each day. The mysterious knockings on the walls and ceilings and floors were heard everywhere, both in the presence of Sister Maria, and without her ; wanton hands had at night turned over furniture and even holy objects, upset the contents of drawers, and created disorder of all kinds both in the dwelling-rooms and in the chapel ; at times it had been as if someone were throwing heavy stones out of the fields at the convent, as though hurling projectiles, which had been very terrifying ; in dark passages the sisters

would feel the touch of invisible fingers or fall suddenly
into someone's dark and cold embraces, which had
filled them with inexpressible tremblings; then the
demons had begun to appear to the sight, in the shape
of black cats, which had appeared no one knew whence
and clambered under the skirts of the meek sisters.

At first the Mother Superior had striven to combat
the sin with exhortation and prayer; then the convent
chaplain had read the prayers appointed for the purpose
and sprinkled all the rooms with holy water; and still
later there had been invited from the town a well-
known exorcist, who had performed exorcisms for
two days and two nights, charming bread and water,
dust and offal, but the confusion had only increased
yet further. Visions had begun to appear at all hours
of the day and night, and in all corners; spirits had
appeared to the sisters during prayer, during dinner,
when they were in bed, there whither they went for
their needs, in the cells, in the yard, in the chapel. The
music of harps had begun to sound from a source
unknown, and the sisters, powerless to master the
temptation, had begun to dance and whirl around to a
pitch of frenzy. Finally, the demons had begun to
enter into the sisters and possess them, felling them to
the floor and subjecting them to spasms, contortions
and torments. Sister Maria, though even she had
failed to escape these seizures, had continued to maintain that they were but the assaults of the hosts of evil,
which, as her angel instructed, must be repulsed with
all strength, and there had yet remained sisters who
continued to believe her and revere her. But only the
more furiously had the others cursed her, declaring
that it was she who had brought the spell upon the
convent, and accusing her of a pact with the devil, so
that there had occurred a great division in the convent,
and shameful and ruinous strife. It was then, in such
an extremity, that it had been decided to appeal to the
Prince-Archbishop, to whom, by prescription from the

Holy Apostles, it is given in this world to bind and release our sins.

This is what Mother Martha related to us in a long and confused speech, though it was obvious that it was not for the first time that she told it, and, as she spoke, I recognised, without possibility of error, the traits of Renata's image, so that terror and despair at once inhabited my soul, themselves like demons— and I listened to the narrative as one condemned listens to the reading of his death warrant. When the Mother Superior had finished her story, the Count, who had displayed throughout it an attention I had not expected, asked whether it were not possible to summon Sister Maria hither, that some questions might be put to her.

" I forbade her "—said the Mother Superior—" to leave her cell for a few days, for her presence causes disturbance, both at meals and during the hours of Holy Mass. But I will send for her at once, and order her to be brought hither."

Mother Martha said a few words in a lowered voice to her sister attendant, and the latter, bowing, left the cell, while I, at the thought that I was now about to see Renata, was hardly able to stand erect upon my feet, and was compelled to lean against the wall for support, like a man dead drunk. And during the time that the novice was fetching Sister Maria, the Mother Superior said the following to the Count:

" Highly honoured Count! Whatever may come of it, I must tell you that for my part I can make no accusation against poor Maria. I do not know whether she be indeed accompanied by an angel of God, but I am convinced that she has not voluntarily entered into any pact with the Demon. I can see that she is very unhappy, and I pity her as much to-day as on the day when, hungry and a pauper, she came to me to crave shelter."

I was ready to fall on my knees before this honourable woman in gratitude for her noble words, but at that moment the door opened, and there entered, following the lay-attendant, with soft tread, her eyes lowered, garbed as a nun, with covered head—Renata, who, making a deep obeisance, paused before us. I could not fail to recognise her even in the grey habit of a member of the Clarissian order, to her so unused, could not fail to recognise those features beloved with all the power of my heart, so familiar, as the image dearest to me in life—though paled and drawn by the sufferings of the last few weeks. Renata was still the same as when I had known her—frenziedly passionate, or in the last hopeless impotence of despair, or seized by ungovernable anger, or calmly reasoning in the midst of books, or the dearest, kindest, most tender, softest, meekest creature, like a child, with the eyes of a child, and the lips, just a shade too full, of a child, and at this moment, losing the last vestige of control over myself, I involuntarily exclaimed, addressing her :

" Renata ! "

All those in the room automatically turned towards me, for until this moment I had not uttered a word, but Renata, not making a move, only lifted towards me her clear eyes, gazed for one moment straight into my face, and then spoke softly and clearly :

" Begone from me, Satan ! "

The Count asked me, in surprise :

" Can it be, Rupprecht, that you know this maiden ? "

But I had already overcome my emotion, and, grasping that the only hope lay in my preservation of the secret, I replied thus :

" No, gracious Count, I now perceive that I was mistaken : I do not know her."

Then the Count himself addressed a question to Sister Maria :

" Tell me, dear maiden ; know you of what you are accused ? "

In her customary, very melodious voice, in which was now, however, unusual humility, Renata replied ·

"Sir! I came hither to seek peace, for I had suffered much, and never addressed my prayers to any but God Almighty. But if my enemies seek to undo me, it may be that I shall not have the strength to withstand them."

After some meditation, the Count asked again:

"Have you yourself ever beheld any demons?"

Renata answered with pride:

"I have always averted my face from them!"

Then the Count put his third question:

"And do you believe in the existence of evil spirits?"

Renata retorted:

"I believe, not in the evil spirits, but in the word of God which testifies of them."

The Count smiled and said that so far he had no further questions to ask, and Renata, bowing low again, left the cell, without looking more at me, while I remained shaken by this meeting more than would have been possible by any, even the most horrible, vision. I do not remember what the Count and Mother Maria then discussed between them, but, in any case, their conversation was soon interrupted, for the sister key-warden hurried in, saying that His Eminence had bidden all the sisters and all those who had arrived in his train to congregate with him in the chapel. The Mother Superior of course rose hastily, issuing instructions, and the Count turned to me and said:

"Let us be going too, Rupprecht. But what has made you so pale?"

This last remark showed me that I had not succeeded in concealing my confusion, and therefore I strove with every means to preserve an appearance of calm, gritting my teeth to agony, and straining my whole will.

As we were leaving the house in which resided the Mother Superior, the Brother Inquisitor, walking behind the Count, asked me:

"What do you think now of Sister Maria—were not the words I spoke to you this morning true?"

I replied:

" I think that thorough investigation is necessary
here, for many aspects of the case seem dark to me."

The Brother Inquisitor gladly picked up my thought,
and began to elaborate it, thus:

" You are, of course, perfectly right, and we can
both perceive that no real investigation has as yet
been made here. In the first place it is necessary for
us to establish which of the two alternatives here obtains
(for already the influence of the Devil in the one form
or the other is not subject to doubt)—possession or
obsession, *possessio sive obsessio*. In the first case
these observants, and particularly this Sister Maria,
would be guilty of a pact with the Devil, whom they
must have admitted into their very bodies; in the
second, they would be guilty only of weakness of
spirit, in having allowed the devils to rule them from
without. There are many means of determining this,
for instance: the flesh of those possessed does not
emit blood if it be cut by a knife that has been blessed;
they can hold a red-hot coal in their hands without being
burned; further, they do not drown in water if they
be thrown bound therein, and so forth. Next, it is
necessary to discover whether those guilty have caused
damage only to their own souls, or also to their neighbours' goods and bodies; whether, by means of their
spells, they have destroyed cattle and human beings,
made women sterile, summoned rains and fogs, caused
storms to rise and unearthed the corpses of babes, and
so forth. And, finally, it is necessary to establish clearly
the identity of those demons that have here manifested
their activity, infamous in the sight of God, their names,
their favourite outward forms, and the invocations they
obey—in order that it may be the more easy in future
to withstand their pernicious influence."

Talking thus, we reached the doors of the chapel,
where already not a few people were crowded, for
there were gathered not only all those who had ridden

327

with the Archbishop, but also many of the neighbouring
inhabitants, and of course there would have been yet a
multitude of other inquisitive persons desiring to see
their prince and his combat with the demons, had not
by his own orders the simple yokels been excluded
from the nunnery, so that they seethed without the
gates. To us, who walked with the Count, of course
the ingress to the temple was open, and soon we found
ourselves beneath the crosswise arches of the ancient
chapel, dark, gloomy, resounding, but not devoid of
grandeur, and I began to study the ranks of the grey
nuns, who huddled like a flock of frightened pigeons,
columbæ ceu, as Vergilius Maro says, all to one side ;
but Renata was not amongst them. The Count, and
with him Brother Thomas and myself, took seats on the
first bench, and for the space of several minutes, while
the general silent and wearying expectancy endured, I
plunged into sad memories of those days, when, myself
concealed behind pillars, I had searched as now for
Renata with my eyes. I knew that she would enter
here, that I should see her again, and, from that
knowledge, my heart beat in my breast like the heart
of a timorous lizard, gripped by the coarse fingers of
a man.

The harsh grating of a door forced me to raise my
eyes, and I saw advance from the sacristy, with her two
attendant sisters, first Mother Martha, and behind her,
her eyes downcast but with firm step, Renata, and then
immediately, scarcely had they reached the other sisters
—the Prince-Archbishop, accompanied by two prelates
and the convent chaplain. The Archbishop was clad
in his solemn robes, embroidered in gold, with a
stole round his shoulders and an ornate episcopal staff
in his hand, wearing an infula, yet more gorgeous than
that which he had worn at the feast in the castle,
bordered at the seams with precious gems, which
glittered in the light of the wax candles, lit despite the
fact that it was noon, and on his entry all fell to their

knees. The Archbishop, with his prelates, walked
straight to the altar, where, kneeling also, he read the
prayer: "*Omnipotens sempiterne Deus*," and when
he had finished the whole congregation intoned with
one voice "*Amen*," in its number also Renata, who
was kneeling, however, away from the others, in front
of the benches, in the sight of all. Then, rising and
turning towards us, the Archbishop, in a loud and
clearly distinct voice, called out: "*Te invocamus, te
adoramus*," and so forth, while we evenly returned him
the responses. Lastly, blessing the water, he sprinkled
the liquid thus consecrated towards the four corners of
the earth, and then, seating himself on the archi-
episcopal throne, he bade Renata approach.

My glances were bound so firmly to the image of
Renata that, methinks, no power on earth could have
served in that minute to avert my head, and I saw each
minutest swaying of Renata's robe, as, rising slowly,
she made a few steps forward, and again when she
lowered herself to the ground before the very throne of
the Archbishop. The Archbishop made the sign of
the cross on her forehead, imposed his hands upon her
head in blessing, and pronounced another prayer:
"*Benedicat te omnipotens Deus, Pater et Filius et
Spiritus Sanctus*," to which Renata listened in meek
submission, and to which we all replied once more
"*Amen*." And while all this ritual lasted, since I saw
that Renata conducted herself as a true daughter of the
Church, and showed no traces in herself of the presence
of the Power of Evil—there was born in me the joyful
hope that all might yet transpire well, as though a
thin streak of the lightening dawn broke through the
darkness of my soul.

After the second prayer, the Archbishop rose once
more to his feet and turned to us with the following
speech:

"Beloved brethren and sisters! It is known well
enough that the Spirit of Darkness assumes often the

shape of an Angel of Light, the more certainly to tempt and undo irresolute souls. But a spiritual sword is given unto us for that very purpose, to sever in such circumstances his hideous head, and we call upon you to fear his wiles no longer. And thou, daughter dear unto us, answer us : what evidence hast thou that thy visions are from God and not from the Devil ? "

And now again I heard Renata's voice, soft, restrained, yet clear, and she said :

" Highly reverend father ! I know not from whom be my visions, but he who appears to me speaks to me only of God and Good, calls me to a spotless life and abominates my transgressions—how can I not have faith in him ? "

But hardly had Renata finished these words when, all around her, on the ground, as if from below, there suddenly sounded quick and agitated knockings, the same as those of which she had said that it was the " tiny ones " who knocked. And at the same moment a great confusion arose in the chapel : screams were heard from amongst the sisters, all set themselves in movement, and I myself was unable to subdue the sudden terror that shook me, while the Archbishop, mightily and angrily striking the earth with his staff, exclaimed :

" Whose be these wiles ? Answer ! "

I could not see the face of Renata, but from the tremor of her voice I realised that she was in a state of the highest excitement, and in a very low voice she uttered :

" Father ! These be my enemies."

The Archbishop, maintaining control over himself, began an exorcism, speaking at first in the vernacular :

" Step forth, dark spirit, if thou hast found thee shelter in this holy place ! Thou—father of lies, and destroyer of truth, and inventor of wrongfulness ; know then the sentence our candour shall pronounce upon thy artifices ! Wilt thou not, condemned spirit,

submit to the will of our common Creator? Thou didst
fall into deadly sin, and wert thrust from the holy
heights into the abysms of darkness and the subterranean depths. And now, hideous creature, whoever
thou beest, to whatever hellish hierarchy thou mayest
belong, if, by God's allowance, thou has thrust thyself
by deceit into the confidence of these pious women, we
name the Father Omnipotent, we implore the Son
Expiator, we invoke the blessed Holy Ghost against
thee! O ancient serpent! We anathematise thee, expel
thee, curse thee, renounce thy works, forbid thee this
place, and mayest thou flee, despised, ashamed, exiled
into places arid and weird, into horrible deserts, inaccessible to man, and there, hiding and chafing the bit
of thy pride, mayest thou await the terrible day of the
last judgment! Thou shalt not mock the servants of
Christ Jesus, thou shalt deceive none of them, fast
flee, quick begone, leave them to worship God in
peace!"

But while the Archbishop was uttering these ana-
themas and conjurations the knockings not only failed
to cease, but yet increased, and began to sound not only
through the floor, but on the benches, from the walls
of the chapel, and even came from its high crosswise
arches, and their strength became so violent that it
was as though the full swing of a mighty hammer were
striking against the building. At the same time grew
the confusion within the chapel, for many of the on-
lookers in terror sought the doors, and among the
sisters there occurred an extreme disturbance: some
of them huddled tremblingly against each other, like
sheep at the appearance of a wolf, others, beside themselves, shouted curses and reproaches at Renata. But
Renata herself remained immobile, like a statue, as if
carved of wood, not rising from her knees, but also not
lowering her head, as though all that happened around
her concerned her not at all.

At last, from the ranks of the sisters, there suddenly

tore forward a nun, young and beautiful, as far as I could see, who ran into the middle of the chapel, making strange movements and shouting something incomprehensible, and then fell to the floor and began to throw herself about in a fit of that possession that it had been my lot to observe previously in Renata. All, in terror and confusion, then rushed from their places, and I too hurried to the girl, and saw how terribly she was contorted, while her belly bulged out from under her robe as though she were with child. But the Archbishop, in a commanding voice, bade all remain motionless. Then, approaching the unfortunate, he ordered his prelates to bind her tightly with sacred stoles, so that she could no longer throw herself about, and, sprinkling holy water over her face, he asked loudly, addressing himself to her:

" Art thou here, accursed sower of confusion ? "

The bound sister replied, the demon entered within her speaking with her lips, thus:

" ' I am ! ' "

We were struck by this answer more than by anything that had gone before, and the Archbishop questioned once more:

" I conjure thee in the name of the living God, answer: art thou an evil spirit ? "

The sister replied : " ' Yea ! ' "

The Archbishop asked :

" Art thou he who seduced Sister Maria in the guise of an angel ? "

The sister replied : " ' No, for we are many here.' "

The Archbishop asked :

" Answer, to what end did you scheme this deceit and seduce with false images the servants of God ? "

The answer was not forthcoming, and the Archbishop asked again :

" Had you the shameful intention of undoing the eternal bliss of these pious sisters, and diverting the whole convent from sanctity to dishonour ? "

The sister replied : " ' Yea ! ' "

The Archbishop asked :

" Answer : had you an accomplice amongst the sisters of this nunnery ? "

The sister replied : " ' Yea ! ' "

At this answer all those who crowded round suddenly shivered, and the Archbishop asked :

" And who was this accomplice ? Not she whose body thou dost now inhabit ? "

The sister answered : " ' Nay ! ' "

The Archbishop asked :

" Then was it not the sister who calls herself Maria ? "

The sister replied : " ' Yea ! ' "

I understood in this instant that thus had been delivered the death sentence of Renata, and the Archbishop, again sprinkling holy water on the prostrate and bound sister, began to exorcise the demon that possessed her, that he might emerge from her body.

" Deceitful and sinful spirit "—pronounced the Archbishop—" I charge thee—abandon this body that thou hast wrongfully chosen as thy residence, for it is the temple of the Holy Ghost. Begone, serpent, defender of cunning and riot ! begone, ravening wolf, overflowing with all filth ! begone, goat, guardian of swine and lice ! begone, poisonous scorpion, accursed lizard, dragon, horned vermin ! I command thee in the name of Christ Jesus, initiate of all the mysteries, begone ! "

At the last of these exorcisms the bound sister began to throw herself about with especial power, and moaned terribly with her own voice :

" He is going ! He is going ! He is in my breasts ! He is in my hands ! He is in the tips of my fingers ! "

As she spoke, the distension of her belly moved first to her breasts, then to her shoulders, then she lifted her bound hands on high, and at last she remained motionless, like an invalid exhausted by a terrible fit of sickness. Brother Thomas told me afterwards that he and several

333

others with him saw the demon, which flew out of the
fingers of the unfortunate woman in the guise of a
manikin, shapeless and hideous, and was carried away
on a smoky cloud through the door of the temple,
leaving behind him a stench, but I, though I was
closely observing all that took place, neither saw such
an apparition nor was aware of any such smell. And
when the possessed sister had quietened down, and it
became apparent that the demon that had possessed
her had left her, the Archbishop gave orders that she
should be carried away, for she could not walk of herself, and himself he turned once more to Renata, and
we all followed him.

During the whole time occupied by the purification
of the possessed sister, Renata had remained apart
from us, still kneeling and not once even making an
attempt to turn her face towards us. Several times I
had been tempted to approach her and speak to her,
but I had been held back by the thought that I should
thus expose my intimacy with her, whereas to help
her, and perhaps even save her, I could succeed only if
people thought me a stranger, or even hostile to her.
Therefore, mastering my passionate yearning, I had
remained apart from her, in the midst of the others, and
approached her only when the Archbishop again turned
towards her. This time I tried to place myself so that
I could see the face of Renata, and so that she could
see mine, but the expression of her features, whose
every play I knew so well, boded no good, for I noticed
at once that the expression of humility had been replaced in her features by an expression at once stern
and stubborn—and a new and sickening fear clutched
at my heart. I must add further, that the mysterious
knockings, which had died down somewhat during the
colloquy between the Archbishop and the demon, had
not, however, disappeared altogether and at times
sounded still from the wall, from the floor, or from
beneath the arched beams.

Returning to the altar, the Archbishop commanded that, as a sign of affliction, the wax candles be extinguished, and then, turning to Renata, he struck the stone flags sternly with his staff and called to her:

"Sister Maria! One of our enemies, whom we, with the help of God and the power granted us from above, have forced to quit the body of one of thy sisters, has informed us that thou art in sinful league with diabolical forces. Repent thee before us thy falling from God."

Renata lifted her head and replied firmly:

"Not guilty am I of the sin you have named."

Hardly had she said this, when suddenly there sounded knockings so shattering that it seemed as though the walls of the temple were sagging apart and crashing to the ground, or as though cannons with their projectiles and battering appliances with their rams were attacking us upon all sides. In the noise and thunder of the knockings, which followed almost continuously upon one another, for a moment nothing could be heard, and all those present fell upon their knees around the Archbishop, stretching out their arms to him, as to the only one able to save them. And he, still not losing the firmness of his spirit, pointed his staff forward, like a magic wand, and addressing himself no more to Renata, but to the demon he believed to have entered her, exclaimed commandingly:

"Evil spirit! By Him Who was brought before Caiaphas, the high priest of the Hebrews, Who was questioned and gave answer, I conjure thee, answer me; art thou the enemy of God and the servant of Antichrist?"

Then Renata suddenly rose from her knees, and, looking straight at the Archbishop, answered, but by whom inspired, I know not:

"By the holy and mysterious name of God, Adonai, I swear and testify: I am the servant of the All-Highest, standing before His throne!"

And again her reply was followed by a terrible rumble, but at the same time several sisters, tearing themselves from the ranks, rushed towards Renata, pressed, kneeling, around her feet, and exclaimed in frenzy:

"And we! and we! we testify! Sister Maria is—holy! *Ecce ancilla Domini! Ora pro nobis!*"

In extreme fury of anger, the Archbishop, all red with strain, the sweat streaming down his face, called:

"Away, false spirit! *Vade retro!* Children, come to your senses!"

But the maidens continued to scream, embracing the knees of Renata, who stood with her eyes gazing at the heights; all around the terrible knockings continued, and the excitement reached such intensity that already none could control themselves, but all shouted, howled, wept, or screamed with frenzied laughter. I saw that the Archbishop himself was, at last, himself shaken, but, once more raising his voice, he began one of the most crucial exorcisms in the following terms:

"*Per Christum Dominum, per eum, qui venturus est iudicare vivos et mortuos, obtemperare! Spiriti maligni, damnati, interdicti, exterminati, extorsi, jam vobis impero et præcipio, in nomine et virtute Dei Omnipotentis et Justi! In ictu oculi discedite omnes qui operamini iniquitatem!*"

He had, however, by no means reached the end, when first one sister, then another, fell to the floor with laughter and weeping, possessed by the spirits who lay in wait around, for immediately many others were unable to withstand the assault upon their bodies of the powers of evil. The unfortunate maidens suddenly fell, one after the other, each with a moan, and flung themselves about terribly on the stone flags of the floor, either shouting out impious words, naming the Archbishop himself the servant of the Devil, or blasphemies, exalting Sister Maria as the bride of an angel of Heaven. Shouts, moans, laughter, blasphemies, plaints, curses—all mingled with the mysterious

336

knocking of invisible hands and the confusion of the other spectators, who, shaken by terror, reeling like men drunk, strove to flee to the doors, and there was not one man in this crowd able to retain mastery over himself: thus mighty was the power of the demons, who unquestionably had seized the whole temple in their sway. I too felt that my head was swooning, that my throat was strangling, that darkness was in my eyes, and I too yearned to throw myself towards Renata, fall on my knees before her, and shout into the Archbishop's face that she was a saint, and perhaps, had this state lasted but one more minute, I should have done so.

There were two who retained a measure of calm in all this frenzy: the Archbishop, who still repeated, though in a shaken voice, the words of the exorcisms, already unheard in the general tumult—and Renata; embracing her faithful followers with her arms, amidst screams and moans, amidst praises and curses, she stood straight in front of the Archbishop, her eyes directed above, and the immobility of her face seeming as the strength of a granite rock amidst the fury of storming waves—but at that very moment when, forgetting my prudent calculations, I was already about to rush towards her, suddenly there came into her eyes a striking change. I saw that her features started, that her lips twisted at first hardly perceptibly, then a sudden convulsion racked all her face, in her eyes was suddenly reflected inexpressible terror, and in this one minute, instantly, I too fathomed what had happened to her, as she exclaimed, in a voice of despair:

"My God! My God! Why hast Thou forsaken me?"

Immediately afterwards she too, in a fit of possession, subsided into the mass of the sisters who were pressing about her, and who at once, as if in obedience to a command, began to fling themselves about, to beat themselves against the floor, and to scream. Then the last vestige of order was broken in this assembly, and everywhere around, wherever the eye could reach, could be seen only women possessed by demons, and they ran about the chapel, in a frenzy, gesticulating, striking themselves on the breasts, waving their arms, preaching; or rolled about on the ground, singly or in couples, twisting in convulsions, pressing each other in embraces, kissing each other in a fury of passion, or biting each other like wild beasts; or sat fast on one spot, furiously distorting their features in grimaces, rolling out and in their eyes, thrusting out their tongues, roaring with laughter, and then becoming suddenly silent, or suddenly falling backwards, striking their skulls against the stones of the floor; some of them screamed, others laughed, a third group cursed, a fourth blasphemed, a fifth chanted; yet others hissed like snakes, or barked like dogs, or grunted like swine; —it was a hell, more terrible than that which appeared before the eyes of Dante Alighieri.

At this same moment, I saw between me and the Archbishop, who stood rooted to the ground, the figure of the Dominican brother, Thomas, who had as if dived up suddenly from beneath the floor, and who exclaimed in a voice sharp and commanding, unaccustomed in him:

" These women are guilty of extreme heresy and obvious carnal connection with the Devil! In the name of His Holiness, I declare them subject to the court of the Holy Inquisition!"

I heard the rattle against the floor of the staff that fell from the hands of the Archbishop, startled by these simple words, in the chaos around him, more than by a trumpet call from Heaven—but his reply to the speech of Brother Thomas I already failed to hear. Like a flash of lightning there cut through my brain the thought that this was the last moment in which to save Renata, and that perhaps it was yet possible for me to tear her from hence, bearing her, perhaps against her will, as those demented are borne from flaming houses. Not thinking of the consequences, of the means of leaving the nunnery, which was surrounded by guards, I rushed to Renata, who was convulsed on the floor, still wound by the arms of her companions, and had already touched her body, so beloved by me, so precious to me, when I felt Brother Thomas softly thrusting me aside, and saw, busying themselves around, several archers who had not been present in the temple, and who had just been brought in, of course by the inquisitor, and were preserving all the calm of soldiers.

Brother Thomas said to me:

"Holy zeal deceives you, Brother Rupprecht! Calm yourself! These men will do everything, as is becoming."

I saw the archers of the Archbishop impassively bind the hands of the now unconscious Renata, and raise her to carry off somewhither. Still hardly knowing myself, I did not heed the words of the inquisitor, but once more rushed forward and was about to engage in personal combat with these men, to tear their precious burden from them, when I felt someone now take me by the arm, and it was Count Adalbert, who said sternly to me:

"Rupprecht! You are losing your reason!"

Commandingly and almost by force, he led me away across the whole chapel towards the doors of the exit; I obeyed him without will, as a child a grown-up, and we suddenly came into the fresh air and into the light of the sun, and behind us still were heard the howlings, and the moans, and the screams, and the laughter of the unfortunates possessed by the demons.

Chapter the Fifteenth

How Renata was tried under the Presidency of the Archbishop

CONTINUING to hold me by the arm, the Count led me across the whole convent yard, beyond the gates, until, crossing a small lawn set with a few silvered willows, we sat ourselves down, as if by accord, on the slope of the hill above the moat that encircled the walls of the convent. Here the Count said to me:

"Rupprecht! Your excitement is unusual. I swear by Hyperion that you are touched closer by this affair than all the rest of us! Explain it all to me as you would to a comrade."

And in truth I had, at this hour, no other comrade in all the wide world, and the fears and hopes teeming in my soul sought exit, like birds confined in a narrow cage, so, like a drowning man clutching at his last support—I told the Count everything: how I had met with Renata, how we had spent the winter together, as man and wife, and how only the caprice of her character had prevented us from sealing this union before the altar, how Renata had suddenly left me, and how I now recognised her as Sister Maria; I withheld only the real reasons of Renata's flight, explaining it by her sorrow for her sins and her desire for repentance—and I ended my narrative by addressing a request to the Count to aid me in this terrible position.

"These last weeks"—I declared—"as you yourself, gracious Count, may have noticed, I had somehow become

340

resigned, or rather, grown accustomed, to the thought that I had parted from Renata for ever. But scarcely did I look once more upon her face, than all the love in my soul resurrected like a Phœnix, and I realised once more that this woman is dearer to me than my own life. But alas, the merciless fate that has returned Renata to me, at the same time has thrown her into the hands of the Inquisition, and all the circumstances of the case cry out to me that I have miraculously regained her whom I had lost only to lose her utterly! What can I undertake for the salvation of my beloved— I, alone against the power of the Inquisition, against the will of the Archbishop, and against his force of archers and guards? If in you, Count, I can find neither assistance nor protection, if in you there is no compassion for me, there remains naught for me to do but to shatter my head against the walls of the prison that encloses Renata!"

Roughly in such words as these I spoke to the Count, and he listened to me with great tenderness, and showed, by the occasional questions he put to me, that he was trying sincerely to comprehend my history. And when I had finished, he said to me:

"Dear Rupprecht! Your history touches me to the quick, and I pledge you my knightly word that I shall render you every assistance within my power."

The events that followed proved that the Count did not trifle with his knightly honour, for, in trying to aid me against the inquisitor, he bravely endangered his high position, but, none the less, I am by no means certain that he acted thus owing to his goodwill towards or his interest in me. Reflecting now upon the behaviour of the Count, I am inclined to suppose that he was urged, first, by the desire to show himself a true Humanist by defending Sister Maria from the fanaticism of the inquisitor, for he would on no account agree to believe in the reality of demoniac possession; second, his dislike, of long standing, of the Archbishop, his liege lord, whose intentions it pleased him to frustrate; third and lastly, his youthful fondness for adventures and all manner of exploits, the same that prompted him to the involved and precarious mockery of Doctor Faustus. These considerations, however, it goes without saying, do not prevent me from preserving a feeling of the liveliest gratitude to the Count, and I think that, till death itself, his memory will ever be for me like a refreshing breeze in a torrid desert.

From the hour of this conversation the Count took upon himself the direction of all my actions, and began to behave towards me like an elder brother to his junior. While, after our talk, we were walking back to camp, I constructed on the way dozens of plans for more speedily securing the freedom of Renata, and all these plans converged to one—that we must tear the captive from her prison by main force. The Count pointed out to me with reason that the means of the other side were far superior to ours, that even should all the Count's men-at-arms obey us without a murmur, yet against us we should find the whole strength of the numerous guard of the Archbishop, his might as a prince, the power and influence of the inquisitor, and probably the whole population of the district, naturally ill-disposed towards witches, so that it would be preferable for us to use cunning, saving the sword till the last extremity. The remnants of sound reason could not but declare to me that the Count in this argument had hold of the stirrup of rightness; and I had naught else to do but yield to those contentions, bowing my soul beneath them, as an ox bows its head beneath the yoke.

Leading me to his tent, the Count ordered me to await him there, and I remained for several hours in a state of inactivity forced and burdensome, yielded a prey to ravening thoughts and merciless dreams. The major part of this time I spent lying face downwards on the bear's skin spread upon the couch, listening to

342

the beating of my heart, and trying not to marshal into rank the images that appeared in my imagination, one after the other, like horsemen on a hillock, and disappeared, after glittering for a second in the light of the sun. First I imagined Renata prostrate on the filthy and cold floor of a dark underground cell, then I saw the executioners submitting her to torment and elaborate torture, then her body being carried to burial without the cemetery walls; then, on the contrary, I imagined myself leading her forth from the prison, galloping on my horse with her across the countryside, sailing with her beyond the Ocean, beginning a new life with her in the New World. . . . At times I would be seized with such terror from my visions that I would leap to my feet, impetuously, ready to run whither only I might be able to do something, but with the power of will and the reasonings of logic I would shackle myself once more to my couch, and force myself once more to watch, like an idle spectator, the scenes enacted before me on the boards of my dream.

It was long past noon, and I was already almost exhausted by solitude and uncertainty, when at last the Count came in, but he avoided giving any reply to my passionate questions, demanding whether he had learnt anything of the fate of Sister Maria, and half-jokingly, half-didactically, he said that, since we had touched no food since morning, we must first partake of dinner. Painful was this meal, while Michael, a servant from the castle, served the simple dishes cooked in camp, which we were able to drink down with red Arbleichert of the best, from the convent cellars, and while the Count, pretending not to notice my gloom, persistently dragged me into a conversation about various ancient and modern writers. And, though forcing my mind, I yet involuntarily confused the names of the authors and books, thus exciting the gay laughter of the Count, which seemed blasphemous to me at that hour. And when, at last, our dinner had come

343

to end, the Count, washing his hands after the meal, said to me :

" And now, Rupprecht, take up your inkstand and let us be going to the convent : they are about to begin the examination of your Renata."

I felt clearly that my cheeks turned white at this communication, and I had strength enough only to repeat the last words :

" The examination of Renata ? "

And the Count, becoming suddenly quite serious, related to me in a sad and compassionate voice that the inquisitor and the Archbishop had decided to begin the inquiry without delay, for the case appeared likely to be important and complex ; that the Count himself was to be present at the trial by virtue of his rank, and that he had offered my services as a scribe, to record the questions of the judges and the answers of the accused ; for, in accordance with the provisions of the new Imperial code, a written record must be kept of the proceedings of every trial.

" What ! "—I exclaimed, on hearing this explanation —" Renata is actually to be tried here, at the convent, without the presence of a representative of the Emperor, without an advocate being accorded to her, without conformation to all the lawful forms of judicial procedure ! "

" You, it would seem"—the Count replied to me— "·imagine to yourself that you live in the happy times of Justinian the Great, and not in the days of Iohann of Schwarzenburg ! I must remind you that, in the opinion of our jurists, witchcraft is a crime entirely exceptional, *crimen exceptum*, in prosecuting which it is unnecessary to conform, strictly and faithfully, to the processes laid down by law. *In his*, they say, *ordo est ordinem non servare.* They so mightily fear the Devil, that they think any illegality justified in fighting him, and neither you nor I am in a position to dispute that custom ! "

344

The Fiery Angel

I did, in truth, understand at once the futility of a juristic argument, but none the less, at first view, it seemed to me monstrous—that I should partake in the trial of Renata, sitting amongst her judges—so that at first I firmly refused the proposal. Gradually, however, partly influenced by the arguments of the Count, partly having myself thought over the situation, I came to the conclusion that it would not be wise for me to avoid the opportunity of being present in court, for there, at the last extremity, I could in any case come to her assistance. So, in giving at last my consent, I yet firmly declared that, should the matter come to torture, I would permit no despoiling of the body so dear to me, but, unsheathing my sword, would free Renata from the torture by death, and, with a second thrust, myself—from the penalty of thus taking the law into my own hands. I discovered later that it would have been better had I not voiced this decision aloud, but at the time the Count made no attempt to dissuade me, only saying :

" In case of extremity you must act as you think fit, though we shall try to prevent it from going as far as torture. But remember in general that we are planning a dangerous game, and that you will ruin yourself for certain if you in any way betray your compassion for or intimacy with the accused. It were best for you not to disclose your face to her, and, if she should herself name you as her accomplice, deny it firmly. Now let us be going, and may Hermes, the god of all cunning, render us aid."

Having thus agreed, we made our way to the convent for the second time.

At the gates there awaited us, by the order of the Archbishop, a monk, who, after gruffly and disrespectfully remarking to us that we were late, conducted us to the eastern wall of the temple, where, near the door of the sacristy, there appeared to be yet another, low and embedded in the earth, a door that led into the

345

chapel vaults. By the light of a torch made of pitch, carried by our guide, we descended down a dark, slippery passage, through musty air, to a depth of more than one flight, then crossed two arched chambers, and at last, through a side arch, entered a subterranean hall, lit sparingly, so that everything within it appeared as if in twilight. In a corner of the wall, where was fixed a long torch, stood a heavy oak table, perhaps equal in years to the vaults themselves, and at that table, on a bench, sat two figures, in whom we soon recognised the Archbishop and the inquisitor, while, at some distance, were visible the dark forms and glittered the arms and trappings of the guards. And when the Count had apologised in elegant terms for his delay, and we had taken our places, also on the decayed bench, eaten away by the moisture of centuries, I distinguished in the opposite corner the vague ghost of a pole with a crossbar and a rope, and, realising that this was the strappado, I involuntarily felt for the hilt of my trusted sword. I shall remark also that the Count took his seat in line with the other judges, while I preferred to sit at the very end of the table, firstly because this was required by my respect for the rank of the Archbishop, and second, because there the light of the torch barely penetrated, and I could justly count upon my face remaining in shadow, and consequently not being recognised by Renata.

After the arrival of the Count, and seeing that I had taken out my field-inkstand, made ready my pen and spread the paper, the Archbishop turned to the inquisitor with the invitation :

" Brother Thomas, proceed with your duties."

Now, however, there ensued between the Archbishop and the inquisitor a polite altercation as to which of them should preside over the case, for each courteously relinquished the honour to the other. The Archbishop referred to the exact instruction of the papal bull, in which the Vice-Regent of Peter confers upon the inquisitors, directly appointed by him, the right to conduct trials of persons accused of the crime of magic, of commerce with demons, of flights to the Sabbath, and so forth, to throw them into prison, submit them to torture, and determine their punishment. But Brother Thomas, humbling himself hypocritically, admitted these rights as being his only by request of the prince of the district in which the criminal is discovered, and pointed out that, moreover, sorcery was a mixed crime, *crimen fori mixtum*, subject both to the ecclesiastical court, as a heresy, and to the civil court, in that it brings damage and ruin to people, and that therefore it was most becoming that the Archbishop, who united both authorities in his person, should take it into his competence. Interrupting this fruitless argument, the Count decided the question by suggesting that the Archbishop preside over the enquiry as seigneur of the Trier Kurfürstendom, and the inquisitor assume the conduct of the examination proper, as one endowed with direct authority by His Holiness, which decision I duly entered at the head of my melancholy report.

This, however, did not complete the preparatory deliberations, for Brother Thomas, dragging a paper from his deep pockets and holding it to his very nose, for it was not light enough for easy reading, made the following communication to us:

" Beloved brethren! In accordance with the recommendations of just and learned men, here is a Summons, which I shall nail to-day to the gates of this convent, should you approve it: ' We, known in the Dominican Order as the humble Brother Inquisitor Thomas, inspired by living affection for the Christian people and prompted by a thirst to maintain it in the unity and purity of the Catholic faith, and purge it of any contagion of heretic error, having to this end the dispensation and commission of His Holiness, the Vice-Regent of Christ, Paul III, and the sanction of His

Reverend Eminence the Archbishop of Trier, Iohann, do, by virtue of the powers with which we are invested, exhort and command, in the name of holy obedience to the Church, on pain of ruinous excommunication from Her, that any body, who knows or has heard of any other body, that he be a heretic, or practises sorcery, enjoys notoriety of doing so or be suspected of it, in particular if he be using various secret means to damage persons, animals, the fruits of the earth, or any part of the earth—that in the course of twelve days he report to us of such, and if in the course of twelve days he shall not have submitted to this our persuasion and command, let it be known to him that he himself, as a heretic and sinner, is subject to excommunication.' "

At this point in his speech, Brother Thomas made a pause, glanced in triumph at his two companions, and, hearing no argument in contraversion, continued :

" But in this particular case we have no need, so I presume, either of a report, or any *inscriptio*, for we ourselves have been witnesses of the appalling infidelity into which Sister Maria has fallen, in yielding to the temptations of the Fiend, and therefore we can proceed immediately to conduct the case by Inquisition procedure. If, during the examination, there should come to light evidence against other sisters in this holy cloister, we shall have a witness against them ready to our hand, for in such a terrible matter as sorcery no evidence must be despised. And let us remember the words contained for us in the precepts of the Saviour Himself, ' If thine eye offend thee, pluck it out.' "

Now I believe that an assured and experienced man could have destroyed the arguments of the Dominican, and snatched, if only temporarily, the prey from his jaws, as, according to the story, Agrippa of Nettesheim once saved, by reasoned arguments, a woman accused of witchcraft from the hands of another inquisitor in the town of Metz some fifteen years before. But who

out of us three could have taken upon himself the part
of the great scientist : the Archbishop, in no degree
less than Brother Thomas, was full of zeal to master the
wiles of the Devil, and being shaken, apparently, by
all that he had witnessed at the convent, was only glad
that someone else had taken it upon himself to conduct
the case ; if the Count had even begun to speak, it is
hardly likely that the other judges would have listened
to him, for he himself was under suspicion as a heretic
and friend of the humanists ; and could I have raised
my voice here, a humble scribe from the castle, only
by chance having been awarded the post of court
clerk ? And therefore no one opposed the inquisitor,
who felt as merry, in this business of the trial of a witch,
as a pike in a fish pen, and who, having concluded his
explanations, gave an order with the air of a commander
addressing his soldiers :
" Lead hither the accused ! "
Once more my heart fell, like a shot squirrel from a
tall pine, and two of the guards quickly disappeared
into the subterranean depths, as if diving into its
damp twilight, and then, after an interval, reappeared,
not so much leading as dragging behind them a woman :
it was Renata, her hair in disarray, in a torn monastic
robe, her hands twisted behind her by a rope. When
Renata had been led nearer to the table I was able to
distinguish her quite pale face in the unclear light of
the torch, and, knowing thoroughly all the peculiarities
of its expressions, I immediately perceived that she
was in that state of exhaustion and helplessness that
always came upon her after a fit of possession, and
during which there always ruled in her soul a consciousness of sin and an insurmountable desire for
death. When the guards released her, she almost fell
to the floor, but then, mastering herself, she remained
standing before the court, bending like a stem in the
wind, scarcely raising her eyes, and only at times trailing
her clouded glance along those present, as if not

comprehending what she was seeing—and I think that, after all, she never noticed my presence in the midst of the collegium of her judges.

For the space of several minutes Brother Thomas silently inspected Renata, as a tom-cat studies a mouse he has caught, and then put his first question, which sounded sharply, and slashed our silence like a knife :

" How are you named ? "

Renata just barely raised her head, but without looking at the examiner, and uttered in reply, softly, almost whispering :

" My name has been taken from me. I have no name."

Brother Thomas turned to me and said :

" Write down : she refused to give her Christian name, given to her in holy baptism."

Then Brother Thomas again addressed Renata, with the following harangue :

" My pretty one ! You know that we have all been witnesses of the fact that you are in league with the Devil. Moreover, the pious Mother Superior of this convent has informed us of the faithlessness that has established itself in this place from the very day on which you came here to live, certainly moved by the intention of seducing and destroying the gracious souls of the sisters of this cloister. Your accomplices have already all repented before us and denounced your shameful machinations, so that your denial will avail you nothing. It were better for you to confess all your sins and imaginings with an open heart, and then, by the majesty of the Holy Father himself, I promise you mercy."

I looked askance at the monk, and it seemed to me that he smiled, for, as I knew, the word " mercy " always means in such promises " mercy for the judges " or " mercy for the people," just as the word " life " in the promises of the inquisitors usually means " life eternal." But Renata did not notice the deceit in the words of the examiner, or perhaps it was the same to her before whom she confessed, only, with that same sincerity with which she had made her confessions to me in the happy days of our intimacy, she replied:

"I seek no mercy. I desire and seek death. I believe in the mercy of God at the last judgment, if here I do expiate my sins."

Brother Thomas looked at me, queried: "recorded?" and again asked Renata:

"So you confess that you have made a pact with the Devil?"

Renata answered:

"Fearful are my sins, I could not enumerate their number, even if I were to speak from morning until nightfall. But I renounced evil, and thought that the Lord had accepted my repentance. I do not seek to exculpate my sins, but, by the living God, I swear to you that I came to this cloister to seek peace and consolation, and not to instil strife! But the Lord permitted that even here I might not hide from mine Enemy, whom I myself gave power over me. Burn me, Master Judges, I thirst for fire, as for a liberation, for I see that there is nowhere on this earth where I may live in peace!"

Overcoming her weakness, Renata spoke these words with passion, and it was well that I was sitting away from the others, for my eyes filled with tears when I heard these terrible avowals, but they produced no effect on the Dominican, who interrupted Renata, saying:

"Not so fast, my pretty. We shall put the questions to you, and do you answer."

After this Brother Thomas took from his pocket a little book, which I recognised, by various signs, as the "*Malleus Maleficarum in tres partes divisus*" of Sprenger and Institor, and referring to this handbook, he began to put detailed questions to Renata, which, as well as the answers that followed them, I had to write down, though at times they made me grind my

teeth in despair. This whole examination I shall record
here exactly as I then wrote it down, for each ruinous
question sucked at my soul like a tentacle of the ocean
octopus, and each melancholy confession of Renata
remained in my memory like the words of a prayer
learned by heart in childhood. Methinks that not a
word will I have altered in reproducing this record of
mine in the pages of this faithful narrative.

I will remark here that Renata replied to the first
questions hesitantly, disconnectedly, and shortly, in an
exhausted voice, as if it were too great an effort for her
to pronounce the words, but gradually she somehow
livened, she even held herself on her feet with more
confidence, and her voice became stronger and regained
all its usual resonance. To the final questions she replied
even with eagerness, humbly explaining every point
about which she was asked, ardently and longwindedly
relating even much that was irrelevant, going into
unnecessary details, not being abashed to touch upon
ignoble matters, as was her custom, and as if intentionally seeking out more and more horrible accusations
against herself. Remembering the experiences of my
life in company with Renata, I am inclined to think that
much of her confession was untrue, and that much was
invented on the spur of the moment, mercilessly to
calumniate herself to some end incomprehensible to me,
if it were not that some inimical demon possessed her
soul the while, and spoke with her lips, to destroy her
the more certainly.

I will observe, also, that the further the examination
proceeded, the more obviously satisfied and yet more
satisfied grew Brother Thomas, and I noticed how his
nostrils quivered as he listened to the shameless admissions of Renata, how taut became the veins of his hands,
as he leaned on them, drawing himself up, how all his
body swayed with an overflow of joy, as he saw his hopes
and suppositions justifying themselves. The Archbishop, on the contrary, already seemed tired very soon

after the examination had begun, and in no degree exhibited that same firmness with which he had astonished me in the morning—he was suffering, no doubt, from the fetid subterranean air, wearied from sitting on the wooden bench, and probably he found nothing entertaining in the revelations of Sister Maria. While the Count contrived all the time to remain stern and dispassionate, his face not betraying the movements of his soul, only arresting me from time to time with a meaning glance, when I, losing control over myself at the horrible proceedings, was about to cry out some imprudent words, or even to commit some demented action, which of course could have led to no other result than my immediate arrest also, as accomplice of the criminal.

And so, this is what I wrote down, question following question, acting in my capacity as a humble scribe of the inquisitorial court:

Question : Who taught you sorcery, the Devil himself, or one of his disciples ?

Answer : The Devil.

Question : Whom did you teach in your turn ?

Answer : None.

Question : When, and on what date, did the Devil wed you ?

Answer : Three years ago on the night of the holiday of Corpus Christi.

Question : Did he force you, in pact with him, to renounce God the Father, Son and Holy Ghost, the Most Blessed Virgin, all the saints and all the Christian faith ?

Answer : Yes.

Question : Did you receive a second baptism from the Devil ?

Answer : Yes.

Question : Have you been present at the dances of the Sabbath, thrice a year, or oftener ?

Answer : Much oftener, many times.

353

Question : How did you transport yourself thither ?

Answer : In the evenings, when night set in, when the Sabbath was gathering, we anointed our bodies with a special ointment, and then there appeared to us a black billy-goat, that transported us through the air on its back, or a demon himself, in the shape of a gentleman dressed in a green jacket and yellow waistcoat, and I held on to his neck with my arms as he flew above the fields. And if there were neither billy-goat nor demon, we could sit astride any object and it would fly like the fastest steed.

Question : Of what substances did you concoct the ointment that you rubbed on yourself in such cases ?

Answer : We took various herbs : hart's wort, parsley, sweet-rush, cotton-weed, banewort, madwort, placed them in an infusion of aconite, added an oil distilled from plants and the blood of a bat, and boiled them all together, repeating certain words, varying according to the different months of the year.

Question : Did you add to this composition the fat of babies you had done to death, and if so which, melted or grilled ?

Answer : No, for it was not necessary.

Question : Did you see at the Sabbath the Evil Spirit seated on a throne in the shape of a He-goat, and had you to give worship to him, and kiss his unclean rump ?

Answer : That has been my sin. And also we brought him our offerings : moneys, eggs, pasties, and some, also, brought him stolen babes. Also we gave suck with our breasts to small demons in the shape of toads, or, by order of the Master, we thrashed them with rods. Then we danced to the sounds of a drum and a flute.

Question : Did you also take part in the service of the ungodly Black Mass ?

Answer : Yes, and the Devil himself partook of the

354

communion as well as administered it to us, saying
" this is my body."

Question: Did this communion consist of one substance or of two ?

Answer: Of two, but instead of the host there was
something hard that was difficult to swallow, and instead
of wine a draught of liquid terribly bitter, and bringing
cold to the heart.

Question: Did you at the Sabbath enter into bodily
connection with the Devil ?

Answer: The Devil each night chose one among the
women whom we called Queen of the Sabbath, and
she whiled away the night with him. And everyone
else united at the end of the feast, as it might befal,
who chanced to approach whom, women, men, and
demons, and only occasionally did the Devil interfere,
himself arranging couples, saying ; " This is he of
whom you stand in need " or " She will suit you."

Question: Did it happen to you to be Queen of the
Sabbath ?

Answer: Yes, and not only once, of which I was
very proud—may the Lord have mercy on my soul !

Question: Tell us, did your lying with the Devil
give you more sweetness and satisfaction than that
with a man ?

Answer: Much greater, without any comparison.

Question: Had he in its course an outflowing of
seed ?

Answer: Yes, but this seed was cold.

Question: Did you not have any issue from cohabitation with demons ?

Answer: One small white mouse, very pretty, was
born unto me, but I strangled it and buried it in the
garden, above the river. Ah, had I but had any
children, how many sins would I have been saved from
committing !

Question: In general, did it give you pleasure to
visit the Sabbath ?

Answer : An extreme pleasure, so that we went to the Sabbath as to a wedding. The Devil held always our hearts so strongly shackled that no other desire could enter into us. It seemed to me then as though I saw at each Sabbath many hundreds of new and wonderful things, as though the music of the Sabbath were more beautiful than any other music, as though it were an earthly paradise.

Question : Did the Devil teach you how to produce thunderstorms, hail, rats, mice, moles, how to change yourself into a she-wolf, how to deprive cows of their milk, how to ruin crops, and make men incapable of marital cohabitation ?

Answer : He taught me all this and much else, in which I acknowledge myself a sinner, before the Lord God and before mankind.

Question : Tell us, how do you produce thunderstorms ?

Answer : For this purpose one must make a little hollow in a field, in a place where banewort grows, and, squatting over it, cause it to become wet, and say: " In the name of the Devil, rain ! " and at once there will come a cloud and rain will follow.

Question : And how do you deprive men of their strength ?

Answer : For this there are more than fifty means, for example, take the male organs of a newly-slain wolf and go to the threshold of him whom you desire to disable, call him by his name, and, when he answers, wind that which you have in your hands around with white tape—and, anyway, I have no wish to tell you more of them !

Question : Did you cause by these means, and also in the shape of a she-wolf, or of any other were-beast, hurt to fields, animals, or human beings ?

Answer : A terrible hurt, that it is impossible even to fathom, for we ate a multitude of lambs, ruined crops and orchards, sent hosts of rats into villages,

356

made many women incapable of bearing issue, and, I
think, had not remorse come upon us, the whole
district would have perished from a failure of crops
and other misfortunes! But why do you question me
further when, however much you question me, I
shall never be able to enumerate the whole number of
my sins! Oh, lead me more quickly to the pyre, for
even here my enemy does not quit me—even now he is
about to seize me! Slay me, quickly, quickly!

With these last words, Renata began to jerk herself
about, as if on the point of flinging herself at the judges,
but the two burly guards seized her arms and restrained
her from this intention. Then the Archbishop, perhaps
rendered uneasy by the behaviour of the accused, or
perhaps merely fatigued by the examination, turned
to the inquisitor with the following words:

" Should not the examination be ended, if the accused
herself admits that she is guilty and deserving of the
stake ? "

Brother Thomas, who had thrown himself into the
inquiry as a merry otter dives into water, objected thus:

" I suggest it as my opinion that it behoves us first
to discover the names of the demons with whom this
slut has entered into connection, and the exact terms
of her pacts with them, and also to worm out of her
the identity of her accomplices in all these ungodly
deeds. For thus speaks the Apostle: they are from
amongst us, *ex nobis egressi sunt !* "

Renata, hearing the words of the inquisitor, exclaimed in a strangled voice:

" You must not ask me any more. I had no accom-
plices! They whom I met at the Sabbath are afar off.
It was not here, but in another land! Merciful Lord
Christ, come to my aid! "

Brother Thomas replied to her:

" Not so fast, my little chicken, when we jerk you
up on the strappado, and roast your heels with a red-
hot iron, you will sing us a song in another tune."

I clapped my hand to the hilt of my sword, but the Archbishop said firmly :

" It were better for us to continue the investigation at some other time, for we have yet to question the witnesses, Mother Martha and the other sisters."

The Count, who had been silent until now, also took part in the discussion, and he too began to insist that the case be postponed until to-morrow morning, pointing out, among other things, that it was not worth while to begin torture when even the judges themselves were already tired by the examination, but Brother Thomas disagreed :

" Have you not forgotten, my lord Count, that it is only prohibited to *repeat* the torture, if no new evidence be manifested, but all the authorities are agreed that it may be *continued* the next day, or the one after next also, and intellects worthy of respect call on us to proceed in such a case *ad continuandum tormenta, non ad iterandum*. We might just have begun to-day, and to-morrow we could have continued. . . . "

Seeing however that his speech met with no sympathy, Brother Thomas abruptly broke it off, like a spinner a ravelled thread, and though he himself would obviously have been happy to continue questioning day and night—he said in a quite different voice :

" However, I am entirely obedient to the will of His Reverend Eminence, who knows better than others how this case should be conducted. But nevertheless, methinks you will agree that we should not let this wench go without first having seen whether she have upon her body the stigmata of a witch."

Brother Thomas loudly called someone whose name I did not catch, and from the darkness, from beside the horrible post that rose in the depths, there stepped forth a man, broad-shouldered and bearded, in whom it was impossible not to recognise an executioner. At this appearance I clutched my sword for the second time, but encountered immediately the staring gaze of the Count, silently importuning me to keep calm until the last possible moment. Overpowering myself, I watched as my horrible dream became incarnate, saw how the executioner tore the dress of Renata, who in no wise resisted him, and how in the moist subterranean twilight he searched all her body with his coarse hands, her body, that once I covered with reverent kisses.

At last the attention of the executioner was arrested by a small birthmark on the left shoulder, which I knew so well, and taking a small awl from his pocket, he touched with it on this spot the flesh of Renata, who did not move. Then the executioner exclaimed in a coarse and gruff voice, as though he were shouting through a trumpet:

" Here it is ! No blood has oozed ! "

For the inquisitor and the Archbishop this announcement by the executioner, even though unverified by them, seemed a last and decisive proof, for Brother Thomas at once shrieked, as in bygone days did the High Priest of the Hebrews :

" What further need have ye of witnesses ! Is it not as clear as God's day that she is a witch ! "

Then he added :

" And now we have still to singe all the hair on her body with fire, for beneath it she may be concealing spells."

However, the Count, seeing clearly that I should suffer no further indignity, intervened firmly, reminding the inquisitor that the Archbishop himself, who presided over our inquiry, had decided to interrupt it until the morning of the morrow, and Brother Thomas, fussing like a mouse in a trap, gave orders for Renata to be led back into her cell. Methinks that at this moment Renata was not in consciousness, for a guard, clumsily pulling over her her monastic garb, lifted her up like a child and dragged her again into the darkness, while I, having no means of following her, almost collapsed, racked by my powerlessness. At this

moment, in my fate, I was like the Spaniard whom the
Aztecs, after taking prisoner, tied to a tree trunk and,
cutting off his eyelids, forced to watch them submitting
his comrades to torture before his eyes.

Despite all my efforts, I was probably not able
entirely to conceal the interest that I felt in the fate of
the accused, for when our small company, having
passed once more through the subterranean passages,
had come out again into the fresh air of which Renata
was deprived, and when the Archbishop, having given
us his blessing, had departed, Brother Thomas asked
me, not without suspicion:

"It must, Master Rupprecht, be the first time you
have been present at the prosecution of such fiends:
you wear so depressed an air one might think you were
sorry for this slut."

And I, who had but just now been patient through
far heavier trials, could not endure these words, and,
suddenly losing mastery over myself, flew at the inquisitor, grabbed him by the collar of his cassock, shouting
at him:

"You are the first to deserve being cast into the
flames, accursed pater!"

Such behaviour on my part might have led to very
serious consequences for me, but the Count, rushing
quickly to the monk's rescue, freed him from my hands
and said sternly to me:

"You too must be possessed by some demon,
Rupprecht, or else you have lost your reason!"

Brother Thomas, whose face had become all distorted
with fear when I flew at him, very soon recovered his
composure, and, though he tried to keep at a distance
from me, also began to soothe me:

"Or perhaps it is that you do not know me, dear
brother Rupprecht? It is I—your meek brother
Thomas. How is it that you have thus granted domin-
ion over yourself to the Unclean? The Fiend is strong,
but one should be able to withstand him by prayer.

Oh, heavy is this task, the combat with the Devil, for he prowls around his judges, and wherever he finds a breach undefended, there he hastens to penetrate : be it through the mouth, through the ears, or through any other opening of the body ! "

I muttered some kind of apology through clenched teeth, and the Count, to dispel the unpleasant impression, entered into a conversation with the inquisitor about the case of Sister Maria, and asked whether it were undoubted that she would here and now be sentenced to the stake. Brother Thomas livened up at once, and began with the greatest readiness to explain to us the law :

" In the Criminal Code "—he was saying—" printed by the will of His Majesty the Emperor for the use of the whole Empire three years ago, and by which we are now governed, clause 109 declares : ' *Item*, if a body by means of sorcery cause evil or misfortune to any other body, he shall be punished for it by death, and execution shall be performed by means of fire. If, however, a body shall have practised sorcery, but yet not caused harm to any other body, he shall be punished according to the circumstances of the case.' Sister Maria has from her own mouth confessed herself guilty of having caused harm to human beings, and cattle, and crops, and thus she incurs death."

The Count also enquired whether one accused must be submitted to torture if she has already confessed all of her own accord, and Brother Thomas answered this also without delay :

" Unquestionably "—said he—" for clause 44 of the same Constitution of the Emperor Charles says explicitly : ' *Item*, if a body has recourse to doubtful matters, deeds and actions which in themselves contain sorcery, and if such a body be but accused thereof, by this fact is given a clear indication of the presence of sorcery, and a sufficient ground for the application of torture.' Apart from this, you are probably unaware that there is no other means against such fiends as witches, to force them to speak the truth, for the Devil is for ever present at their examinations and often helps them to support the most arduous trials. In cases of such weighty crime, one must perforce have recourse to the most powerful countering methods."

I did not listen further to what the inquisitor was saying, for I felt as though I had wandered into some ensorcelled courtyard, from which there was no egress, so that I fruitlessly flung myself from side to side, everywhere meeting stone, insuperable walls. Not saying a word to anyone, I hastened my steps, and almost ran from those talking, having no purpose before me, only desiring to be alone. The Count, however, soon caught up with me, asking me whither I was running, and I replied to him:

" Dear Count! It behoves us to attempt our enterprise immediately, for every hour of delay may cost Renata her life. Till now I have restrained myself from any crucial action, only because you promised me your assistance. I beseech you not to postpone matters any longer, or, pray, tell me straightway that you are powerless to help me. Then I shall act on my own, even though my attempts may lead me to certain death."

The Count replied to me:

" I pledged you my knightly word, Rupprecht, and I shall keep that oath. Go to our tent and there await my call, while I shall work on your behalf."

The voice of the Count was so persuasive, and I was so conscious of my utter impotence, that I had no other course left me but to obey, yet I had not the strength to enter, for a second time, that tent, where, as in a lion's den, would have lain in watch for me, with greedy jaws and sharp fangs, the same thoughts of sorrow as those of the morning, and perhaps many more, not less bitter.

I told the Count that I should await him on the

shores of the rivulet, and, avoiding all encounters, I made my way through the thick willow growths that lined its course, and there hid in the twilight and the moisture, so placing myself that the convent was visible to me through breaches in the foliage. Here, once more in forced idleness, I spent another period of several hours, breathing the fresh fragrance of the running water, and knowing that Renata, ill, exhausted, was spending these same hours upon clammy earth, amidst lichen, spiders and woodlice.

I feared that I might lose the power to act with reason if I gave myself up to the waves of despair that pressed upon me, and, accordingly, I stubbornly forced myself not to lose my clearness of thought. As if resolving some problem, I considered all the possible means of saving Renata, yet could think of none but that of gaining possession of the convent by main force, breaking open the doors of her prison and carrying her off, before the Archbishop could have time to assemble a considerable troop. Transported by such dreams, I already imagined to myself all the particulars of the forthcoming fight between the supporters of the Count and the henchmen of the Archbishop, visualised exactly how I should break down the gates of the cloister, composed from the first word to the last the speech that I should address to the frightened nuns persuading them not to oppose the liberation of Sister Maria, and finally, with tears in my voice, I repeated the words I should speak to the rescued Renata.

From these imaginings, as from a soothing dream, I was roused by a voice that softly called me by my name, and turning round, I saw that near me stood the Count, and behind him Michael, holding two horses by the reins. The Count's face was more deeply clouded than I had ever see it before, and in the first instant, thinking that all was over, and that Renata had already been condemned and executed, I involuntarily exclaimed :

" Can it be that it is too late ? "

The Count replied to me:

" We must ride at once, Rupprecht, I have convinced myself that such forces as we have here are not sufficient for our undertaking. We must seek allies, whom the Romans, too, did not disdain. In the immediate neighbourhood I know a castle, the seigneur of which maintains a friendship with me. Let us ride thither, and bring back with us a score of stout lads."

This appeal accorded so miraculously with my dreams, that I did not for one moment doubt the sincerity of the Count, and it never entered my mind that it would be unwise for us both to leave the cloister; on the contrary, with all eagerness I hastened to my horse and soon both of us were in the saddle. I asked the Count whether our way were long, and he only retorted that we must hurry, but that we had best make the first part of our road along the bed of the rivulet, so that our departure should not be noted in the camp. All this was very convincing, and I was ready at this moment if need be to blaze my way after the Count with my sword.

Having ridden for about a quarter of an hour in the depths of the valley, we climbed up, and galloped due westward along a bad country lane. My eyes were blinded by the sun, which was now setting, and which built before me, by the frolic of its rays, weird castles from the evening clouds, only to annihilate them immediately, and I felt as though it was in those ghostly palaces that we should find the help that we were seeking. I urged on my horse as though in truth I hoped to gallop to the land where Aurora opens wide the flaming gates to Phœbus, and the wind whistled in my ears, either words of encouragement or prophecies of despair. Gradually the west grew dimmer and dimmer, the red sun went down behind the nethermost cloud, and the air around freshened; the country became more rugged, but no sign of human habitation appeared, and in vain did I scan the horizon for the

towers of the promised castle. Several times I asked
the Count whether it were yet far for us to ride, but
each time I received no answer, and at last, seeing that
my horse was tired, and that the road was completely disappearing amidst boulders strewn in disarray, I
suddenly drew rein and thus exclaimed :

" Count ! You have deceived me ! There is no
castle ! Whither have you led me ? "

Then the Count, too, stopped his horse, and he
answered me in a soft, touching voice, which at times he
knew how to assume :

" Yes, I have deceived you. There is no castle."

All my flesh grew cold, my hands trembled, and,
flinging my horse straight at the Count, ready to assail
him in combat, in this forsaken, man-deserted valley,
in the hour of the first shadows, I shouted :

" Why have you done this ? What was your purpose ?
Answer me, or else I slay you where you stand ! "

The Count replied to me calmly :

" *Rupprechte, insanis !* Listen first, and threaten
afterwards. I discovered that Thomas had appointed
a second examination for this evening. Much as I
tried, I could not alter this decision. I did not doubt
that, had you remained at the convent, you would have
committed some rash act, and thereby ruined our whole
enterprise. I resolved to take you away for a time, to
save both yourself and your beloved."

" What ! "—I demanded—" the second examination is
fixed for this evening ? Then that means that it is
being conducted at this moment ? But the examination
will be by ordeal ! That means that Renata is even now
being subjected to torture, and I am far from her—
here, here, here—in this field, and cannot even reply
to her moans ! "

With this, the fit of fury left me, and, jumping from
the horse, I flung myself face downwards on the boulders
moist with evening dew, pressed against them with my
cheek, and, once more, tears streamed unchecked from

my eyes, for, like a woman or a child, I had no other weapons to combat my fate. I at once represented to myself all the forms of torture of which I had even only sometime heard : the press, the screw, the strings, the pincers, the strappado, the goat, the mare, the ladder, the Spanish boot, the collar, flogging, the insertion of pegs under the nails, torture with water, with fire, with pitch, and all the other horrors invented by man against man. I wept uncontrolledly, and at that moment sincerely desired but one thing only: to be with Renata, at her side ; to yield my body to all the torments to which she was being subjected, and it seemed monstrous and incongruous that I should feel no pain while she was languishing beneath her sufferings.

In the meantime the Count dismounted also, sat down next me upon the ground, and also as if seeing in me some child, he began to soothe me tenderly. In the most persuasive manner, he tried to assure me that I must not be alarmed by the torture, which we had no means to prevent, for very many persons can endure it without ultimate injury to their health. The Count himself had known some alchymist, whom the infidels of Mostar had thirty times submitted to torture, and even impaled, hoping thereby to extract from him the secret of the philosopher's stone, which, it was alleged, was known to him. And yet he had lived to a ripe old age. And besides, according to the words of the Count, it was not possible that, in this peaceful and isolated cloister, there could be those terrible implements of torture of which boast such towns as Bamberg, Mecklenburg, or Nürnberg, so that the worst that could happen to Sister Maria was a dislocation of her arm joints on the strappado, which the executioner himself would be able immediately to set. The Count also did not forget to cite for my comfort several quotations from Annæus Seneca, the philosopher, who points out how beneficial it is for mankind to suffer physical pain.

366

Naturally, these words of the Count failed in any way to soothe me, and even provided at times fuel to augment my despair, and at last the Count, noticing that all his arguments and logical deductions were powerless against my emotions, spoke to me as follows:

" Well then, listen, Rupprecht, I shall disclose to you my plan, so that you shall not think me your enemy, but your true friend. Know then, that I have already staged all for the rescue of your beloved. Mother Martha is very well disposed towards Sister Maria and does not believe in her guilt. Moreover, being a Clarissian and consequently belonging to the Franciscan order, she is only too glad to have the opportunity of annoying a Dominican. You know, of course, that all these monastic orders gnaw at each other like dogs. In short, Mother Martha has agreed, after very much persuasion on my part, to help us to engineer the flight of your Renata. But you understand that such an enterprise can be accomplished only at night, *per amica silentia lunæ*. We shall even now return to the convent. On guard at the gates both of the cloister and of the prison will be nuns entirely loyal to the Mother Superior, and moreover revering Sister Maria as a saint. They will unfasten all the locks before us. You will descend into the vaults and lead out your Renata, or carry her in your arms if she have not the strength to walk. At the gates will await you Michael and a couple of fresh horses ; ride straight to my castle. Afterwards we shall see what has further to be done, but I am convinced that not only the others, but Thomas himself, despite his apostolic name, will believe that Sister Maria has been freed by the Devil. Thus, give me your hand, and *ne moremur !* "

The Count's plan contained far more of that fantasy of youthful imagination that habitually governed his actions, than of experience or knowledge of men ; however, this was the last rope by clutching which I might climb out of the abyss of my misfortunes. We again mounted our horses, and again urged them, this time in the opposite direction, finding our way with difficulty in the gathering darkness. Fortunately we did not lose our way, and we reached the camp in the feeble light of an emaciated new moon.

Chapter the Sixteenth

How Renata died, and all that befell me after her Death

WHEN the walls of the cloister within which Renata was imprisoned once more came in sight—I felt in me, despite my fatigue from the senseless gallop, an inrush of energy and courage, for decisive hours always draw my soul taut, as a firm arm tautens an arbalist.

Near our tent we dismounted and gave our horses to Michael, who was awaiting us, displaying obvious impatience, for he replied to the query of the Count whether all was ready, thus:

" Long ready, indeed, and to tarry further is impossible. Jan is posted with fresh horses near the northern wall, I have wound their hooves in wool. And this accursed pater Thomas is prowling around here, and may light on something at any moment."

We all three of us proceeded to the convent, choosing the part of the road that lay most darkly and trying by all means to pass unnoticed, though apparently all were asleep, for we met no one on our road and not a dog barked in the village. Michael walked in front, as if leading the way, behind him was the Count, no doubt vastly inspirited by our unusual adventures, and I came last of all, for I did not want anyone to notice me. The thought that I was now about to see Renata alone, and that within the space of a few minutes she would be free once more and under my protection, made my heart tremble with joy, and I should, without wavering, have fought one against three, if only to realise my dreams.

Having negotiated the hillock, we came to the gates of the cloister, in the black shadow of its walls, and Michael pointed out to us where some distance away loomed the dim outlines of the two horses guarded by one of our men, and said:

"Thither, Master Rupprecht, you must carry your booty—I shall be waiting for you and I know the straight road to the castle. Trust me—falcons would not catch us."

In the meantime the Count knocked softly with the hilt of his sword on the iron of the gates, so that in the moonlit silence the sound came meek and plaintive, like a sob. From behind the gate came a woman's voice, also subdued, which asked:

"Who's there?"

The Count replied with the pass-word agreed upon:

"The land of Judah is no smaller than the provinces of Judah."

At once the gates, as if by witchcraft, softly opened, and at that moment I believed as firmly in the success of our undertaking as if I were already safe with Renata behind the trusty protection of the arrow-slits of the Castle von Wellen. The sister who opened the gates to us looked at us with fear, and was very pale—or perhaps she seemed so only in the light of the moon, but she did not utter a word. The feebly-lighted convent yard was quite deserted, yet we crossed it creeping beneath the walls, like three ghosts, and approaching the rear part of the chapel, we came upon the horrible door giving access to the subterranean world, to Renata. Here, on a flat stone, half asleep, there sat on guard another nun, who jumped up at our approach, trembling all over.

The Count repeated the pass-word and the sister fell to her knees, repeating in a strangled voice:

The Fiery Angel

" Blessed be he that cometh in the name of the
Lord ! March on, march on ! lead from her prison the
innocent victim, heaped with chains by the devices
of the Enemy ! Sister Maria is holy and may her
enemies be dumfoundered with shame ! Christ Jesus
is her Immaculate Spouse ! "

Michael rudely interrupted these mutterings, whispering to the sister :

" Enough cackle, we are not in a hen-house ! Open
the door ! "

The nun, taking out a huge iron key, tried to unlock
the door, but her hands trembled so that she could not
fit the head of the key into the aperture of the lock, and
so Michael, taking it from her, unlocked it himself.
When the black entrance to the vaults gaped open,
Michael carefully struck a flame, lit the small torch that
he had brought with him and handed it to me, while
the Count said :

" Rupprecht, descend. At the back of the hall in
which we conducted the examination this morning is a
door closed by a bolt. Unfasten it : behind it is the
cell of your Maria. Hasten, Michael will wait for
you, and may the mother of love, the Cnidian Cyprian,
come to your aid ! Farewell ! "

I was too excited to make any answer to the Count,
but, clutching the torch in my hand, I rushed into the
dark depths, and hastened, stumbling, along the steps
of the slippery staircase, until I reached the hall of our
inquiry. Our table, at which I had written down the
fatal answers of Renata, was bare and looked like a
huge tomb ; the gloomy frame of the strappado with
its raised arm yet towered in the depths, and as I
looked at it I shivered ; my steps sounded sonorous in
the emptiness, and shadows fluttered around—maybe
they were bats. Having walked a few paces further as
instructed by the Count, I stumbled against a wooden
door with bars forged in iron, and closed by a heavy
bolt, and thrusting this back not without difficulty, I

371

found myself in an arched chamber, low and stiflingly moist.

Moving my torch around, I gradually lit up all the corners of the prison, and distinguished in its far corner a heap of straw, and upon it a prostrate body, barely covered with the rags of clothing ; I realised that this was Renata, and with a sinking of the heart approached and knelt beside her miserable couch. In the swaying light of the torch, I could clearly distinguish Renata's face, pale like that of a corpse, with shut, as if lifeless eyes, her stretched out, motionless, exhausted arms, her breast, hardly lifted by her breath—and for about a minute endured a silence, for I dared not utter a word in this holy place. At last, reminding myself that every moment was numbered, I whispered softly :

" Sister Maria ! "

There was no reply, and I repeated more loudly :

" Renata ! "

At this call Renata opened her eyes, slightly, turned her head towards me, looked at me searchingly, recognised me, and, as if not at all surprised at seeing me by her side, uttered in a weak, scarcely discernible voice :

" Begone, Rupprecht ! I forgive you all, but— begone."

For the moment I was completely taken aback by these words, but then, having reflected that Renata, racked by torture and imprisonment, must be delirious, I replied, putting into my words all the tenderness of which I was capable :

" Renata ! my dearest Renata ! beloved ! my only one ! I bring you liberation and freedom. The gates are opened wide, we shall flee from hence, horses await us. Then we shall sail to New Spain, where a new life shall begin for us. I will serve you like a slave, and in nothing oppose myself to your decisions. For I love you as dearly as ever, Renata, I love you more than my life, more than the salvation of my soul. If you are

372

able, rise, give me your hand, follow me. Or allow me to carry you in my arms, I am strong enough. But we must hasten."

Having spoken these words with extreme emotion, I awaited the answer, bending to the very face of Renata, but she, not having stirred, in the same soft voice, without inflection, without modulation, answered as follows:

"I shall not follow you, Rupprecht! Once you nearly destroyed me, but I saved my soul from your talons! They have tortured me, they have crucified me —oh! but know they did not, that thus they were commanded by Jesus Christ! Blood, blood! I have seen my blood! How good! how sweet! It has washed away all my sins. Again he will fly to me like a large butterfly and I shall hide him in my tresses. No, no, really, he is just a butterfly, and nothing more. How dare you be here beside me, Rupprecht?"

This strange and disconnected speech convinced me that Renata had indeed lost from her sufferings the power of consecutive thought, but I yet made an effort to bring her to reason, saying to her:

"Renata! Hear me, try to understand me. You are in prison, in the convent prison. You are being tried by the inquisitory court and a horrible execution threatens you. To save your life you must flee and I have prepared all for your flight. Remember you said once to me that you loved me. Trust unto me and you will be set free. Then I shall give you your liberty to do as you will; remain with me, or leave me, or enter a nunnery again. I ask of you nothing, I do not ask love, I desire only to tear you from the executioners and save you from the flames. Is it possible that you desire torture and the torments of fire?

Renata exclaimed:

"Yes! Yes! I desire torture and fire! Just now I saw my Madiël and he told me that by death I shall expiate my whole life. He is all of flame, his eyes are

373

blue as the skies, and his hair is of fine gold thread. He told me that he will receive my soul in his embracing arms, and that in the life eternal we shall never part, never. I forgive, I forgive, both you and Heinrich, for Madiël has forgiven me all. I am happy, I desire naught else. Only leave me alone ; let me be with him ; you frightened him away ; begone—and he will return."

With final persistence, I exclaimed :

" Renata, I swear to you by all that is holiest to me, I cannot leave you here ! God and my conscience command me to remove you hence. You are exhausted, you are ill, you cannot reason soundly. Listen to me as a friend, as one older than you ! It is not an expiatory death that awaits you here—you are only delivering yourself into the hands of brutal monks and bigots sunk deep in ignorance. Only come out from hence, only breathe the fresh air, only glance at the sun, and if within three days you should say to me : I desire to return to the prison—I swear that I myself will lead you hither."

Renata raised herself a little with difficulty, and, looking me straight in the face, said, as if fully in possession of her faculties :

" I tell you, that I desire nothing from you ! Your presence inspires me only with revulsion. Go from hence, return to life once more, kiss your Agnes, and I, may they lift me again upon the strappado. You want me to flee with you somewhither ! Oh, dear, dear Heinrich, he would not have insulted me thus ! I should only have said to him that I desired to die, and he would at once have understood me. And you, once a landsknecht, always a landsknecht, all you understand is how to slay an enemy. Well then, slay me, I have not the strength to defend myself ! "

In these cruel and unjust words I recognised the old Renata, she who once made me fall to the earth in impotent despair or grind my teeth at an undeserved affront, but I did not allow myself to yield to impulse and forget that Renata was now not responsible for what she was saying, like an ailing person become delirious, or an unfortunate possessed by an evil spirit. And so I said firmly:

" Renata! I swear by the All Highest, I love you! and therefore I shall save you even against your will!"

Having spoken thus, I carefully leaned the torch against a projection of the wall, and then, clenching my teeth and trying not to look Renata in the face, I firmly bent over her, and, seizing her in my arms, desired to lift her from her couch of straw. Sensing my intention, Renata flew into a terrible excitement, shrank back, pressed into the corner of her cell, and screamed in a loud and despairing voice:

" Madiël! Madiël! protect me! save me!"

Paying no heed to this scream, I did not allow myself to be deflected from the purpose before me, and between us there began an insensate struggle, as Renata, who could hardly use her arms, exhausted by torture, strove to beat me back with her whole body, twisting frenziedly, flinging herself in all directions, using every means to free herself from my embrace. She did not disdain attempting to topple me over, pushing at me with her feet, and also did not hesitate wickedly to plunge her teeth into my hands, and in the intervals of the struggle she shouted into my face furious insults:

" Accursed one! Accursed one! You profit by my weakness! You are repulsive to me! Let me go, I shall shatter my head against these walls! Anything were better than to be with you! You are—the Devil! Madiël! Madiël! Defend me!"

Suddenly, when I already felt myself victor, Renata's movements all at once grew weaker, and, uttering a piercing and horrible scream of pain, she drooped in my hands without movement, as droops the stem of a flower broken off. Quickly guessing that something had happened to Renata, I speedily lowered her back on to the straw, and loosened my embrace, but she was already like one dead, and it looked to me as though she were not breathing. Searching hurriedly round the cell, I found a little water in an earthenware jug and moistened her temples, after which she sighed feebly, but to me, who had so often been witness of the expiration of wounded after battle, there was left no doubt that her last moment was approaching. I do not know whether the efforts that she had made in resisting me had had a fatal effect upon her, or whether her frail being had not been able to support those merciless trials that it had in general been her lot to suffer, but in any case all the signs pointed clearly to the approach of the end, for the expression of her face acquired a special solemnity, all her body became strangely rigid, and she piteously clutched at the straw with her contorted fingers.

I could render no help to Renata, and continued to kneel beside her couch, gazing into her face, but suddenly, for one brief moment, she came to, saw me, smiled at me with her soft and tender smile, and whispered:

" Dearest Rupprecht! how happy I am—that you are with me!"

No curses such as Renata had previously rained upon me could have affected me as those simple words, uttered upon the very brink of the grave—tears poured from my eyes unrestrained, and, pressing my lips to the cold-growing fingers of Renata, as the faithful press theirs to a revered sacred relic, I exclaimed:

" Renata! Renata! I love you!"

At this moment it seemed to me of the most vital importance to engrave in her soul only these words, so that with their echo alone she should wake to another life, but Renata was probably already unable to hear my sorrowful exclamation, for, as she whispered her last greeting, she suddenly fell backwards, and shivered horribly, as if in the last struggle with death. Three times she rose from her couch, trembling and suffocat-

ing, either warding off some horrible apparition or
advancing to meet someone beloved, and thrice she
fell back, and in her chest already sounded the death
rattle, even now like no sound of life. Falling back for
the third time, she remained completely motionless,
and, placing my ear to her breast, I heard no more the
beat of her heart, and realised that from this world,
in which she could have expected only persecution and
suffering, her soul had passed on into the world of
spirits, demons and genii, to which she had always
striven.

When I became convinced that Renata was no more,
I closed her eyes and softly kissed her brow, which was
covered in cold sweat—and though at this moment I
loved her with all the intensity of my being, with a love
no less than that of which the poets sing—yet from all
my soul I delivered a prayer that her hope might be
fulfilled, that she might meet her Madiël, and, if only
after death, know peace and happiness. Then I sat
down upon the floor of the prison beside the corpse of
Renata to reflect on the position, for her death not
only did not deprive me of the ability to reason, but
even returned to me my self-control, broken by the
sight of her sufferings, and the tears even dried in my
eyes. After a short meditation it appeared to me un-
answerable that it would be purposeless to endanger
my life, and the honour of the Count who had so
magnanimously aided me, for the sake of a soulless
body, and that the wisest thing I could do was to
depart secretly. After this decision, I touched for the
last time the lips of the dead Renata with my kisses,
then crossed her arms on her breast, once more arrested
my glance on her motionless face, that I might drink
in her features for ever, and at last, taking my torch, I
directed my steps away from the fatal vault.

I confess that, while I was walking along the dark
halls and passages, the thought several times came
into my head to return and die beside Renata, but by

arguments of logic I contrived to soothe myself, and, having completed the return journey, I came out under the night sky through the door near which Michael was waiting for me. Seeing me, he exclaimed :

" At last, Master Rupprecht ! You were long over-due ! Any moment we might have been seized like mice in a mousetrap. And where is the maiden ? "

Hardly had I had time to reply, when the sister who was keeping guard over the doorway approached us impetuously, and, in a strangling voice, repeated the question :

" Where is Sister Maria ? "

I replied to both :

" Sister Maria is dead."

But scarcely had I uttered these words, when the pious sister flung herself at me, like a maddened cat, clutched at the collar of my jacket, and screamed un-restrainedly, so that she might have aroused the whole convent.

" It is you who have slain her, villain ! "

With all my strength, I pulled the woman off me, pressed my hand over her mouth, and said :

" I swear to you by the immaculate body of Christ that Sister Maria did not die by my hand, but if you howl once more, you I shall certainly kill ! "

After that I flung her away from me, and the nun, dropping to the ground, began to weep softly, while Michael and I quickly walked across the deserted courtyard to the exit gates, which the other portress opened before us silently and without delay. And when we were outside the cloister, Michael asked me :

" This means, the job has failed ? "

I replied :

" Yes, the job has failed, but I shall not return to camp. Tell the Count that I shall ride to the castle and await him there."

Michael did not oppose me with a word, but escorted me to the slope where the horses were waiting us, helped me into the saddle, and at parting I gave him a golden pistole, saying :

" You know, Michael, that I am not wealthy, but I should like to reward you, for you placed yourself in mortal danger for my sake. Had they found us at the cloister, we should both have been marched to the bonfire."

Only then could I at last press spurs to my horse, to urge him into the night and once again be alone, without people, alone with myself, which was as necessary for me as it is for a dolphin to breathe on the surface of the water. I did not know the exact route to the castle of the Count, but, turning the horse roughly in the direction of the castle, I dropped slack the reins, and allowed it to gallop across meadows, rifts and hills. I thought in that hour no definite thoughts, but one realisation in all fullness governed my numbed soul : that on the whole earth, with all its lands, seas, rivers, mountains and habitations, I was once more—alone. At times, too, I vividly remembered the face of Renata, distorted by her death struggle, and at the thought that never would it be given to me to behold it more, I sighed sorrowfully in the silence of the dark fields, and birds, frightened by the sudden sound, fluttered, starting up out of their nests, and flew in circles round me.

When it began to grow light, I found my way and, riding forward on the proper road, I reached the Castle Wellen about the hour of early Mass. The castle retainers were surprised at my unexpected appearance, separate, moreover, from the Count, and at first they suspected me of some crime, though my return itself contradicted such an absurd supposition—but in the end they admitted me and allowed me to occupy my room. There, worn out by the four-and-twenty hours I had spent without sleep, hours during which I had lived through a whole lifetime of hopes, despair, horror, and sorrow, I flung myself into my bed and slept until

the late twilight. In the evening the Countess herself,
mastering her disdain for me, called me to her chamber
and questioned me about our journey with the Archbishop and the reasons for my return, but I still felt
myself so weak that I was unable to compose a truth-
like story, and she probably took me for a man who had
lost his reason. On the following day, everyone in the
castle treated me with a sort of timid caution, and
perhaps, finally, might have thought it necessary to
put me on a chain, if the Count had not arrived towards
the decline of day.

I was as glad to see the Count as if he had been a
blood relation, and, when we were left alone, I told
him frankly all that I had experienced in the subterranean vaults—while he told me what had happened at
the convent after my departure. According to his
words, when Renata was found dead in the prison,
none doubted that the Devil had slain her, and that
served as new evidence against her and her companions.
Brother Thomas, nowise considering the case finished,
had immediately summoned for examination many other
sisters, whom he thought might be suspected of connection with the demons, and all these, as soon as they
had been submitted to the first tortures, had hastened to
assail themselves with the most ruinous accusations.
According to the evidence of the sisters, the whole
convent, and pious Mother Martha herself, were all
guilty of horrible crimes, of pacts with the Devil, of
flights to the Sabbath, of celebrating the Black Mass,
and all the rest. Like a many-ringed snake, the
accusations began to uncoil, and it might well be expected that, sooner or later, our names, those of the
Count, myself and Michael, would be involved in the
inquiry.

" I hastened here especially to warn you, Rupprecht "
—said the Count, in conclusion—" Of course, the
accusations may threaten me as well, but hardly will
this despicable Thersites, Thomas, dare to menace

me directly. In any case, do not concern yourself about me, and know that, remembering the principles of Cicero expressed in his deliberations in ' *De amititia*,' I do not repent in the least having come to your aid. Whereas you may well pay cruelly for our night adventure, especially as your flight serves as weighty evidence against you. Therefore I advise you : leave this land immediately and change your name for a while."

Of course I was not slow to thank the Count for his continuous care on my behalf, and I replied that his advice coincided with my own decision, which in truth it did. There and then the Count offered me a sum of money, partly as remuneration for my services as secretary and also simply as a friendly present, but I preferred to refuse it, for, as it was, I was without it already much beholden to the Count, and this weighed on me. The Count then, weeping, embraced me and kissed me, and though this kiss was given me not as from an equal to an equal, but more like an act of grace or a politeness, yet I remember it with gladness, for all his actions the Count performed without afterthought, and with the simple soul of a child.

In the early morning of the next day, I left for ever the Castle von Wellen, and rode one of the Count's horses as far as Adenau. From there I proceeded on foot, and to questions who I might be I began to answer that I was a former landsknecht, heading for my birthplace, and that my name was Bernhard. I directed my road towards the south, for I desired at all costs to visit my native Losheim, to which I had now come so near, and after a three days' journey I reached the green slopes of the Hochwald, so familiar to me from childhood.

That night I spent at the hostelry " *Halber Mond*," which lay on the very outskirts of Losheim, and, questioning the landlord with circumspection, I managed to find out, giving thanks therefor to the Creator, that my father and mother were alive, that my brothers and sisters lived happily and in affluence, and that all thought me perished during the Italian campaign. At dawn, by a by-path I had known well when still a boy, I walked towards my native town, which for nine long years I had not seen, and which I remembered like a fairy-tale heard in childhood, but the details of which I visualised with such clarity as though I had but yesterday walked all through its streets. If my emotion was strong when, after my wanderings beyond the Ocean, I saw again from afar upon the barge the outlines of the City of Köln, then now the sight of these native walls, these tiled roofs familiar from childhood, was a blow too mighty for my exhausted soul, protected by no shield, and I had perforce, seating myself on one of the wayside stones, to wait until my heart had quietened down, for I had not for a time the strength to make a step.

I did not wish to go into the town, for I did not wish to appear before my parents like the prodigal son in the Evangels, a beggar and miserable : to me this would have been a tormenting shame, and to them it could only have brought unnecessary sorrow, so that it was better to leave them in the conviction that I was no longer amongst the living, to which they had resigned themselves. But I insistently desired to see our house, in which I had been born, and spent the years of childhood and youth—for I felt that the sight of this little old house would be for my soul like some fortifying draught, that would give me strength to begin a new life. Therefore, branching off the main road, I climbed a steep hill that rises behind the village, a place where in the evening pairs of lovers walk, but which was quite deserted at so early an hour, and from thence I could see the whole of Losheim, and especially our small house, which stands near the hill itself. Lying on the ground, I peered, with the thirst of a drunkard gazing at wine, into the empty streets, at the houses, the owners of which I could enumerate by name, at the little house of the apothecary, where of old had lived my Friedrich, of whose fate the innkeeper had been able to tell me nothing, into the deep gardens, around the stern lines of the big church—and then shifted my glance back once more to my native house, to this structure of stones that was as dear to me as a living being. I studied in detail all the changes that the years had wrought in our habitation: I saw how the trees had broadened in our garden; noticed that the roof slanted just a little, and the walls leaned just a trifle crooked; remarked that the curtains had been altered in the windows; I reconstructed in my memory the distribution of the furniture in the rooms, and tried to guess what new pieces were standing there and what old ones had disappeared; but I took no note of how passed the time, of the fact that in the village people had begun to move about, and that the sun, which was already risen high on the horizon, had begun to scorch me mightily.

Suddenly opened the door of our house—on the threshold appeared first a bent old lady, then, following her, an old gentleman, getting on in years but yet trying to be brisk: they were father and mother, whom I could not but recognise in spite of the distance, both by their features and by their carriage. Walking down the porch, and speaking of something together, they sat down on a small bench beside the house, warming their old backs in the warmth of the rising sun. I— the roving vagabond, hiding in the outskirts of the town, I—a failure as a landsknecht, a failure as a sailor, a failure as a gold-seeker even after scouring the forests of New Spain, I—a sinner who had sold his soul to the Devil, who had reached to the edge of inexpressible happiness, and fallen into the pit of nethermost despair, I—the son of these two old people—watched them covertly, like a thief, not daring to kneel before them, to kiss their wrinkled hands, to beg their blessing. Never in my life did I experience such an

access of the emotion of filial love as at this moment,
aware that my father and mother were the only two
human beings in all this universe who concerned themselves about me, to whom I was not a stranger—and
all the time that these two tiny, bent figures sat near
the porch, talking of something, perhaps of me, I did
not tear my glance from them, satiating my eyes with
the long unfamiliar spectacle of domestic bliss. And
when the old people had risen, and, moving slowly,
returned to the house, when our old, squinting door had
shut behind them, I kissed instead of them my native
soil, rose also, and walked away without turning back.

That same day I was already at Merzig.

My purpose was to return to New Spain, but I had
not sufficient money to carry out this far journey at
my own expense. Therefore, in the Imperial City of
Strassburg, I entered, under the name of Bernhard,
the service of a trading house that sent its employees
out to various foreign lands, and they eagerly engaged
me for my knowledge of several languages and my
swordsmanship. As a trader's agent, I spent about
three months, and the story of two encounters that I
had during this time must certainly be added to this
faithful narrative.

We were sent into Savoy to purchase silks, and our
route lay through the Western Alps to the City of
Geneva. As is well known, on the Alpine roads are
encountered a multitude of difficult crossings over
mountain streams, which caused us especial trouble
on this occasion owing to the strong rains that had
passed just before our arrival, transforming rivulets into
turbulent torrents, and in many places tearing down
bridges. Before one of these streams we had to tarry
an especially long space, for it was impossible to ford
it, and our guides and ourselves had to erect a temporary
bridge. Simultaneously with ourselves, the guides of
two travellers who had been riding in the opposite
direction to us and were now standing on the opposite

bank of the stream, busied themselves in the same way. But whilst we were attired very modestly, as befits merchants who ride on business bent, the cloaks and hats of these two travellers denoted their noble descent, and, in conformity with this, they took no part in the work, standing aside and proudly waiting for its termination.

When the structure had, however, been contrived, the noble seigneurs, especially one of them, desired to cross the first, and on this account there ensued an angry quarrel between them and my comrades, though I sought to persuade the latter to pay no attention to so trifling a circumstance. The quarrel might easily have developed into an armed fight, but happily the second of the knights persuaded his companion to cede place to us, and our small caravan was the first to cross, with shouts of victory, and to lead its horses along the logs placed for that purpose. Reaching the other side, I considered it appropriate to thank the knight who, by his courtesy and common sense, had saved us from an unseemly battle, but, when I approached him, I recognised, with astonishment and emotion, in him Count Heinrich, and in his companion Lucian Stein.

For the first moment I felt as though I were beholding one returned from the grave—so removed from me was my past life, and I could neither speak nor move, as if bewitched.

Count Heinrich studied my face, also in silence, for several minutes, and said at last :

" I recognise you, Master Rupprecht, and from my soul I am glad that the thrust of my sword was not fatal to you. I had no cause to slay you, and it would have been a burden to me to have your death upon my soul."

I replied :

" And I must tell you, Count, that I feel not the slightest ill-will towards you. It was I who called you out, and forced you to the combat; in delivering your thrust you only defended yourself, and God will not reckon it against you."

After that for a moment we both were silent, and then, with an abrupt movement, almost swaying in his saddle, Count Heinrich said suddenly to me, speaking gently, as one speaks only to a very near friend:

"Tell *her* that I have cruelly expiated everything in which I sinned against her. All the sufferings that I caused her, God has made me suffer in my turn. And I know truly, that I suffer for her."

I understood who it was that Count Heinrich did not wish to mention by name, and answered softly and sternly:

"Renata is no longer amongst the living."

Count Heinrich started again, and, letting go of the reins, he buried his face in his hands. Then he raised his big eyes towards me and asked eagerly:

"She is dead? Tell me, how did she die?"

But, suddenly interrupting himself, he contradicted:

"No, tell me nothing. Farewell, Master Rupprecht."

Turning his horse, he directed it on to the temporary bridge, and soon he was already on the other side of the raging stream, where the guides and Lucian stood waiting for him, and I galloped to catch up with my comrades, who had ridden forward far along the twisting and turning mountain road.

We remained in Savoy for the space of three weeks, and, having purchased as much merchandise as we required, we decided to return through the Dauphiné, where velvet can be bought at a fair price, its cities being renowned for that material, and with this purpose in view we rode from Turin to Susa, and from Susa to Grenoble, holding road to Lyon. At Grenoble, a small but pleasant town on the Isère, where we spent more than four-and-twenty hours, there awaited me the last adventure that has connection with the story I have related. For when, in the morning, having no especial business, I was wandering through the town, looking over its churches and simply inspecting its streets, someone suddenly called me, in our tongue, by my own name, and, turning, for some time I failed to recognise him who called me, for I expected to see him here least of anyone, and only when he named, himself did I see that it was indeed, the pupil of Agrippa of Nettesheim, Aurelius.

When I asked Aurelius for what reason he was here, he poured out before me in reply a whole basket full of plaints :

" Ah, Master Rupprecht "—he was saying—" very bad days came upon us. The teacher, having left the town of Bonn, thought at first to settle in Lyon, where he used formerly to live, and where he had relatives and protectors. But there, suddenly, they seized and flung into prison the fifty-year-old man, without any explanation of reasons, without any guilt on his part, only, it appears, because in his compilations there are attacks against the Capets ! True, by the intercession of influential friends he was soon released, but many of his chattels have not been returned to him, and, moreover, being an old and feeble man, he has fallen ill. From Lyon we moved hither, travelling light, but here the teacher has taken to his bed completely, and it is now many a day since last he was on his feet, and he is very bad. However, praise be to the Lord, one of the local notables, Master Francois de Vaton, the President of the Parlement, has taken an interest in us and given us shelter and victuals, otherwise in truth we should have had naught with which to buy our daily bread ! "

I asked whether I might visit Agrippa, and Aurelius replied :

" Certainly you may, and further, it is also time for me to return, for I fear to leave the teacher for so long a while."

Aurelius led me in the direction of the Isère, on

the way continuing to complain of the injustice and ingratitude of man, and also bitterly reproaching my friend Iohann Weier, who had left the teacher before the departure of Agrippa for the Dauphiné, and now lived comfortably in Paris. On a corner formed by the quay and a street at right angles to it, stood an ancient house of middle height, decorated, however, with some coat-of-arms hewn in stone—and this was the house in which now lived, by charity, Agrippa of Nettesheim. Hardly had we entered the hall, when Augustin came to meet us, all in tears, which became his broad, round face but ill, and forgetting even to greet me, he informed us that the master was indeed very low.

On tip-toe we entered the room where, in a broad double bed covered by a canopy, in an uncomfortable position, his arms stretched out motionless by his sides, lay the great magus, already like a corpse, for the features of his face had grown sharper, his beard had for long not been shaven and looked as though it had grown after death. Round the bed, in the silence of sorrow, stood the pupils, servants and sons of Agrippa, as well as two, or perhaps three persons unknown to me, so that in all, I believe, including myself, there were about ten or eleven people. At the very side of the bed, there sat on its haunches, its head sorrowfully laid upon the coverlet, the large black dog with fuzzy hair, the same that Agrippa had called *Monseigneur*. The whole contents of the room. gave the impression of a temporary camp, for amongst its furniture left, apparently, by the owner of the house, everywhere were to be seen oddments belonging to Agrippa, and also, everywhere were strewn his books.

Those who had gathered, exchanged several remarks between themselves in a whisper, but I could not fathom what the persons whom I did not know were saying for they spoke in the French language. I only heard Emmanuel, who was also there, say to Aurelius that during the absence of the latter a priest had been called, that Agrippa was then conscious, had confessed and taken the Holy Sacrament, and that he had conducted himself at this shriving, judging by the words of the confessor, " like a saint "—and this circumstance struck me much. For my part I asked Emmanuel whether Agrippa had been visited by a medical man, and he replied that he had, often, and that all the measures prescribed by medical science had been duly taken, but that no hope of recovery could be entertained, and that death had already leaned its scythe against the head of the bed.

I should think that we spent more than half an hour in weary expectation, while Agrippa did not alter his position nor move a limb, and only his raucous breathing testified that he was still alive, and I was already intending to return to my comrades, at least for a short time, to inform them of my whereabouts, when there was enacted before me a scene horrible and beyond my understanding. The dying man suddenly opened his eyes, and sweeping around us his dull, as if unseeing glance, that froze us all numb, paused it upon the dog that sat by the bedside. Then the bony, quite yellowed, and, at the tips of the fingers, already blackened hand separated itself from the coverlet, swayed for some time impotently in the air, as if already incompletely obedient to the will of man, and slowly descended upon the scruff of the dog. Numb with unfathomable horror, we saw how Agrippa sought to unfasten the collar inscribed with cabalistical characters, and how at last he succeeded, and the rattle of the collar falling upon the floor shook us like the most terrible threat. At the same moment the lips of Agrippa, that were as if pasted together, similar in everything to the lips of a corpse, parted, and, through the heavy raucous breathing of the dying, we clearly heard uttered the following words :

" Begone, Accursed One ! From you are all my misfortunes ! "

Having uttered this, Agrippa again froze into immobility, locking his lips and closing his eyes, and his hand, with which he had unfastened the collar, hung from the bed like one of wax, but we had not had time to comprehend the meaning of the words we had heard when another striking circumstance claimed all our attention. The black dog, from which the master had just removed the magic collar, jumped to its feet, bent its head low, dropped its tail between its legs and ran from the room. For a few moments we knew not what to do, and then several, and I in their number, obeying an irresistible curiosity, rushed to the window that gave upon the quay. We saw that *Monseigneur*, running out of the door of the house, continued to run, preserving its humiliated demeanour, along the street, reached the bank of the river, and threw itself, still running, into the flood, to appear no more upon its surface.

And I, and all the other witnesses of this unique act of self-destruction, could not, of course, fail to recollect the mysterious stories which had been circulated about Agrippa's dogs, and about this one in particular, in fact, that it was a familiar whose services Agrippa had employed, ceding in exchange to the Devil the salvation of his soul. I was especially struck by the dying words of Agrippa, and his whole attitude, in view of the stern condemnation of magic he had once delivered to me, mocking the pseudo magi who engage in goety, and calling them conjurers and charlatans. For one short instant, as by a white flash of lightning, I saw Agrippa, though but upon his death bed, as that mysterious sorcerer who led a life different from that of the rest of mankind, as the popular rumour depicted him. But at the time I had no occasion to think over such matters, for the mournful exclamation of those who had remained near the bed of the dying man informed us that his sufferings were over.

At once there began all about the usual tumult and confusion that death ever causes in our lives, falling ever as a heavy stone into stagnant water—and some of the pupils, weeping, kissed the hands of the dead teacher, other persons took care to close his eyes, yet others hastened to call in some women to wash and dress the body of the dead man. Soon the room began to fill with a multitude of people, come to look upon the deceased magus, and profiting by the general commotion, I departed unseen from the house, where my presence was now unnecessary. To my fellows, who knew me as their good comrade, Bernhard, I of course breathed no word of what I had seen, and in the evening of the same day we rode from the town of Grenoble.

On my return to Strassburg, I received as my share a sum of money sufficient to enable me to undertake the journey to Spain at my own cost, and I made it, without any special event, traversing, in the depths of winter, the whole of France. On Spanish soil I felt myself as if in my second motherland, and, at Bilbao, I found without much difficulty persons to whom my real name was not quite unknown, and who agreed to add me, as a man of experience and acumen, to an expedition that they planned into the New World, to wit, to the north of the country of Florida, up the stream of the river of Espiritu Santo, where fortunate prospectors had succeeded in discovering whole fields of gold. Thus my modest plans have come to fruition, and in the spring, with the first sailing caravels, our vessel will set sail beyond the Ocean.

These months of forced idleness, while our ship has been lading, while the crew to man it is being gathered, and while the winter winds yet make dangerous the sailing of the open seas, I have consecrated to the compilation of these notes—a task of painful memory, to which I am now just setting the last binding clamp. It is not for me to judge, gentle reader, with what art I have succeeded in relating to you all these cruel torments and these heavy trials, into which I was drawn by my ungoverned passion for a woman, and

391

it is not for me to decide whether these notes may prove
a useful warning for weak souls, who, like myself,
may be tempted to glean power in the black and
dubious pits of magic and demonomancy. In any
case I have written down my story with all frankness,
showing persons such as they appeared to me, nor
being merciful to myself when it came to depicting
my weaknesses and defects, and neither have I concealed anything of that knowledge of the mysterious
sciences that I obtained from the books that I read,
from my unsuccessful experiment, and from the words
of the scientists with whom fate brought me in contact.

Not desiring to lie in the last lines of my story, I
will confess that, were my life set back by a year and a
half, and did there await me once more upon the
Düsseldorf road my meeting with that strange woman,
maybe I should commit once more all these same follies,
even renouncing once more before the throne of the
Devil my eternal salvation, for even now, when Renata
is no more, there yet rages in my soul, like a scorching
coal, an invincible love of her, and the memory of the
weeks of our happiness in Köln yet fills me with a weariness and a yearning, and an unquenched and unquench-
able thirst for her caresses and her intimacy. *But with
solemn assurance, do I hereby swear an oath before my
conscience that never again shall I yield up so blasphe-
mously my immortal soul, given unto me by my Creator
—into the power of one of His creatures, in whatever
seductive form she may be clothed, and that never,
however weary may be the circumstances of my life,
shall I turn to the aid of divinations condemned by
Holy Church, or to the forbidden sciences, nor shall I
attempt to cross that sacred edge that divides our world
from the dark sphere in which float spirits and demons.
O Lord our God, who seest all, even into the depths of
the heart, thou knowest the purity of my oath. Amen.*